fatal camino

John Douglas Fisher

Abaco Media & Publishing Ltd.

Copyright © 2018 by Abaco Media & Publishing Limited

First published in Great Britain by
ABACO Media & Publishing 2018
Fatal Camino

John Douglas Fisher has asserted his right under the Copyright, Designs
and Patents Act 1988
to be identified as the author of this work.

ISBN 978-0-9927893-1-2

Copyright © John Douglas Fisher 2018
Cover Design and Illustrations Martina Hillebrand
Text, Layout and Graphic Clea Nuss-Troles
Cover Illustration © Abaco 2018

www.abaco-media.com

All rights reserved. No part of this publication may be reproduced or
transmitted in any form or by any means, electronic or mechanical,
including scanning, photocopy, recording, or any information storage
system and retrieval system, without prior written permission from the
publisher, nor be otherwise distributed or circulated in any form of
binding or cover other than in which it is published nor without the
same conditions being imposed upon any subsequent purchaser.

This book is a work of fiction and any resemblance to real persons,
living or dead is purely coincidental.

A CIP catalogue record for this book is available from the British
Library.

ABACO Media & Publishing Ltd
32 North Street
Hailsham BN27 1DW

2018061001

Thanks to all who showed enthusiasm for this story and actively helped by giving free time to read and make suggestions. In addition my thanks to my life partner Clea, who donated so much loving creativity, encouragement, patience and work to this book who lit a fire under my ass to get it finished, as well as Anne, Malcom, and Martina who contributed their creative talents and help. Thanks also to Harry DeWulf for his professional and constructive guidance. Above all, I thank the pilgrims I met along the Camino. Ordinary people in an extraordinary journey who become extraordinary.

fatal camino

John Douglas Fisher

Abaco Media & Publishing Ltd.

A good traveller has no fixed plans
and is not intent on arriving.

                              Lao Tzu

PAMPLONA

Jane stood in a palace without a king. Old, big and cold. Over 140,000 steps had passed under her dusty boot soles in seven long days tramping the Route Napoleon, the pilgrim way across northern Spain. The spanish called it the Camino. Here in the city of Pamplona, her journey was not yet over. Far from it. She walked alone. She felt alone. It had to be that way. It was the only way on her mission.

Disinfectant tinged the air and blended with the smell of charcoaled toast from the Burn It Yourself kitchen. With only a cup of fennel tea in her belly, she shivered from the cold air inside the thick walls of the albergue. She wondered briefly whether the palace had been the home of a king, prince or wealthy merchant, long departed for the shores of paradise.

Beady cunning rat like eyes followed her. The eyes of an unknown cardinal in a red gown and skull cap. White lace cuffs almost shrouded his podgy hands. He sat comfortably in a dark oil painting inside a thick, gold frame as if he owned it. It hung above a huge yawning granite fireplace, its inside big enough to park a pocket Bentley. The cardinal's sensual, fat lips were pursed and suited a Playboy cover more than a noble portrait. *He might even have died as a pilgrim on the Camino,* Jane thought. *Fast Track to heaven.* In ancient times, pilgrims who died along the Way of Saint James were considered martyrs. The thought of martyrdom saddened her blue eyes. She thought of her mission. A self-imposed mission that had brought her to the Camino to repay a debt. A debt of guilt. Her debt, her payment, no credit given. Guilt is not a bank.

'Are you thinking I will deflower my wife or something? Hah!' A gruff male voice echoed up in the high ceiling and dragged Jane back to the present in the once noble hall. He resembled a huge Viking, but without a Viking helmet. Nevertheless, to Jane, his appearance topped with a bull neck looked big and threatening.

'Hah!' His wife barked, as moral support, or perhaps vocal backing.

'Hah!' he confirmed in an accent from somewhere in the Scandi-Teutonic regions. 'Hah!' he again addressed the rough, square hole in a modern, plastic partition that both divided and desecrated the hall.

'Sexual intercourse with *anyone* in our albergue is forbidden.' A severe female voice scolded from the other side of the hole.

Jane got the impression that a ventriloquist wagging a finger was behind the partition, delivering the statutes of a grey headed committee living in the past. Below the square hole, adhesive letters announced it to be the 'RECEP ON'. The partition violated the elegance of an era when only the feet of the well shod, had trodden the marble floor. Now it was an albergue without toilet paper in old Pamplona; its floor trampled by hiking boots dumping the dust of the Camino.

'Men in the men's dormitories. Women in the women's dormitories. That is the rule.'

The man turned ponderously. His ice blue eyes focused on Jane. 'Did *you* stay in a women's dormitory?' he quizzed imperiously.

'Factually, nobody was snoring, so I believe I did,' Jane addressed his cave like nostrils. Her long, thick red hair fighting for space, flipped left and right over her shoulders. Skin round her eyes crinkled slightly as she smiled sweetly at the Viking. She raised her eyebrows, shrugging slightly to show helplessness. 'That is the Camino, I suppose,' she flashed another smile that she didn't feel. The man disregarded her answer and turned his back, leaving her looking at a scallop shell tied to his backpack the size of a covered wagon. They marched out, their white plastic scallop shells swinging like pendulums on their backpacks.

Jane's stomach grumbled for attention pulling her back to reality. She had missed breakfast by trying to sleep longer on a metal bunk that squealed like tram wheels when she moved. She had waited till the communal bathroom emptied. Now her stomach sent an acid Taser prod to remind her that air alone wasn't enough to live on. She hoisted her backpack in her left hand and shrugged one of the straps over her left shoulder like a rifle sling. *I need breakfast before re-joining the Camino or I'll faint with no gallant arms to catch me*, she thought.

She neared the rough-edged hole that looked like it had been made by a drunk with an axe. The voice gained a face. Hatchet features, pale, untouched by sun or make up. Her eyes cast a look as sharp as a harpoon at Jane's shorts, that looked too good on Jane to be wasted on a clothes hanger.

'Goodbye,' Jane smiled with a little wave.

'Buen Camino.' The face wished unconvincingly.

I'll stay at the friendlier private albergues in future, Jane decided and headed for the tall double doors to the street.

* * *

Her nostrils clamped as she plunged into a nicotine cloud, puffed out by the giggling staff standing in a circle by the front steps.

What's this! A smokers' reunion? Jane almost quizzed, but buttoned her lip. She knew she had a quick tongue that had earned more enemies than friends in the last school where she taught for an unhappy year. She held her peace and looked up at the sun cresting over the red and white tiles of Pamplona roofs warming her face. *An oil painting begging to be spread across canvas,* she thought, and suddenly missed the smell of her oil paints. Her shadow rippled ahead over coloured cobbles that she could not feel through her thick soled boots.

Follow your shadow, she thought. *Then you head west. Follow the shadows of the Camino.*

Cars punching music from open windows squeezed by, wing mirrors a centimetre from batting her hip. The smell of coffee was a wild bouquet of roasts swirling with the aroma of freshly baked bread. Her ears filled with chatter from doorways of shops and bars, followed by answers shouted from across the street. A few kids in an alley booted a half-deflated ball about, its bounce long kicked out of it. A scruffy little dog sprang about as piggy in the middle, snapping in vain as the ball passed over its head. Bikes whizzed blindly by while car horns warned people to move. Someone whistled. A compliment for her? She smiled, but not enough to encourage. She crossed Calle de la Estafeta and recalled the long street was the most dangerous place in Pamplona during the Festival of the Running Bulls. Little chance to avoid a bull horn up the behind. She recalled a man who stopped to face the stampede with his camera. He survived to pay his hospital bills on top of the court fines.

Her thick red hair fanned around her shoulders as she turned full circle in Plaza del Castillo. It was the old exercising place of the castle troops and linked the old town to the new. A favourite meeting place for all, including transiting pilgrims enjoying a change from the pilgrim menus in the albergues.

Jane took in the scenes around the plaza. She smiled at a brown corgi watering the base of one of a row of grey plane trees that bordered the square. Clusters of green burst from their gnarled branches bringing in fresh colours to the city. A stone bandstand, its cupola supported by a ring of ionic pillars, stood silent as a tomb. Behind it, an island of old men debated something long past and important only to them. Younger Pamplonians in hostess skirts or razor creased pants hurried by, arms stretched forward carrying café-con-leche-to-go.

Jane turned in a circle again, her eyes like radar. There were no vacant seats outside the cafés lining the square. Pilgrims in jackets of all hues tanked up on café con leche and tapas. Some chatted into palm size screens. Some laughed together. Jane did not feel she was one of them. Her backpack was not the only baggage she was carrying. Her eye roved over them. Like Jane, they would soon hit the trail. The trail, that's what Jane called the 500-mile-long Camino. The ancient pilgrim Way of Saint James, a saint whose life ended without a happy end or head.

First she needed breakfast. Breakfast! The word made her mouth water. She looked for an empty chair. Waiters in black waistcoats quick-stepped elegantly between swollen backpacks and tables, dealing breakfast platters with the dexterity of croupiers. Jane sighed. No vacant chairs and her tummy grumbled that its patience was exhausted.

You should have risen a bit earlier, Jane, she wagged an invisible finger in her own face. *Then you'd have been in time for the albergue's tostada con mermelada*, her Knowing-everything-better-voice said.

Jane pressed her stomach to suppress the noise and the hunger. It did neither. CAFÉ IRUÑA blazed in giant black letters across white awnings like a circus tent, readable from the far end of the plaza.

Her booted feet thudded rapidly towards the palace of food. She did not feel the eyes following her.

* * *

She almost greeted the plastic life size granny in blue pinafore at the door, wearing sparkling lenses of real spectacles. Inside, a good humoured babylon of languages filled her ears and heart. She admired the ceiling high mirrors that visually doubled the number of glowing chandeliers between dark wooden pillars. Her heart hopped. *A table!* A table at a high window overlooking the plaza was free. She almost ran across the café and plumped herself down, suppressing a triumphant grin, like a winner of musical chairs. She relaxed with her back to the window facing a large plasma screen on the rear wall opposite. The newscaster's eyes were intense. His lips enunciated rapidly and mutely. Sound was reserved for football matches, so today it was vision only. An extravagantly dressed girl posed at the long gleaming copper bar expecting to be snapped by a talent spotter. Nobody looked. The Camino is not a fashion show.

A good-looking waiter in well-fitting black pants and shirt, modelling a short, wine red apron, approached with a cocky walk. He had a friendly smile that actually seemed genuine, so Jane returned it warmly.

'Buenos Dias, Señora.' He dragged a cloth across the table and dealt her a menu card. She flipped it open and asked without reading, 'Do you have natural muesli?'

'Sí, Señora.'

'Muesli, a yogurt, and a cup of hot water and a

bottle of still water, please,' Jane slumped back in her seat. She was a week into her pilgrimage that had started in Saint Jean Pied de Port on the French border. Seven days walking through mountains and forest in the same clothes and the same routine; walk, eat, sleep, walk, eat, sleep left her feeling grubby and sticky. Pamplona was worth a two-day rest and the purchase of extra underwear.

Breakfast arrived. She stirred a few teasel drops into her glass of hot water and sipped slowly. Her hand reached into the net side pocket of her backpack and pulled out a red plastic wallet. She plucked out a number of photos and postcards. A young woman smiling from the photos stabbed Jane in the heart. Her eyes lost focus as she riffled through the pictures of earlier times.

* * *

A shadow darkened the table. A tanned face that hadn't felt a razor for days, blinked down at her through red rimmed eyes. *Has he been crying?*

'These seats free?' he asked, dumping his backpack on one of them before she could reply.

'In fact, they are,' she smiled. 'Only the food costs money,' the corners of her mouth bent up some more at his bright orange jeans and poison green rain jacket. *It's true that colour blindness affects only men,* she thought.

'That's a fact, is it?' He spoke with a faint Irish lilt.

'Please be my guest,' she said packing the photos away and sipped her tea.

'What yer taking? Recreation drugs?' His teeth

flashed between his lips.

'Teasel root tincture. I make it myself from wild plants.'

'Interesting, as long as you don't poison y'self.'

'I know the dangerous plants very well, thank you. Factually teasel helps ease aching muscles and fights Lyme disease.'

'Lyme disease! Well, that's a thing!' He pronounced it ting.

'From tick bites.' Jane stirred her tea.

'Friggin' ticks! I didn't know that.'

'Depends on your background, I imagine,' she said and sipped delicately from her cup.

'Is that right?' He reddened. It sounded like "roight". 'Well, let me tell you, that I may not know plants, but I do happen to know other things.'

'Is that a fact?' an eyebrow arched. A hint of a smile curved the corners of her mouth. 'Things? Such as?'

'Well, when I hear the William Tell Overture, I don't think a friggin' Lone Ranger film is about to start.'

A stab of guilt stopped her. 'Sorry, she smiled, albeit a little weakly. 'Just a little slip of the tongue, so to say,' she sipped from her cup again.

'Is that right?' he looked around the café as if sizing up the public.

She put down her cup. Light reflected off a silver metal badge of Mercury pinned to the top flap of his backpack. It reminded her vaguely of some courier company, but she wasn't sure.

'I don't believe in dosin' myself with bits o' flowers an' things,' he nodded at her cup. 'Hot tea or cold beer do f'me,' he slumped deeper into the chair, legs spread out like a starfish. He beckoned to a waiter like a servant and took in the lounge salon. 'This is how I imagine the lounge of the Titanic looked.'

Jane scanned the restaurant. 'I don't recognise anything particularly nautical.'

'But, without the sinkin' feelin'.' Crow's feet crinkled round his blue eyes.

'Is that your taste in humour?'

'It is,' he nodded keeping up his teeth flashing act.

'The risk of icebergs at this latitude is, to say the least, factually remote. I think you're safe here.' She looked at her map. Her long red hair partly curtained her face.

'Hemingway drank here,' he said and looked around nodding in approval.

'True. As a matter of fact, this building also housed a casino when it was built. He probably lost his money here, too.'

'Sure. A casino's a place where y'get nothin' f'something.'

'A fool's hobby,' she sniffed and returned to her map and marked a location. She was conscious of the blue eyes watching.

'Would you be one of these pilgrim people then?' He nodded at her backpack on the seat next to her.

She looked up. 'Except for the waiter, I expect everyone here is a pilgrim.'

'Bunch of lemmin's.' He took the menu and shook his head.

'Why do you say that?'

'Because it's a sort of fashion thing that everyone does.'

'For many it's a serious undertaking,' her voice

was tinged with irritation.

'Spanish!' He let the menu fall on the table.

'We *are* in Spain,' she looked at him from the corner of her eye and marked her map.

'Is that a *fact*? He sneered. 'I'd be after a tourist menu in English.' He clamped his jaw and looked tough.

'A *tourist* menu?' she cocked an eyebrow. 'On the Camino? Maybe an illuminated document in Latin would be more appropriate.' Her smile was getting weaker by the minute. Machos were never her type, genuine or posers.

'I came in here to eat not translate,' he scowled.

Foolish oaf! Jane thought and went back to her map.

'This is double Dutch t'me!' He waved his hand over the page. He turned, scratched his bearded chin and looked for the waiter.

'Dutch *and* double, too? I thought you just said it was Spanish!' She reached and twisted the menu over. 'English is on the back, or would you prefer one with pictures?' she said. Only her mouth smiled. 'I assume you're an exception to your so-called pilgrim lemmings?' Her gaze flitted over his uncombed hair and few days' bristle. She spotted a few grey tufts sprouting among his side whiskers.

'I'm not here just to toddle along dreamin' of miracles that'll never friggin' happen.'

'Is that a fact?' Her polite smile morphed into a frozen mask, making her face ache to maintain it. *Oaf!* she thought.

'I've been here over two friggin' weeks,' Mr Oaf continued. 'Walked from France. Hung around here almost a week. Flyin' back this afternoon, thank

Jasus.' He scratched his hair and wrinkled his nose as if he didn't approve of the menu. Over his shoulder, a row of miniature suns glittered across the large plasma screen predicting a continuance of the hot weather. The waiter arrived with a smile that outshone the beaming TV suns.

'Omelette,' Mr Oaf muttered. 'Coffee. Black.'

'Por favor,' Jane's manners compensated the friendly waiter on the stubbled oaf's behalf. 'And what exactly makes you the exception to these 'lemmings'?' She raised an eyebrow. *Why on earth am I even asking him this?* Her brow furrowed.

'I'm here to work, not walk.' His teeth shone between grinning lips creasing his stubble. 'I'm a sort of journalist.'

'Sort of?'

'No trainin' but I can read an' write and take photos,' he shrugged. 'Not much to it.'

'No qualifications for it?'

'I can friggin' lie, which is enough for popular journalism.'

'Hemingway was a journalist. You're following in great footsteps, if that's any consolation.'

'Yeah, I know. He felt he had made Pamplona famous with 'The Sun Also Rises' but ended up bitchin' about the tourists he'd attracted.' He shrugged. 'Not much chance of me doin' such a masterpiece along the Way of Saint James,' he said. 'Hemingway didn' work for a tweed jacket, dominated by his owner mother, who resembles their horse photos.'

'Working on the Camino sounds great. I'd have thought your colleagues would have simply killed for it.'

'Not in our magazine. It's a sport magazine. The editor thinks he can increase readership. That shows he hasn't a clue or has a great sense of humour'. He yawned.

'Tired?'

'More than tired. I'm knackered. Someone in the albergue sounded like a chainsaw. I lay awake all bloody night thinkin' of ways to stop him.'

'Did you think of any?'

'I did. An all of 'em fatal.'

She smiled imperceptibly and relaxed. The waiter slid a sunny omelette before the Oaf. He nodded thanks and ripped into the meal like a lion over a carcass.

Jane elegantly drank her tea, placing her cup on its saucer after every sip. 'Are you eating that or punishing it?'

'I'm friggin' starvin'!' he addressed the plate.

'Does being a journalist mean one can't be a pilgrim?'

'No. But my editor wants me to troll along the trail and interview pilgrims. I walked from the French border and hung around here interviewin' people. I don't fancy trampin' all day long an' sleepin' in albergues. Had enough of the dormitory shit when I was a kid.'

'Boarding school?'

'Hah!' he pointed a finger like a pistol. 'You're givin' y'background away there,' he scoffed. 'Not f'me. A friggin' home it was.'

'A home?'

He flapped his hand. 'Forget it,' he reddened. 'My schoolin' comes from the past. Past experiences. Past. That's the name of my school. If I decide about anything, I refer to my own past. It's always there, unchangeable. The past is my bible.'

A home? Problem boy? Criminal? Orphan? He does seem rather radical, she thought.

He opened his wallet. His thumb and index finger pecked inside and pulled out two SSD flash cards and lay them on Jane's Camino map. 'Articles, interviews, photos, everythin. All on these little beauties. Mission Senseless accomplished!' a grin slashed his face. 'Now I'm flyin' from here to Majorca for a week, to see my kids without their mother knowin'.'

'Why shouldn't she know?'

'Forget it. Too complicated.'

'Does your editor know you're sneaking off?'

'I'm not friggin' sneakin' off! he reddened. 'I got five weeks and sewn it up in two. Got enough material on those two cards for ten magazines. Why bother with more?' He shovelled a piece of omelette down his throat and reminded Jane of a furnace stoker shovelling coal.

Jane shrugged. 'I'd love to hear what different people had to say about the Camino.'

'Bah. I've had enough of interviewin' people all followin' yellow arrows splodged on trees! Followin' graffiti!' He harpooned a piece of omelette and swallowed. It reminded Jane of her tortoise at home swallowing food whole.

'I rather think the spirit of the Camino has escaped you.'

'Huh. I read a blog where a guy wrote the Camino sucks. He's right.'

'The Camino is part of the planet. If it sucks it stops us falling off, doesn't it?' she smiled sweetly.

'Be positive. I'm Jane, by the way. Jane Downer,' she offered her hand. He nodded and forked more food into his mouth. Jane felt her cheeks flush. She withdrew her hand, lips pressed together in a hard, straight line. *Oaf!*

He sensed her irritation. 'I'm Daniel Brady,' his fork clattered on the plate. His hand shot toward her like a karate jab. 'Pleased t'meetcha, Jane Downer,'

Jane brushed his paw with a light shake. *I like Irish people, but this guy has no Irish charm at all.* His eyes held hers like a gunman at a showdown. He polished his mouth with a napkin as if it was an oil rag, sighed loudly and dumped it on the empty plate.

'Aaah!' He sighed. 'Now I feel fit again.'

'Fit,' she tried to find some common ground. This could be it. 'Fit is a word I hear a lot on the Camino. Did you train to get fit for the Camino?'

'Of course! I went to a different pub every night.'

'Then all men in Britain must be very fit,' she returned to her map. The man called Dan Brady gazed through the window intently, as if mentally counting the pilgrims outside.

Suddenly, they rose en mass, as if someone fired a start pistol. Looping arms through backpack straps, they pulled on floppy hats, pocketed phones, and set off. Backs to the sun, shadows pointing west. Some had sticks and stabbed the stone paving like skiers well off piste and many carried a scallop shell, the Camino symbol, flapping from their backpacks. Viewed from behind, the tall packs of the pilgrims concealed everything except their legs.

'They look like a mob of SpongeBobs on the march,' Brady scoffed.

'They're good people doing something they believe

in. In fact, I shall join them myself.' She closed her map.

'I'd relax until the rest of the lemmin's thin out along the trail.'

'Are you insinuating that *I'm* a lemming?' her eyes shot sparks. 'I suppose you think everyone here is a lemming?' Her breast rose and sank from her sudden heavy breathing.

'Walking the Camino's the *"in"* thing. The latest tra-la-la,' he smirked.

Her livid glare could have ignited gasoline. 'Mr Brady. I'm not walking the Camino because it's my latest tra-la-la!' Tears shot to her eyes.

'Sorry, but...'

'Sorry nothing!' she cuffed her eyes. 'The word *sorry* is a tactical word to avoid changing one's ways! One hears it all the time; sorry I'm late, sorry I lost it, sorry I ruined your dress, sorry I fouled, sorry our government overspent, sorry we started a war, sorry...' she stopped, her mouth hung open. She sat back and stared into space. 'A placebo, nothing more!'

'Oh oh.' He made worried face. 'Quite a friggin' speech.'

'Factually, pilgrims have walked the Camino for over a thousand years! Before them it was an important route for the ancient Celts.'

'Ok, so you're not a friggin' lemmin'. Maybe y'hopin' to find yerself a boyfriend,' he leaned back as if he had not listened to a word she said. His grinning head hung patronisingly lopsided.

'How *dare* you!' She felt her cheeks flush.

'Then why are you alone?' he grinned, eyes flickered about her face.

'I have personal reasons for my Camino.'

'Which are?'

'Which are,' she paused. 'Which are none of your business! I am with two friends who are escorting me.' She pulled her hair through a bobble band into a ponytail.

'Escort? Are you expectin' bandits?' his teeth contrasted with his tan.

'They carry some of my heavier gear.'

'Oh! You employ carriers!' he grinned. 'Very colonial. Camino Lite,' he said.

A bunch of kids bounced across the plasma screen dancing to a muted song that required much crotch and ass rotation. Nobody watched nor cared for moving wallpaper.

'I have a reason, I'm on a...' she stopped herself.

'Whatever,' he flapped a hand. 'I just want to meet my deadline, so I can keep my friggin' job and see my kids again. I need to keep it, so I've interviewed people who quit their jobs, been fired, charity walks, divorced, widowed, or want to get away from things, or they can only pay the electric bill by gettin' laid. Some for religious grounds, or to have fun, and maybe get their leg over. So, what's your angle?'

'Certainly not to get, er, that, leg over sort of thing...' her face flushed red. 'It's private.'

'If I walked the whole Camino, I'd want to break a walking record. I wouldn't want to be held back by anyone in a group.'

'Oh! A little race?' she raised an eyebrow. 'The old gung ho, up an' at 'em type, are we?'

'Only when my testosterone tank's full.' His teeth flashed at his own wit.

Jane rolled her eyes. 'Let me guess. You're Mr Iron man himself,' her face full of false pity.

His face drained of humour. 'Mr Afghanistan-man.'

'Oh! Shoot a kid a day and keep peace away.' She immediately regretted saying it.

'That's way below the fuckin' belt, Ms Downer!' His fist thudded on the table. The table cruet jumped. Jane blinked. Her heart hammered and took away her breath.

'Bit touchy, aren't you?'

His nostrils flared. His words shot like tracers. 'I spent my time playin' rugby for the army and filmin' action since 2001. I killed only blue arsed flies raidin' my food, nothin' more!' he panted, face flaming. 'Now I'm interviewin' pilgrims with touchin' stories for our readers, who kiss more horses than men!' His features indicated an imminent meltdown, attracting unwanted stares from people at the next tables.

'Hmm, poor you!' She tugged a red floppy bucket hat down to her ears. 'Maybe you should have stayed in the army.' She stood and looked down at him, her jaw taut.

'I would have...' He stopped. 'Forget it.' He grabbed his cup like a glass and swallowed it in one. 'I don't need friggin' sympathy.'

'None intended, Mr Brady. Your ego is big enough to survive my disrespect for people like yourself.' She twisted on her heel and left.

Dan watched her leave. He took his seat, cracked his knuckles and checked his tea cup. Empty. He searched the table top as the waiter came with his bill.

'Fuck!' Dan bounced to his feet. 'Fuck!' People stared, but avoided his eyes. His fists clenched into hammers. He rushed to the door.

'Grab that bitch!' he yelled. The waiter called after him. Dan stopped in the doorway and glared across the plaza. Ms Jane Friggin' Downer was invisible among the jazzy gala of pilgrims.

Two waiters with egg shell expressions, one waving a bill, appeared either side of him.

'She's taken my fuckin' SSDs!' He pointed at the column of pilgrims. 'Get the fuckin' police!'

'Ten Euro, Señor.'

'She stole my data!'

'Ten Euro, Señor.'

'Get the fuckin' police!' he roared.

'Ten Euros, Señor.'

'Can't you fuckin' say anything else?' he bellowed.

'Ten Euros, Señor.'

'Can't you say anything else!'

'Ten Euros, Señor.'

'Shit!' Dan's hand dived inside his jacket in a rapid shoulder holster draw. He thrust a crumpled red note at them. 'An' keep the friggin' change!'

'There is no change, Señor.' one said as they melted away.

'Fuck! Now I'll lose everything!' His eyes blistered with hate.

PERDÓN

A pilgrim in bright red tennis shoes shot himself.

Jane watched without any reaction. She thought he had followed her part of the way, but she was more focused on a small, brown, suede sack, clinking as she pushed it into her backpack.

One could say that the pilgrims both follow and are followed, she mused. Everyone is following someone on the Camino.

'Got it!' The pilgrim smiled at his selfie. His background was the rusty, steel sculpture profiles of an ancient pilgrim column on the crest of the Sierra del Perdón, the first mountain ridge west of Pamplona. 'Phew, what a climb that was!' he grumbled in a Yorkshire accent.

Jane didn't answer. Getting up here had been a real knee buckler that left her exhausted. Her mind wandered to what lay ahead after Logroño, then Villafranca, Montes de León, then mountains before Santiago.

'A right savage gale up here!' the Yorkshire man brought her back to the present.

She didn't answer. Her tongue felt like an inch-thick postage stamp stuck to the roof of her parched mouth. After she had clawed her way up the last two hundred yards of an almost vertical, boulder strewn way to the crest, her mouth was dry. She had sweated herself empty of body fluids. Leaning back against her backpack, she drained her water bottle and looked back the way she had come. Pamplona was a dark patch in the distant haze beyond endless green wheat and vine filled plains below the mountains of Perdón. The Mount of forgiveness was unforgiving for the unfit.

Jane found her croaky voice. 'You should take your photo from the West, or you'll get all those windmills in the background.'

'Oh, aye?' The tennis shoe pilgrim shrugged. He stood before the metal sculptures, phone close to his forehead and shot himself again. A pixel coup de grâce.

Three tanned sisters from Ecuador babbled excitedly, snapping photos of each other against the sculptures. Jane had met them on the way up and walked some of the way with them. They appeared close and united in spirit.

'Photo?' One of them offered, holding out her hand for Jane's mobile. Jane handed her mobile to the friendly woman and positioned herself so the battery of white windmills with still blades were not in the background. Rust skinned horses and donkeys with eight rusty walkers filled the screen. *I wonder whether they have little rusty blisters to add to the realism!* she thought.

Stiff winds that always gust and tumble over the crest of the Alto Perdón whistled through the metal figures, flapping Jane's ponytail and almost tugging off her hat.

The sisters' heads dipped below the crest of the descent as they left. Jane sipped a glass of scalding tea at the white kiosk hitched to a Land Rover. A fly cruised around her plastic cup. After burning her lip too often, she mimed adiós to the bored Spanish woman at a small table nearby. Her life was stamping Pilgrim Credentials, the pilgrim passport required to get a bunk in the albergues along The Way.

Mr Tennis shoes stopped fooling with his smartphone. She felt his eyes as she followed the yellow arrow daubed on the road pointing to a drop that only suicidal hang-glider pilots could love.

* * *

Jane made her way along the few long earth steps just below the ridge. The sight of the steep, stony trail that was no longer distinguishable across a field of shale, snatched her breath away. Like a novice skier on her first steep slope. She peered warily down the mountainside that dropped abruptly from the ridge edge, like an avalanche that had skidded to a chaotic halt but ready to roll again. A steep ramp of pebbles and boulders had flowed around battered islands of gorse looked unstable, as if the slightest of tremors would send it thundering down. She watched her feet feeling the way forward as if entering a minefield. It did not feel good. Stones rattled and bounced down from under her thick soled boots that sounded like they were crushing ice.

Steady Janey! This is a way that only fools and the bravest go down.

I know, Jane thought back. Some pilgrims prefer the winding detour road instead.

Simple choice, Janey girl. Short and queasy or long and easy. This is as safe as walking down the side of an iceberg, she thought and stepped gingerly.

Within a few minutes Jane reached a woman lying helpless against her backpack on a patch of coarse grass. Her lips pressed tight in pain. Two kneeling companions bandaged her knee and soothed her in Spanish.

'Do you need bandages?' Jane asked, her feet felt unsteady on a sloping rock. They shook their heads and thanked her in Spanish and then in fractured English.

'Buen Camino!' Jane felt the instant comradeship of the Camino. She raised her hand like an Apache greeting and faced into the steady wind flattening the grass and bushes around her.

After a slow and arduous slippin' and slidin' she gradually reached the gentler lower slopes. Relief chased away the anxiety in her gut. It felt good to walk upright after hours crouched crabbing down the slope. She splashed through a stream that cut across the track to Puente la Reina. As the sun reached its midday peak, she entered the cobbled main street of the town, passing through a narrow canyon of houses leading to La Plaza, the centre. She was a few hundred yards from the bridge that gave the town its name, Bridge of the Queen, financed by Queen Doña Mayor - who introduced the concepts of feminine rights - in the 11th century. *Good for her,* Jane thought. *Her husband, the King, blessed his wife's initiative but continued bestowing his manly blessings on ladies of his court. King of cruds!* She wrinkled her nose showing her feeling for the stinker.

Jane reached the plaza and dived into the welcome shadow of a row of arches and slumped on a bench. She pulled at her yard-long boot laces till they curled like spaghetti around her feet. She sighed with relief at the loosening pressure of her boots. Her socks came off with them. She wiggled her bare toes. Luxury. No blisters! She felt proud of her feet. *Good boots. Fit like a glove. Good choice.* Jane grinned, giving herself a mental high-five and stretched her legs as far as she could and wriggled her toes again. She watched other pilgrims limp by in various stages of exhaustion or pain. A gaggle of pilgrims pulled each other's water bottles from back pouches from their rucksacks. They laughed and chatted between swallowing litres of water.

A short woman in a straw hat settled on the next bench. She pulled off her boots, sighed and peeled off a dirty plaster, dropped it on the ground. A fat fly pounced. Jane frowned. *Hope she takes that plaster with her*, she thought. *At least it's not as bad as the used toilet paper left in some of the ruins.*

The lady pulled out a sewing kit, plucked a needle, pursed her lips and threaded a cotton tail. Flame sprouted from a plastic lighter. She waved the needle through the flame as if conducting music. Her brow furrowed in concentration as she pierced a blister on her foot. She removed the needle and left the cotton protruding each side of the blister. She read Jane's face. 'It's ok. The cotton draws the liquid out. Takes the pressure off.' She rethreaded the needle. Her steady hand repeated the surgery on the next, oblivious to a hysterical burst of flamenco from the bar a few yards away. The fly landed on Jane's nose. She waved it away and it buzzed about her ear before heading back to the discarded plaster. The flamenco player spanked the guitar. People clapped but soon lost their timing that decayed to an uneven patter and petered out.

Jane headed for the gate tower at the end of the street and over the bridge. *I could make it to Estella*, she thought. She pulled the chamois bag from her pack and crouched at the end of the bridge to carry out her ritual. Minutes later, she stuffed the bag back into her backpack and groped for the map in her thigh pocket. The map opened itself in the breeze. Two tiny objects bounced off her boot. She plucked them off the ground. The sun glinted off the row of miniature gold teeth of black SSD disks. 'Brady!' she gasped. *Oh, oh, Janey, girl! Someone is not going to Majorca now, and that's a fact.*

* * *

Fuck! Fuck! Fuck! The purge word flowed through Dan's brain like a Sergeant Major calling a marching cadence, punctuating every furious step across the Pamplona plains. Dan hoped he could intercept Ms Bloody Downer. He cursed himself for not being nicer and asking for her phone number. He knew he was, once again, paying the price for his lack of manners. He reasoned that she was ahead of him, and was sure he hadn't passed her but you never can be sure. She could be feeding her face in a bar. To cover this possibility, he'd darted through the door of every bar along the way. He stood against the wall next to the door, scanned every face, and darted out again, as if searching suspect buildings in Afghan villages.

'Fuck!' The word spat out like a round of tracer. He had to get well ahead of Ms idiot Downer and choose a point where she had to pass. An unavoidable point on the trail. A bottleneck. He marched on.

'Fuck, fuckin' fuck! How could I be so careless? Idiot, moron!' he berated himself. A pilgrim nearby crossed to the other side of the narrow street. Dan realised he sounded as if he had Tourette's syndrome.

He stopped and looked at the bridge he was about to cross over the River Agar. 'Plan B,' he muttered.'

He dug his cell from its holster and pressed a stored number and pressed the hands off button.

'Is that you, Danny boy?' A Welsh voice rasped from the phone speaker.

'Yes, it's me, Gwill. Look I can't join you in Majorca.'

'Ooh, that's no good, is it? Why's that then, boyo?

'Because some stupid bitch took my SSDs with her!'

'Could be a spy, look you?'

'No, she wasn't a fuckin' spy! Just another idiot pilgrim with nothing better to do in life.... Look, Gwill! Don't wait for me on the boat. I'm not gonna make it... I'll have to stay on this stupid Camino to fulfil my job or lose it!'

'That's shit. I won't say anything to your kids, just in case you manage to get 'ere somehow.'

'O'course it's shit! But losin' my job is shittier. I

could lose visitin' rights to my kids; too.... Anyway, thanks, Gwill. You're right about not mentioning it to the kids. Just tell them I'm delayed. Now it's plan B, I'm afraid...'

'What is plan B then, boyo? Hope it's better than some o' the plan Bs we had in the regiment, look you.'

'Plan B is repeat the whole fuckin' shit from the fuckin' beginnin'.'

'Sorry about that, Danny.'

'Yeah, well, next time, Gwill. Next year maybe when my friggin' ex sends them on holiday with their favourite uncle.'

'Yeah, next time, Danny.'

'Catch a big one for me,' he forced a humourless chuckle and pressed cut as if it was the jugular vein of his worst enemy.

'Goodbye kids,' he sighed, holstered his phone and made a bugle of the bottle. His Adam's apple jumped up and down till water trickled down his chin. He sat and looked at the wonderful view. He breathed deep and long, closed his eyes and let himself float in his mind and calmed down. *That's it then. Start again, Brady, you idiot!* He ordered himself. *You might manage to intercept Ms friggin' Downer. Then again you might not. Write it off as lost. Start again.* He took a deep breath and watched the calm Agar River sliding by.

Twenty deep breaths later, his feet touched the far bank of the Puente de Reina. Within minutes he started taking photos. Action is therapeutic, he thought, laying down a barrage of pictures. He had taken a few photos of the side of the bridge and looked at the screen. He whistled as if he had received a precious gift. The bridge and its reflection showed an amazing, symmetrical reflection that transformed its arches into optical circles on the smooth surface of the river below.

'Good angle here.' A deep voice distracted Dan.

A giant, fleshy Teuton with a red jolly face pointed at the bridge. 'That is the most photographed bridge on the Camino.'

'I'm takin' them for a sports magazine.'

'A hundred years ago a statue of Our Lady stood in the middle. Folklore says a small bird cleaned her face, which was believed to be a good sign and bring good luck on the town.'

'Interestin'. May I ask why you're walkin' the Camino?'

'I will tell you. It is something different. Not like going for a long walk where there is no real aim other than getting back home for lunch or the TV movie. Everyone here shares the same aim. You talk to strangers, young, old, men, women, and they reply. Nobody is suspicious or wonders why a total stranger speaks to them. It is ... how do you say in English?' He clicked his fingers to aid his memory. 'Er, unique. Yes, unique! It is like a Kameradschaft!'

'Comradeship,' Dan translated.

'Ah! You understand some German?'

'Only in bar rooms.'

'So,' he waved to Dan from a yard away as if he were a mile away. 'Goodbye.' He turned and marched. Dan imagined a brass band accompanying the oversized Teuton. He poured water down his throat and watched the man disappear along the hard-beaten brown trail into the green countryside. His anger with the stupid Ms Downer began to evaporate. He batted away a fly. *Got a problem, Dan? Deal with it!* He recalled one of his authoritarian step father's endless tips for life. *Well, dad, I am dealin' with it, thank you very much.*

'Hello,' a voice haled and brought him back to the present. A stout woman with a fresh happy face approached.

'Hi,' Dan called back and dragged on his best smile.

'Going my way?' she grinned.

'Don't know. I'm thinkin' of staying here for the night,' he gestured back across the bridge that he had just crossed. Where are you from?'

'Canada, Saskatchewan? I'm on a sponsored walk to raise money for South Sudan to fight against hunger there.'

'Very noble. Have much have you raised?'

'A dollar for every kilometre. I've walked over two hundred kilometres so far. Now I'm hoping to catch up with my family.'

'Are you here with your family?' Dan looked surprised.

'Not my natural family,' she stabbed her walking poles into the earth, scattering the odd pebble. 'My Camino family. While you walk you tend to become part of a loose group. You see these people at bars and albergues along the way for weeks on end. It's awesome! It gives me energy knowing some are ahead or behind me. I never feel alone. This is my Camino family. People who show they care for you.'

Dan thought about her words in a long silence. 'I'd never considered that aspect,' he said quietly. 'I don't seem to have a family yet.'

'You will,' she smiled. 'You already know me.

What's your name?'

'Dan, er Daniel.' He reddened.

'Irish, huh? The gift of the gab. Are you a gabby person, Daniel?'

'I'm not, well, not really. It depends what I have to say. If I'm riled up I am. Otherwise I'm a quiet sort of person. Don't make friends all that easily.'

She smiled and stabbed the trail with her walking poles and looked at him. 'Well, you're gabbing now, Daniel. That's a start, isn't it?'

'Yeah,' he said quietly. 'That's a start, I suppose.' He nodded and stared at the trail powder on his boots. A dark lizard shot into the grass where bees hovered over wild flowers.

'My bedtime. I'm an early riser. I'm done for the day. You?'

'I'll do a few more miles and earn a couple of extra dollars for the cause,' she waved her stick. 'Bye for now, Daniel, the newest member of my Camino family. I'll be looking out for you.' Her smile was radiant and her eyes seemed to shine with liking and respect.

He watched her walking west towards the low afternoon sun. He batted away a persistent fly and headed back over the famous bridge to find food and bed for the night in Puente la Reina. He now felt better despite his angry start to the day. It was strange, but he wished she had walked further with the women. He also hoped he would see her again. A friend walking the Way of Saint James. The words to the song You've Got A Friend, rolled through his mind. He wondered how far Ms snooty Downer had walked and whether he was ahead of her or not.

* * *

'Is that seat free?' A girl in smiley T-shirt under a silver jacket pointed at the empty chair next to Dan at the breakfast table. He had risen early and had his backpack on the floor beside him ready to go.

'Sure,' Dan sipped his cup of albergue coffee. 'Where're you from?'

'Hungary,' she took a swig from her water bottle. 'And you?'

'Ireland and England. Born in one, adopted in the other. Name's Dan. I write for Huntin' and Anglin' monthly.'

'Cool, a life story in two lines. I'm Ida,' she offered a hand.

'Can I interview you for my magazine?'

'Do I look like a horse or a fish?' She reached for a bread roll.

'Blow bubbles in your water bottle. I'll claim it was an interview with a mermaid,' his teeth flashed. 'Just give me your thoughts.'

She searched the sky. 'I believe there always were and always will be pilgrims walking the Camino. Pilgrims have to be here. That's reason enough.'

'There *have* to be pilgrims here? Why?' He sipped from his cup.

'Disused railway tracks rusting and overgrown with weeds look sad. Without pilgrims the Camino would be a ghost road of weeds. Its spirit would die! That's a reason.'

'Hmm, not bad,' Dan said and butttered himself a roll. 'Even my editor might get tears in his eyes when he reads that. Especially about the deserted railway lines. He loves trains. His office shelf is lined with model locomotives.'

'Really? My boyfriend, too!'

'I bet he wanted to be a locomotive driver?'

She laughed. 'But now he's a soldier. His mother always refused to buy him toy guns or tanks when he was a kid. We're getting married when I return. He has red hair like me, so we'll have red haired children,' Her eyes lit up with her smile.

'Congratulations.'

'Do you have kids, Dan?'

'Two.'

'That's cool. How old?'

'Twelve and ten. Girl and a boy.'

'They're pretty lucky having a cool reporter dad.'

Dan grinned. 'Thanks for the compliment. I hope my kids grow up to be as cool as you.'

'And walk the Camino,' she laughed. 'Then you can interview them.'

'I'd like that. Thanks for the interview, Ida.' He stood and reached for this backpack. 'I'll write it the way you described it. It's good.'

'It's romantic,' she smiled.

'It is at that,' He nodded. 'Well, I have to get moving.'

She grinned. 'I'm going to look around the town first. Here's my mail,' She scribbled in a small book and tore out the page and offered it, exposing three red hearts tattooed below her left ear. She took Dan's card and put it in her purse.

'Ok, Ida from Hungary. I hope to see you along the trail.'

'Cool,' she smiled and took another bread roll. Dan looked back and gave a little wave as he reached the door.

* * *

Jane's long early morning shadow flowed over the stone path lined by a blaze of nodding poppies with silky petals glistening among bright yellow flowers of Saint John's wort. White butterflies and bees waltzed over yellow flowers. She stopped and plucked a few to brew her own tea. *Good against depression and muscle aches*, she thought as she pulled a resealable plastic bag from her backpack. She stuffed the flowers inside and resumed her trek. The sound under her boots reminded her of her sister chewing dry cornflakes without milk.

A cuckoo called, making her smile. An invisible tractor engine complained somewhere between the steep olive groves. She looked up at the endless sheet of sky full of heat. A white line trailed across the endless blue. The morning mist had long dispersed, and the back of her neck was warming up. A fly buzzed at her, and a large bee droned past. The dried ground dust floated longer here. The cuckoo called again, answered by birds warning their mates.

The sun became intense. Pores sprung beads across her skin as she began the steep strenuous climb up to the Iglesia de San Román where the pilgrim route leads right through the middle of the church. She paused inside to get her breath back and enjoy the cool air before descending the steep road down to bridge.

Outside, she clutched her shoulder straps, leaned

into the slope and trudged downward over large flat stones that cobbled the surface between an alley of cypresses. Jane watched her boots on the ground, and imagined sandalled Roman troops and traders treading these same cobbles two thousand years ago. The immensity of the time that had passed and sheer number of people over the centuries who were funnelled along this way was staggering.

The path deteriorated into a stony dirt trail heading for the bottom of the valley. Huge fallen blocks of a collapsed Roman bridge made it look as if only mountain goats could pass. After scrambling over the ruined bridge, Jane saw that the trail meandered between red hills of gorse. She crested another hill after another before she paused. A lizard darted under a stone. The trail trickled down to a medieval bridge over a small river.

Don't drink the water here, a voice in the back of her mind warned. *That's the River Salado! The river of death.* Jane's research flooded her head. In medieval times, horse flayers told pilgrims it was safe to water their horses. The horses died quickly, and the flayers skinned them on the spot, forcing the pilgrims to continue on foot.

A figure stepped out from the shadows of a nearby stand of trees and pulled on his backpack.

'Oh, no,' She halted, her brow furrowed. Slowly she walked down the slope.

'Where are my friggin' SSDs?' the man barked as soon as she set a foot on the bridge.

'Here,' she halted a few yards from him and dug her purse out. 'Factually, they were a lot safer than when they were with you.'

'I've been combin' the whole fuckin' Camino for

you to get these back!' His face blazed red through his tan. She looked down at the trickle of water hoping he wouldn't throw her in. It might, in fact, still be very poisonous.

'Now you can now make your editor at Huffing and Aging happy.'

'No fuckin' thanks to you!' He looked as if he might bite her. A small green lizard skidded across the bridge stones.

'Still your charming self,' her heart thumped like a bass drum. She stepped back to get a bit of distance and eyed the bushes. She wanted to get into the privacy of the small woods before she began wriggling in front of him like a disco club dancer.

'Huh, people like you piss me off!' he snarled. 'I suggest you go and wallow in y'friggin' emotional tourism!' He swivelled on his heel and left her standing on the bridge fuming.

'What would you know about it as an emotional cripple!'

'What!' He turned back, venom lanced from his eyes.

Jane's face went hot in a flush. 'I'm sorry! That wasn't necessary..'

'Shove it!' he roared and strode away without looking back.

The adopted cuckoo called. Nobody answered.

Jane watched him. Her mouth opened, but nature called. She scuttled along the river bank and found a private spot. It was quiet except for a slight hum. She squatted and stared unfocused at the greenery surrounding her, hoping nobody would blunder through the bushes with the same intention. Finished, she reached for her water bottle. Air gurgled into it as water fought her thirst. She opened her eyes. Her heart walloped away her breath. Her eyes wide orbs of shock. A figure was watching her. *Pervert!*

'Hey!' Outrage strengthened her voice. Her heart thumped her ribs.

The figure just watched. The mouth moved but said nothing. No sound came.

'What the devil do you want?'

Anger and fear rose together making her heart beat faster.

The figure reclined against a tree stump. Jane's eyes adjusted to the shadows. It was a young woman. Jane calmed down. 'Erm, can I help you?' The woman watched. Jane plucked up courage. Stepped nearer. The mouth kept moving. Jane stopped. Disgust screwed up her face. A humming mass of flies feasted on blood clotted over the woman's mouth and throat.

'Help!' She recognised her own voice calling. She ran. Whipping branches stung her cheeks. She burst panting from the foliage into the blazing sunlight. Her head swivelled left and right. Prickly heat ran up her back. She shivered.

'Brady! Brady!' Only the echo of her own desperate voice answered.

Brady had disappeared.

LORCA

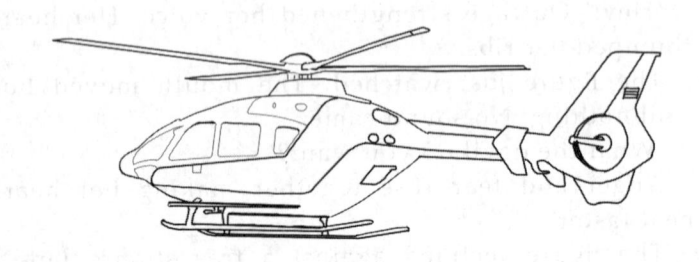

Dan sat in a very narrow street between two Albergues in Lorca. They were three metres apart. One had a half beer barrel on the stone wall above the door. He reckoned he could easily spit a cherry pip into the doorway of the opposite albergue, but he had neither cherries or pips to prove it. The crickets' evening chorus and a bird on the roof talking to itself relaxed him. The landlord had told them the mayor forbade chairs outside these two albergues opposite each other. Dan was not in the mood to please some village mayor after Ms Downer's remark that he was an emotional cripple. Her words had gone through his mind like a poisoned bayonet. Only the paralysing cramp in his leg distracted him. He sat outside, mayor or no mayor and twisted his legs to one side to allow cars to pass, braving the exhaust gas and radios punching through open windows like Wladimir Klitschko's fist. The owner told him to relax and check in later after the rooms were cleaned. He did exactly that.

'You look a bit pale,' said a lady with a six foot staff ticking on the ground. Under a black wide brimmed hat, and a white blouse with a black skirt flowing to her ankles, she looked as if she had stepped out of a history book.

'Cramp. Helluva friggin' climb up to here.'

'I have just the thing. Roll up your trouser leg.' She fumbled in her ancient backpack.

Dan took a magnesium tablet and relaxed while the lady rubbed cream into his leg.

'I owe you, t'be sure.' Dan said after the treatment.

'A cold beer will do nicely,' she dropped the tin of magic cream back in her backpack. Dan called to the bar in a low voice, it was only a metre away, and asked for two fresh beers. They sat with a Dutch couple outside. The man stroked his companion's tanned knee continuously as is if staking his claim. Dan set his right ankle on his left knee and watched his beer. The lady drank and sighed.

'Have you a bed for the night.'

'Yes, she placed her beer glass on the table. 'I'm going up to it now. I want to start early,' she said and hoisted her backpack. 'Sleep well.'

Dan watched her go. A distant thudding filled the hills, and a Euro Copter hammered low over the rooftops.

'He's low,' the Dutchman said.

'Police,' another man said.

'Someone speeding on the Camino.' The Dutch woman smiled. They all laughed.

'May I join you?' a woman nursing a condensation pearled glass of beer stood by the bar.

'Sure' the Dutchman smiled and moved his chair to make room, despite the Mayor's decree. 'Already got a bunk?' he asked.

'No, I'm going on to the next town after this beer.' The sinewy woman swiped her hat exposing grey, wiry hair. She dabbed her brow. 'Where did you start this morning?' She asked the question every pilgrim asks another pilgrim.

'A place called nowhere,' Dan answered. 'I stopped when my feet said stop. What brings you to the Camino?'

'Escape. I had to escape teaching girls subjects they don't like.'

'What don't they like?'

'It depends on their talents. They excel in subjects they like but often drop them if they don't count to get them into university. Math rules. I'm sad at the inflexibility of university boards. This walk is to give me space to think about my future career.'

'I'm writing for a magazine. Could I write about you?'

'You don't know my name to quote me, so you can quote me,' Her smile was Mona Lisa pure. Everybody chuckled then got more beers.

'I've got to get on,' she wrestled her backpack onto her shoulders.

'Have you got a Camino family?' Dan asked.

She cocked her head to one side thoughtfully. 'A Camino family?' her eyes searched the blue sky then slowly nodded. 'I think so. That's a good expression,' she said. 'You should write that down.'

'Not my creation,' Dan grinned and raised his glass.

'Then copy more things,' she smiled impishly.

'Multiple plagiarism becomes research.'
 'I'll try anything once,' Dan grinned.
 'Not once, many times. Good luck!' she waved.

* * *

The clattering rotors spurred Jane out of the copse into the open. The helicopter leapt a gorse crest and headed for her, a giant insect ready to pounce. She shuddered and shrank back clapping her hands over her ears and hat. Instead of devouring her, the insect rotated sideways. POLICIA curved artistically upwards against a broad, blue stripe background. The hammering rotor blades thrashed up a dust storm ripping at the surrounding bracken. Jane blinked rapidly to clear her eyes, as the copter settled on its skids. Behind the Perspex, large Ray Bans watched her, reminding her of a giant fly. She waved pointlessly. Two police officers leaped out and jogged towards her in a crouch, hands clamped on caps. Two impassive men in plain clothes followed with the leisurely gait of authority.

The younger of the two was a handsome, snappy dresser, with green bow tie, cream linen jacket and black hair slicked back like a Tango dancer. His stylish shoes struck Jane as out of place in boot country. A bulky hard faced middle-aged man with a thick moustache followed, stopped, stuck a cigarette in his mouth while patting his jacket pockets. He drew a lighter and moved out of the down draught from the still rotating rotor blades, and carefully stroked the end of the cigarette with a flame.

'Good morning!' The younger man stood before

her, light on his feet. *Athletic. English perfect. Accent American. Texas,* she guessed. But he was obviously Spanish. His face was pleasant, friendly and open. 'Did you call us?' His fingertips ploughed through thick black hair. His smartphone rotated in his other hand as if washing his hands with a bar of soap.

'Yes I did,' she nodded once, wiped her eyes and cleared her throat.

The Detective's eyes flicked from Jane's face to her hair, as if he were not sure where to focus. 'I'm Detective Alonso Amador,' he held out a hand. She took it. Soft. Expensive aftershave wafted from a smile as wide as the Camino. Brown eyes regarded her intently then glanced at his phone. Jane noticed his finger nails; chewed to extreme shortness.

Two uniforms stood behind him, eyes and feet shifting uncomfortably, awaiting orders. The Detective twisted away and coughed, then dabbed his mouth with a handkerchief. 'Excuse me,' he apologised, shoving the handkerchief in his pocket. 'This is Comisario Mendoza,' he indicated the thickset man who had caught up breathing deeply, moisture covering his flushed features. His tired jacket appeared old enough to have its third set of elbow patches and was too thick for the summer heat. He pulled deeply on his cigarette and nodded. A stream of smoke erupted from under his thick, grey drooping moustache, tinged by years of nicotine.

'Good morning,' he bowed his head slightly and ran his finger over his moustache, before plugging in his cigarette again.

'Is it?' Jane choked. She hated cigarette smoke. Her father chained smoked. She never liked it. She didn't like the Comisario. He reminded her of her old headmaster. A dour Glaswegian who flicked the ears of the boys in class when he got a wrong answer. He never went near the girls. He simply ignored them.

Take it easy, Jane. Forget the past. Hold yourself together.

'Did you report a body?' Mendoza stared at her as she was wasting his time with a cheap prank. He picked a bit of tobacco from the tip if his tongue.

'Yes. A girl, er, woman. A young woman.' Jane's voice stammered and irritated her.

'Show me.' He removed his sunglasses exposing bushy salt and pepper eyebrows. His eyes were as devoid of expression as his sun glasses.

'I take it you are walking here as a pilgrim,' the younger Detective's tone was friendly. His eyes continuously flashed from her face to her hair. Jane almost said she was an "emotional tourist," the words from that horrible oaf Brady. It insulted her mission. She nodded to his question. 'Any idea who might have done it?'

'Factually, no,' Jane shook her head.

'Did you see anyone nearby?' Mendoza demanded. He trod the cigarette into the dirt.

'The only person who left the woods was a Mr Brady.'

'Brady?' Mendoza stroked his moustache. 'Who is Brady?'

'An Irish reporter.'

'A *reporter*!' Mendoza's expression was of someone sucking a lemon. 'That is all I need! A damned reporter!' Bad temper narrowed his eyes. Jane was surprised by the anger in the comisario's gravelly voice.

'Please, show us the body,' Amador ordered.

Jane led the way. 'Don't get your shoes dirty,' she said instinctively. 'Sorry,' she flushed.

He smiled. 'No problem.' He pulled a plastic packet from his jacket pocket. He broke it open and pulled a pair of plastic overshoes over his stylish brogues, then snapped on rubber gloves, each with a loud thwack. His hand clenched and opened a couple of times, reminding Jane of a surgeon about to operate.

'Over there,' she pointed and watched him stepping gingerly as if walking on burning embers.

Two Guardia officers followed him, one trying not to look while the other goggled with a fixed grimace.

Engines growled. Two jeeps jumped over a hump in the trail. Wheels locked and skidded to a stop. A photographer in a blue plastic overall got out followed by another two men. They reminded Jane of the Teletubbies. His camera glued to his face while it whizzed without pause. He used a large, long zoom lens that might suggest a phallus complex, but at least he avoided trampling the ground flat and contaminating the scene and evidence.

Detective Amador bent into a cloud of humming flies. He touched the jaw, tried to close an eyelid and then eased his fingers below her wrist. 'Rigor mortis is present' he murmured, flapping flies away. He took out a dictaphone and spoke in Spanish.

Jane turned away, feeling dizzy. She started swallowing and drew rapid breaths, spittle flooded her mouth. Her stomach heaved and gushed its contents leaving her throat raw. She panted. Retched till there was no more to come other than pain, leaving her drained. The Detective looked away and pretended interest in his shoes.

'Do you need help? A doctor?' The Comisario stood before her. His flabby expression tried to look sympathetic but failed. She shook her head and turned away. The horrible discovery made her think of her reason for coming here. It brought a rash of prickly sweat down her back.

'Have you a room booked anywhere?' a competent faced police woman stood before Jane, who shook her head in slow motion. 'Can I please have your passport to take down your details? One of our jeeps will take you to the presidium and then to a hotel.'

'Do you know where the journalist is staying?' Mendoza broke in. The police woman frowned. Jane shook her head.

'Can you identify him?'

Jane nodded, stared at the dry baked reddish soil. The shock had drained her energy. She nodded absently, sank onto a fallen tree trunk. Her mission suddenly swelled in importance.

* * *

In Lorca village the albergue owner called everyone to table. The meal was a perfect Pilgrim Menu with copious amounts of red wine and a choice of four menus and twenty five guests each got exactly what he ordered. Nessun Dorma flowed from an invisible speaker. The music lifted Dan's heart, reminding him of his teacher at music school.

He smiled as he went up to his bunk. A full day, some nice people, a great meal, leg better, and, he had his friggin' SSDs again!

The sound of a hog with indigestion ripped from a large hump in a sleeping bag on the bunk opposite. A smothered fart within the sleeping bag prompted Dan to open the window and stuff ear plugs deep into his ears. He zipped up his sleeping bag up to his nose and lay awake. 'Majorca here I come,' he smiled. The darkness absorbed the brass sunset and the white moonlight slid across the open window. Dan felt warm and secure in his sleeping bag and fell into a deep sleep, banishing Prosser-Jones from his dreams.

LOS ARCOS

Dan's feet pounded the trail like steam hammers under a brain grilling sun. He could have fried an egg on any stone he picked. His boots crunched the trail like Brighton's rattling pebble beach. He was almost expecting mirages to appear. He sweat so much he hadn't pissed since before breakfast. Only his New Zealand Kiwi hat prevented Dan's face resembling frazzled bacon. He thought of his adoptive mother. She had always served frazzled bacon because she always read a book while cooking. She frazzled everything except water. She read a book no matter what she did. She was probably reading when she left his step father; or at least on the bus taking her to her new future, whatever it was. Midday and Estella town were well behind him. His path took him across undulating countryside past rows of fat stubby vines across endless green barley fields, edges full with poppies with shining petals folding and unfolding in the breeze. A lizard sped across the trail and a duck followed him for some minutes before losing interest and settled in the shade of a bush.

'Hello,' a man in his fifties with white hair and high forehead greeted Dan. His skinny legs made his boots look enormous, giving the impression he was wearing ski boots. 'Going my way?' he grinned.

'I think so,' Dan nodded ahead at the trail.

'My name's Oiva, from Finland. You?'

'Dan, from Ireland and the UK.'

'Dan from Ireland and UK,' he pursed his lips. 'Where did you start? Estella?'

'I took a break there. Thinkin' of returning home.'

'To UK? Breaking off?' He looked sad at the idea.

'My job is done. A project for my magazine.'

'Why didn't you take a bus to Madrid or Pamplona from Estella?'

Dan shrugged. 'I ask myself that, too.'

'Did you get an answer?'

'Can't remember.'

'Well you're still here.'

'Need more time. To think.'

'Plenty of time for that here,' the man smiled. 'That's why many people are here.'

'I walked from Lorca this morning. I was ready to leave when I walked a hundred yards away from the Camino path into Estella. I suddenly felt out of place.'

'An alien,' the man smiled with a vigorous nod. 'I felt that a few times. This is my third Camino. I met my French wife here ten years ago.'

'Is she not with you?'

The man's face dropped slightly. 'She died last year, he stared across the meseta. 'I'm here to remember her. I stop at places where we stopped together. I talk to her while we are walking sometimes.' He swallowed and looked away.

'I'm sorry to hear that.'

'He took a deep breath and looked at Dan. 'You felt out of place, you say?

'I'm not sure I can explain it. I got used to being with pilgrims carrying their world in their backpacks.'

'It's a humbling experience,' the man said.

'I started out with a cynical attitude and then the pilgrims I met began to make me think. At first I called it the "in" thing to do.'

'It is for some, but that doesn't have to alter other people's opinions.'

'I wasn't aware of any change in myself until I left the trail and walked that one hundred yards.'

'And what did you find at the end of your one hundred yards?'

'I entered a world of blasé fashion followers, sun glasses perched on hair, occupying pavement cafés, cultivating bored expressions and ladies with permed doggies in handbags. I half expected to be asked to leave!'

'Why that?' The man's eyebrows reached his hairline.

'I felt so out of place, not because I was dressed so differently, but because I saw a sea of shallow consumers, oblivious of the world outside their little smart screens.'

'Like so many modern cities, my friend,' the man chuckled. 'You're suffering from civilisation blues. Isolation in the middle of a crowd.'

'I almost fled. Back to the trail, among my own kind.'

'Your own kind? Who are they?'

'Good question. Nobody in particular. All races, colours and creeds, but they're here!' Dan waved his arm to encompass the countryside around them.'

'Maybe you've discovered something new about yourself. Others are also finding out about themselves. This is my third walk. I discover it anew each time. I find it both enlightening and humbling. This time it's just hot.'

'That's an understatement.'

The man smiled, stirring a few stones with the toe of his boot. 'I walked my second time in the winter. What a contrast! What cold!' he rolled his eyes. 'Snow, rain, mud and more mud. Never got out of my poncho!' he chuckled. 'I almost gave up after my friend got frostbite,' a mirthless grin crossed his features as if remembering pain. 'It makes you tough. Makes you fit. A lot of people are very surprised to find out just how tough they really are!' his gaze fixed Dan's. 'Everyone with determination makes it in the end.' He punched Dan lightly on his shoulder.

'You're going to be part of my article,' Dan grinned.

The man nodded. 'Be my guest, Dan.' He looked along the trail. 'I'm staying here in Azqueta for the night. It's a hundred metre climb from here to the next peak. I'll save that for tomorrow,' he grinned.

'I'll push on to Los Arcos,' Dan said.

'It's a long walk, Dan. No more villages between here and there. Have you enough water?'

'I think so.'

'Here, take mine!' he stuck his hand holding the bottle at Dan. 'I'll get some more here in the village.'

'It looks nice here,' Dan's eyes wandered across the landscape and settled on the village.

'The village was a present. Given to a knight over a thousand years ago because he caught robbers who plundered the monastery in Irache.'

'Well, do a good deed...' Dan began.

'But, they took it back later, so leave your armour at home,' he grinned again.

'How long have you planned to walk?'

'As long as it takes,' the man smiled. 'Buen Camino. My friend.'

'Buen Camino,' Dan realised that he said the words for the first time on the Camino. He turned away. He felt a little longing for company.

The solar furnace forced Dan to cake his face and arms in sun block for the second time. His fingers closed round the two SSD disks in their protective plastic cases in his pocket. He considered breaking off the trip now he had got the SSDs back from that stupid Downer woman.

His deficient right lung slowed him down. 'Fuck it!' he drew a slow breath and sagged to the ground and leaned against his backpack in the shadow of the only tall bush for miles around. He closed his eyes and mulled over getting the next flight out of the Camino.

'Hi, howyerdoin'? an American asked and sat beside him.

'Enjoyin' a rest,' Dan closed his eyes to make the

point.

'This thing's sure heavy! Carried it all the way from California.' His backpack sounded like a sack of cement thudding on the ground.

'What have you packed in there? Dan's boot tip tapped a plastic drum hanging from the backpack.

'Two kilos of protein powder.'

'You'll use more protein carryin' it than it can give back to you,' Dan said. The young man shrugged and pulled out a big hard-back Spanish dictionary. 'Who taught you to pack?'

'My mom.' He grinned and reddened round his ears.

'You should pack for your desires, not for your fears. That's dead weight y'carryin'.' Dan nodded at the young man's things.

'Ah this is nuthin' I passed a group of students from Alabama carrying a satellite dish.'

'What for? To beam down fuckin' aliens?'

'There's no reason to be offensive, you know?' The college boy from California repacked. 'I gotta get goin',' He lugged the pack over his shoulder and almost lost his balance, then walked away. His expression somewhat miffed.

Dan clambered to his feet and walked without any intention of catching up.

After a mile a cheerful, bearded Italian drew alongside Dan. They walked in silence for about ten minutes. 'This is my eighth Camino,' he said suddenly.

'Eighth! When do you have time for other things?'

'This is my last time.' They continued in silence. He was a fast walker. Dan stretched his pace, but his lung hindered the oxygen required for the extra effort. 'The scenery is part of it,' the man said. 'But it's the people you meet that really make each Camino different.' They continued for a while.

Dan was struggling. He croaked a reply. He tried deeper breaths, but the old capacity was no longer there.

'People are changing.' The man continued. 'More tourists,' he shrugged. 'Groups of kids on a day out, chattering like monkeys through the night, shitting in old ruins along the way.' Despite his litany, he kept up a gruelling pace, the sandy surface hissing quick time under his boots. Dan was feeling the pressure. 'I don't know why they come here.'

'Maybe teachers have a bucket list of places to visit for their students,' Dan said and fell back. 'I'm writin' an article,' he called after the Italian. 'Can I quote you?'

'Be my guest!' The Italian waved without looking back. Dan panted like a smithy's bellows and stopped in the shadow of a small tree, idly wondering whether to photograph some turds if he came across them, but decided Prosser-Jones would not appreciate such realism.

* * *

It was siesta time in Los Arcos. A serious business for the Spanish.

'Have you a bunk?'

'Yes, lots.' The girl at the reception was Austrian but still funny. No siesta for her.

'One will do, I'm not plannin' to throw a party,' Dan said tossing her a tooth flashing grin. She smiled back and made his day.

'Or an orgy,' she smiled and made his day again.

'That needs more energy than I've got.'

'Too much walking,' she grinned and opened his pilgrim pass.

He had trudged into Los Arcos with aching calves after thirty Ks without trees or shade. It ended in a gravel track on the edge of town, flanked by roofless stone houses with skeletal rotting beams. Trees jutting out of the windows were the only occupants. Gardens overgrown with yellow flowers and clusters of towering teasel plants, spiny heads ringed with tiny lilac flowers, shared their scents with him.

Dan returned the smile of the receptionist while she hammered his pilgrim pass with a rubber stamp and gave him a room number. He was happy to be here as busses ran to Pamplona airport. His next destination. Maybe. Then Majorca. Maybe.

Dan took the stone stairs two at a time. He passed a bathroom with an open door. A bald man held a hair drier. He saw Dan's curious expression. 'For my wife,' he grinned.'

Three men scraped red faces with yellow plastic razors and all smiled in greeting. Dan found a cool room on the first floor. Backpacks lay on bunks like giant eggs in small nests. Reserved in albergue code. Two pilgrims, mummified in sleeping bags, lay on the beds. Their snores alone testified to life. The early starters - up at five - out before dawn pushed back the night. You never see their faces but hear only the rustle of their packing before dawn, when you wish you had another hour to snooze before "throw out" time after breakfast. Nobody stays two nights, unless you feel unwell, then another night is permitted.

Dan dumped his backpack on an empty bunk, happy that it was a lower one. He didn't like the narrow bar rungs of the ladder that bite into the arches of bare feet. A woman in her underwear sat reading on the other lower bunk.

'Hi,' Dan greeted.

'Hi, yourself.' She looked up. Her smile and eyes were wide open.

'Where are you from?' Dan wondered if he was interested or interviewing people as a reflex action.

'Bavaria.'

'Oh, leather pants land,' he grinned.

She laughed in a sweet tone. Dan liked that. 'They are called Lederhosen. And you? England?'

'Ireland. I'm counting pilgrims for my magazine.'

'Oh, do you want to count me?'

'Only if you want to tell me about your life secrets.'

'Oh. Um.' She clapped her book shut. 'My story is not interesting enough.'

'Are you alone?'

'Ah, yes. That was funny. Before I started I told friends that I am walking alone and they all said "Whaaat! Alone? YOU! A woman walking alone?" She giggled and shook her head. 'People always think the worst! I have met only good people on the Jakobsweg. That is the German name for the Camino.'

'You're sayin' that it's perfectly safe here?'

'Oh, yes. I've lived in many cities. None of them are safe. I feel very safe here. People said I should book accommodation so I know where I'm staying and where I can eat,' her nose wrinkled at the idea.

'That could be reassuring for some people. I'd find it confining.'

'Ya, ya. I often end up in a place I hadn't planned to be and get nice surprises, treasures, that I might have missed.'

'That's good to hear. Do you fancy eatin'?

'No thanks. I buy my food on the way and prepare it in the kitchens of the albergues. It's cheaper that way.'

'Ok. I'm starvin' and on an expense account, so I'll have a quick shave, rinse my things and find a ten-star pilgrim restaurant.'

Downstairs next to a second-hand library, Dan dunked his underwear and socks in a sink of cold water in a large yard. A group of pilgrims loitered with phones on ears, or noses to screens, gabbing to people thousands of Ks away. A small group stood at the far end of the yard, a glimmer at each mouth creating a blue smoke haze, enjoying a pre-cancer reunion.

Dan hung half his entire wardrobe on thirty centimetres of a sagging line. The other half now hung on him. They swayed alongside dripping underwear of all sizes and taste.

'Like a flag day,' a man with a Scandinavian accent plastered Dan with a smile through a long straggly beard that would have prompted a full body search at any US airport. He scratched his crotch.

'I doubt if anyone will salute,' Dan noticed his stuff next to something black, the width of a boot lace with lace frills.

'There's a lively village centre nearby.'

'I'll take a look,'

'Good bit of history here, too,' the beard flapped.

'Did you know that Arcos means bow?' he absently scratched his crotch.

'I do,' he clipped an extra peg on his soggy socks.

'The town supplied a company of archers who won the battle of Valdegón nearby. The king renamed the town after the archers' bows. That's how the bow and arrow became their heraldic symbol. The battlefield was by Rio del Torres. Now the largest wind park in Spain. There's nothing there to see.'

'Unless you like windmills,' Dan said. 'I'm gettin' the bus out of here tomorrow.'

'Giving up,' the man's tone and smile suggested weakling. He scratched his crotch again. Dan wondered if Mr Beard had brought only one pair of underpants for the whole Camino.

'My assignment is completed.' He touched the form of the SSDs in the plastic envelope in his buttoned thigh pocket for reassurance. 'Buen Camino,' he wished for the second time in his Camino assignment.

The Plaza de Maria resembled a beer garden. It was full of tanned pilgrims talking and laughing between selfie sessions. It was the usual happy evening atmosphere along the Camino. Beer glasses sparkled in the rays of the sun slanting through the ancient west archway. He nodded to a pilgrim he had seen a few days before, and practiced stretching legs under a white, square umbrella. Dan checked his phone. No messages. Good.

'Hi, Dan?'

Dan squinted into the darkness of the Bar Comidas. An older Dutch guy with white stubble stepped into the sunlight.

'Hi, man,' his perfect teeth made a piano keyboard

look neglected. 'We met a few days ago.'

'I remember.'

'Had yourself a shave.'

'Quick scrape,' Dan smiled.

'Workin' for that magazine, Huntin' an' Fishin'?'

'Huntin' and fuckin' Anglin',' he searched for a waiter who was not busy hiding.

'Wow, huntin' an' fuckin' an' anglin'! All good sports!' his shoulders danced as if he was on a pogo stick.

'One's an emphasisin' word.'

'Which one?' his shoulders danced again.

'Ask my editor.'

'Ooookay!' His hearty slap on Dan's shoulder almost propelled him from his chair. 'Did you drink the wine from the fountain in Irache? The Fuente del Vino?'

'I stopped for a drop, but two arseholes sucked at the tap as if they'd rediscovered their mothers' tits,' he wrinkled his nose. 'I decided to avoid a dose of whatever they might have.'

'There's worse ways of catching something,' his shoulders jogged again while seeking a seat to grab.

'And better ways, too.'

A cheer echoed across the plaza. They rubbernecked to locate it. A backpack flew in a majestic arc through the air. Some pilgrims grabbed it. The Dutch guy's shoe soles left smoke hanging in the air. He covered a hundred yards and caught it. 'Light as a feather! Full of cotton wool!' he called and tossed it to Dan. A man swore in Spanish, grabbed and missed. Dan pulled a Rugby feint and passed to a man with a hyena laugh. He tossed it back. Dan twisted-passed again.

A woman caught it. Her eyes narrowed in a darts player squint. 'Invented Camino Rugby and incited a little riot, have we?'

'Oh, God!' Dan's smile slithered from his face.

'Mr Brady?' A friendly voice behind asked over his shoulder.

'That's me.' Dan turned. A good-looking male model type face contemplated him. An ID card floated before Dan's nose. He recognised the word POLICIA before the man palmed it with a magician's skill.

'I'm Detective Alonso Amador.'

'Where's the fire?'

'I think *you* might be the fire, Mr Brady.' Another man stepped into view. He stroked his bushy moustache. Arctic eyes cooled Dan's mood. 'I am Comisario Mendoza.' He didn't offer his hand, only an ID card with a badge.

'What's up? Speedin' ticket for walkin' too fuckin' fast?'

'We need you to help with our inquiries, Mr Brady.'

'Inquiries about what?'

'Murder, Mr Brady. Murder.' Dan saw in the Comisario's eyes that he was not joking.

LOGROÑO

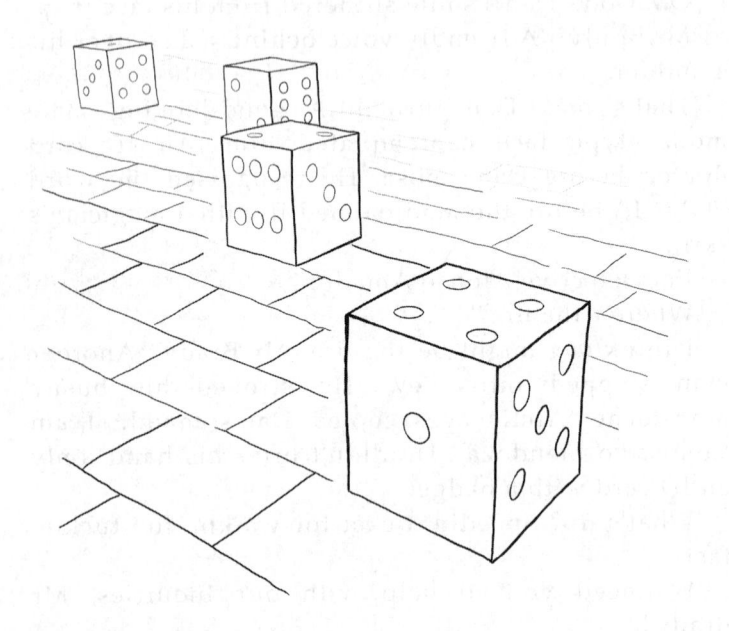

'Get into the jeep,' Mendoza said in such a commanding tone that Dan checked to see if he was holding a gun. He wasn't, but his gaze was hard as a bullet regarding Dan the way a hangman sizes up the condemned.

Jane wriggled into the jeep first, avoiding Dan's gaze. The plastic seats stuck to her thighs like distasteful sticky tape. It made her cringe and instinctively tense her sphincter muscles. Her water bottle was empty. She felt hollow and exhausted.

'Well! Well! Well! Mrs Downer! What's a girl like you doing with such nice policemen on the friggin'

Camino?' He slumped in his seat as if he owned it.

'How should I know? After all, I'm just wallowing in my touristic emotions,' she glared at him. She released an extra loud sigh, wrinkled her brow and tried to make herself smaller as he squeezed up beside her. She winced with her whole body to make her point as Detective Amador completed the crush. Jane was reaching her tolerance limit. Mendoza enthroned himself knees apart on the front seat as if visiting the opera. The gears grated. Everyone winced and glared at the uniformed driver.

'Now you're Miss Marple of the Camino, are you? Giving an emotional cripple the Judas kiss.'

'Don't be impertinent, Mr Brady. My shallow emotions have had enough of you,' she looked out of the window as the jeep pulled away, causing an undignified bouncing lap dance. *One more remark from this man and I'm going to give him a chunk of my mind*, she thought and slumped back against the seat. Angry at the police, angry at the Oaf, angry at the situation, her brain was sparking with a thousand short circuits. She was tired and closed her eyes, which accentuated the sickening, rolling feeling. She prayed her stomach would stay calm.

'I'm sorry if my friggin' remarks offended.'

'Factually, it was uncalled for.'

'I said I was sorry. But your remark was below the belt to say the least.'

'I immediately apologised on the bridge.'

He nodded. They both concentrated on the dust road ahead. 'I hope this won't take long. I've a friggin' plane to catch tomorrow.'

'I'd say your little holiday is factually on ice.'

'Is that a fuckin' fact?' Dan's words spat like hot

rivets. 'This is all your fuckin' fault! He folded his arms bunching the muscles. 'If you hadn't taken my SSDs I'd be in Majorca now! Fuck!' he kicked the back of the driver's seat.

'Violence comes easily to you, Mr Brady.' Mendoza's arctic stare met Dan's eyes in the mirror.

* * *

Sweat glued Jane's shirt to her body like a postage stamp during the drive. She felt her face must look green trying to keep down whatever was left in her wobbling stomach. A fingernail bent in the edge of her seat of the bucking jeep. *God help us! A frustrated Formula 1 driver!*

Messages bursting from the radio filled the car. Both the driver and Mendoza ignored them. The Detective was busy texting on his phone.

What do Detective's text about? She wondered. Has he a mother or wife preparing the evening meal at home? She sensed her gut sinking. She felt so tired. *Who cares? God, I'll be glad when this is over*, she thought. *Maybe I've bitten off more than I can chew.* The pang of homesickness stabbed.

A blue metal sign with rusty dents announced Logroño, the cultural and financial capital of the wine region of La Rioja. They all swayed as the driver followed a slalom course through a car park that ended in an unnecessary emergency stop throwing everyone forward in a collective bow. The driver's foot unglued the pedal from the floor. Jane's cramped grip and stomach relaxed. They parked in front of a shoe box building faced in aluminium louvers. Dan squinted from the blinding reflections of the sun.

'Police Station.' The driver exhausted his English vocabulary.

'Looks like a design for a Mars colony.'

She watched Dan put on tinted glasses. *Mr Cool. What now?* she asked herself. The murder of the girl was terrible, but she could not see how she could be of further help. Not only that, but she felt too exhausted to concentrate.

They followed the police officers into a lift that smelt of farts. Upstairs, the police officers led them into a small conference room where the Detective and the Comisario had already staked their claim at the large table. Their eyes held onto Dan Brady as cold as a machine gunner. The Detective revolved his Smart phone in his hand, glancing at the screen between sentences.

Mendoza got down to business. 'Profession, Mr Brady?'

'Journalist,'

'Journalist,' His expression looked as if he'd discovered a piece of shit in his mouth as he uttered the word. 'Jour – nal – ist. So you are a jour – nal – ist.' His sneer was bigger with each syllable.

'I am. For a magazine called Huntin' and Anglin'. A sports magazine.'

Mendoza nodded and toyed with his moustache. 'Not much hunting and angling along the Camino, is there?' He twisted his hand and surveyed his nails as if they were more important than Mr Jour – nal – ist Brady. 'What did you do before your present job?'

'First tell me why I am here!'

'Why? You were there,' he spread his hands as if

presenting the obvious. 'You. Were. There! At the scene of a murder, Mr Jour –nal – ist, Brady. A place where a girl was murdered.'

'So were many other people. What do I have to do with it?'

'Mrs Downer saw *you* coming out of the woods. We have to follow every lead.' Mendoza twisted his moustache. 'So, what did you do before that?'

'Army. Royal Signals Company in the UK and later Afghanistan. After my discharge, due to a wound, I got my present position.' Jane noticed his sneer showing his opinion of his job.

'Army,' Mendoza turned his flecked hand and looked at it. 'Tell me,' he squinted at Dan. 'What brings an ex-British army man, to play at being a journalist for a sports magazine, on the Camino?' Mendoza's tone was hard edged. Flame sprouted from his fist holding an invisible lighter. It ignited a cigarette tip. The red No Fumare sign was not for him.

'You seem to have something against journalists.'

'Oh! Mr Brady! How very, very perceptive of you.'

'Ok. Well, I'm writin' articles on the Way of Saint James.' Dan tapped the table top with a fingernail.

'A strange assignment for a hunting magazine, isn't it?' Amador twisted his Smart phone in his hand. Jane noticed his chewed nails again. She also noticed his gaze on her hair. He caught her eye and looked away.

'It's not strange. It's fuckin' *stupid*! But I'm not the boss of the magazine.'

'It could be worse,' Detective Amador smiled for the first time. 'We have better weather than England, and better food.' His expression turned serious again. 'What were you doing in the woods by the bridge where Ms Downer saw you?' He turned his head and stared into Dan's eyes.

'Pissing.'

Mendoza stared without expression.

'And a short nap,' he added.

'Or maybe something that can get you a good name and your article in all the papers? Hmm? I know how the minds of journalists work. Bad news sells, raises TV viewer quotes and gets more clicks in the Internet,' Mendoza paused. 'Even if it ruins reputations.' He flicked ash on the floor and stuck the cigarette in his mouth; one eye half closed as smoke spiralled past his face. It drifted before the King of Spain on the wall who maintained a dignified royal smile.

Jane watched Dan clenching his fists. 'I assume this is a free country, isn't it?' Jane watched his lips moving and wished the interview would end. *The man's cigarette smoke stings my eyes.* She looked across the table and out of the window into the distance. She thought of the Camino, and Debbie, and then about the poor girl she had found. She shuddered at the indelible image in her mind. She wanted to go home.

'Sí, Mr Brady. Spain is a free country,' He sucked in smoke and blew it out again. 'If people behave,' Mendoza added. 'So what about the woman, Mr Brady?'

'What woman? Dan's forehead wrinkled.

'The woman Ms Downer found metres away from where you were passing your journalistic water, Mr Brady.'

'I didn't see or hear anything! I have nothing to do

with it!' Dan erupted into a shout. 'I'm here to write articles about pilgrims, not kill them!'

'We will see what the forensic team says. Until then, we will watch you Mr Brady. And don't you dare to write one line about this. I dislike reporters who act like little Gods on crusades against people doing their jobs.' Spittle collected on Mendoza's moustache.

'Murder's a public thing!'

'Then consider yourself under my personal D notice, Mr Brady.' The thud of Mendoza's fist on the table startled Jane, but Dan just blinked slowly and calmly.

'Details of our actions could help the killer evade capture,' Detective Amador smiled. 'You'd be obstructing our investigations if you wrote about the murder before we made an official press release.'

'However, the reason we are here is to discover your role in this young woman's death, Mr Brady.' Mendoza stared Dan out while his cigarette stabbed a coffee saucer.

Dan's Adam's apple bobbed again as he swallowed. 'I didn't fuckin' kill her, so lay off me!'

'You were standing outside the woods when I arrived,' Jane said primly.'

'Come on, Ms Downer!' Dan shouted. 'I had a short nap and came out as you arrived with my stolen disks!'

'Tut! Stolen! Don't be so dramatic. You misplaced them!'

'Then you could have been there when she died,' Mendoza snapped, he reappraised his finger nails.

'No!' Dan yelled. 'My God! I read Logroño was the centre of the inquisition in the middle ages. Are you still livin' in those fuckin' times?' Dan's face flooded bright, red enough to stop traffic.

'Steady on, Mr Brady, please control yourself,' Detective Amador said.

'Control my fuckin' self? Look. I don't like the way you are framing things! I want to contact the Irish embassy!'

'Not the British?'

'Either. I don't give a fuck!'

'Ok, ok,' Detective Amador pressed his hands downward placating. 'We want to establish basic facts. Now, when did you first get to the murder scene?'

'He was there when I arrived,' Jane said. She saw Dan's face staring back at her. 'Well, not there but on the bridge nearby.'

'Now *wait* a fuckin' minute!'

'Nobody is accusing you, Mr Brady,' Amador chided. 'I estimated the time of death to be about eight hours at the most. So she was killed when it was still dark. It was dark when you got there I think.'

'Not dark. After dawn. I started early. Look! I have nothin' to do with this! Nothin'!' His hand chopped the air sideways to make his point.

'We shall see, Mr jour – nal – ist reporter, we shall see.' the Comisario interrupted. Dan looked into hard brown eyes. Jane saw his Adam's apple bob again as he swallowed. He was clearly nervous.

Jane stared at her fingers splayed on the table, her lips pressed together. She looked up, her eyes following the blue smoke curling from Mendoza's second cigarette. She noticed the man's thick, brown fingers and nails. She cleared her voice loudly. They all looked at her.

'Comisario, can I have a word in private?' Jane interrupted.

'About this murder?'

'Yes. About the murder and something else. By the way, shouldn't we be in separate rooms to hear our statements taken, Comisario?'

'Normally, yes. But I wanted to get things cleared up as fast as possible with an open discussion of your joint experiences.' He mopped his brow. 'Very well, Ms Downer. You come with me.' He turned to the Detective. 'Amador, stay with Mr Brady and write notes on anything you ask.'

'I'll record it, Comisario,' he smiled and waggled his mobile phone. Mendoza grunted and left the room. Jane followed.

* * *

'That is quite a story,' Ms Downer,' Mendoza nodded twenty minutes later, his lips pursed in thought. They were in an office two doors down from the conference room. 'Not that I know anything about the incidents you describe.' Mendoza stood. 'I'll look into your case and do what I can to assist, Ms Downer.' He showed her to the door of the office.

'Thank you Comisario. You can understand that I did not want to talk about something about my family in front of Mr Brady.'

'I understand, Ms Downer. You can be sure of my support. Detective Amador shall bring you to a squad car to bring you to a hotel nearby. Tomorrow it can take you to the edge of the city; if you wish to continue your walk that is.'

'Thank you. Will Mr Brady be coming too?'

Mendoza smiled. Jane focused on his brown smoker's teeth and thought of her mother who had paid the ultimate price. I have to return to continue with Mr Brady. Detective Amador will take you to the hotel we have reserved for you.

Ten minutes later, Amador escorted Jane to a gleaming Skoda patrol car. 'We have booked a hotel room in the city centre. If you need anything, Ms Downer, please don't hesitate to call me.'

'Thank you, I shall.' She felt a slight irritation at the way he stared at her hair.

* * *

The hotel in Logroño was perfect for deaf people. The pilgrims with thicker wallets for upscale accommodation were loud. At least the bed was comfortable and she had the room to herself, but the comfort did not lull Jane to deep sleep. It was always punctured by the scene of flies feasting on clotted blood. She woke again with a thudding heart. The top of the sheet was soggy in her mouth. She decided to stay awake. 'God, I'm dry!' she muttered and swung out of bed. The room bar threw a glow across the room. She inspected the row of miniatures on parade inside like a chess game waiting to start. The whiskey didn't anaesthetise the horror she had witnessed. Back into bed her limbs twitched as if electric shocks rippled through her. After some hours, dozing under her third whiskey she got up and stared out of the window, seeing only her own reflection. Do I look drunk? She stared, trying to see herself and leaned forward to peer at her image reflected in the black window. *Either the image is poor or I can't see straight. He's out there.* The hairs on the nape of her neck raised. *He may be in bed. Killers sleep, too.*

The room was stifling. She opened the window to change the still air, letting the sounds of the city flow in. Jane's memory made fast rewind back to the scene. Yes. True. She was dressed in long hiking pants and big boots. Was she assaulted? Or a jealous argument with a boyfriend, or lover? Or robbery? That could be it! It could have been a robbery-murder. She resisted, and the thief killed her. She shook her head, her brow furrowed. Is that credible? Pilgrims carry very little money. *Credit cards? Some look well off, even if they are in debt. But not in Debbie's case. She didn't know what debt meant. Death from robberies tend to be head injuries from heavy object, or a stab wound. And people don't sit around while they are being robbed. She would have been lying on the ground after a struggle, not sitting down. That makes it look as if she knew him. She was sitting and relaxing with someone she knew.* 'Oh, God! Leave it to the police', she sighed. *That's what they're paid for. Get some sleep.* 'I have to know!' Jane muttered.

She reached for her mobile and saw she had missed a call. So what! It was only *him*, her lip curled. Jane phoned the room service. None, out on the town. She grabbed the remote and zapped the TV.

Welcome Ms Downer. She pressed button P.

Zap

Adult movies. Titles will not be itemised on your

bill.

Does Brady watch these? She wondered and thumbed the P again.

Zap

A soap opera featuring female actresses in permanent hysteria, in scratch-her-eyes-out yelling while gigolo types slimed from scene to scene. Their yelling momentarily turned Jane's room into Bedlam.

Zap

BBC World filled the screen. She stared at disasters, floods, babies with swollen bellies and big eyes over jutting cheek bones stared listlessly, then more bombings, people yelling in the rubble, then Dax and Dow, showing the rich west in an orgy of speculation. The show flowed from repeat to repeat.

Zap.

The plasma went blind. Jane stared at the screen and nodded off, still trying to erase the terrible images from her mind. A woman cried out throatily in a long orgasm in a neighbouring room. A man laughed. A dog barked. The woman's cries began again. Jane rushed to close the window and lay down again. She closed her eyes. Her phone rang. Her eyes popped open like a toy doll. It rang again. She stretched an arm. 'Oh, Angie!' she whispered feeling relieved.

* * *

Metal bunk frames squeaked as Pilgrims rolled over to throw venomous glances at Dan's snoring form.

He was deep in the sleep of exhaustion after his previous day's walk and police interrogation till late evening. Finally, the police had finished and called a few albergues to find one with an empty bunk.

Dan's snores rumbled through the stale air within minutes after crawling inside his sleeping bag, much to the irritation of the seven female pilgrims sharing the small dormitory. They plugged in their ear plugs, pulled their hooded sleeping bag tops over their heads and took cover, huddled deep inside. A darker mute shadow edged unchallenged across the room. Nobody is indiscreet enough to question shadowy forms at night in an albergue. A hand slipped gently into Dan's backpack on the floor where he had dumped it.

EMBALSE DE LA GRAJERA

Flashing blue lights of the white and blue police Skoda died. Balls of snowy fluff from cottonwood trees drifted dreamily in the breeze across the ground in a surreal summer snow drift.

'Gracias!' Jane swung her legs out of the car and heaved her backpack from the back seat after herself. She saw the outside of a red brick restaurant on the bank of Lake Embalse de la Grajera, west of Logroño. Here the asphalt road ended and became serious Camino again.

The two police officers in light blue shirts with razor creases and blunt jaws smiled like male models. 'Buen Camino!' they chimed with eyes sparkling, showing they had an eye for a pretty pilgrim. The immaculate car with its immaculate crew swayed away over potholes and passed a ghost town of an amusement park sprawled under the trees. Jane waggled her hands above her head as if the police officers were lifelong friends. The tail lights bucked, dwindled to pinpoints that blended before vanishing into the woods.

A clopping sound attracted her attention. A rider on a white horse came along the trail out of the pine trees.

'Buen Camino,' he wished as he rode by at a slow walk. He had bulging saddle bags and enough equipment hanging from the saddle to accommodate a whole class of kids. Jane watched him go, and thought of Debbie and the horse her father had bought her. She shook her head and made her way over to the restaurant, casting glances into the shadows of the woods flanking the Way. I should have brought a pepper spray, or a gun. A real man-stopper. That's more that awful man Brady's department. He'd probably strangle anyone who tried to jump out and surprise him. She tried to swallow. Her mouth was too dry. The morning was already hot and the glare blinding. A fly buzzed her ears and nose. She swiped it away. Worker bees droned over flowers along the way, their heads ducking into and out of the petals before bumbling to the next.

Inside the restaurant Jane ordered hot and cold water at the long wood topped bar. Another woman took her coffee away and nodded. The barkeeper planted three blue bottles of Solan de Cabras. She emptied one down her throat faster than the Niagara Falls before wedging the others in the net side pockets of her backpack. She dripped a few drops of her teasel tincture in the steaming cup and took it outside and sat under the long back terrace facing the lake.

'Mixing your own?' the other woman with cropped black hair at the next table asked.

'I like to collect herbs and experiment.'

'Walking alone?'

'Yes, but I have friends who are mobile. You?'

'I wanted to walk with my husband, but he said it was to *intimate,* she flexed her fingers to mime quotation marks. 'He didn't like the idea of sharing rooms with lots of other people.'

'Factually, we are going in the same direction. We can walk together, if you like.'

'Thanks but I'm thinking of going back into town. Take a train. My feet can't take any more. Got blisters.'

'Hi!' Jane turned. A pilgrim couple accompanied by their big shaggy dog got up to go. They waved. She stood and waved back. She had met them a week ago. An English pensioner pair who had emigrated to Bulgaria and now walked from there to Spain. He pushed a homemade cart with bicycle wheels loaded with tent, backpacks and battered aluminium doggie dishes. She turned back to her seat. The woman had silently left.

A clean smelling breeze from off the blue water cooled her face. She tried to shake away thoughts of the terrible day before and concentrated on the view across the vast lake surrounded by a forest of firs and chattering birds. A swan on the grassy bank puffed and ruffled its white feathers and watched a raft of ducks bobbing like a moored fleet nearby. Two anglers hunched on the grassy bank, baskets by their side. Dad was a keen angler. Jane thought of Debbie. Her twin sister. She and dad spent hours together angling and coming home in triumphant glee, no matter how small the catch. Jane thought about how mom always swore they bought their catch from a fishmonger near home. She smiled at her mother's humour and stood up. She sprang aside to avoid a mob of cyclists with gaudy helmets as they flashed by. They shouted loudly to one another in French as they stacked their bikes and stormed the toilets as if they were the Bastille.

Jane rejoined the trail behind two marching Koreans. Their poles stabbed the ground ticking like a loud clock. They turned and looked back at Jane, their faces hidden behind surgical masks like pending bank robbers. Jane wondered whether it was protection from the dust, sun, or germs. Many Korean women went on the Camino hoping to meet a man, Jane thought. When singles hit thirty in China and Korea they're called the Leftover Women. A book, written by a man described his romantic dreams coming true along the Camino, increased the popularity of the Camino as if gold nuggets were lying around for the taking.

The rubber thump of her boots on paving changed to crunching as the trail became gravel. She and the two Koreans were the only people in sight, and they were pulling way ahead of her. She looked back. The loud French bicycle gang were mounting their Tour de Camino steeds calling to each other as the first few pressed their pedals and lowered their heads making power. One winked as he flew passed

A cowled monk in a dark ankle length habit stood under a tree. It was hard to see him in detail. He was motionless. Jane screwed up her eyes to focus. She couldn't make out whether he was meditating, or watching the cyclists or maybe her. She moved and waited a metre away from the edge of the trail. The cyclists blew passed, chains whirring, fat tyres crackling, helmets gleaming over teeth clenching concentrated faces. Fluffy cotton balls swirled and waltzed in their wake before settling on the path and on the white and lilac lavender bushes. The Koreans had left her behind, alone again with the birds, the breeze and trees. She looked back. The monk was invisible.

Dust coated Jane's boots like brown talc that hung behind her on the air. She kept up a good pace through the shadowy woods looking left and right. *Are these woods safe?* she wondered. *That girl was attacked in the woods, but she was a long way from the path,* she reasoned. *Nobody would try anything here. Someone to keep you company always comes along.* Nevertheless, Jane kept a roving eye on the woods flanking her. She didn't relax until the trail climbed and the trees thinned out, exposing her to the intense sun. It was an unusually hot May. Her T-shirt was clammy under her backpack and she felt the first feeling of a blister forming on her little toe.

The light of the sun made her feel safer than the gloom of the forest. She put on her sunglasses. Here, higher up, only a few stunted firs offered temping shadows against the scorching sun. The next tree, she thought, the next tree, always the next tree, but the urge to keep moving was stronger. Far away shadows seem cooler. She pulled at her water bottle. A fly settled on her cheek. She wrinkled her nose. She hated flies. Her hand flicked at it. It came back. She swatted again. It dive-bombed her face and arms as she continued the calf cracking climb. The track cut through a vast waist high expanse of yellow mustard flowers flowing away over the hills. She plucked a piece. Pressed it between her thumb and fingers and inhaled the aroma from the juice on her finger tips. *Can't understand why it's considered a weed in some parts of the world. I didn't like that Brady man's remark about poisonous plants. I'm the last person to make that sort of mistake.* She though briefly about her sister. She'd loved Jane's herbal teas

She turned and faced the way she had come and sniffed her finger tips again. A clapper sound made her look up. The heads of two storks in a nest of sticks perched precariously atop a telephone pole watched her. Their long beaks clacked down at her. They must have young or eggs to guard, Jane decided. She took a photo of the pair with her camera. She heard that some storks stay together for life. A symbol for fertility, their increasing population is contrary to the declining Spanish population, shown by the number of decaying and collapsed houses she had passed. One stork rose and launched itself across the sky, its white and black trimmed wings flapped slowly as it dwindled across the fields. She turned and saw a clump of nettles. *Should I collect them to make tea?* she wondered. *Be practical. You've collected enough herbs already.* She lowered her backpack to the ground, opened it and felt for the suede sack.

A shadow fell across her, and two brown eyes

watched her over a black mask. Her heart leaped into her throat choking her.

* * *

'Buen Camino,' The woman pulled the mask from her face. 'You alright?'

'You startled me.' Jane stuffed the sack into her pack.

'Oh, the mask! It's for the dust,' she grinned. 'Hope I didn't throw a scare into you.' The sticks of a woman with a short haircut, tick-tacked in the grit as regular as a clock, even though she was standing still.

'Well, a Buen Camino to you, too. Where did you start?'

'Originally New Zealand. This morning God knows. A sort of church with Albergue painted on the wall. English aren't you?'

'Yes, from Chester. South of Liverpool.'

'I know it. Roman walls. Eastgate clock.'

'Factually, the most photographed clock after Big Ben.'

'What's so bad in Chester that would to drive you to the Camino?'

'A wake up call on life, and…' she stopped to avoid the other reason.

'Man problem?' Her stabbing sticks ticked like a metronome. 'I've met other women here because of a man.'

'Not all because of the same man, I hope,' Jane smiled. 'In fact, some men are here because of women.'

'I found out my husband's gay. When I confronted him he kicked me out. Sold our house!' She stabbed her sticks as if his heart lay on the trail. 'And you?'

'Factually, I reached a point of no return. I left him.'

'Was he violent?'

'Mean,' Jane brushed her hand across the red plastic wallet in her side net pocket. 'Stingy with money, feelings and words. I told him I had a special reason to come here, but he couldn't and wouldn't understand.'

'What special reason?'

'My sister.'

'Is she here?'

'Yes.'

'That's nice.' Water and bubbles flowed through a tube attached to a plastic water bladder hanging from her backpack. The sun glinted on a bottle of Rioja nestling the net pocket of her backpack.

'Wine! That must really increase your backpack's weight.'

'I've got two!' she smiled and twisted her body to show the other side of her pack. 'I carry it in case there isn't any when I stop for the night.'

'That's most unlikely.'

'Oh!' the woman ducked. A gang of cyclists, arses up and heads down, squeezed past without warning. Fountains of dust sprouted from fat chunky tires. Chains whirred under pressure of their pumping feet. 'Buen Caminooo,' they sang out and pressed their pedals westward. The woman looked back.

'Any more coming?' Jane asked.

The woman turned around. 'No. Just a monk.'

Jane looked back at a solitary figure about a

hundred yards behind them.

'A poser,' the lady said. 'He could be the real thing, but there *are* people who dress up to get a real pilgrim experience. The sackcloth and ashes brigade, I call 'em; wearing sandals and habit, like a thousand years ago.'

'Oh!' Jane winced as a solitary bike whizzed by. 'Where did he come from?'

'Two thousand Euro bike and too mean to get a two Euro bell.' The woman's eyes narrowed shooting a look to leave invisible arrows quivering in his back. 'Did you know; twenty percent of Camino fatalities are cyclists?' The swaying cyclists morphed into dots.

'That's a lot!'

'Yes. Thirty percent of deaths are from traffic. Walkers and cyclists together that is. If half are cyclists are added to the twenty percent, it's a high casualty group.' she stabbed her sticks harder. 'Heart attacks sixty percent.'

'My heart's alright, and I haven't got a bike. I should be safe.'

'Oh, you are certain to be safe here. The chances of being victim of a crime is about one percent on the Camino. Sixty percent less than the rest of the country. Statistically the Camino is one of the safest places on the planet.'

A bar ahead looked inviting and it was near. The blue massive mountain chain seemed too far to reach. 'God, it's hot! I'm going to take a break now. What about you?'

'Too early for me. I wish you a Buen Camino,' the lady beamed and piled on the power, and speeded up, despite the extra weight of wine bottles. Jane had kept her backpack below the ideal ten percent of body weight.

'Remember,' the lady called waving her stick over her head. 'Saying Buen Camino to a cyclist means "Break your effing neck!"'

'I'll remember that,' Jane raised a hand and turned toward the bar. She caught a glimpse of another pilgrim. She frowned. *Mr Tennis shoes?* she wondered. He was almost invisible, sitting still in the shade of a tree watching. Jane felt sweat prickling up her spine.

EL PRESIDENTE

Sexy Graffiti haunted the air in Maria Cadorna's office. The tear shaped bottle stood next to her computer keyboard. She had a desk with a great view of the sparkling River Arga below that curved through Pamplona. Maria preferred the view in her mirror. The window with the view was firmly closed against the afternoon heat. The air conditioning hummed lightly. So did Maria, listening to music in her ear pods. She was a mono-lingual, two finger typist, already at the top of her single rung career ladder. It was the bottom rung of the administration of the President of the Cultural Development Council. She wore her hair long and her skirt short.

At her ten-minute job interview, the President had seen all the qualifications he deemed necessary.

Comisario Mendoza padded silently into the high panelled ante room on crepe soled shoes. He stopped before Maria's desk. He inhaled loud and long like a hound, followed by a smile of appreciation. 'Good morning, Maria. A new perfume?'

'Yes. New for three years now, Comisario,' she fluttered her eyelids as if starring in an online dating advert.

'Hm, yes, of course, of course,' his smile drooped from his mouth.

'The President expects you,' she nodded at the old lecher's throne room. 'Señor, Comisario? Please. The cigarette!' she hissed. 'The President hates cigarette smoke. He likes only cigars .'

Mendoza grunted and stubbed it in an art deco Smokador standing by the door.

'Señor Presidente,' Mendoza greeted from the doorway and bowed his head. The President's small black eyes stared from a baggy, grey complexion across his giant mahogany desk. His family clan huddled in a silver framed photo on the corner of the gleaming expanse. A solitary file lay like a giant playing card before him. The President beckoned Mendoza with a lazy wag from the wrist. Wispy smoke trailed from his thick lips pursed above a collection of chins. The President's teeth clenched a fat cigar. Mendoza approached the desk. He stopped, hands slightly cupped before his crotch in a footballer's stance at a penalty kick.

'Sit, Mendoza,' the President stabbed the cigar at two antique chairs before his desk. Mendoza bowed across the desk to shake the proffered hand before he sat. 'Hmm, nice smell,' he nodded at the cigar. He knew they cost over thirty Euros each.

'Cuban,' the President inspected it as if to make sure and nodded without offering one. 'Mendoza,' He said it at two different tones. Higher then lower. 'I read your report on this latest killing. Not good. Not after two bodies last year,' He shook his bald head and flabby chins and looked with Spaniel eyes. 'This could damage the Camino, Mendoza. And the Council.' He regarded Mendoza over the cigar as if sighting along a smoking gun barrel.

'We contained the situation last year as you wished, Señor Presidente. We convinced the people who found them that the victims died of exposure after a night in the open. Their relatives accepted the story as well.'

'Bah! This is the hottest May for years!' He mopped his brow with a silk handkerchief to make the point. 'Exposure won't wash now, Mendoza.' He frowned at the dead cigar tip, pulled an ornamental lighter on the table towards him. A flame sprouted. His cheeks puffed like a Smithy's bellows to revive it. He leaned back and opened his mouth. Smoke drifted out. His cold gaze returned to Mendoza. 'But this incident, Mendoza! A body left in the open to be found like that!' He stared as if Mendoza were the culprit.

'Difficult situation, Señor Presidente. A woman stumbled across the body.'

'How?'

'Wanted to pee.'

'We should apply to the EU to fund more toilets along the Camino, Mendoza. There must be a grant for that.' He assumed a cash register expression.

'Toilets are a good idea, Señor Presidente.'

'All this scurrying around in the bushes, Mendoza. Not hygienic!' He sucked the cigar till it glowed enough to replace Bilbao lighthouse. 'Do you think it is the same perpetrator, Mendoza?' His hand jabbed the cigar at Mendoza in a spear throwing gesture.

'It is the same man, Señor Presidente.'

'You arrested a man did you not?'

'We released him. Detective Amador is the police correctness generation, habeas corpus...'

'Aaah! Stop, Mendoza! Stop!' the President raised a hand. 'Say no more, Mendoza! These Do-Gooders will have all the criminals running around free. Tell me, Mendoza, what sort of killer are we dealing with?' More smoke expanded in the air.

'It does not have a sexual motive.'

'But she was female like the two last year. People add two and two and make five. Most pilgrims are female,' the President raised a finger. 'Mendoza! Keep it quiet! If it does become public, I want a prisoner, or a body, to show we've done our job.'

'Then we need to keep the body away from the Public Prosecutor's office, Señor Presidente.'

'Do that. Declare it was a suicide. These are not subject to an autopsy and will stop an enquiry. Then they can keep her in a morgue under the guise of gathering evidence.'

'That is possible, Señor Presidente. The people in the morgue are always under pressure to hurry. They'll be happy to put a job off.'

'Then they won't be curious,' he blew more smoke and smiled at Mendoza for the first time.

'She must have parents, relatives, even a husband, Señor Presidente.'

The President hand flapped a dismissive wave. 'So what? Lots of people disappear. Some of them want to drop out of sight.' His smile stretched his capillary riddled cheeks.

'I have a plan, Señor Presidente,' he mopped his brow. 'As long as this Englishman thinks I am after him, but feels he can stay on the Camino, I have a person who we can pick up any time we want. If the damned press starts to make life difficult, we have a suspect.'

'Good, Mendoza. Either way, close the case before the fields turn yellow!' He raised a warning finger again. 'Our Council could collapse if the clowns in Brussels looked further than the brochure we produce!' He leaned closer across the table and lowered his voice. 'I took the last brochure to Brussels myself.' He sucked at the cigar and blew a smoke ring. They both watched it as the President poked his cigar through the middle. Mendoza had seen this party piece a hundred times. 'Our grant is always just below twenty million Euros, so the birdbrains don't even open it! I don't want to wake them up through bad publicity.'

'It *is* a nice brochure,' Señor Presidente.'

'Hah! It's stored in an old building in Waterloo! Imagine! Water-loo!'

'The famous battle!'

'The very same place, Mendoza.' He unwrapped another cigar. 'Almost where the Duke of Wellington stood.'

'Please bear in mind, Señor Presidente, I haven't many men at my disposal to contain this.'

'My cousin has a security firm in Madrid. He has a man called er...' He held the bridge of his nose with his brow furrowed, trying to recall the name. 'Um, Ram, Rambo?'

'That's a Hollywood film, Señor Presidente.'

'Ah, Ramos! Yes! Ramos. He has a company. Rough types. You'll get them as a special team. Nobody will ask questions; you have my guarantee.' His chest expanded prior to launching a new cloud. 'Don't let anyone leave the scene of a crime before you check and erase any photos. The team will be the first at any future crime scenes of this kind.' The President lowered his voice. 'The next twenty million Euros are due in early June, Mendoza. Don't fail me.'

'I understand, Señor Presidente.'

'We all have a lot to lose, Mendoza. Fail, and you lose your pension and a future as my successor! Everything!' He blew another stream of cigar smoke across the desk. 'Use any methods you choose. But. Do. Not. Fail.'

'This Englishman...' he stopped.

'Use him, Mendoza!' the chins wobbled. 'If we need a body, let it be his, and not another pilgrim. That's bad for business. Remember,' the cigar poked again. 'There is twenty million Euros at stake, Mendoza! Twenty million!' his finger raised and his lower lip quivered. 'Your cut is substantial,' he slumped back and blew another ring. They both watched it float through the glowing chandeliers. 'Fail me, Mendoza, and your family will suffer.' The President leaned back and released another ring and poked his cigar through the middle.

'I can find him any time, Señor Presidente.'

'Do that. For your family's sake.'

* * *

'Are you ok?' An American voice broke into Dan's dream of himself in a small, sinking rubber boat while Admiral Prosser-Jones shouted down from the bridge of Puente la Reina that Dan was fired. He blinked up at a figure looking down on him where he lay in a pile of hay near the trail. 'Are you ok?'

'Taking a nap.'

'Sorry. I thought you had fallen over. You're still wearin' your backpack.'

'Quicker that way. Do it all the time,' Dan grinned. The impassive twenty something face remained serious.

'Well, if you're alright, sir.'

'The "sir" made Dan feel very senior, or old or ancient.

'You're American?' Dan clambered to his feet.

'Yes, sir.'

'Where do you hail from?'

'Washington DC. This is my first pilgrimage. And you, sir? Is this your first pilgrimage?'

'First and friggin' last I hope. What brought you from Washington to the highway to hell?'

'A film called The Way.'

'The Way,' Dan nodded slowly and hung onto his eyebrows from inside, to resisted rolling his eyes.

'Yeah. But it's sure not like the film, no sir.'

'Life is not Hollywood. Hollywood's not life.'

'I worried that people might have negative feelings for America and its government, so I was kind of worried how people might receive me.'

'Don't worry. You meet people on the Camino, not governments.'

'Glad to hear that, sir.'

'Ah! Umbrellas! Shade! Beer! You thirsty?' He grinned and was beginning to enjoy being addressed as "sir." He took a seat outside a bar under an umbrella. The student sat opposite.

'I'll get some beers,' Dan headed into a bar. The queue was long. He came out fifteen minutes later with two Estrella beers wetting his hands. The seat opposite was empty. Dan sighed, shrugged and swigged his beer. He chased it down with the disappearing student's beer, leaned back in the shade and let his eyelids droop.

SUGAR

It was a small room without pictures. It made a phone booth look like a ballroom. Only the outline of a missing crucifix marked the wall above the grey, tubular metal bed bolted to the concrete floor.

'Hi, Mommy,' a figure sank in the hard mattress at the foot of the bed. There was nowhere else to sit in the room devoid of furniture. A black baseball cap hid his features.

'Sugar?' a woman's voice crackled from under the sheet over her head. 'Is that you, my little Sugar?' The sheet over the figure's mouth trembled like a damp diaphragm when she spoke.

'Yes, it's me, Mommy.' The figure sat hunched, knees pressed together, feet turned inward.

'How are you, my Sugar?' The sheet pulsed.

'Not good, Mommy. I came to tell you I saved

another Eva.'

'Another Eva?' The cracked voice, slowed by its lazy southern states drawl came through the sheet. 'That's good, Sugar.'

'No! Not good, Mommy! I saved her, but...' the voice choked back a sob. 'Another woman stopped me...'

'What! What you sayin' Sugar?'

'A woman found her in the woods before I could take the Eve away to her burial. '

'A wasted sacrifice, Sugar!'

'I followed the girl for three days!' the petulant voice whined. 'I talked to her a lot! Prepared her. Got her away from the Camino. Then before I could save her body the way I should, the woman came before I could process her.' He sighed. 'The woman called the police. Mommy, I let you down.' The head of the figure drooped.

'No.' The whisper was raw. 'You know I'm proud of you. You can still fix it, d'you hear that?'

'The other woman, Mommy. She's...' His voice stopped. His figure rocked to and fro.

'Tell me.'

'She is also an Eva.'

'What! What are you telling me?' The head twisted as if it could see through the sheet 'Another Eva! This is Satan's work! She could be a guardian! Do you understand? Satan has substituted the Eva you saved. He's played this trick through eternity! He's created another Succubus! You must save her, too! Save them both!' The head twisted left and right. 'I'd kill them myself if I could get out of here!'

'If you could see, Mommy.'

'Yes, if I could see.'

'That was a bad thing she did with the acid, Mommy.'

'She paid. I made sure of that.'

'But now you're paying again, Mommy. Locked in here.'

'The will of the Lord,' the voice hissed. 'Get them, Sugar and save us both.'

'Yes, Mommy, I will. I won't let you down.' Soft sobs were the only sound.

'Good. Go home and sleep now, y'hear? The Lord is with you, Sugar, because you're doin' his good work an' every Eva you save will get you nearer to God on Judgment Day.'

'I know that, Mommy. I'm gonna do my bestest best.'

'How many crosses are left along our Camino, Sugar?'

'Two.'

'Still two to bless with Eva's.'

'Then I've finished my mission on the Camino,' he said.

'*Our* Camino!'

'Our Camino, Mommy.' He nodded a long time.

'Do your duty! Then you'll have a place next to the Lord. Go!' The voice gasped. 'Make them pay!'

'They'll pay, Mommy, they'll pay.'

NAVARRETE

The clock tower of Navarrete pokes above the roofs of the village like a rocket awaiting the launch and ready to fly. The only thing flying for Jane was the time. The tower was the first thing she saw when she crested a hill. *I'll stop there*, she decided and descended the hill along the trail that curved away from the noisy motorway beside her. She entered a landscape of chunky vines flowing in every direction around her. Rioja wine country.

She reached the ruins of San Juan de Acre, a medieval hospital separated from her by a sea of lilac topped thistles on her left. A man shot photos from various angles.

'Nicely kept,' he nodded at the ruins.'

'Yes. So clean it makes me ashamed of the state of my kitchen back home,' she smiled. He chuckled. 'It makes me wonder about the millions of feet that tramped passed here. I wish I could go inside.'

'Yes,' his accent was French and cute. 'It is a sobering reminder of the courage and tenacity in the face of discomfort and illness. These hospitals were crucial for survival.'

'Factually, some died from attacks by thieves.'

The man nodded. 'You are right but, half of deaths in the middle ages were from drowning, and often doing mundane things, like washing clothes in rivers or falling from a boat. They were unable to swim!' he spread his hands in amazement. 'Where did you start this morning?'

'Logroño.'

'Oh, not so far.' He packed his camera and long phallic symbol telephoto lens away in a shoulder bag.

'Far enough for my feet.' Jane sat for a moment.

'I want to reach Azofra,' he said taking the first step.

'Good luck. I'm going to take it slowly,' she smiled. His eyes were nice. He smiled and walked off at an impossibly fast pace. Jane hobbled a few steps further and stopped at a giant Rioja wine bottle that towered over her head. It dominated the field and the bottling plant behind it. A large sign saying Born on the Way failed to inspire her. She stood and looked at the bottle for a long moment as if meditating. Debbie was here, Jane thought about one of her postcards she had sent.

Footsteps crunched behind her. Two men deep in conversation in a Slavic tongue while looking at their phones walked by without noticing the giant bottle. Jane took a step and froze. Her leg muscles were knotted tortured strings. *I need an extra strong herbal tea*, she thought. She had collected dandelions and nettles, and some pine needles along the way to ease muscle pain and cramps. She knew some laughed at her and her herbal teas. She didn't care. *I'm healthier than most people.* She winced. Her boots felt tighter with every step. Her toes felt raw. A fat fly fastened itself to her arm. She wrinkled her nose as it rubbed its forelegs together as if washing hands. She felt too tired to swat it. *Why am I damned well doing this?* She suppressed a small sob. *I'd rather go home.* She stopped and stared at the hazy horizon. She stood panting and aching.

Fighting her inner weakness, she dragged each foot up a steep flight of concrete steps and entered the town. She came to an elegant fluted cast iron water fountain in the street. Jane had heard it is law in Spain for every village to provide drinking water for travellers. *Good law,* she thought, and pressed the bronze tap, cupped her hands and flooded her stomach. The relief was immediate as a cold wave flowed inside.

Five minutes later she arrived under a low gallery with beams. She stood with several others before the locked wooden door of the municipal albergue. A long bench was crammed so tightly thigh to thigh with pilgrims that they could feel each other's pimples. While they compared experiences of the day, Jane and other late comers stood around or sat on their packs killing time. The cobbles were as round as tennis balls making the soles of her boots difficult to keep level. She considered walking to the next albergue but wasn't sure how far it might be.

No sense waiting here, she mused. And went to find somewhere comfortable. She walked with wobbly steps up the cobbled walkway. Hairs stood on the nape of her neck. She looked back. The other pilgrims sat waiting for the doors to open. Nobody new had appeared. Nobody followed. Her imagination again?

* * *

She emerged from the gallery blinking at the glare in a square full of the ubiquitous grey trees with pruned gnarled branches.

'Well, well, well. Look who's here!'

Jane pressed her lips together and narrowed her eyes. She slowly turned her whole body in the direction of the voice. 'Out of gaol and up early?'

'Habeas Corpus. Someone from the British consulate arrived and sprung me.'

'I called them after I left,' Jane said examining her nails, a haughty smile creased her lips.

His eyebrows shot upwards. 'Well, thanks for that.' He grinned and held up a beer bottle in a "Cheers" gesture. 'I owe you a drink!' His teeth shone across his tanned face. 'Heard anythin' from Batman an' Robin?'

'Batman?'

'Mr moustache and dicky bow boy.

'Mendoza? God, why did you have to mention him?' Jane's thoughts returned to the woods. 'That terrible, horrible scene. I couldn't sleep thinking about it.' She shook her head as if to clear it. 'It's factually branded on my mind. I've tried to push it aside, but...'

'Takes time,' he swallowed some beer and looked into the distance.

'You're probably used to it after being in the army.'

'We don't see dead bodies every day, and, you never get used to it.'

Jane sighed. 'God. I wish I hadn't bumped into you again. It's brought the memory back.'

'Sorry, wasn't planned on my part.'

'It'll pass I suppose.' By now the solar furnace was cooking her alive. Too hot to be proud, she took a seat in the shade of the umbrella. 'My feet are killing me.' She looked for the waiter. She waved. He came. She ordered hot water.

'That's how you know you're livin',' Dan's teeth split his tan as he watched her place her teasel drops on the table. 'Think of somethin' else if you can. Try and look on the bright side of life,' he smiled.

'You sound as if you're about to sing me a song.'

'Everythin' is possible.' He raised his glass. 'Welcome to Navarrete, town of pottery and that sort of stuff,' he said.

'I was glad to get here. The way parallel to the motorway was deafening before I reached the ruins of the Hospital de Peregrinos.'

'What hospital?' he grinned. 'I had eyes only for the gigantic bottle of wine by the side of the trail.'

'I'm surprised you didn't hi-jack it.'

'Too heavy, otherwise...' His teeth flashed like polished ivory.

Dan slouched even more on the chair under the big umbrella to stop sun pelting him outside the Bar Deportivo. His self-assurance both irritated her and impressed her. 'I thought you'd have been in Santiago de Compostela by now.' The paving under her feet radiated BBQ temperatures.

'Why are you always so friggin' sarcastic?'

'It only sounds that way to men who are insecure.'
'It sounds sarcastic to anyone.'
'How are the articles coming?' She sucked in her cheeks to hide a smile, determined to have the last word. 'National Geographic, wasn't it?'
'Oh, piss off!'
'Your charm is irresistible. Now our relationship is back to what it was.'
'Back to you bein' a snotty madam, you mean?'
She shrugged. 'Something about chasing and splashing, wasn't it?'
'Huntin' and Anglin',' he growled. 'My editor, Prosser fuckin' Jones isn't happy with what I've sent so far. He says he's under pressure because of a possible printing strike and wants my material earlier,' he scowled.
'Lift something from Canterbury Tales. Change the names of people and places, and voila! Compostela Tales!'
'Copyright is copyright in my book. I don't copy other people's work.'
'Factually, that was a joke. Look, didn't you even research the Camino?'
He shook his head. 'I got landed with the job at very short notice. I'd have preferred doin' the Blackpool bikini contest,' his smile splashed his tan again.
'Bikinis for a day can't be as good as sunshine for weeks.'
'Either way I had no choice. My friggin' editor has a hire and fire mind-set. I can't risk my job.'
Why on earth am I listening to his problems? she thought. She loosened boot laces and his fingers started twisting the white scallop shell hanging from

her rucksack. 'Listen,' she changed to a reasonable tone. 'I can give you some background, if you like. That scallop shell is found along the shores of Galicia.'

'Yeah, symbol of the Camino. Shells belong in the water; anglers can identify with that,' he swigged his beer and held two fingers up at the waiter, who nodded.

'Factually, the grooves of the shell coming together symbolise the many routes that pilgrims travel to the final destination.'

'And it gives 'em a little souvenir to take home.'

She sighed. 'Must you be so cynical, Mr Brady?'

'Dan. My name's Dan,' he swigged again.

'Very well, Mr Dan. Shall I give you some background or not?'

'Ah, the teacher reverts to type,' he grinned.

'Do you want to take notes?'

He shrugged. 'If it's good, I'll remember it.' He took another pull on the beer bottle and squinted across the square at a passing pilgrim woman in hot pants. Jane ignored his straying glance. Hot pants turned the corner as the waiter placed two golden glasses of beer on the table. Dan nodded thanks and took one and returned his gaze to Jane.

'Saint James' followers sent his body to Spain but it was swept overboard in a storm.'

'They should've used FedEx.'

'Listen!' Her forehead wrinkled. 'The sea washed his body ashore covered in scallops...'

'Ouch! Arrivin' after bein' lost is a miracle,' Dan chuckled. 'When my luggage is lost it stays lost.'

'The other version is the body came on a ship without a crew as a wedding took place. The groom sat on his horse at his wedding. The horse saw the ship and shied and they fell into the sea.'

'Maybe it shied when it saw the bride's face. And why sit on a friggin' horse at a weddin'?'

'Legend has it that the horse and rider emerged from the sea alive and covered in seashells.'

'At least they got a meal out of them afterwards,' Dan grinned. 'Why did he come to Spain?'

'To preach the Gospel. Then the Virgin Mary appeared in a vision.'

'A vision! Mary was always good at that.'

Jane sighed. 'Oh, forget it...'

'No, no, no!' Dan leaned forward. 'The Horsey Fishy folk of Merry Old England will love this horse and scallops bollocks.'

'Oh, go and read it yourself.' She turned away.

'Ok. I'm sorry. I didn't mean to be so... Oh, I dunno.' He ran his fingers through his hair. 'Sorry.'

'Well,' Jane swallowed some beer. 'Mary told him to return to the Holy Land. When he arrived King Herod ordered him to be beheaded.'

'Hah! Never listen to a woman about career moves!'

'That's beside the point.'

'Makin' Saint Jim a head shorter was a helluva a point, if you ask me.'

'Do you wish me to finish or not?'

'Okay, Herod didn't allow burial, I take it.'

'Yes...'

'Typical! The friggin' authorities not only fuck up your life but even your death...'

'His followers boarded a ship to take the body back.'

'Wait a minute!' Dan's poked an accusing finger.

'You said the ship was crewless...!'

'There's a lot of myth involved. The story goes that they discovered his remains when the Bishop followed a star to the spot. That's how Compostela became known as the Field of Stars.'

'And a few relics can push tourism.'

'I wonder why you're even here!'

'To keep my friggin' job!'

'If the job is so bad why didn't you stay in the army and shoot people?' she stuck her nose in the air.

'Shoot people! I was the one who got fuckin' shot!'

'Shot yourself in the foot, I shouldn't wonder.'

'I was shot here! Here!' he bellowed knocking his chair over. Two tables away two pilgrims bounced to their feet. Dan tugged at his shirt. A button skittered across the table.

'Everything alright over there?' An Australian voice called over.

Jane waved and smiled at the two pilgrims who stood at their table, faces aimed at Dan like hunting dogs. She goggled at Dan's chest and reddened. 'Sorry. I didn't realize.'

'Through the fuckin' lung!' His finger prodded the purple crater scar on the bottom rib. 'Blue on fuckin' blue. American terminology for friendly fire, but it's not so fuckin' friendly.'

'Someone shot you?' Her voice was a weak whisper. Her jaw sagged.

'A drunken arse hole fired all over the place. One bullet caught me. My mate next to me took him out.'

'My goodness! You mean he...? In fact...?'

'In fuckin' fact, yeah. I took my mate's pistol and the blame. The army discharged me as medically unfit. I went through a bad time of it. I took this crap job to keep a wage comin' in to keep up support for my kids and make a good impression and retain my visitin' rights.'

'Impression with whom?'

'The court that wanted to suspend my visitin' rights, after my ex-wife made up stories about me,' He buttoned up his shirt.

'I remember you saying you have children.'

'A boy and a girl. I bloody miss them.' His gaze was unfocused in thought.

'From your marriage?'

'Of course from my marriage. I don't lay eggs, you know?'

'Don't be so touchy.'

'I'm not touchy. Just pissed off.'

'Have you sent the articles to your editor, to keep your job safe?'

'I sent what I had up to now as E-mail attachment, including some pictures. He's accepted that I'll bring the rest of the data with me when I have more material. I could transfer it, but when he gets it he'll expect me to be in the office almost the next day. My kids are in Majorca with their uncle and aunt and their kids. I wanted to see them. So I'm keeping the data to take it back to England myself. That way I buy myself a bit more time.'

'Halleehalloo!'

Jane's eyebrows shot upwards. She jumped to her feet and took a step towards a tall man and a dark haired woman about her own age. 'Hi, Angie, old girl, hi, Karl!'

'We came as fast as we could after your call,' the woman said. 'How terrible!'

'It was. Horrible. So horrible you can't imagine.'

'Well, we're here now,' she hugged Jane.

Jane mwaa mwaaed on each cheek of the beautiful girl with long black hair and liquid movements. Her looks were better than any Photoshop session could create. She dressed snappy, as if going to a fashion show. Jane transferred her hug to a tall spidery guy with a slight limp and shaved head. 'Dan, this is Angelique and Karl.'

'Angelique,' the woman purred. The sun twinkled on a small silver arrow piercing two parts of the helix at the top of her ear. Her accent was French. Her wide smile promised French things. Her green eyes sharp enough to unleash a man's mind. She offered her hand as if it should be kissed.

'Hi,' Dan wiggled her fingers with his fingers.

She raised an eyebrow. 'Puh! Is that an Englishman's way of shaking hands?'

'He's Irish,' Jane said.

'Is there a difference?' she cocked an eyebrow and smiled.

'I am Karl, friend of Jane,' the tall spidery man offered a hand on a long arm with loose joints. He spoke with a German accent. Steel rimmed spectacles hooked over jug ears that flanked his bare head with a binary code tattooed above his left ear. The man ran his fingertips over the tattoo with brown stained fingers showing a history of too many cigarettes.

'You'll be the friends that Jane mentioned,' Dan said.

'Yes. We are her back-up,' Binary man said.

'Back-up? Like bodyguards?' Dan frowned.

'Ach, not bodyguards,' he shook his head. 'Bodyguards make me think of violence. I am against violence. We are here to help Jane.'

'Help her with what?' Dan sounded curios.

Nobody answered this question and Karl was suddenly busy with his phone.

'We have known each other for a long time, researched together in London and I got to know Mr King Hacker here during a computer course.'

'A Hacker! And a King Hacker at that? How interestin'!' Jane saw Dan looking at Karl's hands. They had thick fingers on paws that looked as if they had found work on a building site and not at a keyboard. 'Are hackin' skills somethin' you need on the Way of Saint James?' Dan asked.

Karl rubbed the tattoo above his ear and took a slow breath. 'I think you are making a mickey of me,' his eyes wavered about Dan's face as if deciphering alien sounds.

'Sorry,' Dan winked. 'You don't have to answer if you don't want.'

Angelique waved her manicured hand with a small green dragon tattoo that started on her fist and a tail sneaking up her forearm. 'We have other skills, too.' Angelique threw him a heart-warming smile.

'Maybe I can interview you sometime,' Dan said absently.

'Why not now?' she said, eyes shining with curiosity. 'I've got time,' Her eyelid flickered.

Jane noticed Angelique's subtle wink that let a man wondering if she was flirting, or whether he had imagined. 'Cool it down, Angie. Mr Brady mustn't get hotter with a walk under a hot sun ahead of him.'

Her long lashes stroked her cheeks as she semaphored Dan. 'Next time, when you are not in such a hurry.'

'Got it,' Dan blinked back. 'I have to get movin' along.'

Jane felt relieved. *That's all I need with him and her getting involved. Then I'll never get rid of him*, she thought, happy to see him ready to go. He tugged hard at his backpack straps as if preparing for a parachute jump.

'Ach your big backpack looks like a PLSS,' the German said.

'What's PLSS?' Angie purred in her lovely French accent.

'Primary Life Support System,' Dan added. 'It's the big backpack on astronaut's space suits. I need a large pack for all my photo equipment. Weighs a friggin' ton.' He tugged the shoulder straps tighter. 'Well,' he nodded to them. 'See you along the Way.'

'Buen Camino, then,' Jane added with relief. They watched him march across the square.

'The energy I feel from him is that he is somehow kaputt inside,' Karl said, rubbing his Binary tattoo again. Angelique cocked an eyebrow at Jane, curious for confirmation.

'He has a story behind him,' Jane said under the shade of the umbrella.

'Everyone has a story of some sort,' Karl said, checking his phone screen.

'Like the story of the world?' Angie said.

'The world that God created in six days and since then nobody's heard from him,' Karl grinned.

'Puh! Mr Joke man,' she slapped the back of his head and waved to the waiter. 'That's the first time I've seen a monk with a big doctor's bag.'

Jane followed her gaze to a monk walking past.

His face concealed by a deep cowl. Was he the monk she had seen earlier in the day?

'Buen Camino,' the two Aussies got up to go and waved to Jane.

'Buen Camino!' she wished. They smiled and nodded with both thumbs up and followed Dan. She looked for the monk again, but he had disappeared. Her gaze settled on Mr Tennis shoes reading a Spanish paper and idly harpooning salad bits in a large bowl.

'Ok, Jane, now we're alone. Tell us about this body you found. I cannot believe it! Are you *sure* you saw a body?'

'For God's sake, Angie! Of course I'm sure!' People at other tables glanced in her direction.

'No need to shout.' She smiled at the approaching waiter. 'Four beers,' she mesmerised the young man.

'Ach, you ordered for me without asking.'

'You always drink beer,' she said and wrinkled her nose at him.

'I still liked to be asked.' He turned to Jane. 'You know you sounded very hysterical on the phone.' Karl rubbed his tattoo above his ear. The waiter came back with the beer.

'We thought you might have mistaken it from something else.'

'I'm surprised at you both! I know what I saw. Ask the police!'

'Ach, I think you should go home.'

'Never!'

'I think you should wear a disguise. Whoever murdered the girl might have seen you.'

'That could be bad for you, Jane,' Karl wagged a warning finger. 'That could have a bad end.' He went back to his E Mails.

'Karl's right. You should call the whole thing off.'

'Never,' the glasses wobbled, slopping beer from the blow of Jane's fist on the table. 'Never!'

AZOFRA

A smartphone bursting into Nuthin' But A "G" Thang in the darkness, woke the local cockerel. The song choked off, replaced by a monotonous Scandinavian litany.

A moron of the first order, Jane thought and opened her gummed up eyelids. Reflex screwed them shut against the criss-crossing display of piercing LED head lamp beams. Their weaving through the darkness, reminding her of the opening scene of the film ET when he was chased through the forest by stupid Earthmen.

Another selfish pilgrim completed the wake-up transition by crunching plastic things into his backpack in the darkness. Jane looked across the dorm from under the hood of her sleeping bag. Phone screens illuminated the greenish profiles of sleepy faces around the room. Somebody nearby farted. Sleeping bags rustled as owners pressed the air out of the filling, followed by backpack zips, zipping and buzzing her into another Camino day.

She thought of Angie and Karl and felt angry that they had not quite believed her account of the body she had found. It wasn't until Karl had heard it three times that they really accepted Jane's description of events. They had left her and driven ahead to a more comfortable hotel. *Ok for them. Money no object*, Jane thought. Karl with his programming firm seemed to earn money that flowed without end. He was financing the whole mission and would have willingly paid for Jane's hotels, too. Jane didn't want that. It clashed with the aim of her pilgrimage. They were not here for the Camino experience like her.

She heard a window shutter squeak. Dawn seeped into the dorm. *No sense in lying here much longer.* She crawled out of her sleeping bag and climbed from the top bunk on the cold metal ladder rungs digging into her bare soles. The bunk below was already an empty creased mattress.

She zombie-walked to the communal bathroom wearing her waterproof document wallet around her neck. Four toilet door locks showed red occupied signs. Someone in a cubicle farted like a tuba. A row of shaving men occupied all the wash basins. The shower cubicles all hissed busily with flip-flops before the doors. Her forehead wrinkled in frustration.

Maybe a cat lick later, she thought and sighed, returning to her bunk to pack. She threw on her few clothes and fled the stale air.

She wanted to leave before Mr Lobster, a very sunburned Argentinian flirt champion, woke up. He had clung like a limpet the day before and filled her ears with insincere flattery after Angie and Karl had left for Azofra in Angie's colourful car. She wanted a good start on him to walk in peace.

She screwed up her face in disgust as a squadron of flies rose in the kitchen. The buzzing dragged her mind back the scene of the dead girl. Two pilgrims entered the messy kitchen.

'Greetings,' one smiled. The other looked round, frowning. The big table was hidden under vegetable peelings and empty tins left by the pilgrims who had cooked the night before.

'Phew! Looks like a hurricane's swept through here,' he waved a fly away as he muttered to his companion who poured coffees. 'Damned flies,' his hands windmilled around him.

'Some people don't know how to behave. They leave their rubbish for the staff to clear up.'

'No wonder volunteers are getting hard to find for some of the albergues,' the taller guy said. 'Good morning!' he greeted noticing Jane for the first time.

'Morning to you,' Jane drank her fennel tea breakfast with her own muesli stored in a sealed plastic bag. She preferred it, even if it was another 300 grams in her backpack.

'Is that muesli you've got there?' one man asked. 'Don't see it on the counter.'

'I carry my own,' she said between chews.

'Oh! Then good appetite and Buen Camino,' he smiled and turned away to help his companion bulldoze vegetable peelings with his hands to clear a space.

* * *

Outside the cold air rinsed Jane's lungs in oxygen,

waking her completely. Spanish music came from an open window. The orange sun split the horizon. The cuckoo welcomed her like an old friend and made her smile. Other birds joined the chorus and dogs barked long distance to one another. Dogs! *Never mind the dogs. They're far away.* A cat watched her from the top of an ancient rusty tractor. She passed a cemetery full of shadows.

The asphalt ended at the edge of the village. The tone of her boots soles changed on the packed dirt into a crispy march. Flanked by the endless swaying corn, the smell of the fields wafted over her and awoke all her senses. A short concrete post with a yellow oyster symbol sprang into the beam of her Petzl lamp.

'Buen Camino,' a shadow wished as it passed Jane, boots chewing up the trail. Light across the horizon levered day from the night throwing long shadows across the world. Within an hour the sun burned away the thin morning mist still hanging in hollows. Another day on the Camino trail had started. She felt good being one of thousands of pilgrims, all spread over 500 miles of The Way, all setting their feet on the trail together at this very moment. Comrades, she thought. Debbie was here, too. She let her pack slide from her shoulders and crouched to rummage inside. Her fingers felt the soft suede and drew out the baize sack. It rattled a little as she set it on the ground. *She was here. I feel it.* She reached into here backpack to begin her ritual.

* * *

Jane's lunch time was shorter than a long burp. One big glossy tomato hurridly stuffed into her mouth on the river bank of Nájera, leaving juice and seeds on her chin. A stork sailed serenely on wide white span wings with black trailing edges fluttering against the blue above. *Wish I could fly,* the thought as she relaxed and dozed. She opened her eyes and looked at her watch. Forty minutes had fled. *God I'm tired! I shouldn't have stopped.* She groaned as she stretched. Muscles always lose their power and go floppy once relaxed. She recalled how often her trainer had warned her when training for the swimming Olympics. She stretched each limb slowly, then walked. She decided to minimise her aims for the rest of the day. Concentrated on placing each heel before the toe of the other boot without thinking of anything. Staying awake after a night of sleep broken by blood splashing across her dreams. She tuned in to the endless crunch of her boots for hours on end. The tone varied with the surfaces; bumping on asphalt, thudding on hard packed earth, crackling on sand, crunching on stones. It was steady and relaxing to listen to her cadence. The Camino was dry in the boundless green fields of short corn edged with blood coloured poppies with fragile petals fluttering like flags in the light wind under a sky wider than forever. Her gaze stretched to the blue-black mountains along the shimmering horizon, then back to the hills ahead, where she would be in a few hours. The hill slopes looked reachable and less daunting. They moved nearer as she walked, giving her more sense of movement. The flat land reminded her of the long distances between villages she had covered, sun without shelter, boredom and sometimes loneliness. The constant walking sucked her leg muscles empty and aching. Her gut feeling made her wonder whether she had overestimated her strength and resolve. Uncertainty slowed her pace. *I'd love to just lie down and sleep*, she actually considered doing it. *Can't stay here*, she told herself. There are only two ways out. Walk. Or give up. *Walk or give up on Debbie?* 'Never,' Jane muttered, and threw each foot forward to increase her speed.

Go Jane! She ordered.

No! March! She ordered herself like a drill sergeant.

She marched. Her heels dented the trail. A lizard slipped away under a rock. A flock of birds sailed north. Thirty thousand feet above a condensed trail scratched the endless blue. A fly landed on her brow to plunder a sip of her sweat. She flapped a hand. It persisted. Its whine annoying her. She tried to distract herself; *Walk, eat, sleep*. The words hammered in her head. *Walk, eat, sleep. Walk, eat, sleep.*

Four exhausting hours later, following the same walker who stayed half a kilometre ahead of her, she climbed without pause through miles of stocky vines and olive trees. She kept up the pace until her boots pounded the shimmering street of Azofra, a one street village somewhere in the middle of nowhere. Dusty old houses bearing coats of arms flanked the Calle Mayor, the original pilgrim way through the village. She paused in a shadow. She pulled her water bottle and sucked it dry. She stretched her back a few times. Horseback, cat's back, horseback, cat's back, to ease her back muscles. Her mobile buzzed. She grabbed at the side pocket of her backpack. 'Ow, damn!' she gasped. She had pulled a back muscle. 'To hell with him!' she muttered. Its complaining buzz persisted. *Everyone must be able to hear it*, she thought. A wasp, a hornet, a buzz saw. In this case it was her pain in a scallop shell, future ex-husband.

An island of chairs and tables under fluttering white umbrellas filled the left side of the street. Green plastic chairs with San Miguel emblazoned on the backs propped up six tired pilgrims, slumped with feet on their backpacks. Six was a big crowd for a village like Azofra. One of them lathered sun blocker over his red lamp face that would keep him awake that night.

'Finally made it.' The hairs on the back of Jane's neck bristled, as if the air was charged with static before lightning strikes. She'd prefer a lightning strike. She clenched her jaw to bite off any insult to Mr-Fast-Foot-Hero of the St. James international racing trail.

'Hello, Mr Brady,' she muttered formally with the enthusiasm of a dental patient awaiting a root canal operation.

'Beat you!' he grinned. She stopped under the sunshade. Her forehead matched the condensation on the large glass of Estrella on the table. She frowned with a head shake at Dan's inane face split by gleaming teeth as if expecting a dog biscuit.

'I wasn't aware this was a race, Mr Usain Bolt of the Camino.' She looked pointedly at his dusty hiking boots perched on the chair opposite. 'Have you already been awarded a trophy?'

'Take the weight off your feet,' he moved his legs and bit into a Tapa as elegantly as a raptor.

She sat. Her nose wrinkled 'Pooh! It smells here!'

'Shit. I stepped in it.'

'Dog dirt?'

'Man shit.'

'A man?'

'Man as in human. Human shit. On my boot. I had to dash behind the only bush I could find.' He shrugged. 'Couldn't get it all off on the grass.'

'I had that same experience in a small ruin. In fact, there was more paper on the floor there than confetti at my wedding.'

'Must have been a great weddin'.'

'That's a matter of opinion;' Her face had the same expression as when Dan mentioned shit. She changed the subject and reverted to every pilgrim's standard question. 'Where did you start this morning?'

'Nájera. On a river. Nice place.'

Jane yawned. 'I had lunch there. You haven't walked far today.'

Dan shrugged. 'I got up slowly, breakfasted slowly, and visited the monastery slowly. Guy called Sancho The Great...'

'King Garcia.'

'Yeah, that's the fella. He followed a dove into a cave and discovered a statue of the Virgin Mary,' he grinned. 'A little extra somethin' for my article.'

'You'd better be careful, Mr Brady, you might end up writing a good article.'

'I almost did once, but my editor stopped me in time.'

Jane smiled. 'And Majorca?'

'Still thinkin' about it. My brother in law and ex-army pal chartered a boat and are spendin' ten days tryin' to catch somethin' they could order in a fishmonger in three minutes,' he pulled a silly face. 'My kids are there with him, his wife and his sons. Santo Domingo has bus connections. I'll leave the Camino from there.'

'Hi, Jane!' A tall Dane she had met a few days before waved.

'Hello. Lars. Want to join us?'

'Got to get myself a bed first. Catch you later,' He patted Dan on the shoulder and walked on.

Jane pulled off her neckerchief and wiped her forehead. Her back was damp from her backpack and her feet swollen inside her boots.

'Have a beer and you'll be right as rain. Liquid bread, they called it in the middle ages. The bread of the poor.'

'Ah! That's why the pubs are full. Poor men getting their daily bread to survive until their lionesses come home.'

'Yep,' he emptied his glass, printing a white moustache above his lip. 'Señor! Dos cervezas!' The waiter nodded.

'Two beers in *Spanish*! You're really mastering the language, aren't you?' She raised an eyebrow in mock admiration.

'Only the important words. Luckily "Sex" is an international word. That eliminates half the vocabulary I need,' he winked.

Froth quivered on two new sweating glasses landing on the table top. Dan peered through the prism of the blond fluid.

'Beer was not only the bread of the poor but a

reason to go to church. Monks had a monopoly on brewin' beer. They offered it to the congregation, who went to church out of fear and for the beer.' He raised his glass. 'Guzzle up!' he renewed the white moustache.

'Look, er Dan. Were you really shot? In Afghanistan? I know I saw that scar, but...'

Dan stared unfocused into the distance. His thoughts on another planet. 'I was,' he said quietly and took short absent sips looking into nowhere.

Jane sat in silence wishing she hadn't asked and concentrated on the table top. A giant wasp rioted in her backpack. She ignored it, pretending it was silent so she didn't have to answer. Mr Tennis shoes appeared and took a seat at a nearby table and started talking animatedly with another equally sunburned man. The buzzing persisted.

'Aren't you goin' to answer your phone?' Dan shaved away his foam moustache with his forefinger.

She exhaled with an irritated huff and plucked the cell out of the side pocket between her finger and thumb as if holding a stinking fish. 'Yes?' She answered quietly, her expression vacant. 'I'm traveling.' Her fingers plucked at the sides of her shorts. 'If it costs so much then don't phone. Save your beautiful and precious money!' She pressed hard on the cut off button.

A harsh metallic voice echoed along the street. A metal coned speaker on the roof of a white transporter pulled people from the doors along the street. A row of dresses on hangers lined the sides, fluttering in the breeze. Women surged from doorways and surrounded the mobile shop, plucking at clothes and twisting price tags.

Dan downed the rest of his beer. 'So, you were tellin' me why you are here.'

'I wasn't.'

'Weren't you?'

'It's private.'

'Maybe I can help.' He raised his eyebrows.

'It's *private*.'

'Ok, ok,' he held up his hands in surrender and stood up and opened his wallet.

'I'll pay for my own beer,' Jane said.

'There's enough dough there,' he nodded at the blue twenty soaking in a blob of beer foam.

'My husband and I always pay for ourselves.'

'Och, I'm not him.' He blinked as sun flashed on the windscreen of a green SUV pulling out from a row of parked cars. The driver's black bill cap hid his features The car rolled towards the albergue.

'Dan!'

'Yeess,' Dan turned in slow time. Jane got up and grabbed her backpack.

'You asked me why I am walking the Camino. I'm following my sister.'

Where?' He gave the street a quick once over.

'Here,' she drew level. 'She disappeared over a year ago.'

'How do you know she was here?'

'I have cards and photos she took along the way and sent home to my parents. I have to find out what happened to her.' Her eyes searched his, then turned away. 'I'm sorry. I don't know why I've told you. As I said, it's private.'

'Bit late now.' He watched her dab her nose with her neckerchief.

'What about the police?'

'British and Spanish cooperated. No clues. No witnesses. No suspects. No results. No Debbie.'

'Fuckin' hell,' he whispered. 'I'm sorry to hear that. It must be a terrible shock for your family.'

'It's taken me a year to bunch up the courage to come here. Debbie is my mission here. It will end in Santiago de Compostela.'

'What will happen there?'

'Can't say right now.'

'Can't or won't?'

'Both.'

His face darkened. 'Suit yourself,' he turned and left her standing.

'Oaf!' her eyes threw spinal nerve killing lightning bolts between his shoulder blades as he strode away.

A car engine roared. She turned and was blinded by the sun bouncing off the windshield. Her heel snagged a parked backpack. She fell and landed on another backpack. Wheels passed at face level. Her eyes blinked away the dust from the slipstream.

'You're sitting on my backpack,' a woman whined.

'So sorry! That car almost hit me!' Jane struggled to her feet.

'What car?' she gazed vacantly along the street.

'There!' Jane pointed. They both looked at nothing along the shimmering street.

* * *

'Hi, Mommy.' The figure entered the white room. He dropped his black trucker cap on the foot of the bed and sat. The feet under the sheet shifted to one side. The shadowy outline of the crucifix still marked the wall. He had smuggled it out of the clinic long ago. It lay on the piano at home and reminded him of Mommy. He had his own holy cross, made from the wood of the original cross. The cross upon which the Lord Jesus died. His cross held the power of life or death. It saved Evas. His thoughts returned to the room. Nothing had changed in the bare room in six years.

'Hi, Sugar,' said the scratchy voice.

'I wanted to tell you what I did.' The little voice answered. Mommy listened. 'I found the Eva who found the other Eva.'

'The one who stopped you processing the saved Eva?'

'Yes, Mommy. I tried to run her down. Satan saved her!' He entwined his fingers and cracked his knuckles.

'Don't do that, Sugar!'

'Sorry, Mommy.'

'She must be a powerful Succubus, Sugar. Only very evil helpers are protected so much. She is the one you have to save, Sugar!'

'I know, Mommy. But I saved another! I found another Eva, Mommy,' he answered after some hesitation. 'I saved her, too, Mommy!'

'You know Mommy's so proud of you. One day I'll return to God, too.'

'I know, Mommy! I saved another Eva and got her to a way cross to help you!'

'Each Eva you save gets us both nearer to the Lord in heaven, y'hear?'

'I know, Mommy. And I know time is short.'

'Don't think about that, Sugar. Just carry out your mission and earn a place next to the Lord with your

Mommy.'

'I followed the other Eva, too. She is walking the Camino on a quest.'

'A quest? On *our* Camino, Sugar?'

'Yes, on *our* Camino, Mommy.'

'You gotta save her, Sugar! You gotta save her!'

'I will, Mommy. I'm tired, but I am following her, Mommy.'

'Rest, Sugar. Save your energy to finish your mission and save us all from Satan.'

'I'm so tired,' he stood and slapped the trucker cap on his head and pulled the peak well down. He had a false police ID to get access to the unit, but he did not want people to see his face.

'Fail and your death will be followed by the fires of hell,' she croaked.

A STAINED SHELL

The blue mattress on the bunk in the Azofra albergue was an empty nest. Jane accepted that walking buddies from the day before often melt away. They pursued the steel-grey dawn alone. Everyone has his or her own pace on the Camino. Listen to your feet is the advice on how to walk.

Pilgrims seldom waited unless they were a pair. Loners never wait. In this case it was different. Jane drew in her breath, tight lipped in irritation. The empty bunk next to her had been Dan Brady's "doss nest," as he had called it. He had slipped away in the dawn. *Was his action bad manners, or consideration?*

A widow shutter rattled open. The day light reflectèd off the shiny blue plastic cover of the vacated mattress. His silent departure irritated her.

Not that he is any loss, she thought. *Forget him,' she ordered. He's not your type. Actually, he's probably nobody's type.* Hunger stopped her thoughts that were not going anywhere useful anyway. She pulled on fresh socks and panties, washed the day before under the shower. Her outer clothes had clung to her skin since she set out on the French side of the Pyrenees two weeks ago. She rolled her sleeping bag into a sausage and thought briefly about bed bugs. She hadn't seen any so far. She packed. Two T-shirts, two pairs of undies and two pairs of socks. Weight saving was everything on the Camino. Every gram counted. Anything more is a waste of energy. She felt that the hundred-gram bar of dark Swiss chocolate in her pack didn't count. *It gives back energy!* she told herself and jerked her phone charger from the spaghetti of cables sharing a multi adapter connected to two more multi adapters, hanging from the single wall socket like mating octopuses. *I could write a guide book*, she mused. *Under suggestions I'd insert: bring a multi adapter, so others can charge their phones, too.* She smiled at a young Brazilian woman struggling to dress herself inside her sleeping bag. *Latin prudery,* Jane thought. All the north Europeans stripped into underwear next to their bunks.

She humped her backpack down to the breakfast room. A large table filled the spice scented room. A radio whispered Adele's voice Rolling in the Deep. Jane loved her voice and the lyrics she wrote.

Two cheerful women prepared thick sandwiches with tomato wedges and bricks of cheese. A third sat, head on her backpack on the table, keeping her eyes closed until the last possible second before leaving.

Jane thought about relaxing a bit longer over breakfast. Pilgrims entered, greeted everyone, and queued patiently at the coffee machine whining and spluttering above the music. Her eyes searched the buffet in vain for anything resembling muesli. She swallowed her tea. It was good. The machine whined as she thumbed the button again to gurgle a refill into the plastic cup. 'Damn!' She pressed her lips together. Mr Lobster had entered the breakfast room. Jane simulated a tortoise by ducking her head into her imaginary shell. She had not expected, nor wanted to see him again. Mr Lobster's ego was the size of Argentina, his homeland. His face had the glow of a road worker's hazard jacket. She was relieved that he was focused on the breakfast buffet while chatting up a blonde girl who nodded vacantly, her attention on the food. Jane left her coffee on the table, a tendril of steam swaying up like a snake before a charmer.

In the boot room, the tang of leather and foot odour thickened the air. Each pair of boots bore marks and scars; each with its own story of pain and certainly a few tears to tell. She located her own grey Lowas. Karl had insisted they all buy them from Globetrotter in Cologne. 'Why not?' they had thought. He was paying. She freed the endless laces that she had tied together and round a radiator to discourage any attempt to take them. Consequently, she had to thread the laces again through the row of metal eyelets and hooks. She pulled them tight until her ankles felt like the plaster cast she had worn after a skiing accident two years before. No wiggle-room. No blister room.

Jane decided to minimise her aims again for the day and concentrate on walking. *Think about nothing,* she reminded herself. She would try and get an early night somewhere. She raised herself by her thigh muscles and stood still, boogieing her toes to stimulate circulation. Heavy booted astronaut like steps carried her into the freshness of a new dawn.

* * *

Minutes later, rucksack high on her shoulders, Jane followed the rough yellow cross, a careless splash of graffiti blazed on a grey stone wall. Birds shared melodies. A distant cock crowed. A dog barked. A tractor growled to life. Her boots thudded, her breath rasped. She followed other pilgrims passing by the botanical gardens dedicated to the Virgen de Valvanera, the patron saint of La Rioja. The air still held enough moisture from the night air to suppress the dust and freshen her lungs. Glistening diamonds of water clung to a large cobweb stretched between two bushes. Her boots soles changed tone as asphalt gave way to brown earth flanked by the familiar corn and short vines and olive trees. Yellow flowers sprung from the grass along the edge of the trail, flooded by the slanting rays of the dawn's sun reflecting orange under the bottom of a few clouds hanging like puffy islands above her. Birds melodised in their new day and Jane felt at one with them. She hummed quietly, feeling in harmony with nature around her. A pair of abandoned boots with yawning laughing soles were parked, heels to the trail, as if the owner had placed them by his bedside prior to a nap.

The sun was soon high enough to give the air pizza oven temperature. Jane dragged down on her bucket hat brim to shade her eyes and protect her neck. An overweight cyclist with the puff gone out of him and unable to talk, leaned against a stunted tree. His bike lay unattended at his feet. He nodded at Jane, his face glistening from rivulets of sweat. He grimaced and panted 'Buen Camino.'

'Buen Camino,' Jane smiled back and increased her pace between dirt banks that sloped either side of her. In a short time, the sun was high enough to shrink her long shadow to dwarf size. *Follow your shadow and you'll arrive in Santiago de Compostela.*

Footsteps crunched behind her, growing louder by the moment. A faster walker? Boot heels loud. Mr Lobster? *Don't look back*, she told herself. *Maybe he won't recognise you*, she tried to be invisible, tugging her bucket hat deeper over her ears. She turned her head away from the trail and stared across the swaying corn, without interrupting her steady pace.

'Buen Camino, eh?' A female voice at her elbow relaxed her. A tall woman drew alongside. Jane blinked at her Flamingo pink pants with matching jacket, backpack and lipstick and a red plastic visor jutting from her forehead. She resembled an exotic astronaut. 'Buen Camino, eh' the vivid red thick lips pouted again.

'Buen Camino,' Jane nodded back at the lips that shone like a beacon across the woman's pale, thin features.

'Where are you from?' The accent was Canadian.

'England.'

'Well, I never! My grandparents came from England, eh!'

'Where in England?'

'Cardiff.' Her lips pouted when she stopped speaking

'That's in Wales.'

'Well I never!' she said as it didn't matter. 'And you?'

'Chester. Do you know it?'

'No. Never been to England,' She stretched her neck to focus into the distance. 'What's that light?' She nodded along the straight way ahead, her lips pouting the way. A pulsing blue light sent a sense of urgency across the fields of corn.

'A vehicle. A car, or an ambulance,' Jane looked ahead.

'Someone's fainted from heat stroke, eh?'

Jane shielded her eyes and squinted along the baize earth beaten trail. A stone pillar formed in the haze and grew taller as they neared - a sentinel among the bushes.

'A police car! Some sort of kerfuffle, eh?' The lips opened and closed, mesmerising Jane for a moment.

'Looks like it,' Jane nodded and saw the blue and white police car parked on the grass a few yards beyond a grey stone pillar. They approached a pillar mottled with lichen and crowned with four eroded faces. Their expressions bore a hint of urgency, keeping watch across the swaying sea of green corn. It stood two yards to the right of the trail in an island of long grass. Splashes of yellow flowers and purple thistles vied for room around a wild cherry bush thrusting to the light from behind the old pillar.

'Those are police cars! Definitely a kerfuffle, eh?'

Four police uniforms flanked the column. They stared down into what appeared to be a large hole under the cherry bush. Worry niggled Jane's brain. Something was wrong here! Her stomach was suddenly queasy.

'It's a Way Cross,' isn't it?'

'The Rollo de Azofra,' Jane said. 'A punishment pillar, where local justice was once heard and served.'

'Looks strange with cops standing round it.'

The police officers looked up as Jane waded through the high grass towards the pillar. A wide yellow tape fluttering at waist height stretched before her. Her eyes followed the text, 'LINEA DE POLICIA POR FAVOR NO CRUZAR'. Her glance bypassed the tape and froze. An arm and a limp hand protruded from a hole under the cherry bush. String twisted through the fingers, supporting a scallop shell splashed with blood.

'No! No! No!' A tall police officer with a panic covered face jerked into action. He stepped over the tape, hand outstretched towards Jane.

'Avanzar, por favor. Continua, por favor!' he gestured the way ahead. 'Please, do not stop. Please continue,' face tight with strain. Other police officers, young with anxious eyes, unrolled a long grey canvas sheet cutting of her view of the hand. Jane sucked in air as if her tongue was scolded. Her stomach soured with nausea as she lurched back to the trail, the shock stole her orientation and clarity of vision. A revving motor under the foot of an impatient driver behind shocked the Canadian lady into springing to one side.

'Well, I never!' her lips pouted more than before as a van with darkened windows rocked to a halt on the trail. A dust cloud rolled around its wheels as the doors flew open. Men in overalls tumbled out. A powerful stocky man with a jagged Grand Canyon scar from his bald head to his jaw line flipped an ID. The police officers stood aside. Whether from the authority of his ID or the scar, Jane couldn't be sure.

'Such driving, eh!' She looked at Jane and her mouth hung open before she found her voice. 'My dear! You're as white as a sheet!' The pink woman's eyebrows arched with concern. Two other pilgrims ambled by, cast short glances at the police officers and continued a little faster. The tapping of their sticks accelerated their rhythm on the stony earth.

'Come. Let's go.' Jane passed her.

'Why m'dear? What have they found?' Her lips opened into a perfect O, reminding Jane of a life ring hanging on the tiled wall of the swimming baths at home. Despite her shock, Jane wondered whether the lips had been botoxed, then bashed the irrational thought out of her head. Rapid sounds like a carpet beater thrashed the air. A copter approached and followed the trail ahead. Jane moved on with a sour feeling in her stomach.

'Are they landing?'

Jane's answer choked stillborn. Mendoza stared at

her through the Perspex.
 'Do you know that man?'
 Jane nodded. 'I wish I didn't.'

SAN DOMINGO

Dan felt he had eaten the Magna Carta. In the midday break his omelette looked and tasted like a piece of brown parchment curling at the edges. Now, walking under the big hot sky, he felt he resembled that omelette, frying on the wide open plateau in drenching heat. The distant mountains were only a dark blur along the shimmering horizon. Azofra lay well behind on a distant hill. Dan felt barbecued and poached from the sweat soaking his shirt. At the top of the next ridge a single mushroom shaped tree in the distance promised shadow. It seemed such a distance away. It can be hard to gauge distances along the Meseta.

'I think it's a good idea to stop early in this sun,'

said a Swedish woman walking alongside croaking for air.

'Stop where? Here? There's no cover at all on this part of the friggin' trail.'

'I thought I'd made a good head start on the sun. This is sauna air.'

'It's bakin' m'nasal passages dry as sandpaper,' Dan breathed through parted lips. Time and their feet dragged on, backpacks heavier, shoulder straps cutting collar bones. The green corn stood as motionless as a photo in the still air. Dust from their boots hung above the trail. Raps lined the fields and scarlet poppy petals fluttered like silk butterfly wings against their ankles as they passed close enough to cause a slight eddy of air. Dan pulled his hat lower and listened to his footsteps.

'It is boring here,' she said after some time.

'Isolation gives me time t'think.'

'My boots feel as if they are dragging me backwards.'

'An illusion. Look,' Dan nodded at a single tree. 'We're doing better than we thought.' The woman looked at the broccoli shaped tree with the eyes of a drowning sailor spotting a lifeboat.

'There are people standin' there.' He nodded at two figures sagged in the shadow under the tree. They approached. Dan recognised them. A Mexican lady and a Filipino man from an albergue two days before. Dan recalled he had been drunk and dropped a bottle of red wine in the hall of the albergue. They had covered for him and helped mop up. He stopped in the soothing shadow. They all nodded. Too tired to smile. Too dry to speak. An empty Cola tin lay nearby. 'I wonder if there's anythin' left in that,' Dan unstuck his tongue from the roof of his mouth.

'We looked already,' the man joked.

'I think we started out too late,' the Swedish woman said.

'You are right,' the Mexican woman who had rested against the rough tree trunk, got to her feet. Buckled cans and wrappers from previous visitors lay around on the dry earth.

'Hi,' a voice behind them announced a new arrival. Dan noticed how often he had been alone, with nobody in sight, and then a short pause for a pee or a rest and bingo! A pilgrim appeared out of nowhere.

'God it's hot!' A dark-haired girl with a wet face under a wide straw hat dropped her backpack at her feet. Her long, bare arms matched her red backpack.

'Hola,' the Mexican lady greeted. 'Where did you start?'

'Norway two months ago, and Nájera today. I'm with a group of teachers. They left earlier. I bathed in the river and lost time and the group. She sat on her backpack, ripped off her left boot with a loud, 'Ouch!'

'Doesn't look good,' the Filipino said, wrinkling his nose at the weeping ragged blister skin dangling from her heel.

'I'll be ok,' she sniffed and pulled a small box of Compeed plasters from her pocket and got to work.

'What's the next town?' Ms Mexico said.

'Chicken church town,' the man answered before Dan could.

'Chicken town?' The woman's round face tried to smile, but it disappeared in tiredness.

Dan remembered his research about Saint Domingo who built a bridge for the pilgrims. The town was named after him. 'Chicken church is the irreverent nickname for the cathedral of San Domingo.'

'A fable claimed that in the 14th century a German Pilgrim boy and his parents stayed in a nearby inn,' the Norwegian teacher slipped into her teacher mode. 'The landlord's daughter liked the boy, but he ignored her. She planted a silver cup in his bag.'

'And shopped him,' Dan said, eager to impart some of his knowledge.

The teacher shot him a severe teacher look. 'Theft carried the death penalty,' she appraised Dan as if she wanted to administer it herself.

'He was hanged,' Dan nodded slowly with a solemn expression, as if to warn them to keep their eyes on their bags.

'But!' the teacher pinned them with an intense gaze. 'His parents found him alive on the gallows. He said Santo Domingo had performed a miracle and saved him. The parents asked the Mayor for permission to cut their son down. He was dining and said their son was as dead as chickens on his table. Thereupon, the birds sprouted feathers and flew away, and the Mayor allowed them to cut down the boy. Now white roosters live in a cage in the cathedral.'

'What many people don't know,' Dan interjected, 'was the landlord and his daughter were hanged together on the very same gallows!'

'I think the moral is: never lie,' the Filipino smiled. He picked up his rucksack. 'I think we can risk going now,' he said to the Mexican woman. She nodded and heaved her backpack onto her hunched back. The man patted her backpack.

'I'll be goin' now.' Dan kicked the Cola can again and pulled on his pack.

'Not me!' The Swedish woman said. 'I going to wait till it's cooler.' She dumped her pack on the ground and sat on it, her blond hair plastered to her sweat covered face down to her determined jaw.

'Mind if we walk together?' the Norwegian teacher asked.

'Why not? We can swap dirty history stories.' He grinned. She didn't.

After walking the walk and reaching melting point they came to a sudden green oasis of lush cut grass under oak trees. Four comfort-free concrete loungers lay unused around a bronze drinking fountain. Dan filled his bottle and emptied it three times and lay down for just a few seconds.

'Dan?' He blinked at the blue sky. 'Are you staying?' The voice asked.

'Did I drop off?' He looked up at the teacher with her backpack already on her shoulders.

'Twenty minutes ago,' she nodded.

'Ok. Be right with you,' he closed his eyes for just a split second. When he opened them again the sky was where he'd left it. The teacher was not. Only rustle of leaves above his head and a distant tractor kept him company. He dozed again.

'Are you alright?' A gentle hand grasped his shoulder.

Dan's eye blinked open. 'God!' he shouted.

'Not quite,' a girlish voice chuckled. He saw the outline of a nun. His heart jolted and jaw sagged. A bad dream? Four of them looking down at him.

'Your eyes remind me of headlights,' the nun chuckled, the others giggled nudging each other. He took a second look at the African nun with beautiful winning smile. Amber rosary beads hung from their belts round pale blue habits that trailed the ground hiding their feet.

'God, you shocked me!' He staggered to his feet.

'We thought you might have suffered heat stroke,' another nun joined in.

'No. No. I, I'm all right. Thank you.'

'Take care,' her eyes sparkled. 'We'll leave you in peace now we know you're alright.'

'Where are you from?'

'Nigeria. Have you been there?' Dan shook his sleepy head.

'You should come. You would be very, very welcome.'

'Most welcome,' said another.' Her eyes sparkled with more humour and kindness than Dan had ever seen in his life. He stared, open mouthed. Something tugged inside his breast. Something he had never felt before. Something he could not name. 'You would be welcome. Have a beautiful day.'

'Thanks for the invitation,' he almost stuttered.

Their laughter was tinkling water. 'See you along the way, brother. Buen Camino,' they chuckled again and walked back to the trail. Dan watched them go. Their pale blue habits dusting the ground. His eyes followed till they were out of sight and stay fixed on the crest over which they had disappeared. 'Well, I'll be...' he sighed, for the first time in his life, he was lost for words. A slight smile creased his cheeks as he again filled his bottle at the fountain. These were nuns from another world. They had *actually* friggin' helped me! He shook his head to clear the whirling thoughts. They were *actually* worried about me!

An hour later, Dan caught up with a half-naked pilgrim who held an umbrella against the sun. The trail turned to asphalt. The right side was a line of crappy looking building yards and warehouses that ended on a large piece of industrial wasteland. On the left lay fields of corn scattered with glossy poppies. He had reached Santo Domingo; chicken church town. The torso of the umbrella-man gleamed under a sheen of sweat. It highlighted his intricate green and blue tattoos that resembled a mass of interwoven snakes. A scarf tied around his head reminded Dan of a pirate. Other pilgrims were strung out along the Way. A yard full of long steel pipes with connections to extend over miles of terrain indicated that irrigation was big business here.

'Hi!' Jane appeared out of nowhere. 'Why didn't you wait this morning?'

'I'm in a race, remember? Mr Iron man?' he panted. 'And besides, I didn't think you desired my company,' he snatched his Kiwi army hat and dragged it across his brow. He scanned the desolate warehouses and watched some workers coming out of a side door, oblivious to the tired pilgrim column as they chattered among themselves. 'It's nice to see real people comin' of a buildin' again.'

'What are you talking about?'

'I passed through a ghost town. It was more eerie than a ghost town in ruins. It's modern! A small, modern, intact town that's dead.'

'I didn't see it.'

'You can't miss it! Smart, snappy houses. Front lawns. Village green with empty swings and slides. Windows stare at you like square eyed skulls.

Modern but dead. It's as if aliens had lifted the people off the face of the earth.'

Jane nodded. 'It's the property building bubble that burst in Spain.'

He took off his sunglasses at squinted at her. 'When did you get here?'

'Oh, about three hours ago. I got a taxi ride in a helicopter.'

'Wow! Big spender!'

'In fact, it was a *police* helicopter.' He followed her nervous glance across the wasteland.

Dan's breath expelled loudly as his jaw sagged. A helicopter with sagging rotor blades stood next to a black limousine. A group of kids had gathered to gawk. But it was the two men who stood next to it that made Dan's stomach swirl like an imbalanced spin drier. 'Shit!' he growled 'What happened?'

'There was another body. Near Azofra.'

'Where we spent the night!' Dan saw twin anxious faces – both his, mirrored in the lenses of Jane's Ray Bans.

'Just outside the village at a way cross.' Jane grimaced. 'I caught a glimpse of an arm.'

'Shit!' Dan passed his finger through his hair. 'Now we have a repeat of the fuckin' moustache and dicky bow show. They have it in for me, that's for sure.'

Her glasses swung in the direction of Dan's gaze. 'You haven't done anything wrong.'

'Neither had Jesus, nor Saint James.'

'Well, you're not either of *them*.' She watched the ground as they approached the Detective. Dan tried a smile. Mendoza didn't. He regarded Dan through narrowed eyelids in stony features. The tip of his tongue brushed his thick moustache like a hungry cat. Dan felt mice scurrying through his bowels. This did not look like a social call.

'Good afternoon, Mr Brady. Please be kind enough to get in the car.' He wasn't asking.

'Why? We're not tired at all, are we, Jane?' Dan's stiff smile did not reach his worried eyes.

'We wish to ask a few questions in the local office. There are some new developments. We have more questions. Please, get in the car!' Mendoza's tone of voice made it clear it wasn't for a joy ride.

'I'm coming, too!' Jane heard her voice and could not believe what she was saying.

'That is not necessary, Ms Downer,' Mendoza reached for the door handle.

'I think I should, or I'll have to call the British embassy,' she held her phone up to show it.

Mendoza's hand froze in inches from the handle. 'I said it is not necessary.'

'It might be useful, Comisario,' the Detective broke in. Mendoza glared at him and opened the door. 'Let me help.' The Detective held the rear door open.

'Thank you,' Jane said quietly. She looked up. The Detective's eyes were fixed on her hair. 'Thank you,' Jane repeated.

'Not at all, Ms Downer. Not at all!'

The door thudded and clunked. She had the impression that the doors had locked with a louder sound than her car. She felt trapped.

* * *

The limousine turned off the tree lined Avenida de

Haro and braked in front of grey metal double doors of a cream plaster building. At her side, Dan practiced a string of muttered profanities in case he might need them.

Jane noticed a web of hairline cracks that resembled a road map running in all directions across the wall. She felt queasy at the sight of wrought iron bars guarding boarded windows. *It's a ghost house!* Her brow wrinkled.

'Where the hell is this!' Dan growled. 'It's got a fuckin' pillbox with machine gun slits on the corner. Looks like a poor man's Alcatraz!'

Jane saw the small bunker jutting from the corner of the building. 'It's certainly not the Ritz.'

'Your sense of understatement never ceases to friggin' amaze me.'

Mendoza ignored him. The Detective avoided looking at him. The doors opened, and they drove inside. Jane recognised the bald, thick man as wide as he was tall flicking away a cigarette stub. He spat on the floor before he opened the car door. His face was round but distorted by the ugly scar.

'He looks like second place in a friggin' sword fight.'

Jane shuddered. 'He reminds me of a cheap nightclub bouncer,' she whispered.

'Yeah? How many cheap nightclubs have you been to?'

'Not enough to give me a bad reputation.'

'Cheap or not, he looks dangerous,' Dan muttered.

Jane felt goose bumps rise. The insect eyes sunglasses weighed up Dan for some moments. Dan stared back.

'This is Ramos.' Mendoza nodded towards the

stocky figure. Jane recognised him from the way cross that morning. Ramos looked neither Latin nor north European. Just brutal. He followed on their heels into a depressing office furnished with wall to wall dust, its walls decorated by light coloured squares from missing pictures. Mendoza placed himself behind a grey metal desk that looked as if someone had thrown it from the top floor.

A burst of machine gun fire ripped the room. Jane saw Dan crouch, as if about to pull a gun.

Ramos clapped his cell to his ear. 'Sí?' he grunted and stepped out of the room and muttered monosyllables in the corridor.

'How tasteless,' Jane muttered.

'I'm sorry, Ms Downer,' Detective Amador arched his eyebrows and glared at the open door.

Jane took a deep breath. She shuddered. It was cold within the thick stone walls. She shivered and felt only half dressed in her shorts. She tried to massage her legs without drawing attention. *Should I go to the bathroom and change?*

'You stayed the night in Azofra, Mr Brady,' Mendoza began.

'Correct.'

'There was another body near Azofra.'

'Ms Downer's already told me,' Dan said. 'But why are you tellin' me?'

'Two murders and you near both scenes.' The Comisario fingered his moustache. His eyes flickered across Dan's face as if reading his mind.

'So were a few hundred other fuckin' pilgrims.'

'The other pilgrims do not own this,' Mendoza lay a red object on the desk.

Dan frowned as he picked it up. He flicked it

open. A stern face looked back at him. His own, from a dog eared passport.

'Yours I believe,' Mendoza looked at Amador and back at Dan.

'Where did you get this?' Dan gaped.

'It was under the victim's body. How do you explain that?'

Ramos returned to the room and sat backwards on a chair, cowboy saloon style. He stared Dan out. Inner violence simmered on a short fuse.

Dan looked at Jane's shocked features. 'That's not possible! I know nothing about it!'

Jane clenched her knuckles and took another deep breath. She didn't know what to say. She saw perspiration on Dan's brow despite the coolness of the room. She was confused. What if Dan was guilty, despite all he had said to her? *A passport can get into wrong hands*, she thought. *But, under the body!?*

Dan shrugged and shook his head. 'I hadn't noticed it had gone from my pack!' He looked at Jane again and saw doubt in her eyes.

Mendoza leaned towards Dan, raised his hand and flicked a small card on the table like a poker dealer. 'How do you explain this, Mister Brady?' Dan stared down at his own visiting card.

He cuffed his damp forehead. 'This is some sort of set up...!'

'You must be mistaken!' Jane heard her own shout at Mendoza, surprising herself at her reaction.

'All the facts fit, Ms Downer.' His eyes cold as ice. 'What can I, as a policeman, say?' He spread his hands.

'Factually, Comisario,' Jane cleared her throat. 'Things do not fit as well as you claim,' Jane was quiet and calm, although her heart thrashed like a hooked fish. 'I don't know how Mr Brady's passport came to be with the girl, but I am sure he was the whole night in the Albergue in the next bunk. Remember, the Albergues have a curfew. In fact, they lock their doors at ten o' clock, so he had to be inside.'

'Mr Brady is ex-military, fit and resourceful. An ex-soldier with service in Afghanistan.'

'Huh?' Ramos grunted and said something in Spanish.

'A locked door would not keep him in or out,' Mendoza continued.

'That's not true! If I had let myself out I would not have been able to get back in, no matter what you think about my experience as a soldier.'

Jane saw him turn and look at Ramos, who muttered something to Mendoza.

'As a matter of fact, Comisario,' Jane broke in, 'my sister disappeared a year ago along the Way of Saint James. Now two girls have been murdered and I feel that my sister has suffered the same fate.' She dabbed her eyes. 'Factually, I think it was covered up!'

'What are you suggesting, Ms Downer?' Detective Amador's brows furrowed. He frowned at Mendoza.

She turned to the Detective. 'When my sister disappeared, the British and Spanish police cooperated. But it all came to nothing. I thought it strange that nothing appeared in the press.' She took a deep breath. 'Comisario, I think my sister's disappearance is connected to these two murders. That's why I don't believe Mr Brady is guilty. I think Mr Brady needs a lawyer.'

Mendoza entwined his fingers and stared at her.

'Sorry, but I had no idea, Ms Downer,' Amador frowned.

'Mr Brady shall have a lawyer!' Mendoza raised his voice and his glare cut off Amador's tongue.

'Ms Downer,' Mendoza's voice took on a new tone. 'I am sorry, but I see nothing to prove that your sister's disappearance was linked in any way to these murders.' He spread his hands and looked with an innocent expression.

'In fact, Comisario, I find it rather strange that you didn't seem surprised when I first told you back in Logroño.'

'No, no, no, Ms Downer,' he held up both hands. 'Let me assure you that you are mistaken,' Mendoza's tone became softer. 'There is no connection,' he held his hands open in a gesture of sincerity. 'No connection at all.'

'I am convinced that Mr Brady is innocent,' Jane's thumb stabbed buttons on her Smartphone out of sight under the table, hoping not to make too many typos.

'Mr Brady, I am obliged to see the facts before me. We found this visiting card of yours in the first victim's pocketbook.' The Detective tapped the visiting card.

'It's all a fuckin' coincidence!'

Mendoza pursed his lips. 'To sum up. A dead girl had your visiting card in her purse, and a second dead girl lay on your passport.' Mendoza shook his head. 'Mr Brady, it seems that violence is your second name.'

'Rubbish! Where did you get that shit!'

'I have checked up on your background.

Afghanistan where violence was nothing new for you!' Mendoza spat the last words out like bullets. With a brusque gesture he passed a sheet of paper to Detective Amador.

'And do I get to read the friggin' thing?'

Alonso nodded at Mendoza and laid the papers on the desk. Ramos, rocking on the chair, snatched them and eyeballed the contents. Mendoza looked sour but turned his attention back to Dan.

'The report says that you...'

'Puta Madre!' Ramos roared. He uncoiled from his chair like a spring. His hand dived inside his jacket lapel. Amador flung himself between Dan and Ramos. Ramos' eyes blazed in rage that increased within milliseconds.

Jane cried out and bolted for the door.

Amador held Ramos' arm up high, a grey pistol pointed at the ceiling. 'Puta Madre!' Ramos' vulgar language filled the room. Mendoza rushed round the desk to help.

'Come on!' Dan hissed. 'Out, out, out!' She felt Dan tumble her through the door. Furious voices bellowed inside the office. Dan slammed the door behind himself. Twisted the key. Ducked as a thunder clap filled the office. Wood splintered above their heads.

Go! A voice in her head commanded.

Jane felt Dan's hard grip boosting her along the corridor.

Another explosion resounded behind them. Little wood splinters stung her neck.

* * *

Dan pulled Jane from the building at a run. They were quickly breathless. They jumped aside from a trumpeting horn. Explosions of backfiring followed by a screech of tyres stopped them on the spot.

Dan registered a matt coloured car with different coloured doors swerve in front of them. It stopped, rocking on its springs. A figure erupted from a red door. Dan recognised the face.

'Angie!' Jane cried. 'We were...'

'Get in!' Angie shouted. Dan sprawled along the back seat. Jane's weight winded him. Tyres squealed, and the door slammed under the force of a sharp right. Dan twisted - recognised the tall man called Karl with his shaved head and the binary code tattoo above his ear. Karl's eyes regarded Dan in the mirror. Angie's large candid eyes flickered over Dan's features sizing him up.

'Thanks, Angie, old girl,' Jane panted.

'Where did *you* friggin' come from?'

'We've been following you. Karl fixed a tracking device to Jane's backpack,' Angie's lashes hugged her cheeks.

'In this!' Dan surveyed the tatty interior. A spring dug into his backside. 'Is this old bucket safe?'

Karl stabbed a radio button. Heavy Metal filled the car, matching the backfiring exhaust. Angie rolled her lovely eyes and turned it down.

'And I sent an SMS,' Jane said.

'Very friggin' James Bond! There's a crazy asshole after us. He's wavin' a gun about!'

'He wanted to shoot you!' Jane stared at Dan.

'So I noticed,' Dan breathed deep, charging his depleted lungs with oxygen. He stared at Angie's tanned, oval face as she stabbed the radio button. Brahms filled the car. She wound back the volume.

'Puh! Did you provoke him?'

'O'course not! I was just sittin' there while a stupid Comisario asked stupid questions.' Another tyre squealing curve pressed Dan against the door. 'Is this door safe?'

'Of course! I service this car myself,' Angie said high and haughty.

'Feels loose to me.'

'These cars last a lifetime,' she stuck her nose in the air.

'I hate that noise!' Karl pressed a select button and killed Brahms and the radio smashed their ears with Heavy Metal.

'Did he lose his job as a Getaway driver?' Dan nodded at the shaved head. He peeked out of the cracked back window. Nobody followed.

'Careful, Karl!' Jane said as the car swerved to avoid a pedestrian.

'Always am,' he grinned pulling the car in a series of suspension cracking swerves, throwing Dan and Jane together like the stars in a Punch and Judy show.

They screeched to a nose standing stop between two cars. They sat and listened. 'They will never search here.'

'Why not?'

'Police station car park,' he grinned.

'Good for you, my Formula One hero.' Angelique patted his arm and looked at Dan.

'I doubt if they'll mistake this multi coloured

friggin' death trap for one of their own.'

'Made in France.' The tip of her tongue flashed in a hint of mischief. 'Drives forever.'

'It looks as it already has,' Dan took in torn upholstery. 'It looks as if it's been made of ten different cars.

'It has,' her eye twitched – or did she wink? Dan wondered.

'She dents it so often it always needs new body parts,' Karl said. 'Like Frankenstein,' he pressed the button for the Heavy Metal station again and nodded in time to the driving beat.

'Allez!' Angie shouted and turned it down. 'My father says never buy a spare part when you can get it from a scrap-yard,' she turned back to the radio and changed back to classic.

'That is nerd music!' He changed channel back to Iron Maiden

'You *are* a nerd.' She smacked the back of his head.

'She buys replacement doors and fenders so often it makes no sense to spray them.' He rubbed his scalp on his binary tattoo.

'Puh!' she smacked the back of his head and turned back to Dan. 'You have to get your name cleared!' Angelique tapped Dan's arm making the hairs rise.

'Sure, but how? That Comisario doesn't seem to be the listening kind, and as for the crazy guy in there..!'

'Jane said you are a journalist!' Karl interrupted. 'Journalists are dogs. When they have a bone, they can't let go, no? These murders are a juicy bone for a journalist, right? You could use your journalist contacts to help you.'

'Did you tell them the name of the rag I write for?' Dan raised an eyebrow in Jane's direction. Jane shrugged. Dan looked back at Angie. 'It's a sport magazine. Nothin' *you'd* want to waste your money on.'

'Depends on the sport,' her eyelid flickered.

'Ach, Angie! We must organise a place to sleep.'

'Or a good place to friggin' hide with Ramos on the loose.'

'We will find something.'

'Oh, fuck!'

'What now?'

'My backpack! My passport, money, SSDs! They're still in the fuckin' police station!'

ON THE RUN

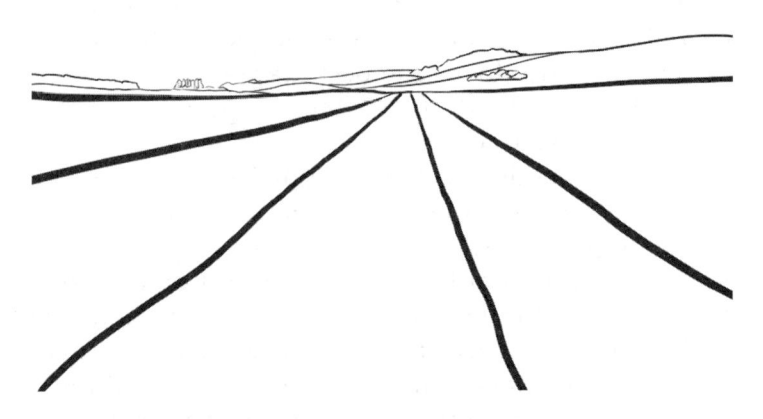

Darkness swallowed the day, relieving Santo Domingo from the withering heat. Windows of shops and restaurants threw glowing oblongs across the paving of the old town while waiters threw tableclothes across dining tables.

Dan led the way into the pedestrian zone, slightly crouched as if stalking. Two policemen leaned against a wall, their thumbs busy on their Smartphone screens. Dan boldly walked past as if he owned the street. The uniforms didn't look up. The others followed into a square full of cafés and noise.

'I reckon those policemen are supposed to be guarding the friggin' place, so nobody will come looking here.'

They found seats and gradually relaxed with the

music and soothing aroma of food steaming on the plates of pilgrims around them. Locals wore blue neckerchiefs for the town festival of Santo Domingo and handed them out to pilgrims. Some sang, some danced, most gossiped, and savoured food with an endless flow of vino tinto. The pilgrims ate heartily and quickly before they had to hurry back to their albergues, where, after the ten o' clock curfew, strict custodians marooned them outside locked doors.

'Are you sure this is the best place to hide?' Jane's eyes slid side to side like a tennis spectator, taking in the whole square.

'They'll search all the friggin' busses and the station, not the middle of a festival.'

'You hope.'

'Ach, they are not looking for me, so I don't mind,' Karl touched his tattoo as they took a table in the middle of the square. They hunched and took cover behind menus. Jane watched the crowd. Karl fiddled with the olive oil bottle as if considering whether to take a swig.

Dan spoke, his voice edged with irritation and hardness. 'Ok, I'd like some more information about how you and I came to be here after we met in Navarrete.'

'After Jane's sister disappeared on the Way of Saint James and Jane decided to walk the Camino in order to find out what happened to her, I wanted to help and protect her.' Karl answered the way Germans expand short answers into logistical reports.

'I came to help Karl,' Angelique explained. We're working together to solve the case of this poor missing girl.'

'Debbie,' Dan said.

'Ah, you told him,' Karl looked at Jane without expression and scratched his tattoo again.

Angelique touched Dan's arm 'We weren't getting anywhere until you got in the way.'

'Got in the way!' Dan spluttered crumbs from a bread roll he had taken. 'That's rich! I've been dragged into this friggin' mess against my will, and now I've gotten in the way!' His eyes vivid in anger. 'That's the friggin' laugh of the friggin' week, if you don't mind me sayin' so.'

'Allez! It's a compliment,' Angelique smiled. 'You getting to know Jane...'

'Gettin' to know? Hah! You make it sound like we're fuckin' datin'. Quite the fuckin' opposite, I'm glad to say. She pinched my SSDs and screwed up my summer plans. Me bein' near that body was a shitty coincidence. Nothin' to do with me gettin' in the fuckin' way.'

'I think it is better to stay calm,' Karl warned.

'I just wanted to say that it triggered a series of events that seem to involve you and the killer.'

'*And* the fuckin' police,' Dan glowered. 'And, even worse, brought me together with this loony Ramos who suddenly went berserk with a pistol! And all because *she*,' his finger almost lanced Jane, 'took my fuckin' SSD cards!'

'Hmm, I love the way you tell it. So, expressive,' Angie's eyelids flickered, she cocked her head. Lights glinted on the small arrow piercing her ear.

Jane rolled her eyes and looked at the menu.

A hand clapped firmly on Dan's shoulder. He froze. Eyes ignited. His chair clattered backwards. He twisted like a spinning top, into a boxer's defensive crouch.

* * *

'Ola!' A grinning woman with a toothless mouth held out a blue festival scarf.

'Jesus! I thought that was the police!' Dan's fists opened and dropped to his sides. His face relaxed. He righted his fallen chair and the old woman lay the scarf round his neck and gave one to each of them.

'I thought I'd been copped by Mendoza,' he panted and felt the scarf round his neck and grinned to people watching from neighbouring tables.

'It's alright, Dan. Just part of the celebrations.' Angelique giggled.

Jane saw Dan outwardly relax. *He's jumpy*, she thought as the flame of angry fear in his eyes subsided. *Why not,* she mused. *After his escape he's got half the Spanish police searching for him.* She saw a Mexican woman and a blonde woman walk by. Dan flapped a hand. The teacher nodded in recognition.

'You finally woke up then?' she smiled. Dan gave a thumbs-up.

Jane's eyes followed them and wondered why they were so nice to Dan. She squinted at the rapid movement of red shoes. Mr Tennis shoes took a place at a table across the square where some of the locals linked their arms in his and offered wine. *Him again.* Her brow furrowed. She felt a little twist in her stomach. He seemed to be everywhere. She watched his shoes cutting a red arc as he was practicing his leg swinging.

Two waiters arrived and distracted her. One

hunched with sad bloodhound expression under the bossy remarks of the other. He hopped around the table, covering it with plates of Tapas while the bossy one opened a bottle of wine. All four stared at the mass of food and devoured everything in silence, driven by hunger from their adrenaline upsurges. Finally, they slumped back on their seats. Dan held his stomach and suppressed a burp.

Karl also stretched and rubbed his belly. 'That meal reminds me of two cannibals eating a clown. One said to the other 'I think he tastes a bit funny,' he chuckled at his own joke. Angie slapped his head. Dan rolled his eyes. Karl went back to his mails.

Around them, pilgrims and the local people danced and sang to a group of minstrel-like musicians.

Jane watched but didn't feel like joining. The day had been too much. She was still shaken by Ramos' actions. She worried that he might find them here. Her eyes scanned their surroundings. 'We need somewhere to sleep.'

'We must find a room for you alone,' Angie warned. 'The police will think it's strange if you disappeared with Dan.'

'I certainly do *not* intend to disappear *with* Dan!'

'I can camp out,' Dan said. 'Just drop me outside town.'

'The countryside is so flat they would pick you up in no time at all,' Jane said.

'Ooh!' Dan pulled an expression of mock surprise. 'Nice of you to worry about my safety.'

'He can hide with us,' Angie smiled at Dan. Dan smiled back and noticed a long scar along the back of her forearm. 'They don't know us. As long as Jane is on her own they cannot be suspicious.'

'We already have a place booked,' Karl said. 'But I will need some peace and quiet to deal with things on-line.' He stared at Dan. 'Maybe you should leave the country.'

'How?' Dan rolled his eyes. 'They'll be watchin' the airports. And beside that the police still have my rucksack with my fuckin' passport and credit cards as well as my SSDs!'

'Then I'd say you're stuck here,' Jane said.

'You'll have to do it all again.'

Dan stared across the square. Jane could see he was weighing up the odds. Try and get them back from the police or try and repeat everything.

'I have a job to do.'

'Writing about pilgrims? Huh!' Jane rolled her eyes.

'I just changed my original mandate.'

'Let me guess; you're trying to break your sister's record *and* race the police to Santiago.'

'Don't be fuckin' stupid,' he shot back at her.' There's a serial killer on the loose. I've got to help! I'm guilty in the eyes of Mendoza. Even if I got out of the country, he could extradite me from England. Then I lose my job, my kids! That's not how I see my future.'

'Ramos could also come after you.'

'You think so?' Dan asked. His eyes showed he agreed with her.

Jane nodded. 'I feel it. In fact, he could be mad enough to follow you to England! Something made him lose control. I wonder what happened there in the police station that drove him so crazy.' Jane regarded him a moment.

'Ach, we should get some early sleep!' Karl touched his tattoo.

'What about Dan?' Angelique plucked at Dan's sleeve. 'He needs new clothes. I'll go and buy something with a little more street cred.'

'You don't know my size?'

'I can estimate.' She looked him up and down and winked.

'Something tasteful!' Jane said. 'That'll really fool them.'

'What's wrong with these colours?' Dan frowned. 'Green's my favourite colour.' Even fashion indifferent Karl rolled his eyes.

'Allez. Wait in the car with Karl,' Angie ordered. 'You can plan how you can get out of your predicament.'

'I hope there *is* a friggin' way out!'

* * *

An hour later Angelique pulled open the rear door of the car and pushed four plastic bags at Dan. 'These will stop you assaulting people's eyes.'

Dan twisted in contortions trying to change clothes in the confines of the rear seat. 'I will dislocate my fuckin' arse in the back here!' he growled. He finished his sartorial transformation into long beige hiking trousers and a blue jacket.

'It'll disguise you from the police.' Angelique glanced out of the window at the street.

'Factually, he almost resembles a human being.'

'Huh, still got the same face,' Dan muttered.

'Nobody's perfect,' Jane shrugged.

'Anythin' else?' Dan's sullen eyes flickered from one grinning woman to the other. They stared back in silence. He stared in Angie's eyes and let himself slowly topple back against the seat and creased up in laughter for the first time for what seemed forever. Angelique joined in and slapped his knee and ruffled his hair. Jane glared at her. Dan smiled like a spoiled brat.

'Factually, Angie, this *isn't* a party!'

ALBERGUE IN THE WOODS

'I checked us in to the Parador in town. With its big foyer as it's more anonymous.' The car rocked and springs complained as Karl slumped into the seat. 'I checked in three of us.'

Jane looked through the car window as a cloud slid from the moon and lit up a long, two story farmhouse south of Santo Domingo. The building lay at the edge of a wild wood, held at bay by an overgrown lawn. The eerie call of an owl raised goose bumps. 'And who are the happy threesome?' Karl switched on the internal light. The building was replaced by Jane's refection in the glass.

'Me, Angelique and Dan,' Karl's poker face glance flitted from face to face. Only Angelique nodded in satisfaction.

'How cosy,' Jane glowered at her angry

countenance in the glass.

'We agreed that you should check in alone as the police know about you and your relationship with Dan...'

'There *is no* relationship between Dan and me! I wouldn't have him even if he were the last living man on this planet.'

'Hah! Don' worry. You'd be killed in the friggin' rush.'

'He means that events connect you,' Angelique said. 'Not sex.'

'I'm glad we've all got *that* clear,' Jane drummed her fingers against her thigh.

'The police expect Dan to be with you. If they find where you're staying, they'll come and search your room,' Karl scratched his tattoo. 'They would find Dan.'

'They wouldn't have to search. I'd tell them,' Jane muttered.

'Dan can sleep in our room on the sofa.' Karl said.

'We can order a meal so Dan can eat.' Angelique smiled at him.

'He's just eaten enough for a regiment!'

'I get hungry in the night,' Dan said meekly.

'I'd hate you to starve on my account.'

Angelique placed her hand on Jane's. 'I'd share your room with you, Jane, but if the police did a check and found me with you...'

'It's okay, Angie,' Jane flapped a dismissive hand. 'I just can't believe I'm on the run with Mr Marathon man!'

With a tight smile Dan said, 'don't take it so hard on yourself, Jane. Many people would've had a nervous friggin' breakdown by now.'

'There's still time. The night's still young.' She forced a weak smile.

* * *

Inside the Albergue, Jane's face dropped faster than a bent coin in a parking meter. It was a sparse albergue with a dormitory suitable for garden gnomes with bunks close enough to twiddle thumbs with one's neighbour. She released a long breath of relief when the landlady showed her a room. It was an albergue that boasted the unusual luxury of twin bedrooms. Something for the upscale pilgrims.

Once in her room, Jane dozed on a downscale lumpy mattress. The room was stuffy and smelt of mothballs that were strong enough to keep the whole province moth free. She got up and pulled open the French windows as wide as possible and wriggled her fingers through the wooden slats of the shutters.

The owl's haunting cry echoed again from the trees. Jane imagined Dracula flapping through the night on leathery wings. *He wouldn't waste his time on my tired blood,* she thought. 'God, I'm thirsty!' she whispered, listening to voices drifting from downstairs. A clumsy hand strummed an out of tune guitar, fumbling the same three chords, E A D ad nauseam. The large empty bottle of Solan mocked her. She had guzzled it half an hour before and its content had long popped out of her pores, leaving her limp and damp all over.

The pilgrim cowboy started again. *Now I know why lonesome cowboys are lonesome,* she mused and perched on the edge of the sagging mattress and sucked on the water bottle again. The last drop slid onto her sandpaper tongue. She pulled on her jeans to get more water.

A strong smell of stale beer greeted her in the bar

downstairs. Her feet stuck to the carpet, showing where much of it had slopped. *God, I'll get up drunk from the fumes in here.*

'Dos botellas de agua, por favor,' Jane held up two fingers in a V sign that could have got her in impolite answer back home. The landlady plonked two large bottles of Solan on the bar, each with a beautiful skin of condensation. Jane's fingers pecked at the coins in her shabby purse, chosen for her trip to appear worthless to itchy fingers.

Outside at the front door, she nursed the cold bottles and stared at the clear black sky. Stars multiplied with each second she watched. Aliens switching on their lights. Apart from the Milky Way, she recognised none of them. So much for astronomy at GCSE level.

That was why she had studied languages and music instead of physics like her sister Debbie. A whiz kid who got her pilot license in record time. Jane clicked the seal and sucked on the bottle. It vibrated as air fought its way in with each gulp.

The cowboy guaranteed more loneliness by murdering three other chords.

'Your phone's ringing.' A pilgrim smiled and blinked.

'I know,' she recognised the ring tone.

'Don't you wanna speak to him?'

'Who says it's a he?' She frowned at the speaker.

'Only men make women so angry,' a woman said.

'Do you want to talk to him?' Jane challenged.'

'Er, nope.'

'Then that makes two of us.' She upended the bottle against her lips.

* * *

Back in her sticky room, she tried to pull the tall French windows open wider. They stuck. She pushed the slatted wooden shutters outward and stepped onto the narrow balcony. She felt a thousand invisible eyes in the dark woods staring back. A gentle breeze carried to her the scent of the woods and cooled the film of sweat raising goose bumps. She yawned and exhaustion sucked the energy from her body. Her muscles melted away. She went back into the room and let herself fall on the bed, rolled on her back and lay like a starfish. To clear her head and sleep, she tried to meditate where she lay. Something at which Debbie always scoffed. Calm seeped through her till sleep slid through her body.

* * *

'Ah, Mendoza! Sit! Sit!' The President was only partly visible under the low glow of his desk lamp, apart from the glow of his cigar. The rest of the large office disappeared into the shadows. 'Thank you for coming at this late hour, but I thought it better when no other personnel are around.' His hand illuminated by the lamp gestured to the two lower chairs before a desk that had cost a mahogany tree its life. 'Especially Maria.'

'Is she a risk?'

'Possibly,' the glow partly lit up the Presidente's face.

'Why did you employ her?'

The cigar glowed again. 'Nice face for visitors, nice ass for me,' he chuckled like a gurgling sink.

'Anyway thanks for coming.'

'I was returning to Pamplona anyway, Señor Presidente,' Mendoza said, trying in vain to imagine a situation where he could be offered a job because of the shape of his arse.

'Were you really, why?'

'I live here, Señor President.' They both fell silent.

The cigar glowed. 'Mendoza, this latest murder...'

'We have it under control, Señor Presidente.'

'Have you, Mendoza? Have you?' He paused. 'I am told the English suspect escaped!'

'Ramos, the man you gave me with his team made a real pigs arse of things. He went wild when he found that the Englishman was in Afghanistan and could have something to do with the death of his brother. The man is out of control, Señor Presidente, I cannot take responsibility for him.'

'Like you, Mendoza, I'm retiring soon. No scandal shall blemish *my* career. These murders not only endanger our EU grant from Brussels but a scandal like this could lose it all and cause an investigation of the Council and our past.'

'Señor Presidente, may I switch on the light? I cannot read my files.'

The Presidente grunted. Moments later the room was a blaze of light.

'Please bear in mind I cannot claim the new killing is a suicide.' Mendoza looked worried.

'Ah, so what do you suggest?' he pursed his prominent lower lip and arched an eyebrow. 'If people think there's a serial killer on the loose, they'll stay away from the Camino. We cannot afford that. The whole region relies on the income it brings! And,' he wagged a warning finger. 'If they hear we have covered it up, that'll be a double scandal! That would finish both of us.'

'I understand, Señor Presidente,' Mendoza dabbed his brow.

'Tell me, Mendoza, is the English man guilty or not?'

'Not guilty.'

'Damn!'

'But, there is nobody else! I am watching him. If we pick him up we cannot do or prove anything to hold him. I prefer to leave him in the belief he is successfully evading me, then he'll stay and I have a scapegoat in reserve.'

'If we don't catch the real killer, then give me a culprit when we need him, Mendoza. Even if he be later proved innocent, or had a sad accident...,' the Presidente smiled without humour in his dark eyes. He steepled his fingers and rotated his chair to see out of the window across the Plaza where the lit up statue of General Espatero sat on his trusty steed.

'If anything untoward happens, my successor can sort it out after we have retired and have what we want, Señor Presidente.'

'Yes, exactly, Mendoza, exactly!' The old Presidente swivelled back to face the Comisario and pointed his finger like a pistol. 'Make sure no murders become public. The annual EU payment of twenty million Euros will soon be transferred to the Council's bank account. Nothing, Mendoza, nothing, must hinder that payment. Do what you have to do. Don't bother me with the details. Fix it! And fix this Englishman if you must. Leave any dirty work to Ramos.'

'Gladly, Señor Presidente, as long as I am not held

responsible for his actions.'

The Presidente acted as if he had not heard and asked, 'How is your family? The two boys? Doing well at school?'

'They are in America. University.' Mendoza's face was sullen.

'America! Good place. Good for them!'

Mendoza shrugged slightly. 'If you say so, Señor Presidente.' His voice was tired. He had heard this theme a thousand times.

'And your wife?' The cigar glowed.

'My wife is still living in Buenos Aires, Señor Presidente.'

'Hm,' he puffed his cigar and watched the smoke. 'Will she come back to Spain?'

Mendoza reddened; his gaze drooped toward the floor. 'I cannot say, Señor Presidente.'

The Presidente peered over the top of his glasses, sucked on his cigar and leaned back to let an unseen smoke ring float upwards into the darkness. 'You know something, Mendoza? When a man has a restless Argentinian wife, he should perhaps learn to tango.'

* * *

The mattress sank on one side of the bed.

'What?' Jane murmured, floating between sleep and waking. The room was almost black.

A hand closed round her wrist.

'Who...? she murmured. The hand gripped tighter.

'Cursed Succubus!'

'Hey!' Jane jerked upward and sat with hammering heart. A second hand pushed her down. Panic flooded her brain. She struggled. 'Mmmpph!' She tried to shout. A pad clamped over her nose. Dizzy, she twisted her head free. Gulped in air. 'Stop!'

Sweat and hot breath made her retch. Bile stung her throat. The soft pad covered her nose again. She felt dizzy, weightless.

Jane! The voice in her head yelled. *Jane! Twist! Kick!* She was falling into space. *Fight! Kick!* Her lungs burned for air.

She kicked.

'Succubus!' Saliva wet her ears. Her lungs began to absorb the last precious remaining air. She kicked in a frenzy. The gauze pad slipped. She sucked litres of air. Kicked wildly in every direction. Lashed out in the darkness against a hooded figure silhouetted against the moonlight.

'Help!' she yelled.

A fist banged on the wall. 'Cut out the noise!'

The door burst open like a thunderclap.

A form rushed into the room. The meaty sound of a fist connecting. The two shadowy figures parted. An agonised cry burst from one of them. Jane smelt CS gas. Her eyes watered.

A shadow bolted through the French windows in a confusing blur of movement.

Footsteps thundered through the open door.

'Help!' she yelled. 'Help me!'

'You OK?' a voice asked. An arm supported her.

'A man,' she gasped. 'A man in my room.'

Light flooded the room. A couple appeared from the corridor. 'What happened?'

'You shit!' A pilgrim knocked Dan, half blinded, to the floor.

'No!' Jane cried. 'Not him! she shouted, eyes wide.

'It was another man! Another man!'

'Ain't it always?' a woman grumbled in a New York accent.

'Someone got in over the balcony.'

'Call the cops,' the New Yorker said.

'No!' Jane looked alarmed.

'Why not f'chrissakes?'

'Er, yes. Yes, I'll do that.'

'Wanna witness?'

'No. No thanks, I'll er manage.

'Up to you I guess,' the woman said. 'Some women never learn,' she muttered as she left. The audience in the corridor melted away as they headed back to their bunks in the dorms.

'Who d'you think it was?' Dan asked.

'How should I know? Maybe someone's twittering about his exciting night.' Jane sighed loudly. *It's not right to attack him.* Her head was spinning. She found it hard to believe that less than twenty minutes ago she had been attacked. In this room! She felt close to a nervous breakdown. She tried to grab onto something real. Change the subject. 'Anyway,' she tried to steady her breathing. 'How come you're here, Mr Brady, er, Dan?'

'I woke up with an uneasy sort of feeling. Call it what you like, but it's saved me in the past.'

'Sixth sense?'

'Dunno,' he shrugged. 'But the feeling was there an' I thought I'd better come over to check on you. I asked Angie for the car. She said yes, an' here I am. Looks like I can still trust my intuition after all.' His smile looked tired. 'Right now I need to relax.' Dan closed the door and wedged a chair under the doorknob.

Jane felt a shudder through her whole body. *This Brady's not my type of fellow, but rough as his manners are, he seems to be a straight type who can look after himself and could be relied on.* She crossed her arms, in an effort to wrap them round herself. 'Actually, er, Dan, you can use my bed. I'll sleep on the couch.'

'No. I'll take the couch, it looks bigger than the one I was already sleeping on in Karl's room.'

'Factually, it's a better hotel.'

'This is about your protection, not how many friggin' stars a hotel has.'

'Thank you. I'll just send Angie a quick message that you'll stay here and tell her what happened. I'll close the window.'

'Don't friggin' bother. It's friggin' stuffy in here, an' he won't be back. Not tonight anyway.'

Jane stared at Dan. 'Not tonight! Are you suggesting he'll come another night.'

Dan didn't answer, but pushed the couch in front of the window. 'He'll have to climb over me, if he wants to get back in,' he grinned.

Jane relaxed and switched off the light. In minutes she was listening to his snoring.

* * *

The door was blocked with a chair as the original lock hung loose on two screws in the torn wood. On the other side of the door, thudding feet of pilgrims marched along the corridor on their way to breakfast and almost drowned the sound of the cuckoo. Jane yawned. Her wrist hurt. The bruises on her arm flooded her mind with the horrible memory of the night. *I should report this to the police. But how?* Her brow furrowed in consternation. *I'm hiding the man they're seeking!*

Her phone buzzed. She pressed green. 'Morning, Angie,' she sighed and listened. 'Yes, Dan slept alright,' she glanced at the cocooned form on the couch. 'Yes, I am alright, don't worry. Just some bruises. And I feel tired. See you at that café for breakfast in half an hour. Can you ask if they have any muesli?'

'Good mornin'.' Dan had risen silently and was on his feet looking at her. 'Are you alright?'

'We have to tell the police.'

'I know.'

'But they're looking for you! God! What a dilemma!'

'I'm innocent and us reportin' this is friggin' important.'

'I know, but let me think about what to do,' Jane said. She jumped in fright as a thunderous drumming of fists shook the door.

'Who is it?' Jane called, eyes on the turning handle.

'Policía!' a voice bellowed. The door shuddered again.

'That takes care of your dilemma,' Dan said. He faced the door and braced himself in a boxer's crouch.

SAN DOMINGO JAIL

Dan winced from the deafening metallic crash of the grey steel door that could be heard all the way to Madrid, two hundred Ks away. It sounded permanent. Permanent like the Tower of London during the Inquisition. The thin, baggy eyed jailor seemed to love his job

Even though innocent of any crime, Dan felt cut off from hope. The feeling that had clutched his vitals with icy fingers when locked in the Sinners Room came back to him. The Sinners Room was without lights, deep under the orphanage run by the nuns.

'Mornin' an unwelcoming voice came from behind a newspaper on the top bunk. The tone sounded pissed, as if Dan had robbed him of the exclusiveness of his own room or interrupted a great spiritual meditation.

'Mornin' to you, too,' Dan grumbled. He turned and stared at the closed peephole. He felt on the wrong side of a giant safe. The ceiling lamp was bright, but not effective against the light from the small glass window with stubby bars. 'Stayin' long?'

'I don't know. Is there a choice? Sorry if I'm disturbing a friggin' luxury vacation:'

'What you in for?' The newspaper lowered to reveal a long face, made longer by a high bald head. *East end London*, Dan thought.

'Nothin'.'

'That's what they all say,' the newspaper raised again.

'And you? Also nothin'?'

'Yeah, takin' nothing from pilgrims backpacks.'

Dan immediately disliked the man. He was not from Dan's world. Dan's upbringing had been hard, but honest. He sat on the bottom bunk next to scratches on the wall commemorating earlier guests' time served. None went more than five or six days. These were holding cells for drunks and petty thieves, before kicking them out or moving them on to larger cities for serious court cases. He still felt the past fear of the Sinners Room where the solitary key had hung from the belt of Sister Faith. He shuddered.

'You don' look like a bleedin' Tea Leaf,' the man outed himself with Cockney rhyming slang for thief.

'No, I'm not a Tea Leaf, that's f'certain.'

'Drunk in charge of a Jam Jar?' The man sneered round the side of his paper.

'Murder.'

'Wot!' The paper dropped. The face lost its smart-ass expression. 'Murder? Who?'

'People who ask too many friggin' questions.'

The impassive face studied Dan. The only movement were two blue irises flickering warily. A grin spread slowly from the mouth showing teeth like piano keys with many more black than white keys. 'Yer havin' me on!'

Dan nodded and smiled for the first time that day. 'Had a run in with a Comisario without a brain over a misunderstanding.'

'Comisario? The man's eyes looked upwards to one side. 'Who might that be?'

'Guy called Mendoza.'

'Mendoza! The man's jaw sagged to his chest. 'Old guy? Bout sixty? Big moustache?'

'That sounds like my favourite Comisario,' Dan pursed his lips. 'You know him?'

'I'll say. He led a big crack down on stealing along the Camino. Made it his mission. I don't think he ever solved any cases before an' saw that as his big chance to make a name for himself before he retired.'

'Now he's teamed up with a young, sharp sort of fellow. Amador.'

'Never 'eard of 'im. So what did you do to be in 'ere?'

'Nothin' much. Bit of a punch up in one of the albergues.'

'An altercation,' he pulled a face. 'They don't like that. This Mendoza seems to have a thing about protecting the Camino's good name.'

'What brought you here?'

'Mendoza.'

'Stealin'?'

The man swivelled on his bunk, jumped down and landed nimbly. Slim, fit, sinewy. He had restless rat's eyes. 'I left the trouble and strife, wife to you, and came 'ere. Saw how careless them pilgrims was wiv their bloomin' backpacks. Went into business, din' I?'

'Stealin'?'

'Well, it was the family business back in London, wannit? Y'could say I opened a branch office, din' I? Good little number. I'd lift about five or six wallets a day. Amazin' 'ow much money some of 'em are carryin'. Especially Orientals an' Asians. They got the most cash on board. Little gold mines, they are.' He read Dan's expression. 'Never lifted from a Brit!' He wagged a raised a finger. 'Nor Aussies or Kiwis, or Canadians, and never a Yank. They were always allies of ours. Selective, that's what I am,' his expression showed pride as if doing a public service.

'Did all your family steal?'

'Most of 'em,' he nodded as if talking about a long line of doctors or lawyers. 'No!' he raised a finger. 'I tell a lie.' He looked at Dan with an altar boy expression. 'My great grand uncle was one of assistants in Winston Churchill's business office.'

'Not the Prime Minister Churchill?'

'The very same, mate, the very same. Me great grand uncle organised many of his social engagements. He said he had to always buy three tickets when ol' Winnie went to the theatre. One for Churchill himself, one for his daughter and one for his hat.'

'Rubbish!'

'It's true, I tell yer! So 'elp me God!'

Dan smiled and didn't believe a word. 'Where did

Mendoza come into the picture?'

'Bleedin' churches, wasn't it? I started doin' churches with a Spanish guy. Statues, ornaments, gold. Big stuff. Heavy stuff. The Spanish guy fenced the stuff in Barcelona an' Madrid. Then bleedin' Mendoza came on the scene. We were caught with a van full of stuff. Mendoza led the investigation. I skipped bail and got picked up again,' he said. Dejection creased his features. 'Case comes up in a few days.'

Dan listened. Felt no sympathy. Made no comment. 'And Mendoza? What's he like?'

The Cockney pulled a face. 'I heard he's not so clean. But nobody can put a finger on him. He might even be Ok,' the Cockney shrugged. 'I heard he was about to retire. I'm surprised he's botherin' with your case over a little punch up.' His gaze fixed Dan, waiting for more details.

'Strange world,' Dan said. 'I think I'll have a kip.'

The Cockney took the hint and clambered back on this own bunk.

Dan lay still. The rustle of the Cockney's newspaper was relaxing and took him back to the days when he lived in the barracks long ago. He dozed off, in a shallow half dream about Sister Faith with the key to the Sinners Room refusing to give Churchill his hat.

* * *

King Felipe VI of Spain smiled nicely at Jane. Normally she would have smiled back. *That beard suits him*, Jane thought facing the picture of him on the wall above Detective Amador. She thought Amador looked a little similar, but without the beard. She stood opposite Amador in front of his desk. It resembled a miniature paper city of apartment blocks made of stacked files.

'Thanks for coming, Ms Downer,' he offered his hand across the papers.

'I had no choice.' She gave her hand but kept back her smile.

'Please take a seat.'

Jane was lightly dressed and shivered from sudden cold of the air conditioning. She saw a sheet music book open on the chair. 'You're a musician I see,' she said, just to say something. She placed the book on a free edge of the desk.

'Piano. A hobby.' He shrugged. 'Bit of boogie after dinner,' he smiled. 'And violin. Father's wish, not mine. He played in an amateur orchestra. Very good. Great man.' He tugged his tartan bow tie. 'Not that I play well. Time to practice is always short,' he flashed an expression between sadness and helplessness. 'I have to take care of my mother. That takes a lot of my time when I'm off duty.'

'Is she ill?'

Amador nodded gravely. His cheeks reddened.

'That responsibility comes to most of us in the long run.'

'Is your mother well, Ms Downer?'

'She died. Christmas day.' She and her father decorated the tree that day. Loaded it with everything they could find. New and old things, in a glittering memorial, to try and ease their grief.

'I'm sorry. One should always take care of one's mother.'

'I did.' The pain of her mother hovered before her. She pushed the thoughts away and released a loud impatient breath. 'Mr Amador, can you tell me why I have been brought to your office at this late hour?'

'I want to talk without other ears around.'

'Walls can have ears?' Jane remarked.

'Not these walls, Ms Downer. The police budget doesn't stretch that far.' His eyes flickered over her red hair.

Jane smiled and relaxed a little. She was outwardly cool, but her stomach felt things with a million legs crawling inside. 'What, then, do you want to talk about? The weather?' she cocked an eyebrow. A show of bravado she didn't feel. She felt the pressure of wanting to pee, and wriggled slightly, wanting to bring the conversation to an end.

'Your accomplices.'

'What accomplices? I haven't any accomplices, Detective!'

'Your helpers, Ms Downer. I was born in the morning, but not this morning, Ms Downer.'

'Tut!' Jane's eyes rolled followed by what she hoped was a Not-a-care in-the-world expression. 'You make me sound as if I'm part of the Gunpowder Plot.' She had a hard job keeping the lies out of her eyes.

'Gunpowder Plot?'

'A catholic plot to blow up the Houses of Parliament in 1605.'

'Before my time, Ms Downer.'

'Mine, *too*!' Her cheeks heated. 'You are catholic, are you not?'

Amador cleared his throat. 'Ms Downer, it's not about me. It's about Mr Brady's escape.' He paused.

'Escape,' the word hung as a challenge in the air between them. Jane blinked. 'There is no way Mr Brady could disappear after he ran out the police building in San Domingo. Somebody drove him, hid him, disguised him, and fed him, hmm?' It was Amador's turn to cock an eyebrow.

'That was me!'

'Ms Downer,' Amador gave a slow shake of his head. 'You were with us when Brady escaped. And I am sure you didn't have a car concealed in your backpack,' he smiled.

'Taxi?'

Amador sighed and looked pityingly at her. Jane's felt her cheeks flush. 'Please, be serious, Ms Downer. Believe me when I say you are a potential target. You are female with red hair, like the other victims. And you discovering the body could have placed you in the sights of the man who performed the act. I believe that is why you were attacked in your room. What you told us makes me think it was the same man.'

Jane swallowed. Her heart was a Rock band bass drum. No words came. Her mouth dried. She knew she sounded trite, even stupid, and she was beginning to feel it. She tried to swallow. The killer might want her! Suck a stone, her father had always said. That brings saliva. There were no stones on Detective Amador's desk. She felt his pupils fixed on her. Her mouth opened. No words came out. Her gut wobbled, as if at sea. She was frightened.

'Ms Downer, I believe you are in danger. That means your helpers, too,' his level stare unnerved her. 'It's a matter of time until your attacker finds who they are. I would hate anything to happen to them!' He stared with appealing eyes. 'I can help. I can protect them.'

'Do they need protecting?'

'They do. I am sure. Besides the killer, Mendoza is furious. He has been made to look a fool by Brady's escape. His wrath against Mr Brady is dangerous.'

Jane swallowed hard. She thought of Angelique, wild, but good hearted. Karl, easy going. Clever. Funny. Both friends sucked into this because of her! Her feelings were caught in a whirlwind. *Would the killer be interested in her and her friends?'*

'Ms Downer?' Amador's voice pulled her back on track. She focused on his arched eyebrows. She looked at the smiling King. He remained silent, impervious to her slightly pleading eyes. *Never mind the King. He can't help.*

'Alright,' Jane found her voice. 'I'll get them.' She really wanted to pee.

'Thank you, Ms Downer. You might just save their lives,' his eyes were double barrels aimed at her head. 'Your sister was a beautiful girl.'

'How do you know?' Jane saw his brown pupils flicker left and right.

'Twins!' he laughed. 'I assume she looks like you. Her twin. You must have loved her a lot.'

'As a matter of fact, I didn't.'

YUDEGO CROSS

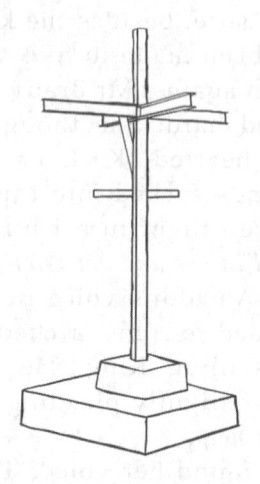

Boredom dumbed the features of two police officers. One was like a sculpture with fine aristocratic features and chin. The taller was fleshy with a face like soft bread dough. They slouched next to a white, rust mottled steel cross. The Cruz de la Encina. Unique with its four arms, each pointing to the points of the compass east of Yudego, a dying farming village with few young people remaining. The village hung on for its life a few kilometres north of the Camino.

The officers' luminous yellow vests blazed against the desolate brownish hill. Red and white plastic tape fluttered on short metal stakes; they had done their job and staked out the scene. Now one sucked cigarettes to the butt to catch up on his chain smoking. The other counted the butts and plucked at a single nostril hair with one eye on his phone messages. A stray sheep and two mountain bikers with an ear racking terrier were the only public. Even the stray sheep looked bored.

In black and yellow sausage skin tight biker bibs and shorts, the men sat on the ground knee hugging, backs to the breeze. Waiting. At their feet lay two helmets which resembled psychedelic ostrich eggs. One biker smoked. One chewed gum. Neither spoke.

The smaller officer looked at his phone. He sighed like a steam engine.

'What's up?' the other trod on the latest ciggie butt on the ground.

'My wife wants me to buy a frozen chicken from the supermarket. Where the shit do I find a supermarket up here?' he waved his arm across the ploughed fields.

'Listen,' the other said. A rapid bass drum beat drew their eyes skyward. They rubbernecked. Sunlight glinted on the Perspex, giving away the copter's position.

'I hope we can get going after they land. I've done enough shit overtime this month.' Both Guardia men clapped their hands on their green bill caps to cheat the downdraft. The hyperactive terrier bobbed about, yelping at the deafening chopper blades. The motor turbine cut with the tone of a weary banshee dying away and only the zippy dog was audible, showing the characteristics of a kangaroo. The long black rotors subsided in swishing waves. The sagging yellow tips became visible.

Detective Amador jumped to the ground, followed by Mendoza. Three men and a woman in light blue overalls tumbled out after them. They hunched into a duck-walk below the rotors. The two Guardia officers straightened their posture. A boot ground out a half-smoked fag.

'Comisario Mendoza,' he thrust his ID forward like garlic against vampires. Heels clicked, hands touched cap brims. The bikers stood up, looking unsure as to whether they, too, should salute.

'Where's the body?' Mendoza demanded.

'Not a body, Comisario,' the champion smoker flashed teeth that resembled a row of walnut pegs.

'Bones,' the shorter policeman said. They tramped towards the mound and stood round a shallow hole. Rich red earth scattered outward in a fan shape from the edge. A long thick bone lay among a few crushed water bottles and chocolate wrappers quivering in the breeze.

'It's not human, is it?' Mendoza's tone prompted a negative answer.

'We think it is, Comisario,' the taller Guardia sounded apologetic. 'It's not the bone of a small animal such as a fox nor a large animal such as a cow or horse...'

The corners of Mendoza's mouth slouched with his mood. He watched the forensic team examine the bone, then took out his small note book. 'Do you have a pencil?' Amador shook his head and flashed his phone. 'Puta Madre!' Mendoza walked away a few paces.

'It's a human femur by the length and thickness,' a woman with chins on her double chin said, 'This is a rib,' another of the forensic team held up a piece of curved bone in his rubber gloved hand. 'Human.'

'A femur is about a quarter of the height of an adult human,' her fleshy hands opened a centimetre measure and checked the length of the femur. 'She was a female between one meter sixty and one-sixty-five centimetres.'

'A female you say?' Amador asked.

'I just uncovered the pelvic bone.'

'Who found the bones?' Mendoza interrupted.

'The cyclists, Comisario,' a Guardia pointed with his chin.

Mendoza glared at the bikers as if they were guilty.

'Pilgrims, or lost on the Tour de France?'

'Germans,' the taller Guardia man shrugged as if that explained everything.

'I'll wait for your report,' Mendoza told the woman who headed the team.

'Sí, Comisario,' she beckoned to the others who started to mark out an area around the hole that the terrier had created. A photographer lay down a barrage of photos.

'He's taking more photos than at the Mercedes-Benz Fashion Week in Madrid.' Mendoza said, looking at the photographer. His gaze shifted to the cyclists. 'Let's see what they know.' Mendoza idly fingered his moustache as they approached them. The two sportive guys looked at each other, shifting from foot to foot.

'Do you speak English?' Amador asked. The young men nodded. The terrier sprang on its hind legs, and shagged Mendoza's leg.

'Sasha! Hier!' The shorter man tugged the lead.

'How did you find the bone?' Amador began.

'Sasha found it,' the tanned man nodded at the terrier, eying Mendoza's leg romantically. 'We had a rest and let the dog run around a little. Then we saw him digging,'

'Did he dig up the big bone?'

'Yes.' The taller man rubbed his nose. 'From biology lessons I think it's a human leg bone. So we called the police.'

'Very well,' Mendoza tugged his moustache. 'Give your identification documents and phone numbers to Detective Amador.'

'Are we in trouble?' the taller asked.

'You will be if you talk to anyone about this,' Mendoza's voice had a menacing edge.

'It's just that it's a police matter,' Amador cautioned.

'Was she murdered?' the smaller asked, anxiety in his eyes.

'How do you know it's female?' Mendoza quipped. 'Are you a detective?' his lip curled.

'We overheard the woman. We speak Spanish.'

'If you speak to anyone about this in English, Spanish or German, you'll be in big trouble.' Mendoza wagged a finger. The two young men glowered. The panting terrier attempted another quickie on Mendoza's leg. 'Give me your cell phones.' His foot shoved away the sexy Sasha.

The tanned biker backed away a pace. 'They are our property.'

'We will check them here, or in the police station.' He glared at the panting dog.

The pale man handed his phone over. 'Yours, too!' The tanned cyclist sullenly handed over his phone to Amador. 'Erase any photos of the bone or this area.'

'Is that legal, Comisario?' Amador whispered.

'Do it.'

Amador coughed and turned away.

'I don't like that cough, Detective.'

Amador pulled a handkerchief from his pocket and coughed into it. 'I'm alright, Comisario. Summer flu.' He cleared his throat and turned back to the cyclists.

'Puta Madre!' Mendoza cursed again and snatched a young Guardia's bill cap and used it to brush the yellow drops off his trouser leg.

'Comisario,' the woman in the forensic team called. 'We've freed most of the skeleton.'

The Detective handed the phones back to the bikers. 'Give your names and home address to the police officers, then you can go.' He followed Mendoza.

The woman pointed at the enlarged hole. Gaping sockets in a grimy brown skull stared at them. Dirt matted hair under it resembled a nest. 'She's been here well over a year.'

'What colour is her hair?'

'Red, same as the other victims.' Amador said as he approached.

'How do you know?' Mendoza said. 'You haven't looked yet.'

'Just a feeling,' Amador said.

'You can check if Brady was here in Spain a year ago.'

Amador watched the two Germans riding away, their heads riveted straight ahead, as if fearing they might be stopped if they looked back. 'It is probably pointless. The body was buried long ago...'

'I shall decide what is pointless or not pointless, Detective.'

* * *

'Mommy!' The bare room had a slight echo. 'They removed an Eva!'

'What you sayin' Sugar? They emptied her grave?'

'Yes, Mommy. They took her bones away from her resting place at a way cross! Where I buried her to save her!'

'You must replace her! Replace her or lose your place in heaven.'

'Nooo! That's not fair! I saved her!' he yammered.

'Get another Eva, Sugar. And get the woman who caused this. It's your only chance!'

'I know, Mommy! I knoooow!' The voice was desperate.

'Time is running out! Do the Lord's work, for your own sake, Sugar.'

'Both our sakes, Mommy.'

'Sugar? Do you love your Mommy?'

'Above everything, Mommy! You know that!' He snivelled. The figure's shoulders shook.

'I spent my life educating you myself to believe without question,'

'I do, Mommy! Always! The Lord is our saviour!'

The voice sighed. 'Then bring Mommy some more of those pills.'

SAN DOMINGO POLICE STATION

San Domingo's large, new police building stands bold and modern, in contrast to the shabby old abandoned station around the corner in Haro Avenue. The difference is day and night. Palace and slum.

Jane and Detective Amador waited in a bright well-lit room with blank white walls and white and black chess board floor designed by architects who used shoe boxes for inspiration. Conversation had dried up after a few polite pleasantries. Jane listened to the Detective's heavy breathing, interrupted by periodic coughs. A policeman with a boxer's face and trouser creases capable of peeling potatoes knocked and entered, followed by Angelique and Karl. They looked as happy as someone who had been arrested.

'Hi, Angie, Karl,' Jane smiled. Karl nodded, his poker face betrayed nothing as he rubbed his binary tattoo. Angie nodded warily, looking round the room, but not because of it's magnificent decor. She looked at Amador. 'Nice tie,'

Amador smiled. 'Thank you.' He touched the light blue bow tie.

'Where's Dan?' Karl asked.

'The guard is fetching him,' Amador tugged the ends of his tie. 'I'm Detective Alonso Amador,' he offered his hand. 'I asked Ms Downer to invite you here.'

'Why?' Karl's face was that of a poker player. 'We have not done anything wrong. I have to tell you that we are free to walk out of here at any time and demand an attorney before we answer any...'

'Slow down, slow down, please.' Amador's hands moved in a pressing calming motion. 'First it depends how one defines wrong,' Amador said. 'Mr Brady ran out of an interview. Someone aided and abetted him to escape.'

'Puh! He's innocent!' Angelique stared at Jane as checking that she was alright.

'It was more a brawl than an interview,' Jane said haughtily. She was determined not to feel subdued or intimidated just because she was in a police building.

Amador pulled a file out of his leather bag. 'I have his release papers here, so let's stay calm. I am here to help, not criticise anyone.'

The door opened. 'Hi fans,' Dan's eyes crinkled in triumph, despite an escort glued so close to his heels they could have almost shared the same pants.

'Dan!' Angie bounced to her feet like a Cheerleader and clapped her arms round him.

'Wow!' he grinned. 'Are you thinkin' of marryin' me?' His chest expanded as he got his breath back after she released him from her Boa Constrictor hug.

Jane stepped nearer. 'Are you alright, Dan?'

Amador handed the papers to the guard, who handed over Dan's backpack and left. Dan ripped it open and foraged through his stuff. 'Gotcha, me little darlins,' he held up the SSDs.

'Everything there? Also your passport?' Jane asked.

'Yes, indeed. Northing's missing.' A smile slashed his face.

'So you can go home. Keep your job, see your kids.'

'Not so fast, Jane. There's a job to be done an' I can spare a little time.'

'Not if you get caught by all the people who don't, in fact, love you.'

'Mensch! At least you are not in prison uniform. You look very Spanish,' Karl tried to be amusing. 'Good disguise.' He gave a thumbs-up.

'My shopping choices,' Angelique waggled her head smugly.

'And much appreciated,' Dan bowed.

'Can we?' Amador took his place at the end of a long table that matched the wall and had three bottles of water surrounded by a ring of glasses.

'Ok, ok,' Dan suddenly looking tired. He sank onto

a chair and reached for a glass. 'I'm thirsty and friggin' starvin'.'

'Now you can eat some good food after eating prison slop,' Angie said.

'Oh, it wasn't all that bad. A hundred friggin' flies can't all be wrong.'

Detective Amador coughed and cleared his throat. 'I have invited you...'

'Invited? Huh!' Jane rolled her eyes. Karl poured himself some water in silence. His face was blank as a dead PC screen.

'I want to speak to you while you are all together.' He looked at the guard and waved him away. Then he tugged the ends of his bow tie again.

'What about Mendoza?' Jane interrupted.

'He's under pressure from someone. Big pressure.' Amador said. 'Listen. One of the reasons for bringing you here is to say that I'm prepared to help you.'

Dan looked surprised. 'Are you tellin' us y'goin' to work *against* Mendoza?'

'No. And I can't tell you all my reasons, but,' he regarded Jane, 'one of them is justice.' Silent seconds ticked by. 'I'll do my best to keep Comisario Mendoza off Mr Brady's back. He's convinced that Mr Brady is violent and guilty in some way of the murders, although he can't prove it. If we can't prove the contrary, we could have a dangerous situation. Especially with this Ramos and his security team.'

'We already have a dangerous situation,' Karl's breath passed across his fingertips, as if about to crack a safe.

'I know. I want to prepare for the worst and

update you all on the situation.' He took another buff file from his bag and flipped it open on the table and pulled out a page of scribbled notes and read. 'Both victims were female and red haired.'

'Oh, my God,' Jane clutched her hair. Her nervousness flooded back through her body.

'Both had identical injuries.' He saw that Jane turned white. 'I'm sorry Ms Downer.' Jane shook her head and waved for him to continue. 'After the attack on Ms Downer, we believe he is an American. She identified his accent.' Jane sat and took a deep breath. She felt vulnerable. Her back prickled in cold sweat. The thoughts of continuing her walk on the Camino provoked a slumbering feeling of panic. Her mouth was dry and her forehead wet. She drank some water. *Maybe it is time to quit*, she thought. The expression of Angie's face told Jane that she felt the same. Her gaze switched from Karl's blank look, to Dan's grim jaw and three-day beard. *No shock in his features,* she thought. *Just anger. He looks determined, despite the problems he's experiencing.* She admired that and felt a little safer.

'He is a mission killer with a certain ritual attached,' Amador said.

'Like a serial killer of prostitutes, blacks, or homosexuals?' Dan grunted.

'Exactly,' Amador nodded. 'The girl you found would've been moved by the killer. You interrupted him and thwarted his ritual!' Amador frowned.

'Are you saying the killer wants to get back at us?' Jane's voice cracked, her throat still dry despite emptying a second glass of water. She saw Amador nod and felt cold shivers up her spine.

'You messed up his plans.' Amador said. 'You were

attacked because he was angry. That would be understandable.'

'Understandable?' Angelique's jaw dropped. 'How can you say that it's under-stand-able?'

'No!' Amador shook his head. 'I meant not understandable to *us*, of course.'

'What do we do now?' Jane asked them. 'Dan can't hide and we can't stand still, and I want to know what happened to my sister. It took me a year to pluck up courage to follow Debbie's footsteps. I have all the postcards she sent me and photos in my mobile. They are from the places I'm visiting. Factually, giving up is not an option. Not for me.'

'Brave words,' Amador pursed his lips with an impressed expression on his face.

'I'll accompany you.'

'Why you?' Jane stared at Dan as if he had suggested visiting a swingers' club together.

'I know the score, and you won't find any escort services along the Camino.'

'I agree, Ms Downer. As long as I know where you are, I can protect you as well. You could continue along the Camino. In fact, it would be logical. It could put the killer off his guard.'

'Or make him attack one of us,' Karl spoke to his empty glass in his hand.

'Factually, what's our next move?'

'We need a friggin' profile. After the attack on Jane, we know he is American from his accent.'

'But you have an American accent,' Karl's blue eyes lasered Amador.

Amador grinned. 'Guilty,' he spread his hands. 'My mother is American. She met my father on the Camino. It took her so long to learn Spanish that I grew up bilingual. I was also an exchange student in the USA. I hope you won't hold that against me,' he smiled.

'We'll forgive you,' Angelique smiled back and fiddled with the gold arrow piercing in her ear.

'I have a good friend at the FBI in Washington. With the new laws about tracking terrorists, they may well have data that could help us.'

'Hopefully before another girl is murdered.' Karl said.

'Or one of us,' Jane rubbed her upper arms as if the air conditioning had made a nose dive.

'Why are you doing all this?' Angelique asked.

'When I heard Jane talking about her sister and the poor police work, I felt angry. My father was a great policeman. That's why I am a cop. I want justice. The same as you, Mr Brady,' he smiled. 'Frankly, you need me nearby.'

'Mister! Mister! Always friggin' mister! Just call me Dan.'

'Very well, Dan. I'm Alonso.' They shook hands. The others reached across the table with outstretched hands.

'Alonso, aren't you risking your job by helping us?' Jane's voice was small.

'If I keep my job, Jane, you may lose your lives.'

BELORADO

'Quite a wedding present,' Jane said. The dark brooding ruins of the citadel on the cliffs above Belorado held her attention. They looked up from the Plaza Mayor in the centre of Belorado town.

'Don't like lookin' at friggin' weddin' presents,' Dan growled. 'Brings back unhappy memories.'

'Factually, you're not alone in that club.'

'It looks Norman.'

'It was Celtic and later a Roman settlement. It once boomed with a population of Christians, Muslims and Jews who all lived here in peace.'

'And it was a present for whom?' Dan threw a cursory glance at the ruins glowing orange in the rays of the late afternoon sun.

'El Cid. The castle was a royal wedding present.'

'All I got was a mortgage on a semi in Dorset,'

Dan's phone pinged. He gazed at his screen. 'Bloody-Prosser Jones wants to know what I've written for his horsey rag,' he muttered.

'Photograph some horses.'

'He wouldn't recognise a horse if he fell off one. He plays with trains all day.'

'Then why has he a horse magazine?'

'I imagine he couldna' get a job anywhere else. His mother is the owner. She should start a magazine about dragons. She'd be in all the friggin' pictures herself.'

Jane's shoulders shook slightly in a squeaky chuckle. 'And your house is in Dorset? There are worse places to live than Dorset.'

'I know. But my friggin' ex is sittin' in it.' Dan stared up at the citadel ruins again but failed to show more interest. 'I'm starvin'.'

'And I feel as elegant as a zombie,' Jane plucked her sticky shirt from her body where sweat stains blazed from under her arms, chilling her as a breeze sprung up. She tugged at her shorts, now crumpled into hot pants length. 'I can feel every single one of those twenty thousand yards under my boots. That's about forty thousand paces!' She tilted her water bottle to her mouth like a herald's trumpet. It gurgled till empty. She kept sucking.

'It was over thirty degrees and cloudless,' Dan said. 'We left it too late startin' out.'

'Your big breakfast made us late,' she said.

'What! You insistin' on muesli made us late. I'm surprised they went to the trouble after that French custodian locked us out as curfew breakers.'

'Until you almost knocked the door down.' She grinned.

'I was surprised Mr Stalag Albergue man went to buy muesli for you after that.'

'I like to eat healthily.'

'What I need now is a beer and food. Junk or gourmet, I'm flexible.' Dan checked his map. 'Here,' he tapped the map. 'Cuatro Cantones Albergue. That's where Alonso booked us in.'

'He's been very good to us,' Jane said. She smiled at a Dutch woman who had slept in the bunk above a week before. The woman waved back and was accosted by Mr Lobster, the Argentinian Camino flirt. His face still resembled a tomato.

'Lonsy's a good man. The friggin' police could use more like him, instead of stupid old farts like Mendoza harassin' me. Look!' A giant painted pilgrim figure with yellow shirt and black hat stood in the narrow street and identified the albergue. The foyer was wall to wall with pilgrims. They went and sat near the pool in the garden. A Spanish mother called endless advice to her son in the shallow end. He wasn't listening.

Jane's phone buzzed. She read the screen. 'Angie sent an sms. Karl wants to meet us here later.'

'Has somethin' turned up?'

'She didn't say. We'll meet opposite the Bar Kais in the square in the evening.'

'He can't keep away from us, can he?' Dan joked.

'He isn't the only one,'

'Yeah? Who else?'

'Our wild Angelique,' Jane pressed her lips together as if in disapproval.

'Aw, she's alright,' Dan smiled.

'A typical male remark. A sweet smile from a pretty face and they make fools of themselves.'

'Would I make a fool of myself?'

'She's a complete contrast to her older brother, the priest.'

'You and Angie are also very, very different. '

'Opposites attract. We met at university when I met Karl. Angie was a hobby stock car driver.'

'She was what?' Dan's eyes stared like headlamps. 'I wonder why that doesn't surprise me,' he grinned. 'And Karl?'

'He took time off from his programming business in Cologne. He lives online. He helped fiance this whole thing.'

'Now that does surprise me. Good f' him.' He looked at his watch. 'We'd better get checked in,' Dan picked up Jane's rucksack, 'God! Your makeup weighs a ton!'

'Don't be so sexist!'

A dark SUV gleamed in the sunlight in the plaza.

* * *

After a generous pilgrim dinner that could put some top London restaurants to shame, Dan and Jane sat on the stone steps of the concrete bandstand facing the north side from where they had come. They were shielded by the double row of cropped grey planes that ringed the centre island in Plaza Mayor.

'Mr Tennis shoes.' Dan watched him cross the plaza and walk passing the bandstand toward the bar.

Jane felt her heart beating faster.

'Again? I've seen him more often than holy crosses along the Camino. I don't like him showing up everywhere I go. This can't be a coincidence anymore.'

'One bumps into people again and again. Look. There's a German guy I interviewed back in Puente de Reina.' Their eyes followed the hulking figure stride across the plaza and disappear into a bar.

'If I had to cook for him, I'd need a truck for my shopping. But maybe you're right. I've bumped into the same nun about three times so far.'

'Huh! Don't mention nuns. I was brought up in a friggin' orphanage by them.'

'I didn't know you were an orphan.'

'A single mother and a God knows who, father. When my sister was born, she left the house and never came back. Social services put us in a home run by nuns,' he cuffed an eye. Jane looked away.

'I'm sorry,' she whispered.

'It's ok. I should concentrate on my future.'

They waited in silence. Spanish music flowed from the Bar Kais. The sun dipped below the roofs and shadows slashed across the plaza, but there was enough daylight to see. The air was as warm as a blanket around their shoulders. A couple of Derbi mopeds passed farting, the helmet-less riders' hair ruffled like flames in the slipstream.

A car spluttering and backfiring entered the plaza.

'Ah! They're comin',' Dan mimed an exaggerated whisper from the corner of his mouth.

'Ok, Mr James Bond. I hope that M isn't M for Mendoza.' she said. 'Angie!' she called. Angie and Karl stopped, eyeballed the trees and sauntered over to the island.

'Hallo, people,' Karl and Angelique stepped under the trees. Karl's T-shirt boasted that he had been to a well-known Café in Stockholm and survived the food.

'Hola,' Angelique wrinkled her impish nose at Dan. She almost tripped on the curb.

'Careful, Angie old girl!' Jane caught her arm. Angie pulled it away.

'Jane told me you have somethin' to tell us,' Dan said.

'Ach, ya. I have spent my time researching.' He sat on the steps up to the bandstand and rubbed his leg below the knee.

'Friggin' lock picking,' Dan said.

Karl ignored Dan and said, 'I have been researching...'

'Hacking,' Angelique slapped the back of his head.

'Have you found out more about why serial killers murder?'

'Mensch, no! I was too busy having some romance on Facebook,' he grimaced.

'Karl! Dan!' Angie glared at them. 'Grow up! You are acting like two big school boys.'

Dan turned his back and stared across the plaza across folded arms. Karl held his iPhone inches from his face and tipped as if he were alone in the world.

'Men!' Jane muttered.

Forget it, Janey girl. They're all the same. Take Angie's example; love 'em and leave 'em.

Angie knocked on Karl's tattoo. 'Hello! Anyone in? We're waiting for your message from outer space.'

Karl jerked his head away. 'Stop that!' he muttered. 'The reason for my meeting is that I found something about Ramos, the man you described. If you're interested, that's what I did.'

Angie placed herself hands on hips before Karl. 'Tell them what you found!'

'Ach, well, I had finishing dealing with my customers on line and had some spare time. I decided to trace a few families with the name Ramos. I found a man called Ramos in Facebook. Is this him?' Karl twisted the tablet round. A man looked out at Dan. Dan glanced and shook his head. 'Alright, wait.' Karl did another search. 'Him?' Dan shook his head. After three more tries a face came up and triggered a gasp from Jane. Mr Tough Guy sneered out of the screen at them.

'Look.' Jane tapped a photo of a younger Ramos in combat uniform. Karl searched friends and produced a group photo entailed "Comrades FFL"

'The friggin' French Foreign Legion.'

'Gut.' Karl searched more and read what he found. 'French Foreign Legion in Mali. Some more friends who are comrades.'

'Ramos in the FFL... That explains a lot. Men who join the Foreign Legion are willing to do anything for money. They have no limits nor ethics. But it still doesn't explain why Ramos went mad when he read the report. You might find more under FFL. Can you lock pick the friggin' FFL?'

'Ach, ya. Just a matter of time. I can call Alonso and tell him what we know.'

'Why bother? We can sort it out for ourselves.'

'Ach, don't think you can do everything, Mr dynamic Dan.'

'Dynamic Dan? What's that fuckin' mean?' Dan's faced flushed up.

'Dan, stop!' Jane pressed her hand against his hard chest. It felt... She cut the thought before it began.

Careful Janey girl! You're married to trouble already. Be a nun in your next life.

Karl drew himself up. 'I know you see yourself as the man of action who sees me as a computer nerd who polishes a chair with my ass,' he scrubbed his tattoo with his fingernails.

'Karl! Stop! Men and boys! I can't tell the difference at times.'

'Hey!' Dan grimaced showing his teeth and stabbed a finger at Karl's face. 'It's not friggin' true! Got it?'

'Dan!' Jane grasped his arm.

Dan pulled away. 'Sorry, but I don't like bein' told what I think. I had enough of that in the fuckin' orphanage by fuckin' nuns!' He swung away and folded his arms again.

'Ach, forget it. It doesn't matter. I am used to people like you thinking that way.'

'What the fuck d'you mean by people like *me*? Dan stepped towards Karl, fists balled. Angie blocked his way, her back pressing Karl's iPhone to his chest. 'Karl, I don't fuckin' think that way or any fuckin' way!' Karl blinked at the thud of Dan's fist. They all stared at the blood mark and chipped bark on the tree next to his head. 'We're different! So what! There's nothin' fuckin' wrong with that!' He clenched and unclenched his fist.

'That's how I see it,' Jane tugged Dan's arm and spun him round. 'Dan's a bit fed up of hiding I reckon,' Jane's weak smile angered Angie.

'Idiot!' Angie whispered staring at the tree where Dan's fist hand impacted. 'Don't do that again, Dan. Listen all of you! If we break up now, the killer can pick each of us off alone. One by one.'

'Ya gut. I don't want to fight you because I am a Mensch who is against violence. But I'm not the nerd you think I am. See these hands?' Dan looked at the big splayed rough hands. 'My father was a plumber. He thought I was wasting my time on computers, so he started me as an apprentice in his little firm and showed no mercy. I had to do as much as three men, to show there was no favouritism. I cut, welded, dug, carried heavy objects, and got these hands.' He held them up. Dan could see the callouses and a finger that had not set straight.

'It's ok, Karl.' Dan held his hand up in a Red Indian peace sign. 'Believe me, I never made any judgments about you.'

'Ach, it's good, Dan.' He offered his hand. Dan felt the roughness of the programmer's fingers. Jane saw blood from Dan's bleeding knuckles leave a stain on Karl's hand. 'You could hide in a brothel,' Karl grinned to change the subject. 'Nobody would think of looking there.'

'Do they have them here?' Angelique raised an eye brow.

'There *are* men in the town,' Jane stared at Dan and Karl.

'Nothing wrong with brothels,' Karl said. 'A neighbour told my mother she saw my father going to the local brothel. My mother said; "So what? He goes to the football stadium, and he can't play football either!" Angelique slapped the back of his head again as Karl and Dan snorted, shoulders shaking. The tension lowered a few degrees.

They checked out the plaza. Cars cruised in and out of the square and pilgrims lounged at the two bars.

'How about a coffee at Kais bar?' Angelique pointed at the bar with its baize marquise.

'We need an early start tomorrow,' Dan shook his head. And the albergue will close in some minutes. You two go to the café. We're tired.'

Angelique shrugged. 'Coming, Karl?' He nodded and followed her towards Kais bar.

It was almost ten. The moon climbed among the stars, throwing silver beams through gaps in the leaves above, projecting a pattern on the ground. The church clock struck as a car brummed passed. A baritone dog barked - a soprano yapped in reply. A frantic guitar galloped through a clever sequence of chords in Café Kais. Jane watched another Derbi moped whine passed spurting fumes, which mingled with some Spanish mama's garlic oil. A loud laugh echoed at a joke going the rounds - maybe from Karl. A car passed pumping the beat of the street. Voices from Kais Bar started singing Happy Birthday.

'The Milky Way,' Jane stared up at the studded sky. 'The Camino follows the Milky Way. It was believed that the Milky Way was formed from the dust raised by pilgrim's shoes. Did you know that, Dan?'

'I didn't,' Dan grunted. They left the shelter of the trees. An engine simulated an enraged lion. Tyres shrieked, painting rubber on the cobbles.

'Dan!' Jane tugged him. They fell. The slipstream plucked their clothes. A dark blur thundered away. Stressed tyres screeched in agony from the ally that swallowed the car.

'Fuckin' idiot!' Dan yelled.

Jane's back hurt. The cobbles pressed against her. She saw Dan roll over and kneel next to her. 'Ouch!'

she arched her back and let herself be pulled up on her feet. 'Did he try to...?'

'Yes he fuckin' did!'

Jane steadied herself.

'Nothing broken? Bruised?' His face showed anxiety.

'Just my pride,' Jane wheezed.

The tyres screeched like stuck pigs. Revving and gear crunching echoed and grew in the alleyways. 'It's after us!' Dan pulled her hand and they sprinted as hard as they could down an alley.

'Ouch!' Jane hobbled. 'My foot!' Headlights swept the plaza.

'Fuck it! Come!' he dragged her along. She hobbled, slowing them down.

Caterwauling tyres echoed off the narrow walls of the alley and stopped. They were lit up in the blinding headlight beams. Jane limped, heart bursting. Nausea made her dizzy. They ran. Jane cried out with every step. The lights followed.

'Go!' Dan yelled. 'Run for the albergue!' She felt his hand push between her shoulder blades. She ran, turned the corner at the T junction and looked back. Dan stood by a row of different coloured wheelie bins lined against the alley wall for collection. He dragged one after the other into the middle. The car roared into the alley and hit the first with a booming crash, which bashed into the next then the next. Jane ran. Behind she heard a deafening bam bam bam bam, like a giant bass drum as the car shunted the bins together. A jumble of bins erupted from the alley. Dan sprang aside as they piled up, showering him with rubbish. The car stopped, wedged firmly against the pile of crushed wheelie bins.

She reached the albergue door and looked back. 'The key!' she panted. 'The key!' She fumbled in her pockets.

'The bastard's stuck!' Dan reached her panting with his hand pressed against his right side. She recalled the bullet scar. The car gears grated like a chainsaw and backed up the way it had come. Lights came on in upstairs windows. A car came from the other direction and screeched against the crushed bins. Windows on the upper walls flickered like a pinball machine. Voices above bellowed and hollered with the force of an angry football crowd.

Jane opened the door. They fell inside. A blonde angel stood before them, and eyebrow raised in curiosity.

'Sorry we are late, but we had an accident!' Jane panted.

'Then do come in!' a cultivated voice invited in perfect English. The woman smiled and slammed the door. 'I am Hana, by the way. Is there something strange going on?'

'Just a problem with the rubbish collection back there,' Dan grinned.

'Are you in a dangerous situation?' her expression was suspicious.

Jane, too breathless to answer, nodded.

'I'm a journalist an' think I've poked a friggin' hornets' nest.'

'Have you told the police?'

'Too busy running!' Jane panted.

''Not necessary,' Dan said, getting his breath back.

'Could we get some sleep and be on our way early?'

'No,' Hana said.

'No?' They chorused.
'No.'

BURGOS

'Burgos, my sleeping beauties,' Hana's voice dragged them out of their sleep.

Dan's eyes popped open. 'Where are we?' he yawned.

'I'm glad you said 'no' to us staying the night in Belorado.' Jane blinked at the lights. 'It was better to move on quickly after what you told me!'

'You're booked in here in my name. No passports needed.'

'Thanks, Hana!' Jane squeezed her arm.

'Single room. That's all they had available,' Hana said. 'Where are you going next?' We have to go to a place called the Tachu Café.'

'I know it,' she smiled. 'It's run by a man who is a missionary in Africa. I'll tell Alonso where you are. Good luck!' She waved and drove into the warm night.

'What a woman,' Dan watched the receding tail lights swallowed by the night.

'Wake up dreamer, it's me you're sharing with not her.'

'Better than nothin', I suppose.'

'It's worse than nothing, Iron man. You're on the floor.' She strode into the hotel as if she owned it.

'Jane!' he called. She turned. 'The man who tried to run us down...'

'What about him?'

'I don't think he was the killer.'

* * *

'Mommy,' the figure closed the door to her room and locked it. 'I tried to follow the man with an Eva in Belorado. Then a car chased them!'

'Who chased them?'

'I don't know, Mommy. It came out of nowhere and tried to run them down!'

'And then?' the voice quivered.

'They disappeared! Just disappeared!'

'He must be Satan himself! He has used his satanic powers to disappear in the past. Be careful of this man, Sugar.'

'He is an Englishman, Mommy. He's helping the Eva.'

'Find him. Kill him.'

'I know someone who want's him killed. I'll fix it, Mommy.'

'Find him. Kill him.'

'I, I'll find him, Mommy. I will! I'm fixin' to find them, Mommy. I promise to punish them. Both of them.'

'Do your duty, Sugar!'

'I will, Mommy. But my strength is leaving me.'

'Overcome your weakness! Fail and you lose your place next to the Lord in heaven.'

'I shall not fail, Mommy,' he tugged his cap peak over his eyes.

'Did you bring those pills, Sugar?'

* * *

Burgos had fallen. The oldest city in Europe had withstood many sieges over many hundreds of years by the Romans, Visigoths, Moors, French and English. Now Field Marshal Cheapie Trips sends legions of tourists and pilgrims to achieve what generations of armies failed to do; overrun this magnificent university city.

Dan and Jane had enjoyed a large breakfast and left the hotel to meet Alonso. Karl and Angelique would join them.

'God! It's flooded by tourists!' Dan waved a hand at chattering tour groups blocking the sidewalks.

'It's a fact of life, Dan. You can't live in the past,' she turned and pushed her way through the crowded medieval old town dominated by its twin spired granite Gothic cathedral.

'Jane, it's not a case of livin' in the past. It's the

contrast after walkin' the Camino!'

'That's quite something, coming from you,' she watched his face. 'What's wrong with it?' she said skipping round a group of Japanese tourists in the middle of a mass selfie orgy, with her neck craning to take in a shoe shop window.

'It's such a jump from the quiet world of friendly pilgrims with all their belongings in their backpack, and, wham, we're in a world of indifferent fashion addicted shoppers loaded with bags from designer shops.' He sniffed. 'Probably see a dog with a perm.'

'It's just city life, Dan. Where have you been living?'

'In a room over a stable,' he pressed his lips together.

'Have you?' She stopped. 'Is it nice?'

'Not really,' he said. 'Right now, I'm missing the trail.'

'Why over a stable?'

'Cheap. Just a single room. It belongs to the magazine.'

'Hasn't it occurred to you that some people enjoy a break to see the cultural parts of the Camino?'

'Yeah, but not friggin' parts sandwiched between hamburger and coffee shop chains.'

'As a matter of fact, I enjoyed a good night's sleep on a proper mattress last night.'

'I hope my floor level discussion with the mice didn't disturb you.'

'I thought soldiers love the tough life,' she smiled.

'I'm not a soldier anymore.'

Jane stopped and turned to face him. 'You loved the army life, didn't you?'

'My first family.'

'I'm sorry,' she squeezed his arm.

'Not your friggin' fault, Jane.'

'This is the place.' They fell through the doors of the Tapelia restaurant with tour stickers like a stamp collection on its window. A bang echoed. Jane clutched her heart. A cork bounced off a table landing at her feet. Cheers blasted from a group at a big table a short distance away from them.

'Over there!' Jane pointed to a table in the back.

Angelique's arms semaphored their location. Karl confronted a plate of crumbs. The remains of a ravaged chocolate cake. His fingers did a drum solo on one of his smartphones.

'Hi, Angie old girl,' Jane said. Angie frowned and rolled her eyes.

'Are you going to say anything in real time, or are you sending us a fuckin' message,' Dan stood with folded arms next to Karl.

'Customer problems,' he mumbled. His hands danced on the keyboard and made Jane think of two spiders doing a tango.

'*I'm* not typing, Dan' Angelique patted the seat next to hers. 'Welcome to Burgos. It was the birthplace of El Cid.'

'I know,' Dan said.

'According to Hollywood he was a sort of Terminator among medieval knights.'

'Hollywood doesn't know its arse from its Burgos,' Dan muttered. 'Did you know Napoleon's troops dug up his body and buried him in France, in case he rose from the dead.'

'They returned him some years later,' Angelique said. 'We French don't keep other people's property, unlike some London museums,' her smile was sweet.

'And,' Karl raised his finger. 'Burgos cathedral's twin spires were inspired by the twin spires of Cologne cathedral. *My* home town!' Karl beamed.

'Who friggin' cares?'

'Dan's rather narky today.'

'You'd be narky after a night on the floor.'

'Didn't Jane share with you?' Angelique mimed mock shock. 'You could've come to me,' her eye lid flicked in one of her mini winks that left a man wondering whether he had really seen what he had seen.

'His snoring would've kept you awake,' Jane waved at a waiter who looked the other way.

'Lonsey's friggin' late again.'

'What do mean *again*?'

'He's always friggin' late.'

'He does have a job you know.'

'So. Have. I.' Dan said as if talking to an imbecile. Angelique poked her tongue in reply.

'Ach, he is here,' Karl unglued his fingers from the keyboard as Alonso entered, followed by Mr Tennis shoes. Jane thought they were together, but the bright red shoes walked by to the back of the restaurant. Jane's gaze followed. He took a seat near the back and busied himself with his phone. *Should I tell Dan?* Her mind explored the option. She shook her head. *Why bother? He would say that lots of people catch up on the Camino and that's a free world.*

Alonso sat down and looked round the group. 'I've come from a meeting with Mendoza.'

'Good or bad?' Dan watched Alonso's expression.

'Ramos and his thugs have a free hand without police control.'

'That cannot be legal!' Dan thumped the table

shaking the condiments.

'I wondered about that until I dropped Mendoza off at the Council offices in Pamplona. Then I got to know the president's secretary. It seems the President is under stress about something that involves EU funds for the Camino.'

'What funds?' Karl dragged his eyes from his phone.

'She didn't say.'

'Ask her out,' Dan grinned.

'I'd rather not.' Alonso's eyes avoided him.

'Don't you fancy women?'

'Of course,' his brow furrowed.

Jane noticed a slight wince at the edge of his mouth.

'But that is my private life and I prefer to keep it that way.'

'Let's hope Mendoza doesn't grab you again on the Camino.' Jane hugged herself as if a Siberian wind had crossed her back.

'Don't worry,' Dan patted her hand. 'He needs a good reason to grab me again. The embassy lawyer will spring me. Our biggest threat is the killer right now.'

'And Ramos,' Alonso eyes fixed on Dan. 'I have more information about him.' He pulled a buff folder from his big leather bag.

Jane saw Dan's brow crunch in lines. He grimaced. 'Yeah, we saw his mugshot in Facebook. He was in Mali in the FFL.

'He is in a rage about something, Dan. You should think about going home. Or go to another Camino. The Camino Nord. You can still interview...'

'No way,' Dan shook his head. 'What I begin, I

finish,' his fist bounced on the table top. 'I *have* to finish this! For Jane's sake.'

Alonso sighed. 'Very well. I'll keep an eye on you all the way to Castrojeriz. You should walk tomorrow. Today it's too late to do it on time and you need some rest. But, frankly, after you told me about yesterday's attack in Belorado, I'm thinking it might not have been the killer.' He flipped open the folder.

'Jasus, I thought that, too.'

'Puh! You mean Ramos!'

'Exactly. I wonder if what we're doin' is so fuckin' clever. I'm frustrated that we're not movin' ahead faster and speedin' things up with Karl's car.'

'No! No! No!' Jane's clenched jaw jutted. 'I have to walk it and I'm *going* to walk it! No discussion. I promised my dying mother I'd visit every place that Debbie mentioned in her postcards. Factually, this is part of my mission.' She stared at them round the table. 'I'm going to finish it.'

'Ya, but Jane,' Karl said. 'You have to accept that you're in a dangerous situation. Nobody would criticise you if you broke it off.' Jane shook her head, 'Break it off before something happens to you, or Dan. Especially now as this Ramos is freaking out.'

'Sorry, Karl, but if you want to quit, I'm not stopping you. In fact, it was never your mission in the first place. I appreciate your support, but don't stay if you're worried.'

'Ach, I want to help with my skills if I can. So I stay, Jane.' He rubbed his tattoo, as always when he was nervous.

'And you, Dan?'

'I think we should press the gas pedal. Use Angie's

car and get it over A. S. A. P.'

'If either of you did leave,' Alonso smiled, 'then, as a Detective, I have the freedom of movement and authority to keep an eye on...!' A convulsive cough interrupted his sentence. 'Sorry.' He put the handkerchief back in his pocket. 'to protect Jane,' he finished his sentence.

'That's great.' Angie's perfect teeth flashed. 'Then Jane can complete her mission. But I won't leave her,' she rubbed Jane's arm warmly.

'Whoa! Just steady on!' Dan's neck and face flushed. 'I didn't say I'd fuckin' quit!' He breathed as if spitting fire. 'I just wondered aloud whether or not every single friggin' yard should all be on foot.'

'Dan!' The condiments shook from Jane's fist thumping the table. 'My sister did it on foot! And. So. Will. I!' The condiments wobbled again. Alonso's hand steadied the shaking bottle of olive oil. 'I. Owe. Her!' Jane panted.

'Okay by me,' Dan held up both hands in surrender. 'Thought I'd mention it.'

'Understood.' Jane slumped back in her seat, arms folded, her lips pressed in a hard line.

'Look, Jane, I can watch over you,' Alonso's voice was gentle.

'Thanks Alonso. It's good to feel that there is *someone* I can trust along the Camino.'

'No problem, Jane,' Alonso patted her arm. 'Just move on tomorrow morning.'

'OK, that's doable. What's in your friggin' folder?'

'I want to update you on my inquiries about Ramos.' Alonso spoke. They all fell silent. 'I found details about him. He's Barcelona Slum born. Four brothers. All bad. French Foreign Legion in Mali.

Dishonourable discharge. Suspected corruption, but not proven. Extreme violence and,' he paused and looked round the table. 'Suspected mental disorder.'

'Now tell us the friggin' bad parts.'

'He might be hanging around, so keep an eye open,' Alonso raised a warning finger.

'We have also found stuff on Ramos,' Dan said.

'I found it,' Karl corrected. 'Now I can update you more. Last night, I lock picked the French Foreign Legion computer in Marseilles.'

'What! I don't friggin' believe it!'

'It was not difficult. The records of the soldiers don't appear to be high on the secret list. It wasn't difficult to see into them. Part of them are almost public records.'

'Don't keep us in suspense!' Angie slapped the back of his head. 'Tell us what you found!'

'Three elder brothers. One works for him. One in jail. The eldest joined the French Foreign Legion. He was in ISAF.'

'Puh! Always letters. What is this I S A F? A club?' asked Angie.

'It's a unit that operated with units of other countries in Afghanistan.'

Jane studied Dan's impassive features. 'Weren't you in Afghanistan, Dan?'

'Loads of people were in friggin' Afghanistan.'

Alonso clapped the folder. 'I'll tell you if I learn anything new.' He coughed and turned away and fumbled in his jacket pocket. Then summoned the waiter who looked the other way.

'I don't like that cough you have there,' Jane said.

'Neither do I,' he grinned. 'Summer flu. It'll pass.'

Angie patted his arm. He smiled at her. 'Did you

come here only for Jane?' Alonso asked Angie as if trying to make small talk. He cleared his throat and got his breath back.

'Yes, but I also wanted to see the Camino for fun.'

'Fun!' Alonso frowned. 'There's only one reason alone to come on the Camino. It's to honour the Lord! Not fun!' His jaw tightened and pumped up the veins in his neck.

'Why so tense?' Angie punched his shoulder. 'Everyone has their own reasons, Lonsey!'

'Sorry.' He looked sheepish and took a long deep calming breath. 'But one shouldn't joke about the Camino.' He turned and summoned the waiter again. The man nodded and took another table's order. Alonso sighed and looked at his watch as if it were a Fabergé egg.

'Don't worry, Lonsey.' Angie flapped her hand at Alonso. 'I'll get the bill.'

'And thanks for all your help, Lonsey,' Dan said. 'We all appreciate it. We couldn't manage without you,' His playful punch split Alonso's face with a big smile and reddened his ears.

'Dan,' Alonso's forehead was ridged with concern. 'Don't underestimate Mendoza or Ramos. Ramos is highly unstable. I fear you are running from two hunters, so keep your head down.'

'No sweat, Lonsey. I've spent my life keepin' my friggin' head down.'

'I think Ramos prefers you under the trail rather than in jail.'

'What did you study at Police College? Fuckin' poetry?'

Alonso smiled and snapped his leather bag shut. He stepped a pace and looked back, his eyes

quizzical. 'Dan, he held steady eye contact.
'Now what?'
'What unit were you with in Afghanistan?'
Dan poker faced Alonso.
'Well?' Alonso raised an eyebrow.
'ISAF. What about it?'
'That is what I feared. What worries me is that Ramos knows, too.'

CASTROJERIZ CASTLE

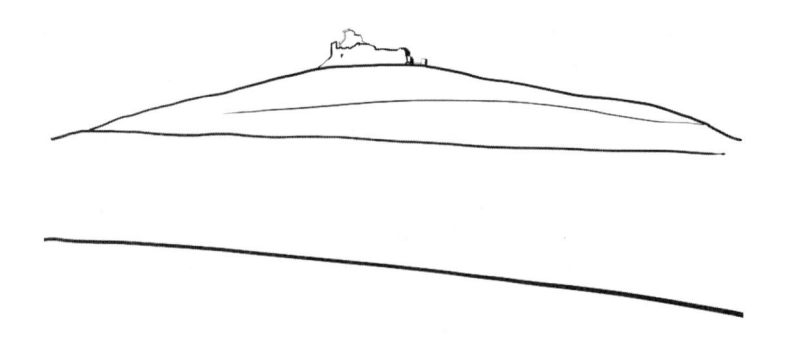

Jane and Dan stood in the doorway of a house that did not offer breakfast. Jane heard Dan's stomach rumbling. She felt the same. They had not slept well. Even the birds weren't greeting them.

'You need a shave,' she looked at his three day stubble.

'Water was cold.' Dan grunted.

'I didn't think much of this place,' Jane said as she looked over the little terrace house.

'It was better to stop than continue with your foot hurtin' from the incident in Belorado. Wasn't your fault that everything was full.'

'I must say the municipal albergue round the corner was chaotic. The kitchen! What a mess!'

'It resembled a friggin' battlefield with pilgrims

cooking in a learnin' by fuckin' up session.'

'And they still charged the full price for this cold little den they stuck us in,' Jane said as they walked along the main street, barely wide enough for small cars without wing mirrors.

'I thought we were in a bed store with every square foot filled with beds and friggin' matrasses.'

'Factually, the jungle garden was a graveyard for abandoned cars!'

'Angie could have parked her heap there without bein' noticed.'

'You've got a thing about that car, haven't you?'

Dan shrugged. 'What really pissed me was the café and the long wait to eat and then bein' asked to leave to make room for the next group of pilgrims watching us through the doorway.'

Jane nodded and thought of her bunk trembling as the man in the bunk above her masturbated. It reminded her of her husband in recent years. She pushed away the memory and held her face into the bright sunbeams. The warmth was wonderful after a cold night.

'Let's eat at the café,' where we ate last night,' Dan said. They walked back. It was closed.

'God! I could eat a fuckin' horse.'

'Why do you want to eat a horse having intercourse?'

'Very funny,' he growled and started to follow the street out of the one horse village.

'Ah, the wonderful intensifier word again,' she caught up with him. 'Your only intensifier, in fact.'

'Swearin' is a fundamental necessity. If you hit your thumb with a hammer, you have to let it all out, don't you?'

'I've never hit my thumb with a hammer. I had a husband to do that.'

'Mark Twain wrote; if you're angry count to four, and if you're furious, swear,' he grinned at her.

'You never count till four! You start at F!'

'I hope we find somewhere to eat soon so I can enjoy the day.'

'Enjoy the day? I thought you hated it here.'

'I didn't like my original reason for comin'. But I've seen a lot that's gradually changed my mind,' He looked around and breathed deeply as if the air was purifying his lungs. 'Despite everythin', I've begun to sort of feel part of the Camino and the people on it. You saw how unhappy I was to be in the city back in Burgos.'

'Wow! That's a big change, I must say.'

'Everyone has the same aim and the same hardships. It's amazin'!' He stopped and reddened. 'Jasus! Listen to me!' he shook his head. 'I'm talkin' like a fuckin' great softy!'

'Well, I often think of Debbie and the millions of pilgrims that have followed this same way and walked where she walked.'

'There seems to be little or no wildlife!' he changed the subject. 'I've been here four weeks and all I have seen are cows. I've been through woods, mountains, and now the Meseta. I haven't seen any rabbits, deer, or squirrels. No wildlife,' he blushed and gabbled without pausing for breath, to avoid further sentimentality.

'This is exactly what Debbie must have seen.' Jane pulled a small red nylon bag the size of a large wallet from a side pocket of her backpack. Dan watched her extract a dozen cards held together by a green rubber band. She riffled through, took one. 'Here.' she held it out to see.

Dan took it and saw the picture. He flipped the card and read a hand-written message;

This is Hornillos. So friendly here.
Met a jolly friar. Such a laugh!
Wish you were here to see this...
Debbie

'Now you *are* here to see it,' Dan smiled and handed the card back. 'You see what she saw.'

'Not that Hornillos was worth seeing,' she murmured as she read the card again – as she had scores of times already. She pulled a tissue from her pocket and blew her nose. 'I should've gone with her, as I promised,' she dabbed her eyes. 'If I'd kept my promise she'd still be here!'

'Don't beat yourself up. It's not your fault.' He lay his arm on hers. 'What you are doin' now is good. If she can see you, she'll know how you feel and she'll love you all the more for it. She'll feel proud that you've taken the time to walk her walk. No matter what fate befell her, she had some great experiences. By finishin' it for her, you make her experience complete and worthwhile.' She nodded. He saw the wet below her blue eyes. 'You're completin' it for her! Understand?'

She nodded again and swallowed and took an enormous deep breath. 'Thanks, Dan. I didn't think you would be the person to rebuild my resolve. You know, I still feel guilty because I didn't like her much. She was always Daddy's little girl, while I had to fight for everything. In a way I feel that I come to peace with her while following her path. Does that sound strange to you?' She wiped her eyes again and marched off toward the ancient ruins of Valdemoro on the trail ahead.

'Not at all. We all have to make peace with our past in some way. Walking the Camino seems to be a way to get rid of a lot of anger and regret. Look at me; it even has a mysterious effect on me. Although this was the last thing I had in mind when I started to walk.'

They came to a rubble wall, the remains of a small house.

'Please wait a moment.' She walked behind a pile of rubble and stepped into what had been a small room, now open to the sky. She started to take off her backpack. Flies buzzed aerobatics round her head. She inhaled. Gagged. Her face puckered up closing mouth and nostrils. The floor littered with pieces of crumpled tissues in various stages of decay showed the origin of the stink. Then she saw the reason; years of excrement littered the earth floor. 'Phew!' she held her breath and clamped her mouth shut. A fly settled on her face. She batted it away. It returned faster than a Wimbledon tennis ball and clutched her lip. She spat three times, disgusted at the thought of where it had been. She scooped her backpack. Another fly buzzed her and one landed on her cheek. She fled.

'What's up?' Dan was waiting outside.

'I went into the ruin to answer the call of nature.'

'Good. I will, too.'

'I wouldn't if I were you. It smells like a stable that's never been cleaned. Full of...'

'Shit?'

'Tut! Well, yes. And used paper everywhere!'

'Not everyone on the Camino is a saint. And, if

they were, even saints still have to...'

'It's alright, Dan. I don't need pictures.' She continued to walk her walk, still flapping her hand at a few persistent flies that had become extremely fond of her.

* * *

Dan's teeth tore at a Snickers bar. He stood under the pointed ruins of San Antón on the road to Castrojeriz. Its soaring archway straddled the road where cars zipped by, forcing pilgrims to hug the edge.

The idyllic dirt path through fields dappled with vivid poppies and yellow mustard plants had joined the road. Jane plucked Dandelions to create her next herbal tea brew.

'My feet are killing me,' Jane stopped.

'I learned to put up with pain.'

'Good for you. All the men I know seem about to die of a common cold.'

'How many do you know?'

'None. They all died of colds.'

'Lucky for them, I'd say,' he grinned. and photographed the towering ruins of San Antón.

'There was an illness called Saint Anthony's fire. It drove people mad.'

'Yeah, some friggin' fungus, wasn't it? Made them blow their minds better than an LSD trip.'

'Imagine a medieval town with most people with gangrene blackened limbs collectively hallucinating because of a fungus in rye grain.'

'Yeah. I read grain was easily infected.'

'The order of Saint Anthony here specialized in

treating the illness. In fact it caused women's miscarriages, convulsions and gangrene that killed many. The Ergot is the source of LSD so it blows one's mind, as you put it.'

'I read that, too. Black robed monks with the privilege to allow their friggin' pigs to run free in the streets. Must have stunk.'

'So what. They saved the lives of many pilgrims. In fact the illness alone was a reason for the pilgrimage for these poor people. You could put that in your article for Dogs and Cats.'

'It's Huntin' and Anglin', but thanks for the elucidation, Ms teacher,' he said snapping his camera at the arches and then followed a long straight road flanked by shade giving trees. Dan swallowed another chocolate bar leaving only the shredded wrapper in his fingers. A middle-aged woman and a younger woman plucked bits of litter lying on the Way and dropped it inside plastic blue sacks. Dan's hand reflexively closed round the paper wrapper as if to conceal it.

'I see the Camino relies on volunteers to avoid it becomin' a 700-kilometre trash trail.'

Jane said nothing but winced with every step. Two pilgrims ahead were always in sight, the gap neither narrowing nor increasing. They were overtaken by a solitary masked Korean woman who walked as if she were late for an appointment.

'Look. Castrojeriz Castle,' Dan said after a period of silence. He nodded along the straight asphalted way with trees lining up towards a conical hill.

'Queen Eleanor of Castile was murdered there on the orders of Pedro the Cruel.' Jane broke her silence, eying the light beige stones of the castle ruins dominating the steep hill, ringed by terraces of pine trees, part of Spain's mammoth tree planting programme. 'Pedro the Cruel's daughter married John of Gaunt, the Duke of Lancaster,' Jane continued with her impromptu history lesson. 'That made her the Duchess of Lancaster and her husband tried to be crowned king here, but to no avail.'

'Poor him,' Dan said without meaning it. The double beep of a car horn startled them. They smiled at the familiar rubric cube paint job.

'Yoohoo!' Angelique waved from the window, as fresh as a daisy after thirty kilometres in an air-conditioned, rolling stereo lounge listening to Beethoven's 5th which switched abruptly to Iron Maiden. She scowled at Karl.

'Now I know what heaven looks like,' Jane grasped the handle of the rear green door with a fresh dent.

'Heaven?' Dan kicked the tyre. 'This is hell on wheels!'

'My feet are telling me it's heaven' Jane clambered into the back. Dan tumbled in after her.

'Jesus! These backseat springs are friggin' flattened.'

'They get a lot of exercise,' Angie winked and punched the radio button. Violins set a romantic mood. Karl turned the volume to minimum and stamped on the gas.

Minutes later they parked in the long Plaza Mayor with its raised sidewalk under a long shadowy arcade in Castrojeriz centre. People walking by eyed the car and nudged each other. They checked in to a hotel with a foyer resembling a castle hall dominated by a yawning fireplace big enough to party inside. Jane enjoyed the surroundings of the cool stone walls keeping the outside heat at bay.

'We're sharin' again,' Dan told Karl.

'Mensch! Then please do not snore.'

A group of Italian cyclists rolled up in their skin tight genitally emphasising suits, all talking at once, with lots of 'Eeh! Ooh! Beh! Aii!' punctuated by wild gestures as they piled fat panniers against the wall.

'It'll be quieter if we find a café somewhere,' Dan said. They headed for the Plaza Mayor and found a nice bar under the arcade. Dan nipped into a shop along the Calle Mayor that supplied everything a pilgrim needed except souls.

Jane slumped at a coffee table outside the building, sighed and stretched her legs. She watched Dan approaching.

'Here,' he dropped a small box of Compeed plasters on the table.

'For your blisters.'

'Oh! Thanks, Dan.' She watched him slump in the chair next to hers.

'Hello!' Jane waved to a Danish Pilgrim. He raised a walking staff in salute. She saw Dan nod at a girl he seemed to know. She acted as if she hadn't seen him. They sat in a circle with cold drinks while an old Cliff Richard song warbled in Spanish. Karl idly murmured the words to Summer Holiday, written well over a generation before him.

Jane noticed Mr Tennis shoes striding passed. He caught Jane's eye and raised his eyebrows and walked on. He was followed by a Monk in deep conversation with a willowy girl with red hair.

* * *

Castrojeriz was soaked in darkness. They spent the evening on the warm terrace restaurant of the hotel with the tang of good food while the moon rose. The Italian bikers shouted at each other as if attending a convention for the deaf. Corks erupted like a mortar barrage and Rioja swirled into gleaming glasses at every table. Grinning flushed faces flushed even more with each glass. Jane looked up. The moon floated higher, illuminating the streets of Castrojeriz better than the dull street lamps. Mr Lobster came onto the terrace, his tan peeling made an unfinished jigsaw effect. He sat at a table with the Dutch woman. She looked content and sure of herself and took over the wine ordering.

He seems to have latched on to her alright, Jane mused. *At least he'll leave me in peace and spare me his dumb remarks.*

They both saw Jane. She waved. He winked. Jane nodded.

A French group occupied the next table. One leaned over. 'May I have the salt?' His accent was more attractive than his face.

'Natürlich!' Karl handed it to the man who focused on a little pin badge on Karl's lapel.

'Tut! No salt on our table,' the man raised his eyes and shook his head slow motion with a life-is-such-shit expression while looking at Karl, 'And the bread! Tasteless!'

'Ours was alright,' Jane smiled.

'And some of the albergues!' his wife sighed as if about to swoon. Jane half expected her husband to put smelling salt under her nose.

'Do you know?' the man nodded towards the kitchen lowering his voice. 'We had a steak in Burgos, and the pan had been used for something else first!' He stared at them as if expecting an uproar to become a cowboy saloon brawl.

'He seems traumatised' Dan whispered.

The man stared at Karl's lapel pin. 'What is that?'

'Ach, just a secret society.'

'Aha! And what secret society is that?'

'They didn't tell me. It's a secret.' Karl grinned. Angelique slapped the back of his head.

The Frenchman stared at Karl, jerked his head back to focus. 'Is that a binary code on your head?'

'Part of the secret,' Karl stroked it and smiled.

'I suppose Steve Jobs is one of your heroes.'

'He will forever inhabit my iPhone!' Karl made sad eyes.

'Waiter!' the Frenchman called. The canny waiter cut a swift curve away from them as if he hadn't seen them. 'Typical!' the man grumbled. His angry wife puckered her lips.

Dan whispered in Jane's ear. 'She's got lips like a cat's arse hole.'

Jane's jaw dropped, looked at the woman, stared at Dan and burst out laughing, unable to stop.

Dan spotted a Spanish acoustic leaning against the wall. He took it and plucked the strings. 'Needs tunin'.'

'Don't break it.' Said Angie

Dan twisted the tuning keys and hit a few A chords and then C.

'You can play!' Karl's eyes raised from one of his phone screens. By way of an answer, Dan sang; I Don't Wanna Be Your Hero, which, in a way, seemed appropriate. Everyone joined in, their voices rose to the silver moon.

* * *

The same moon lit up the street outside. Dan's music from the terrace made a passing pilgrim girl in the street smile. She sauntered passed the restaurant along the Calle Real de Oriente, drawn towards the chords of another guitar ahead, where a woman's voice sang Volare outside an albergue. Others joined in the chorus, their voices echoed from the walls of the narrow street. She smiled again at what was a typical Camino evening.

'Good evening.'

'Oh!' Her hand clapped over her heart. 'Oh, it's you!' her teeth contrasted against her deep tan in the moonlight 'Hi! I didn't see you in the shadows.'

'Moon shadows,' he chuckled.

'Yes, moon shadows. It's nice to see a familiar face again.'

'You remember me then.' His perfect teeth flashed back at her.

'Sure, sure!' she giggled. 'Your red habit is very hard to forget.' she giggled again. 'It's sure distinctive compared to the brown other monks wear.'

'It's an order that helps and saves souls. It's, er, Barbara, isn't it?'

'Sure, sure! Friends call me Babs. But, hey! You got a good memory.' Her eyes and teeth reflected the moonlight.

'I always remember distinctive people, Babs. I can call you Babs, can't I?'

'Sure, sure! Babs is for friends, and you're a Camino friend,' she gave a tinkling chuckle. 'Distinctive sounds a bit over the top though,' she chuckled again.

'Your red hair. That makes you stand out. So I remembered you.'

'Well, thank you. Your cause to save souls sure sounds noble,' her teeth slashed the dusk again.

'Aau!' The monk winced and clasped his knee. 'Could you hold this package of bibles for me?'

'Oh, sure, sure!' she looked concerned. 'What's wrong with your leg?'

'An old football injury from high school days,' he clasped his knee theatrically.

'Oh, dear. Can I help?'

'Maybe you would be kind enough to help me carry that package of bibles you're holding over to my car? They are for an orphanage.'

'Sure, sure! Cool! Where?'

'My car is in the shadow just around the corner.'

'In the shadow?' she chuckled again. 'Oh those shadows of the Camino.'

'Right! The shadows of the Camino.'

'Shadows can hide good and evil,' she said.

'Yes. Good shadows and bad shadows and everything between.'

'That sounds mysterious,' she chuckled again.

'My car's over here. Just follow me,' he said and limped toward the dark side street. 'Can you manage that package, Babs?' His hand groped inside his leather bag.

'Sure, sure!'

* * *

Back on the terrace Dan plucked at the guitar as the pilgrims retired to their nylon cocoons in the dormitories.

Karl's fingers danced on the buttons of his iPhone. Angie rose from her seat and lurched against Dan.

'Whoops! Sorry, Dan. Bit too much wine.' She left wet lipstick on his cheek and tottered away to her own room. No bunks for Angie girl.

Karl stood without taking his gaze from his mobile. 'Gute Nacht,' he murmured and strolled away.

Dan placed the guitar back in the corner. 'Quite a walk today,' he yawned.

Jane nodded. 'It was good to talk to you about, um…,' she paused.

'Um?'

'This and that, and um.'

'And um?' Dan smiled.

'You've changed since we first met,' she nodded rapidly, her eyes searched the room.

'O' course I changed. I didn't pack two pairs of underpants f'nothin', m'girl,' he grinned.

'Tut! You know what I mean. You said nice things about my following in Debbie's tracks.'

'I meant it.'

Yes, um.., her brow wrinkled in a puzzled look..

'Um, factually, you're not my type.'

'Well! How about *that* for a friggin' change of subject?'

'Sorry.'

'Why did you friggin' say that?' His stare was armour piercing.

Jane shrugged. 'Just in case you were being nice to me, um, just to, er, you know…'

'I wasn't trying to "er you know" as you put it.

'Sorry.'

'I said only what was on my mind. Your determination despite not loving your sister very much impresses me. Plus, the actions of this killer made me feel your mission was a worthwhile thing to help.'

'Thanks. I'm sorry if I offended.' She rose from her seat.

'I hope we find more about Debbie. She seems to have been quite a character.'

Jane turned and said, 'Actually, she was a bitch.'

A FIELD

The black van with darkened windows blocked the scene from hikers on the trail. Plain clothes men stood along a plastic tape that cordoned off the cross.

Alonso followed Mendoza to a police jeep at an iron cross near the edge of the field. People stared from behind the fluttering tape with expressions of curiosity, and then moved on after a few minutes.

'Another redhead, Comisario.'

'Puta Madre! I'm not blind, Detective!'

They looked at a girl on her back in a shallow grave, partly covered by a few centimetres of soil.

'Who found her?'

'The farmer.'

'Give him the usual talk.'

'Tell him what, Comisario?'
'Road accident.'
'What???'
'She was obviously a night walker. Probably hit by a motorbike. These things happen, Detective.'

Alonso frowned. Mopped his neck and nodded.

'Just keep the people back!' he snapped at Ramos.

A forensic team member flapped away the flies swarming to lay eggs on the bloody gash in her throat. Alonso laid two fingers on the girl's neck opposite the jagged red gash. 'Cold. Rigor mortis has set in. Tache noir has formed.'

'Tache noir! More mumbo jumbo?'

'That blackish bar across the whites of her eyes. It's caused by the eyes drying out if they stay open after death. It forms several hours after death. She has been dead eight hours at least.' He glanced at his watch. 'Killed late last night, I'd say. She was brought here from somewhere else before post death defecation, because that has taken place here.'

Mendoza kept a metre distance and covered his nose with a handkerchief against the stink of excreta and urine discharge. 'Cover her up! For God's sake!' he shouted at a white-faced Guardia officer.

'Comisario?' A police officer held a small object in his rubber gloved hand. I found this underneath the body.' He dropped a green round object into a plastic evidence bag.

Ramos snarled. 'That sick English bastard!' He slapped the evidence bag into Alonso's hand.

'It's military! Brady's ex-military!' Ramos shouted stabbing Alonso's chest with his forefinger in time with his words.

'Comisario, a woman is asking what happened,'

one of Ramos' team asked. He ignored the Detective.

'Traffic accident,' Mendoza muttered. 'We always warn pilgrims to be careful of the traffic.'

'Do you want to talk to Brady again, Comisario?'

'I'll pick him up, Comisario.' Ramos broke in, his cold brown eyes glittered.

'He's bound to resist and get the embassy involved!' Alonso said.

'If he resists it will be very bad for him.' Ramos leered, increasing the ugliness of his scar.

'Ramos.' Mendoza called. Ramos turned. 'Ramos! Forget Brady!'

'Never,' Ramos turned away.

'Ramos!' Mendoza's face flushed. 'Ramos, come back here!'

The van door slammed. Mendoza's face flushed almost purple. He stared open mouthed as the van lurched and jolted away along the Camino, chased by a cloud of dust.

* * *

Dan looked around at the top of the plateau an hour from Castrojeriz. They reached a tall notice board with a million messages scrawled or pinned to it. A shelter stood next to it.

'Let's rest,' Jane gasped.

'Jasus, we just started!'

'Factually, hours ago and uphill all the way.' She took a pull on her bottle.

'Was Debbie here?'

'Yes,' Jane said and walked to the side of the trail, dropped to one knee. Dan heard a rattle of glass as she fumbled with the mysterious suede sack. He had ceased asking what she was doing. He knew it wasn't gardening.

People arrived in ones or pairs and obligingly photographed each other. He took out his camera and shot a few pics of the smear on a distant hill that was Castrojeriz in the rising sun.

'Ready?' Jane disturbed his shot.

'Yeah, ok,' he packed the camera and shouldered his pack.

They walked the walk. Other pilgrims dropped behind or forged ahead. They reached a cross of beige earth trails. East, West, North and South.

'Which way?'

'West.'

'Where's west?'

'Follow y'shadow. Sun's behind you in the East.'

'When will we get there?'

'When we're friggin' there.'

'What time is it?'

'Now.'

'When shall we stop?'

'When y'feet bleat.'

'Sometimes I hate you.'

'Welcome to the friggin' club.'

She sighed long and loud. He stared ahead, eyes roving the horizon.

'He's out there, isn't he?'

'He is.'

'I know he's out there.'

'Me, too.'

'I can feel it.'

'Me, too.'

'I really can feel it.'

'Save your breath f'walkin'.

'I do hate you.'

'So, y'said.'

'Factually.'

'I believe you.'

Her fist thudded on his shoulder. He grinned. 'You're ok, Jane.'

They walked the trail. Long, hot, dry, straight to the horizon and silent, except for crisp sounds of their footfalls. Fields of knee high corn stretched in all directions as far as they could see, and further.

* * *

The form under the sheet jerked as the door slammed.

'They've stolen another Eva that I just saved!'

'What! What?'

'The police desecrated her grave and removed her body!'

'You *cannot* allow this, Sugar!'

'How?' he bellowed in a strong man's voice. 'I can't stop them!'

'Don't raise your voice to Mommy, sugar!'

'I'm angry Goddammit! They've got help from people in a crazy coloured car!'

'Crazy colours? What d'you mean, crazy colours?'

'Every part is different, red front door, green rear door, blue hood, white fenders, silver trunk. The driver door is mauve!'

'Mauve! Who the hell makes a car like that?' she snarled. 'Perverts!'

'Of course they are.'

'Sometimes, Sugar, I think the world's full of perverts!'

'It's French.'

'Ooh!' The wet patch of sheet fluttered. 'French! Well they always were avant-garde.'

'That's not the goddam point!' his manly voice roared.

'Sugar! Don't raise your voice, and don't take the Lord's name in vain!' The damp patch in the sheet over her mouth palpitated violently. 'I will not stand for it. If you were small I'd wash your mouth with carbolic soap!'

'I'm sorry, Mommy,' the little voice was back.

'This could lose you your grace with the Lord! You must replace them!'

Yes, Mommy, but...'

'Do your duty, Sugar! You gotta catch up!''

'I will try, Mommy.'

'No, Sugar. You will not *try*. You will *do* it! Fail and you will lose your place next to the Lord in the next world! Do anything! Anything it needs! Time is short, Sugar. Your time is short!'

'But, Mommy...'

'Do anything, Sugar! And I *mean* anything!' she panted. 'Anything, even above and beyond your own personal safety.'

'Yes, Mommy.'

'Mommy?'

'They need to change you again,' his nose wrinkled.

* * *

'This man,' Ramos turned from the picture of Dan. It hung on the wall of a tobacco smoke filled room behind a shabby bar in Pamplona old town, 'is your target.' The group of muscle men nodded. 'Here are smaller versions for you to carry with you,' Ramos' sneer made his deep cheek scar even uglier. He dealt out the postcard size pictures with the dexterity of a professional poker player. 'Work in pairs. When you find him, contact me and trail him. We shall be at the scene as soon as possible.'

'Can we expect resistance?' a man built like a road block asked, one eye closed against the smoke from the cigarette between damaged lips.

'He's ex-British army.'

'I thought he was Irish!' Mr Road block said.

'English, Irish. Who cares?'

'Is he armed?' A tall thin man with a vicious face and mad eyes cracked his knuckles while he talked.

'Doubt it. But he's resourceful.'

'Is there a bonus for the man who gets him?' Road Block wiped his nose with his finger.

'One thousand Euros for the man who spots him first.'

'That's a lot of beer,' Road Block grinned.

'We cannot allow him to get away, otherwise our firm will get a reputation of not fulfilling its assignments.'

'What about our assignments to cover dead body finds?' The tall man spat on the floor.

'That stands. That is an order that my firm was given by someone high up.'

'Higher than that Mendoza prick?' asked the Tall-and-thin.

'Higher. Much higher. And, other security firms are watching. If they see this man Brady can fuck us about and get away with it, we could look incompetent.' Ramos' sneer moulded his face as he stared at the group. 'We are not weak!'

The group grunted among themselves. One slapped his pistol in his shoulder holster. The man next to him nodded and cracked his knuckles again.

'We are not incompetent!' Ramos shouted.

Again, the murmurs were louder. They were all Alfa Machos with records that disqualified them from the values of decent folks.

'Listen to me!' His fist slammed the table in front of him. 'He's traveling with three people. They are mobile. He might be walking the Camino or be in a car driven by a German man and a French woman,' Ramos added. 'He's accompanied by a British woman called Jane Downer.'

'Is he screwing her,' Vicious face leered and flashed a middle finger with a skull tattoo.

'I doubt it. She's a rich bitch, or her family is. Father's a scrap metal dealer.'

'Maybe we should just kidnap *her*!' A toothless guy snorted. The rest cheered.

'What if she gets in the way?' demanded a cropped head on the shoulders of a dedicated weight lifter with veins bulging on his muscles.

'No witnesses,' Ramos grinned. They laughed like a hyena's congress.

'I mean, *no* witnesses. Just make sure that we get him alone and teach him a lesson so our employer and our competitors will not forget how good we are. I don't like losing contracts through a smart-ass bastard like Brady. Especially as he owes me a personal debt. The bastard owes me! And I will collect!' His hammer hard face made even the toughest men in the room avoid his demonic stare. 'Get Brady!'

CAFÉ TACHU

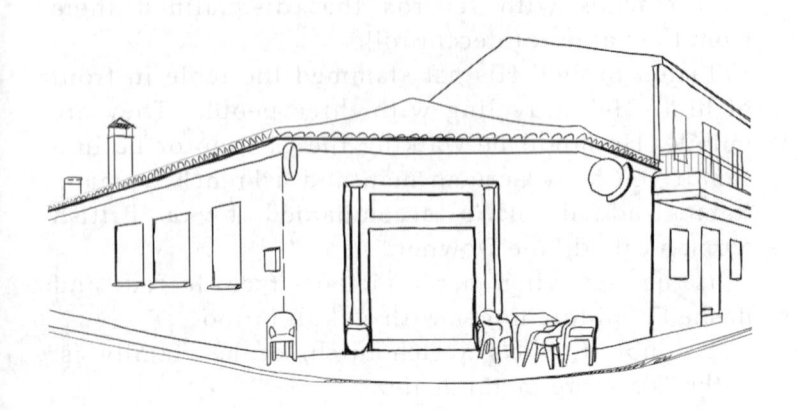

A brown haystack rested like a beached container ship in a field of shivering blue flowers. It was the middle of the Meseta ocean. The province of Palencia lay ahead.

'You don't see haystacks like that in England,' Dan said.

They stopped, pulled their bottles from each other's packs and swallowed enough water to irrigate the Sahara.

A pilgrim stepped into the field and lay flat as a sniper. His weapon was harmless. A DSLR camera. He focused on extreme close ups of the flowers.

'That camera cost more than my friggin' house,' Dan sneered.

'Come on.' Jane resumed their walk. The grit track led to a beige stone Roman bridge arched across a river to a line of trees on the other bank.

'Let's rest,' Jane said, eyes following a stork

gliding elegantly across the endless blue. Its white and black trailing edge wings flapped slowly in no hurry at all. Her eyes narrowed against the sun following the big bird in a graceful curve towards the ground, its long beak pointed down at its prey in a ploughed field.

Dan nodded and clambered down the bank into the shadows under the arch of the bridge.

He unlaced his boots in a flash and splashed his feet into the icy crystal water.

'Is it cold?'

'No. It's friggin' freezin'.'

Tiny dark fish darted round their bare feet dangling among the white stones. The river chuckled over stones pushing an abandoned hiking boot, bobbing against a stout broken branch as the current played with it.

'These are moments that Karl and Angie are missin' in their car,' Dan said. 'Cyclists too, for that matter.'

'Something for your tooting and splashing magazine,' Jane smiled.

'Why d'you keep denigrating' my job?' His eyes shot sparks. 'I know it's nothin' special, but I *need* it. If it wasn't f'my kids I'd be doin' somethin' else, and less respectable at that.' He scratched his head.

Jane's conscience prickled and reminded her not to keep needling him. *He's done alright for you up till now,* she thought.

'Sorry, Dan,' she lay a hand on his arm.

'It's ok,' he mumbled and watched at a fish nibbling at his big toe. 'Maybe you're right,' he nodded. 'Maybe it is a nothin' magazine.' He lay back against the grassy bank. Footsteps passed overhead. Sometimes a single walker, sometime pairs or small groups. 'Camino families,' he said.

'What's that?'

'Nothin'. Just somethin' someone told me about a thousand years ago,' he smiled and closed his eyes.

Jane packed her postcards from Debbie away and watched Dan sleeping. *He seems so harmless asleep. So different from when he's awake. Or angry. He's quietened down since the day we met. But he's not your type.* Jane thought about it some more. *As a matter of fact, nobody is my type. As soon as I've got my divorce I'm going into a convent. Oh, come on! You're joking,* she scolded herself. *It's time I let my hair down the way Debbie always did. I always held myself back and missed out. I'm not getting any younger. Forty comes faster than an express train. What about kids? Short of laying eggs or having an affair, there's not much chance of that any time soon. Dad would love to be a grandpapa. Not that dad was the perfect dad. Not the way he was to Debbie,* she thought. Tears dropped onto her hands. She twisted them to let the tears roll into the stream and be carried away with her sudden sadness. Jane frowned. Dragged her cuff across her eyes. *Once I've done this favour for mum's memory and for dad, and even maybe find something out about Debbie, then I'm off. Dad loved her more than me. She was his favourite and made her what she was. He doesn't really want me.* 'Jane time for Jane,' she murmured and watched the water fight with the branch for possession of the hiking boot. Boots drummed above her head reminded her of the distance still to go to the albergue. A low buzzing from Dan's open mouth made her think of her husband when she woke in the mornings. He hadn't tried to reach her for the last few days. Maybe the divorce papers had arrived. *I hope he's got the message at last.*

She clambered to her feet and nudged Dan with her toe. 'Wake up, dozy.'

'Oh! Was I sleeping?' He sat up in a flash, as if doing a sit-up. She watched him pull the towel from his backpack, dry his feet, pull on his boots, lace them up, pack the towel and stand ready to go in what seemed one continuous movement. A fly landed on her hand. It rubbed its forelegs together. She blew it away while she slowly threaded her first boot. He sat again and waited. 'Need any help?'

'No, thanks,' she felt irritated that he was so much faster. She tied a double knot, grabbed her pack. Her boots were tight. A blister hurt and distracted her. She gritted her teeth and followed him up the grassy bank. As they reached the top two women passed over the bridge. Their eyes met and they giggled.

Dirty minds, Jane thought of one of Angie's favourite remarks; *At least you can take a dirty mind with you everywhere*, she smiled.

'Palencia,' Dan said as they reached a square of shimmering red stones. A large tombstone shaped monument displayed a coat of arms topped by a crown engraved in the baize local stone above a chiselled text; PROVINCIA de PALENCIA.

'Goodbye Navarra,' Jane said to the province across the bridge. She knelt by the track and pulled out her suede sack.

'What are you doin'?

'Nothing.' Glass clinked and rattled.

'What's the glass for?'

'It's private, Dan.' She twisted the top off a small glass jar.

'Are they those little marmalade jars you get in hotels for breakfast?'

She nodded. A spoon appeared in her hand.

'Are y'plantin' somethin'?'

She shook her head and scooped a piece of earth and shovelled it into a jar and sealed it tight with a twist of her wrist. It clinked as she let it drop inside the small sack.

'You takin' soil samples, or what?'

She silently pulled a marker pen and printed letters on the jar.

'Then what the fuck *are* you doin'?'

'My ritual. My mission. My business.'

* * *

'There's the café,' Dan broke the silence. Jane's face was caked in a thin veil of dust on her perspiring features. He nodded at the single-story corner building ahead. She followed his nod. It had a large sign with TACHU in red letters over the door. A big board next to the door showed twelve pictures of menus available inside. A riot of abandoned backpacks and hiking sticks lay strewn along the foot of the walls, resembling the aftermath of a routed army.

'God knows who we'll meet in there,' Jane stopped and stared at the café bar as if it might be the Minotaur's labyrinth.

'Whoever it is, I doubt if he'll try anythin' in a crowded café in daylight.

'You hope.'

'Hmm!' Pictures of eggs and bacon hypnotised

him. 'I'm starvin',' Dan let his backpack drop from his shoulders and shoved it against the wall with his foot. Jane placed hers next to it as Dan reached for the door. It opened alone. A giant stepped out.

'Hallo!' a loud voice greeted. 'Have you printed my story yet? In your magazine?'

Dan recognised the big Teuton he had interviewed. 'Not yet. Got to get back to England first.'

'Hah!' He patted Dan's arm. 'Only joking. Send me a copy! Buen Camino!' he roared like a captain on the poop deck of a galleon and strode off along the white trail.

Inside, fried bacon blended with coffee. Several high black barstools paraded along a gleaming black marble bar almost the length of the café. A few pilgrims sat at tables on the left with their feet up on their backpacks, sipping beers and chomping tapas. Some had yard long laces pooling round their open boots, wagging in time to Sweet Home Alabama.

Behind the bar, a kitchen that looked so small they had to step outside to even crack an egg, created mouth-watering aromas. On the left, a noisy group of Spanish housewives sat with cups full of coffee behind a carved wooden rail that divided the room. Che Guevara watched from a poster in a black frame by the door to a beer garden.

'Look. Mr Tennis shoes again.' Her whispering voice sounded frightened.

'Yes, we've seen him around a few times. Don't worry, he doesn't look like a killer.'

'Oh? How does a killer look?'

'Like you an' me,' Dan's head weaved, his nose hunting the air. 'Hmm! Smell that bacon!' he stopped at the bar.

'That's useful to know, detective Dan. I think I'll still keep an eye on him to be on the safe side,' she said.

'I'm starvin',

'You eat something if you want. It looks like there's a courtyard at the back where I can see to the blisters I'm breeding.' A dense curtain of multi coloured hanging beads slid over her shoulders as she entered the courtyard. Dan ordered breakfast and asked where he could charge his mobile. The man behind the bar took his phone and plugged it into a socket on a shelf behind the bar and Dan joined Jane in the yard. He idly watched through the door into the café where Mr Tennis shoes continued to score goals.

'Easy game, playin' alone,' Dan remarked.

Jane gave only a short glance, too busy peeling back her socks. 'Ouch!' she exposed a flat bubble on the inside of her heel. Dan preferred to read his map while Jane carefully laid out needles in a neat row in operating theatre precision.

'Señor!' the waiter beamed presenting the egg and bacon above as if it were the World Cup.

'Aha, nothing better than a good Irish breakfast to set you up for the day!' Dan's eyes glittered as he grabbed his knife and fork.

'It's afternoon and we're not here for a picnic,' Jane spoke without looking up from her needlework.

'But I'm starvin'!' Dan frowned. 'I'll faint if I don't eat.' He moved to the next table and tucked in, trying to ignore Jane's little operation.

After his breakfast, they went back inside the bar. Mr Tennis shoes had gone. Ellie Goulding was telling everyone through the loudspeakers to *Love*

Her Like You Do. They admired a wall collage of a man passing from boyhood to old in various jungles and primitive huts in the third world.

'That's the owner of this bar,' a woman's voice turned their heads. A pretty young lady in tight jeans and blouse with hair in a ponytail tapped a photo. A tall, robust man smiled out of a photo with his arm round the shoulder of an African boy. 'He's a full-time missionary in Africa. The money this bar earns finances his projects to help children,' she said proudly.

Dan stared, mouth open. 'Amazin',' he whispered. '*This* is what I should write about. The good people silently helpin' others.'

'We also have the Tachu rock festival here,' she beamed proudly at the wall of photos.

'Rock festival! Oh boy! I'd love to be back for that.' His eyes shone with enthusiasm.

'He plays guitar,' Jane said. 'In fact, he's not bad.'

'Not friggin' bad!' Dan reddened. 'Listen! I played in my town orchestra and later got offered a job in a Dublin orchestra. I was goin' to transfer to the army string orchestra when I was...' He turned away.

'Oh, I didn't know...' Jane's cheeks flushed.

'Doesn't matter. Not anymore.'

'We'd love to see you here,' the woman said.

'Sure! I'll spread the word,' Dan looked sincerely at her. His smile was as warm as the rising sun. She handed them a card. 'Where is you next stop?'

'Boadilla.'

'That's not so far from here. Great nude paintings along the garden walls and even greater food.' She smiled. and went back to the bar and waved goodbye as they left.

Outside Dan grabbed his bag. Jane took her pack and froze.

'Dan?'

'Ready to go?'

'No.'

'Why?'

Jane was staring at her backpack. 'Someone's messed with my bag. She crouched and tugged up a net side pocket and held up a brown leather shoulder bag. 'God! This is Debbie's!' she said and looked around with wild anxious eyes.

Dan's eyes eyeballed the street in two seconds flat. 'Hey!'

Jane watched him run after a pilgrim and grab his sleeve. The pilgrim turned and smiled. They talked. The man smiled, shook his head and spread his hands helplessly. Dan nodded, patted him on the shoulder and returned. 'He didn't leave it, and he didn't see anyone.'

'There's a note inside!' Jane pulled out a piece of paper. Dan watched her read. She swayed on her feet. Dan caught her and lowered her onto a plastic chair.

Dan read the note. 'Oh my fuckin'...'

'Let's get away from here,' Jane fumed, shouldered her backpack and started to march so quickly that Dan had difficulties to follow her.

* * *

Village for Sale. The words were fading. The weather beaten notice was already three years old and peeling from the leaning bill board that nobody had seen. No bidders. The legal documents would cost more than the asking price. Nobody wanted it. Nobody knew its name. Nobody lived there. Nobody except Sugar, and then only when on his special missions for the Lord. In his other life, he lived elsewhere. Respectable. Popular. Clever. Fashionable. Cool. Accomplished. Admired and respected.

A red tiled roof peeped above a high stone wall that isolated the farm house from the abandoned village south of Portomarin on the Camino. It was a village without a church, which meant it was a hamlet more than a village. Hamlet or village, nobody wanted it. It was too far for a pilgrim to bother to hike, even if the location hadn't fallen off current maps.

A shiny silver chain in a plastic sheath held the solid steel doors together with a new padlock. A sign warned that dogs were loose within. Another sign warned that the house was alarm wired.

Inside was as simple as the outside except for excellent oil pantings of Camino landscapes. Sugar's figure stood before an eisel dabbing a brush on a partly completed scene of the Meseta. The open fire crackled spitting sparks from the burning logs. A fluffy cat rubbed against his legs interupting his work.

'Hungry my little Daisy?' he chuckled, lifting her up and walked to the kitchen. Daisy purred loudly in his arms. He popped a tin and scooped food into a plastic bowl. Minutes later he returned and picked up a cross on a table. His hands picked up a piece of sandpaper and stroked the cross with a rasping sound. 'Gotta make you sharp again, sharp again, sharp again,' he crooned. He held the cross up to the light. It was a crude crucifix with its bottom end sharpened to a point. He touched the point. 'A little bit more. That naughty Succubus broke off the point against her jaw bone, didn't she? Naughty girl,' he said and applied the sandpaper again. 'Gotta be sharp to do the Lord's work.' He fingered the point again. 'Good,' he whispered and stood with the cross held high like a dagger. He threw the sandpaper into the fire and carefully replaced the crucifix dagger. 'Perfect,' he whispered. His eyes glittered in the flames for a few seconds then he walked across the simple tiled living room and hooked fingers behind an antique wardrobe. He pulled. Felt pads under the feet slid with ease over the red tiles and exposed a dark, heavy oak door. A push swung silently open on well-greased hinges.

The figure took a candle from a stand and held it high. Dust crunched on each of the steep stone steps that melted into total darkness that pushed against the sputtering flame. His hand touched a switch. Neon light tubes buzzed and flickered and glowed along the vaulted ceiling. Mildew and decay hung in the air disturbed only by the figure's breathing.

'Evas,' he whispered. 'So many Evas saved by me!' He coughed in the dank air. A row of small cardboard labels twisted in his unseen wake. Each label bore a one-line history in elegant block capitals. Fingers pincered one and twisted it toward the flame. Released it. Another and another. He stopped. 'There you are.' He chuckled. 'Soon your sister will be joining you,' he chuckled again. 'Reuniting families is such a good deed,'

He returned to the sparsely furnished living room

and placed a backpack on a grand piano, next to a large dusty crucifix. The figure sat at the instrument. Opened the lid. Looked up at a poster of Monty Python's Life of Brian. He smiled. The room acoustics were good. His strong voice filled the room 'Always look on the bright side of life,' he smiled and played the little riff. He was happy.

* * *

'This feels better.' Dan lay on the grass in the gardens of Boadilla. A glass of beer stood on the grass at a slight angle near his head. 'Great art, too.'

Jane had been staring at the grass. She looked up at the naked female forms daubed along the walls. 'It's alright, I suppose.' Her gaze travelled higher, attracted by the movement of a stork in its nest in the church belfry outside the garden.

A guitar played nearby. A man hung his washing over a tree branch next to them. Laughter echoed across the garden. People greeted each other from earlier encounters. More laughter. Someone started singing.

'Great meal, wasn't it?'

'Factually, you seem to be addicted to pilgrim menus.' She let the setting sun play on her face, although she was cooking inside after the last note she had found back in the café earlier that day.

'I've had some friggin' good ones. Especially in the smaller albergues. They're especially great when you're fed up with your own cookin' like I am,' he grinned.

'Can you cook, Dan?'

'When I'm desperate. I can crack open a tin of soup with the best of 'em.'

'Sounds adventurous.'

'Come on, Jane! Don't let that last friggin' note get at you.'

'It *has* got at me, Dan. As a matter of fact it's got me to the point where I want to hit back. I want to tell him what I think of him. I want to… I want…Uuuuug!' She shook her fist in the air.

'You can stand up and shout. He's probably watchin' us right now.'

'I know where he'll be,' she tugged thoughtfully at her lower lip.

'And where's that may I ask?' Dan said propping himself up on his elbow.

'Where we're headed tomorrow. He could be playing a nasty game of dropping clues to get me to go where he wants. That's where he'll be. Waiting, watching, and laughing at us before he tries something.'

'Like he friggin' has done already.'

'I'll be ready. I am bloody well boiling inside.'

'We'll see tomorrow.' Dan nodded.

'Yes, we'll see.'

'I called Karl. We'll drive.'

'Drivin'! We'll that sounds good to me. Give m'feet a rest.'

'And I'll find the coward who is playing with us.'

ELVIS BAR

Reliegos is a one bar village. The Elvis bar. Half the village buildings are grass mounds reminding one of a Hobbits' village, or a collection of bunkers covered with grass. They are above ground cellars for the wine produced in the area. Most are closed, sealed and bolted; unused and derelict. Unblinking blue eyes are always watching the approach' road. This is the Elvis bar. A cult café that celebrates Rock'n Roll as much as the Camino.

'That's the place,' Dan nodded through the windscreen.

'As "Bar Elvis" is painted across its facade, your powers of deduction don't exactly dazzle me,' Jane said from the back seat next to Angie.

'It looks cool,' Angie said.

'I'm glad you persuaded me to drive with you after yesterday's shock,' Jane said.

'Yeah, we just need some friggin' seats that are softer than planks.'

'Puh! Don't look a gift horse in the mouth!'

'It's like sittin' on spikes,' Dan grunted.

'Well, I'm still glad we drove.'

'Ach, that's why we're here,' Karl touched his tattoo and switched Beethoven to Metal. Angie slapped the back of his head. 'I'm the driver. Like the captain of a ship, I'm the boss,' he looked sideways at Angie, grinned and turned up the volume and winked at Dan. Jane rolled her eyes.

A huge face with a piggy snout nose and smiling mouth and eyes on two bricked up windows, watched all pilgrims approaching. The baby blue building was daubed with sayings; Bar Elvis, No Pain, No Glory is sprayed above a tilted wine glass and a happy sun.

Ubiquitous red plastic chairs crowded around the tables outside. Most were empty, except for three pilgrims under an umbrella, picking noses and blisters between a coffee breakfast. The popping of the exhaust attracted their attention and smiles. One took two crouching steps, miming someone diving for cover. The other aimed his phone. It clicked.

* * *

'Oh!' Jane leaned backward, twisting her head, mouth open to take in the multi coloured texts covering the yellow walls. They entered the cult pub, eyes oscillating, drinking in details like kids entering an Aladdin's cave. Gypsy King is the best. Camino is life, Brian loves Mary, Viva Mexico. Greta mit Liebe, the way is the aim and Leslie loves Leslie. No pain no gain, Camino is not a way of life - it is life! Countless other messages from thousands of pilgrims across the globe were on every surface available.

'There must be a thousand thoughts on these walls!' Dan turned full circle to take in handwritten messages in many languages of the world. The wonderful inheritance of thoughts and feelings of countless pilgrims who had passed through to enjoy the cool bohemian bar for bocadillos, beer, and Rock 'n' Roll.

'Hi!' Angelique patted the shoulder of a slim fit man. His black beard tinged with white, framed a broad grin. He made a mock salute.

'Buenos Dias!' He set four beers on the bar without being asked.

'I need this,' Dan gasped and emptied the glass in one go. He glanced at the T-shirts of all colours hanging along the wall. A red shirt showed the face of Che Guevara. 'Reminds me of Jesus' face on the Veil of Veronica.'

'Ach, cool,' Karl nodded and sank the rest of his beer, his eyes on a TV high on the wall, running non-stop music videos.

'He is a famous character of the Camino,' Jane whispered. 'Debbie wrote me about him.'

'Maybe she wrote somethin' on the wall,' Dan nodded at the wall behind the bar.

'The writing on the wall behind the bar is mine,' the man smiled, waving his hand at it. 'Then pilgrims asked if they could write their thoughts, too' he spread his arms. 'Now the whole room is full of their wonderful words and feelings. I built this bar out of two old stables,' he laughed. 'Now I work twenty hours a day and get the right to be the cleaner!' he chuckled.

'Busy man,' Angelique smiled, focusing on his biceps and fiddled with her arrow piercing, as if aiming it at him.

A car screeched to a halt out side and a second later roared away. The door opened and a medium sized giant pilgrim entered. He had a smear on his chin that could have been a beginner's goatee. 'Has anyone asked for a backpack to be delivered here?' A red backpack dangled from his huge hand. Jane gasped her hands clapped over her mouth, her eyes grew like lakes. 'Is it yours?' the man grinned eyeballing both Jane and Angie with a connoisseur's appreciation.

'That is Debbie's!' Jane's lips trembled. She grabbed the pack and grasped tatty little bear in the net pocket. 'We chose our backpacks together!' She sniffed it. 'Mildew.' She looked at the jolly giant. 'Thank you. Where was it?'

'A car stopped. Dropped it from the window. Very shoddy service I'd say. Anyway, good luck and buen camino. See you around,' he smiled, winked at Jane and left.

'Thank you! Thank you!' Jane called after him, clutching it to her chest letting tears roll all over it. Angie placed her arm across her shoulders. Karl wrinkled his forehead and scratched his tattoo. After a moment's silence she pulled out a single flip-flop and placed it on the bar counter. She plunged her hand inside and groped and brought out a silver metallic cosmetic tin, its enamel lid discoloured from moisture. A pair of mildewed brown socks, a quick-dry towel and a moon cup. 'Oh, my God!' she dropped the bag on the counter and buried her face in the backpack while her shoulders jerked in body-shaking spasms. Angelique took her elbow and led her back to the chair. Jane's head sank onto Angelique's chest and she bawled her eyes out. Everyone watched, helpless at her grief.

'Can you leave us?' Angelique ordered more than asked. Dan and Karl looked sheepish and went outside.

* * *

Dan had swallowed a full bottle of water when the door finally opened. Jane came out. Dan opened his mouth to speak, saw Jane's expression and stilled his tongue. Her eyes were red but dry. Her jaw was set. Her demeanour had, in some way, changed. Her jaw was set firm, lips pressed together, eyes fixed like a hunter.

'I'm taking this home.' She hugged the backpack.

'I'll lock it in the car,' Karl said.

'Wait! I found this inside.' She held an envelope out. 'You read, Dan. Please.'

Dan took the envelope from her shaking hand and drew a folded sheet out of it. Her eyes stared at him as he read. 'It's a name,' he said. 'Cruz Santo Justo.'

Karl tapped his laptop, googled the name, traced a finger along the trail. 'Here! Santo Justo!' he stared at Jane.

'We're friggin' pawns in a friggin' game. We are

told where to go and we go! I don't like it.'

'Mensch! We do not know who is playing with us,' Karl said.

'Bastard, bastard, bastard!' Jane snarled, snatching it back from Dan. They gaped at her. 'You're right, Dan. The bastard is playing with us. Until...'

'Until what?' Karl rubbed his tattoo.

'Until he can kill one of us.'

'Who?' Karl looked alarmed.

'Me,' she said.

The silence was long.

'Right!' Jane snapped. 'We'll play his little game. I know he's always watching and I'm not playing it *his* way anymore. From now on it's *my* way.'

'Don't you think your mission's accomplished, Jane?' Dan murmured.

Jane's eyes grew wide. 'What!' Her eyes bulged in fury. Girls are being murdered!' she blasted. 'A man on the Camino is a serial killer and you say; We. Go. Home! God dammit, Dan!' Her mouth snarled and yelled. 'I'll go home when this monster is dead or caught! Understand?' She panted in rage. 'Didn't you hear what I said before?' she bellowed.

They all shrank back from her rage filled eyes.

'Well, Jane, I'd say you've made your point friggin' clear on that.'

'It couldn't be clearer,' Karl blew on his fingertips. 'But, it's a long walk to San Justo. Let me at least drive you to the location of Debbie's next postcard. Where was the next postcard from after she was here?'

'León,' Jane answered without looking.

'Gut! Everyone aboard and I will drive you to León.'

'Karl's right,' Angelique added. 'And think of the shopping!' she grinned. Nobody grinned with her. Karl touched his tattoo and shook his head slowly.

'But I do think you should consider how long this friggin' walk should continue.'

'Till we get the killer.'

'Catch the killer? How can we do that? We haven't one per cent of the resources of the police, and they can't even catch him,' Karl spread his hand helplessly.

'We have to contact the next potential victim.' Jane's jaw was set for confrontation.

'How?' Dan asked. 'We don't know who she friggin' well is!'

'I am.'

'You?'

'Yes. Me.'

'How?'

'He wants redheads. I'm a red head. He tried once. He'll try again.'

'Then I'll fuckin' stay. Some idiot has to protect you.'

'Oh! And you're the idiot who'll protect me, are you?'

'Well,' he shrugged. 'I can't see any other friggin' idiots here,' he grinned. 'Can you?'

'I don't need an idiot!'

'OK. Shall I go? I do have better things to fuckin' do, y'know!'

'Then go!'

'Jane!' Angelique cried, as Dan turned away. 'Dan! Come back here!' Her finger stabbed toward the ground at her feet.

Dan turned and sneered. 'Why? Ms-Clever-knows-all doesn't fuckin' need the likes of us!'

'Puh! Men!'

Dan hooked his pack over one shoulder. 'Can you give me a lift, Karl?'

Karl rubbed his tattoo and looked at Jane for approval.

A motor revved nearby. A car leaned as it jumped round the corner opposite the Elvis bar. It rocked to the other side in a tyre wailing curve and drove past backfiring. Dust flew in Dan's face. The car peeled rubber. A solitary cloud of blue smoke hung a few seconds in the hot air. The screaming engine dwindled into the distance.

'What are you doing down there?' Angie looked down at Dan lying prone.

'Didn't you hear it?'

'Ya, a car backfiring,' Karl shrugged.

Dan climbed to his feet and dusted his jeans. 'What d'you fuckin' think this is? A wormhole?' his eyes were wild with fury. He stuck his penknife into a mini crater in the wall just above his head. He wriggled the blade and drew out a squashed tiny object. They gathered round and looked at a small piece of brass and lead fused together in Dan's palm. He plucked it between his finger and thumb and dropped it into Angie's hand. She made a face and passed it to Karl. 'That's a fuckin' 32 calibre bullet and it just missed my fuckin' head, like the second one there,' he pointed to another small crater in the wall. 'Someone tried to kill me!' He looked at Jane. 'D'yer still think you don't need an idiot to escort you?'

'Puh! They might have hit my car and made a hole in it!'

Dan plastered her with a huge grin. 'Angie, nobody would've noticed another hole.'

SAN JUSTO CRUZ

Dan slumped behind a hot strong coffee. It steamed on the edge of a rough-hewn table under a small arcade of round wooden pillars in a cobbled courtyard. Above, on the first floor, a glasshouse of blue frame windows looked down upon an ancient metal well with a black metal lid. The house was the pilgrim Hospital de Órbigo in medieval times. Now it is the "Albergue Parochial". A stream flowed from mountains in a huge urban art wall mural ending at the edge of a real pool and a riot of plants that clattered everywhere. He was waiting for Jane to unglue herself from her bunk in the women's dorm. Another "We protect morals" type albergue. Jane was quite miffed when they had arrived the night before. Dan could not understand her irritation, as neither of them were getting their leg over in their functional platonic relationship.

'Hi Dan,' Alonso entered and sat opposite across Dan. His shirt looked as if it had come directly out of the drier. Dan assumed it was clean.

'Hi, Lonsey. Where's your bow tie? You look like the end of a bad night.'

'Yeah, sort of.'

'Too many girlfriends?' Dan grinned. Alonso was impassive.

'Can't stay long,' he gave Dan a slip of paper. 'I booked rooms in San Justo de la Vega just before Astorga.' He looked around. 'Where's Jane?'

'Still in the women's dorm.

Alonso's face hung tired. 'Dan. Can we take a short walk?'

Dan abandoned his coffee. They walked like friends in silence, to the endless bridge spanning the Órbigo River. Below them the hammering of the constructions for the medieval jousting festival echoed against the pillars.

'Wonderful, isn't it?' Alonso said. 'It's a 13th century. The main bridge in those times. It became part of the Pilgrim's Road.'

'Helluva a length!' Dan took out his camera as he set foot on the cobbled bridge.

'It was known as Passo Honroso. Honourable Crossing,' Alonso's eyes shone, he was now on his favourite subject. 'Don Suero, a knight from Leon, swore to be a slave to his lady love. An iron collar was fixed around his neck. He swore to remove it only after he and nine other knights won 300 jousts against foreign knights. The bridge was declared a Passage of Arms.'

'That's a lot of fighting. Did they win three hundred?'

Alonso shook his head. 'After a hundred and sixty jousts they were so badly injured that the judges stopped the challenge. They decided that honour had been satisfied and removed the collar.'

Dan hung over the bridge. 'What a fantastic spectacle,' he aimed his camera.

'It was destroyed to hinder Napoleon's troops, but later rebuilt exactly as it was.

'Look.' Dan pointed. 'The river flows under the first three arches only. Sixteen arches span dry land.'

'A hydro-electric dam reduces the water flow.'

Dan pushed his camera back in its case. 'I'm sure you didn't just come to tell me about this bridge, Lonsey.'

Alonso looked down at the crinkled surface of the river sparkling below them. 'I ask myself if you're doing too much for Jane. You put yourself at risk with Mendoza and Ramos. Now shots were fired at you.'

'I know all that, Lonsey.'

'Frankly, Dan, it's getting too dangerous for you. And Debbie was Jane's sister, not yours.'

'Should I leave Jane to walk alone?' Dan stared hard at Alonso.

'She has Angelique and Karl.'

'Jasus, I don't know Lonsey.'

'Look. I am here, too! I could even walk the trail with her, if it made you feel better.'

'Aw! Come on! Your friggin' time is cut out with your own job!'

'I am due some leave,' Alonso stifled a cough.

'With that friggin' cough you need a bed and not a

walk on the Camino!'

'Summer flu,' Alonso waved his hand. 'Nothing much. But what about my idea?'

'Super to offer for you to walk with her. But you don't look up to it.'

'Should she just give up?'

'Fuck, no way! She's now one fuckin' stubborn lady. Hate has given her unlimited energy.'

'I understand, but I'm still not happy. For your sake as well as Jane's.' Alonso cupped Dan's elbow as they walked. 'You have Mendoza on your back. And Ramos is most dangerous. I've checked his record.' Alonso rotated his phone in his hand. 'He was definitely discharged due to his mental instability. He uses any method to get what he wants.'

'Even if you accompanied her, I'd feel bad dropping her.' Dan sighed.

'I know how you feel, Dan. But she could hardly be referred to as your great friend.'

'No, but...'

'But what? You didn't even like each other at first!'

'No, but...!'

'You've known her for a very short time, Dan. Not what you could call it a life-long friendship.'

'True but...'

'You'll probably never see her again after this is over.'

'I promised...'

'Promised? Promised what? Be realistic, you're in a bunch of trouble here, and you've still got your job to complete.'

'That's true, but...'

'And what about your article?'

'To tell the truth, I haven't sent very much so far.'

'You could spend more time writing. I heard it's important to keep your job otherwise you lose visiting rights of your kids. You are risking a lot, Dan. Think about it!' Alonso's brow furrowed with worry as his eyes sought Dan's. 'Think of yourself for a change, Dan.'

'I know,' Dan shrugged. 'Jane's a royal pain in the ass, but I promised to help her. No matter what, no matter how. And, to the bitter fuckin' end!'

Alonso glanced at him out of dark brown eyes. 'I wonder why your comments do not surprise me one little bit. Just think about it. And your kids. Think about them.'

'I will,' Dan nodded. 'By the way, the knight of the bridge. Did he win his bride?'

'Yes, they married.'

'And lived happily ever after,' Dan smiled.

'One of the defeated knights harboured a grudge. He challenged Don Suero to a joust and killed him.'

'Jasus. How long after was that?'

'Over twenty years.'

'Twenty friggin' years!'

'We Spanish hold grudges a long time.' Alonso smiled without humour. 'Let me talk to Jane. She would understand if you left. I'll walk with her.'

'I don't friggin' know...'

'Look, Dan. If she agrees that it makes sense for you to leave, would you do it? For your kids? Your own kids, Dan? How old are they?'

Dan looked at the blue sky in silence. His eyes followed a stork launching from its nest on a nearby church tower. 'Twelve and ten. Girl, and a boy.'

'Their names, Dan. What are their names?'

'Lisbeth and Antony,' he said quietly, and ran a fingertip under each eye.

'Dan, they need you. You gotta go.'

'Ok, then. Just for my kids, as long as you keep a friggin' close eye on her.'

'You do not have to worry,' he clasped Dan's arm in comradely reassurance. 'I'll watch her every step of the way,' Alonso's teeth flashed against his tan. 'You can count on it. Even if it is the death of me.' He grinned again.

* * *

The trail opened out into a broad red earth way as wide as a motorway. Jane and Dan walked in the scorching lunar landscape edged by trees resembling dark giant broccoli. It was the way to Astorga.

'Dan!' Jane stopped.

'What?' Dan stopped and pulled out his bottle and took a swig of lukewarm water. 'What then?'

'In the trees! Behind me.' She had turned her back to the forest. 'There's a man. Near a cross. Watching!'

'Alone?' She saw his eyes scanning the baked landscape. 'Pretend to talk to me,' Dan looked over her shoulder. Her lip quivered.

'Ramos?' she whispered. She saw his eyes stop and narrow. For once she was glad of his army background.

'Got the bastard. He's not movin'. He's still near the cross.' His hand slid into a thigh pocket and drew his penknife. He opened the longest blade. Her eyes widened like headlamps, trying to read his eyes.

'What are you doing with that?'

'Nothin' I hope.' His eyes narrowed. 'He's standin' stock still.' He pulled out a pair of small field glasses and looked over her shoulder.

'What if he has a gun?'

'Then we'll see how useless a knife is at a shootin' party, won't we?'

'Oh, God!' She clenched her pelvic muscles as a tiny drop dampened her panties.

'No, it's not him either, nor Ramos,' Dan slipped the glasses away and closed the knife. 'Let's go.'

'What about the man?'

'It's a dummy,' he grinned and started walking towards the solitary figure.

He's not the only one, she thought, feeling foolish. They approached a life sized scarecrow wearing a realistic mask and straw hat with a pilgrim's staff in its hand. 'Camino for dummies. Very realistic.'

Jane said nothing and kicked one of the stones from the stone mound round the stone cross. *Good thing I wasn't alone,* she told herself. *I'd have had a heart attack.* 'Just a moment!' she almost leaped into the bushes. Dan waited patiently until she emerged. 'Ready,' she said and fell into step beside him. She didn't look back as they left the scarecrow behind.

The trees thinned as they climbed the trail onto a plateau of reddish desert wilderness scattered with bush and occasional trees.

'What's that?' Jane pointed at a long hump. A solitary tree guarded it. As they drew nearer, dots moved before the form that now resembled a ruin. The dot elongated into a cluster of figures outside the ruin.

Something indefinite in the middle of the pilgrims

wobbled in the heat currents. It solidified into a coloured market stand in the middle of nowhere in the dry gorse countryside. The ruin, golden in the afternoon sun, resembled an adobe fort, rounded and softened by the winter rains that drenched everything along the Camino. The tree became two, one each side of an old gaping entrance. They created an oasis of shadow, increased by large heavy white blossoms hanging low. Pilgrims were gathered round like shoppers. Sunburned hands pushed fruit into tanned faces as if looting a store. It was good to drink in the hot air. Jane's nose felt dry inside. She sneezed and drank as quickly as she could and then refilled her water bottle. Dan took a carton of orange juice. 'How much?' he asked a thin guy in bare feet with jet black hair tied in a bun.

A young man on a makeshift bed under a lean to shelter raised his head from his meditation. He rested against a white curtain on the wall displaying a black inked female face in the middle of a twelve-pointed star.

'Free or donations. You choose.' His eyes closed again.

Dan's coins resonated in a metal box. It resonated like an empty tin drum. He looked at Jane. 'Here we are in the absolute wilderness, surrounded only by earth, bush and sky, and wham! A man is givin' away free fruit and drink! His generosity is intimidatin'. I love it!' he turned his face to the sky.

'He's following the true traditions of the pilgrim way.' Jane smiled and fell silent.

'You're thinkin' of Debbie,' they sat on the ground.

'She stopped here. Everyone stops here. She drank here. Can we just rest here awhile? Before we continue to San Justo? This is a place where she was. On this very spot.'

He nodded. They sat under a tree in silence. Each looking out across the arid red earth dotted with hardy bushes that stretched for the 360-degree empty horizon.

Jane closed her eyes and thought of her sister and imagined her sitting on the very same spot. She wondered if this brought her nearer to Debbie or her spirit. *Would dad be thankful that I'm doing this? Even risking my life! I hope dad can respect what I've done, or at least tried to do. Not that I've had much luck with him in the past.* Her heart sank. *Why? Why am I even trying?* She heard Dan stir. The ground crackled under his boots. She opened her eyes and watched him staring across the arid landscape. Her gaze took in the wiry bush and grasses. *He's out there,* she told herself. A shiver went through her thinking that his eyes might be looking into her eyes from a distance. She felt exposed and vulnerable. A target.

'Jane?' Dan's voice pulled her back to the present.

'Yes?' she pulled her gaze away from the horizon against her will. Like being the first to look away when someone stares you down.

'Can I ask you a personal question?'

'How personal?'

'Very personal.'

'How in fact do you define *very* personal?'

'Well, Jane,' he paused.

'Yes?' *God! I hope he's not about to propose!* Goose bumps ran all over her. She rubbed her arms.

'Fuckin' personal.'

'Oh! *That* personal.' She sucked in her cheeks. 'Very well. Go ahead, Dan.'

'I'm friggin' puzzled.'

'I'm curious.'

'The other day you said Debbie was a bitch. That made me wonder why are you friggin' botherin' to do this.'

Jane stared at the toe of her left boot. The surface had a deep scratch. She took a deep breath. Looked at the sky. Looked at Dan. 'Guilt.' She watched him. 'I felt guilty because I refused to go with her. She got everything paid for by my dad. I had to earn everything I needed. She wanted me to go with her. She said it was a cool thing to do. I simply couldn't afford it. Just to be cool. Just to keep her company. My old car needed major repairs. And I had a job interview to get the job I have now. I decided to use my money on that.'

'That's a rational reason.'

'Debbie couldn't understand. Didn't want to understand. Dad bought her everything; new car, clothes, flat, pocket money, even though she had a good job. She was the apple of his eye.'

'Spoilt,' Dan nodded.

'I hated her when we were young. She flirted with every boy. She even took away a boy I loved,' she shook her head. 'I thought I'd got over it. But when I said I couldn't afford it, she got angry and called me a bore who was too dumb to handle my husband. I walked out and left her. So she walked the Camino alone.' Her foot drew a half circle on the ground. 'And never came back.' She clapped her hand across her eyes, but the tears crept through.

'It wasn't your fault.'

'But if I had gone with her, she would still be here!'

'And you'd be broke without a job.'

'That's not the way my parents saw it.' Her tear-filled eyes looked at Dan. 'They never *said* that they considered me in some way guilty of her disappearance, but I could feel it in every cell of my body when they looked at me.'

Dan's hand squeezed her arm. 'Jane. It's fate. Fate presents us with many forks in the road of life. Nobody can know which the true way is. Sometimes there is no true way.'

'Mum died, never knowing what happened to her daughter. I promised them I'd find out.' She looked at Dan with red rimmed eyes.

'Dry your eyes.' Dan tugged his neckerchief from his neck. 'You're here for the wrong reasons. You should live for yourself and the one's you love. Not for others who misuse you. I get the impression you sacrificed enough in the past. Don't sacrifice your future to guilt. Debbie was adult and responsible for her own actions. Not you.'

'I can't stop now, Dan. I have to complete my mission of paying homage. This is my pilgrimage. My father would never ever forgive me if I quit. I must do this, don't you see? I must make the killer pay. Not only for what he did with Debbie, but for the other girls I may save.'

She knelt and pulled the suede sack from her backpack. The sack rattled as she took out a small empty jar and a spoon. Dan watched a spoon full of earth wander into a tiny jar. He bent and looked closely at the silver metal lid on the trail. He recognised the lid of the little breakfast jars of jams found in hotels.

'What are you friggin' doin'?'

'I promised my parents' I'd bring back some soil from every place where she had possibly stood.'

* * *

'San Justo cross,' Dan pointed at a mighty fifteen-foot white stone cross contrasting against the bright sky. It dominated the widest part of the trail before the Way dived down to chocolate town Astorga in the valley below. The cross stood on a stone plinth of four broad circular steps. Each step was covered in stones placed by passing pilgrims.

Jane had recovered her composure. She searched the surrounding baked terrain. Apart from a few pilgrims ahead the area was empty. They approached the white cross.

'Dan!' Jane grabbed his arm. 'Look! At the top of the cross.'

'What is it?'

'It's Debbie's hat!' They stared at a green bucket hat placed on the very top, like the helmet of a fallen soldier on a battlefield.

'It's Debbie's!'

'How do you know?'

'I know!'

'The bastard!' Dan's jaw was on the floor, but Jane's clenched like a vice.

'It's her fishing hat. She took it with her.'

'I'll get it down.' Dan said.

'No!' She grabbed his arm, 'No you won't, Dan!' Her irises blazed sparks. 'It stays there.'

'Why? If it's Debbie's!'

She grabbed his collar. His eyebrows shot up to

his hairline. 'Because he's playing with us! Chasing us from place to place with these bloody clues. Now *I'm* calling the shots!' she jabbed her chest with her thumb. 'Me! I'm changing the rules of play. Right now! The game is over! He's watching. Now he can wonder why I'm not doing what he wants. In your own delicate expression Mr Dan Brady. This game is fucking over!' They stood face to face like gunfighters. 'Watch!'

Stones from the plinth base clattered to the ground as Jane climbed. She swept some from the next step and climbed till she reached the top. She looped her left arm round the cross. Her eyes were ice cold as she dominated the terrain. Contempt creased her upper lip as she drew in a slow, deep breath through nostrils flared by anger.

'Go on, Jane,' Dan smiled and nodded. 'Let the bastard have it.'

'I know you're out there!' she hollered. She clung to the cross like a sailor to a mast and pointed over Dan's head at the bushes beyond. 'Bastard!'

'Great, Jane! That's fuckin' cathartic!' Dan punched the air. Several pilgrims gathered and looked at Jane and then Dan.

'Yes, you! You cowardly little worm!' she yelled over Dan's head. 'You,' she pointed. 'You pathetic, ignorant, dumb, moronic, brain dead pitiful excuse for an impotent half-man!'

'Yeah!' Dan punched the air.

'You coward hiding in the dark, abusing a religion and women like a sick pervert!' More pilgrims gathered with tennis spectator eyes. Some gave Dan puzzled looks.

'You! Yes, you!' she pointed again directly over

Dan's head.

'You have an IQ lower than a worm! You are a dumb, blind, ignorant, moronic, cowardly worm that belongs in a dog's excrement!' She shook her fist like a politician. More pilgrims gathered and looked in Dan's direction. 'You. Won't. Get. Me! Understand, worm? You. Won't. Get. Me! But I. Shall. Get. You! You big er, er, FUCK!'

'Whoooeee!' Applause burst out from a crowd of pilgrims who had gathered unnoticed in a semicircle around Jane on the plinth. Many threw scathing looks at Dan. Jane jumped, caught by another pilgrim who gave Jane high fives. The woman Dan had met in Los Arcos sneered at him and turned her back. Dan glared at Mr Tennis shoes grinning among the crowd.

A Chinese pilgrim patted Dan's shoulder and looked sadly in his eyes. 'Don' be sad my friend. Maybe she no mean everything she say about you.'

* * *

Half an hour later they had descended the hill to Astorga and its famous Gaudi palace. They passed an old man playing guitar at the edge of the Way, whose hat lay open at his feet. Coins flowed from Dan's hand and tinkled in the hat. The cement way hit asphalt. Cars swished by on the road that became the main street of San Justo de la Vega, on the outskirts of Astorga.

'There's our accommodation for tonight,' Dan poked his chin at the Café Bar Oasis, a red brick corner building in front of them.

Inside, Angelique and Karl were catching up on their drinking.

'You missed a fuckin' great speech up at the cross,' Dan grinned. 'She told Mr Shit and a load of pilgrims exactly what she thinks of him.'

'If he was there to listen,' Karl rubbed his tattoo.

'He's always there, Karl.' Jane said. 'Up till now, I've been scared of him,' she stared them all out. 'Now, he'd better watch I don't see him first.'

'Good for you, Jane,' Angelique clasped her arm. Jane's eyes gleamed with pride.

'Let's eat and get to bed early,' Jane grabbed the menu. They ordered quickly and ate in silence.

'I wonder what he'll try next,' Angie pondered.

'He can try what the hell he likes,' Jane pinned her eyes with hers. 'Whatever he starts, I'll finish it. Then it's going to be game over for the bloody bastard.

'I like that.' Karl gave a thumbs up and smiled. 'I better see that I get enough sleep. Good night.' He left the room.

'I'll be off, too,' Jane followed him.

Dan and Angie sat and listened to the sound of Jane's feet on the wooden stairs.

'Drink?' Dan offered.

'Only if it's strong,' she wrinkled her nose.

Dan went to the bar and returned with two whiskeys.

'Jane's changed a lot in the last few days.'

'I get that feeling, too,' Dan said. 'She really gave it to the killer, if he was listening,' he chuckled.

'She used to be a bit, how do you say, timid?'

'Not any more. She's really grabbed the reins now.'

'Her sister was very different.'

'So I believe,' Dan nodded and thought of Jane's remark. He looked at Angie as she sipped her drink. 'Angie, did you know Jane's sister?' Angie looked at him and nodded.

'What was Debbie like?'

'Trouble. You'd have liked her.'

'What do you mean by that?' Dan's forehead wrinkled.

'She took what she wanted. Friends, clothes, holidays, men... She didn't care whose men.'

'Including Jane's?'

'Often.'

'Often?'

'Life was a game for Debbie.'

'That must have hurt Jane. But why? Jane's a good-looking woman, too?'

'Debbie was brash, brazen and bold. Jane's confident but quiet and reserved.'

'Who dares wins,' he quoted the SAS motto.

'Debbie always dared. And she won. Always.'

'Competition for you, too?

'Let's say, she made me look like a nun.' Angie smiled and plastered Dan with eye contact.

'Not any more,' Dan smiled.

'No. But Jane feels guilty.'

'That has to end sometime.'

'Her parents made her feel that way. Her mother died not long ago. It almost destroyed Jane. She even blamed herself for that, too.'

'Broken heart at losing Debbie?' Dan asked.

Angie sipped her drink. 'That and cancer. Lungs. I met her a few times. Very funny most of the time,' Angie smiled at a memory.

'What about her father?'

'Rich. Accountant for a scrap metal firm. He got rich through a management buy-out. Clever.' Angie stared at the floor, eyes distant. She looked up again. 'Debbie was his darling. His little princess' She couldn't do a thing wrong in his eyes. Subconsciously he held Jane responsible for her disappearance.'

'That must have hurt one hell of a lot.'

'Yes. Debbie was not worth it.'

'Then why are you here?'

'Well, not for Debbie.'

'And the killer? Doesn't he frighten you?'

'Merde. He was already here.'

'What does Karl say?'

'Ask him.'

'He doesn't say much.'

'Text him,' she smiled and rose from the chair. Dan took in her figure. Her smile grew. 'I hope I haven't said too much.'

'I appreciate it, Angie,' Dan's eyes creased when he smiled.

'Good night, Dan.' She bent and kissed his forehead. He smiled some more and watched her walking through the door to the stairs. The sound of Karl, chain-sawing the whole Black Forest, echoed from the room above.

RAMOS

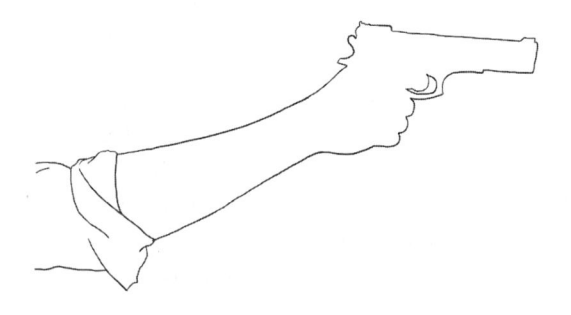

Midnight. The room smelled of stale sperm and alcohol. The lights were dimmed for sex. But no sex was happening in the crappy single room apartment. A late-night movie punched through the thin wall from a similar hutch next door. It was the sixth floor of a cheap Pamplona housing project designed by architects with a grudge against people. The sort of public building that should have been demolished the day it was completed as a favour to people of taste. A beer bottle, sucked half empty, stood on a low table next to a photo of a soldier with a mean expression. Another three dead bottles lay together on the floor leaving blobs of froth on the rug next to a tatty porno mag.

A hand flashed inside a jacket lapel. It reappeared in a split second. A matt grey SIG SAUER pistol pointed at the figure in front of the muzzle. He aimed for the chest. Paused and returned the pistol to his shoulder holster. He was drunk but still fast. He sneered. His facial scar twisted from ugly to repulsive. He ran his finger nails inside the deep cut. The owner of the knife had died slow and hard.

'I give you one more chance,' he hissed through clenched teeth.

He drew again. His hand was a blur. 'Hey, my friend? Fast enough?' He grinned and repeated the action three more times, trying to outdraw himself in the full-length mirror. A burst of machine gun fire erupted in his pocket. He grabbed his phone 'Sí?' He rubbed his hand across his bald head and listened. 'Sí, Brady. Sí,' he nodded. Grunted. Pressed cut off. He held the pistol in front of himself, pulled out the magazine from his pocket and slapped it into the handle of the pistol with a solid click. He pumped a round into the breech and snapped on safety.

'Bastardo!' Ramos spat the word like a bullet.

* * *

'Mommy? Are you awake.' He looked around the room. It depressed him. Her covered form lay as always under the outline of the missing crucifix.

'I'm always awake, Sugar. That whore cost me my eyelids, remember? I can never get to sleep with these damned lights on twenty-four seven.' The figure in the bed lay with the sheet over her face.

'I know, Mommy. It was a viscous attack,' he sobbed quietly. 'I made her pay for her deed, Mommy.'

'I know. You're a good boy, Sugar. Nobody else

visits me here.'

'I feel so bad, Mommy.' The crack of his knuckles was loud in the small room.

'Don't do that, Sugar.'

'Sorry, Mommy. But I still feel bad.'

'Bad? Why is that, Sugar? You ain't bad. You're full of grace. How can you feel bad?'

'The Eva. She called me things. In front of a load of people! It was terrible!'

'What things did she call you?'

'You can't imagine. She called me things as if I was the lowest thing on this earth. A worm, a dog, slime and all sorts of nasty things. She insulted me so badly and even called me dog poo.'

'She's a powerful Succubus. You have to save her at all costs, Sugar.'

'She is protected by others. She is never alone!'

'It's because of a Succubus like her that I am locked up in this damned clinic. She's gotta pay, Sugar, so I can come out of this place.'

'I'll get her Mommy.'

'You gotta take risks, Sugar. The Lord will protect you. Nobody can hurt you.'

'But I can't kill on the Camino. Never on the Camino. I always make them leave the Camino before I save them.'

'That's good. No blood on the Camino, Sugar. Not on our sacred Camino,' she croaked.

'I feel bad in my body, Mommy. Getting worse.'

'That is your test!' she hissed. 'The Lord will reward.'

'I don't think I have long, Mommy...'

'That's not an illness. It's a test to be ready for the Lord's embrace. Only by suffering can we enter heaven. Saving others makes you more secure, Sugar.'

'I am so tired.'

'Go home! Sleep, Sugar. Do some painting. Relax and gather your energy for your mission.'

'I'll sleep now. I'll sleep for strength.'

'Yes. You need your strength. She is dangerous for us. For you. If she desecrates us, you will lose your place in heaven at the side of the Lord.'

'No! No! Don't say that, Mommy,' he sobbed. 'That's my only hope.'

'Then go and save her, Sugar. Kill that goddamn swine from hell!'

'I shall, Mommy! I shall!' he wept.

'Choose a place that leaves a symbol, so everyone knows what she really is. Choose a place to show the world, even if you sacrifice yourself, Sugar.'

'I shall, Mommy.' The figure paused. 'Mommy?'

'Yes, Sugar?'

'You asked me for something you need.'

'Do you have it?' Her hand slid from under the sheet.

His hand drew out a small white, cardboard box and pressed it into the acid scarred palm.

* * *

Silence. Alonso felt confronted with a mini Mount Rushmore. Four impassive faces stared silently like the presidents tight lipped stoney faces in South Dakota. Only the barman of the Bar Oasis dared to hum a Spanish love song while he cleaned the bar top, but then he did not hear what Alonso had said.

Coffee scented the room. A mountain of scrambled eggs quaked on Karl's plate, threatened by the fork in his left hand. Right forefinger suspended over his tablet. Alonso faced four stunned faces, mouths agape, eyes lasering him. Food cooled on forks suspended in stilled hands.

'What did you say, Lonsey?' Jane finally broke the silence.

'We arrested the killer.'

'Yeah!' Dan shouted and punched the air. 'Woweee!'

'Who is it?' Jane sounded breathless.

'I don't know much. He's an American who lived in Spain for more than twenty years. He's not talking yet.'

'Ach, gut!'

'Merde! I can't believe it!' Angie dabbed her eyes.

'Just lemme at the bastard,' Dan hissed through clenched teeth. His fist thudded into his opposite palm with a thud. 'Then he'll fuckin' talk!'

'No, Dan,' Karl shook his head, the corners of his mouth turned down. 'Violence breeds only more violence.'

'Where was he caught?' Angie said.

Alonso shrugged. 'A man is helping us with inquiries.'

'There is nothing in the Internet,' Karl tapped on his tablet.

'There won't be. Not before he's charged.'

'Why don't you know, Lonsey?' Angelique squeezed his arm.

'I'm suspended from the case,' his eyes were vacant. 'That is my bad news for today.'

'Fuck! That is bad shit.'

'The positive side is I can help you.' Alonso cocked an eyebrow in an attempt to look light hearted. 'You can all relax! Dan can catch up on his interviews. You can relax, walk at your own speed, Jane. No hurry. No worry.'

'But I could still get picked up by friggin' Mendoza.'

'I've thought about that, too,' Alonso said. 'You could return to the beginning of the Camino and interview pilgrims there. Mendoza will not expect that.'

'Ach, gut! Now Jane can finish her mission in peace.'

'I can help out along the way.' Alonso smiled. 'I can get Dan out of the country, too. If you want, Dan.'

'God! What a relief!' Jane dabbed her eyes. 'Even if it doesn't change the past. I'll be happy to continue in peace.'

'Ach. I'm glad the killing is over.'

'The fuckin' killer should be strung up!'

'No,' Karl wagged his finger at Dan. 'History shows that violence does not work! We live in a democracy with democratic processes. He has to be tried and serve his sentence.'

'My instincts tell me otherwise,' again Dan's fist connected with the palm of his hand with a meaty thud. 'He should still taste a bit of what he meted out to others.'

'I don't agree...' Karl began.

'Oh! Fuck off with your fuckin' Do-Gooder crap!' Dan's chair clattered to the floor in a back flip. He stormed to the bar as if he wanted to knock it over. 'Whisky!'

'How do you like your whisky, Señor?' the barman smiled.

'In my friggin' stomach!'

'Dan!' Angelique called and rushed after him. 'Danny,' she whispered holding his elbow, shaking it slight to make sure of his attention.

'Only close friend call me Danny,' he growled.

'I want to be a close friend Danny. I think I already am.'

Silence.

'Danny?'

'Yeah?' His lips were tight. Eye hard as stone. Hand shook, making the whisky swirl slightly, catching the light like a semaphore. 'Yeah, Angie?'

'I know how you feel,' she whispered sadly.

'How would a girl who spends time havin' *fun*, know how I fuckin' feel? Huh? Tell me that!'

She blinked back sudden wet pearls. Her jaw set hard. 'Merde!' she hissed and punched his arm. He looked hard at her. Her eyes widened to his challenging eyes 'Look! Mr Why does the world hate me!' She rolled up her sleeve. 'Look!'

Dan sipped his whisky and looked at the bottle behind the bar. 'I noticed before. Didn't want to ask.'

'I tried to save an old man from muggers in a back street in Lyon. One pulled a knife and...' She rolled down her sleeve and hid the scar. 'He slashed tendons that ruined my career as a pianist. Can you understand? I was not a *fun* girl! I practiced every day till my fingers felt as if they were falling off!' She stabbed his chest with a strong finger. 'So don't dare call me a little *fun* girl!'

'Sorry, Angelique,' Dan's voice was quiet. 'Did the bastard get caught?'

She nodded. 'Five years prison. He served three. It took me two years to get my courage back to walk a dark street again.'

'Three years inside! That's friggin' peanuts!'

'I met him. He was sorry! He cried. Then we both cried.'

'Angie, you're amazin' I have to admit and I apologise for misjudging you.'

'Dan?' She searched his eyes. 'Dan!' her voice lowered. 'I forgave him.'

His eyebrows hit his hairline. 'What the fuck for?'

'To take back my future, Dan. The past is past, and the future can be worth more if you try. One should learn from the past and be wiser, and not see it as a photo that is always the same. Looking at the same old photo means you see the same thing again and again and again. It never changes, so you won't either.'

'I dunno...' he shook his head.

'Hate holds you in the past and becomes a model for the future. It's a destructive spiral. I don't want that. Dan, I know you've had a hard life as a child but lose it, Dan! Forgive them! Don't go down that road anymore, Dan. Please.' Dan touched the tears that coursed down her cheeks. His fingers stroked them away.

Dan closed his eyes tight. He stood stock still. Silent. Breathing deep.

'Dan?'

His eyes popped open. He looked at her. 'Angie, I think I just fully realised what a good person you are,' he wiped his own eyes and squeezed her in a crushing bear hug.

'You're stronger than I thought,' she stepped back,

smiled and pressed her lips to his.

'Wow! What a kiss,' his face almost disappeared in his wide grin.

'Promise me you'll get into the present, and stay there, and think of the future! Don't go into the past anymore! Look forward! Understand? If you look backwards you miss the future! Danny, a guy like you could make it magnifique if you tried.'

'Jasus, I know. You're both right.' He slugged his whisky. His eyes glittered. 'I've known violence, too. I never forgave them,' he said and closed his eyes and took a long, slow, deep breath. 'It's hard.' He opened his eyes. They were wet. He swallowed, hugged her again, grabbed her hand and led her back to the table. 'Sorry, Karl,' He held out his hand. 'I was seriously out of line just then. I acted like a complete prick,' he said blushing. 'Sorry, Karl. Sorry everybody.'

'Ach, it's ok, Dan.' Karl said. 'You're an impulsive man, but that's alright, too,' he grinned and scratched his binary. 'Now let us think of our choices.'

'I walk my walk,' Jane was resolute.

'Dan, you can leave Spain,' Karl suggested.

'Or hide along the Camino from Mendoza or Ramos,' Angelique said.

'Or we all go home,' Karl rubbed his tattoo.

'Or we friggin' well carry on as planned.'

'I'll finish my mission, no matter what.' Jane's look challenged them.

'We'll stay with you,' Angelique said. Karl nodded in slow motion.

'Dan, why not catch up on your interviews before you get fired?' Jane said. 'It could affect your visiting rights with your kids. Why risk that, Dan? We'll manage alright,' she patted his arm. 'Don't worry.'

'Ok,' Dan looked at the floor.

'Actually...' Jane began.

'We walk the walk,' Angelique smiled. 'If Dan is doing his own thing, then I'll walk with you. Especially the next bit to the Cruz de Ferro.' She linked her arm in Jane's. 'Should be fun!' her nose wrinkled. 'Just like old times.'

'I'll drive ahead with all your stuff and meet you there,' Karl said.

'Oh, you with your flat feet!' Angelique slapped the back of his head.

'I'll walk as far as Rabanal with you,' Dan said

'But remember,' Alonso looked at him. 'Ramos is on the loose. Mendoza fired him, and he blames you. Keep your eyes open.'

Jane pressed her lips tight together. 'Can't he be arrested?'

'He has not broken the law so far.' Alonso shrugged. He will strike, but I don't know where or how.' Alonso sat down short of breath.

'Ach, he already has,' Karl said. 'That bullet didn't come from heaven,' he rubbed his tattoo.

'All I want to do is complete the final part of my mission,' Jane said.

'What is the final part, Jane?'

'I have to finish something in Santiago de Compostela.'

Nobody said a word. Jane outlined her plan.

SANTA CATALINA

Jane sat in the garden of the albergue and watched the sun, red like Mars. The shadows of the Camino grew as it sank behind the roofs of Santa Catalina, dragging the darkness towards it. For a few seconds it silhouetted the peaks they'd climb tomorrow. She shivered slightly and hugged herself. Birds ceased their songs. A dog barked. Another replied. A car door slammed like a drum. Someone in the next house called and laughed. Three shadows at the next table sipped beers. Jane went inside the albergue to find her bunk.

Two snoring heads were breaking the sound barrier in the small dormitory. Before the moon flooded the window, she heard Dan already competing with the best of them.

Jane felt endless relief after Alonso's good news. Weight had dropped from her shoulders like a coat of chain mail. *A man's been apprehended*, she thought. *He's off the Camino! Gone! Super! You're safe. Relax.* A picture of a dark faceless shadow figure formed in her mind. *Will he admit to the killings? Will he tie himself in knots and confess?* she wondered. *Would he be insane and proud? Boast about his exploits? Lead the police to graves? To Debbie?* She shivered as the thoughts ploughed through her mind leaving her on an ocean heaving with speculation. She floated in wish dreams, forcing a happy end, or at least an end with some relief. Possible closure for herself and her dad back home. *Will dad forgive me?* she wondered. After a while she lost all feeling for time and woke in starts; her T-shirt wet and clammy. Her leg itched. She thought of bugs, but felt too tired to do anything about it. She was half aware of shadows drifting to and from the communal bathrooms. At some point, she couldn't recall when, her heavy eyelids drooped and stayed closed.

Moments later she woke. It had seemed like seconds. The sun had pushed the night away from the moon and pulled Jane out of her slumber. Where did the night go? She felt hot and clammy. Itchy things on her skin. Rubbed and scratched. She wriggled out of her nylon refuge.

'Very elegant,' Dan's voice came from the next bunk. 'You look like a giant moth wriggling out of its cocoon.' He grinned at her.

'You're not so elegant yourself, Mister,' She yawned.

'Four Korean girls on the top bunk are watching

me.'

'They're meditating,' Jane said. 'They're just four of the thousand odd Korean girls hunting the Camino for a guy.'

'I wish them luck.' His mouth opened in a tonsil waving yawn. 'Why are you up so early?'

'Your snore concert kept me awake for the first half, my dreams for the rest.'

'It was Alonso's news that kept you awake, didn't it?'

'The hunt is over. It changes the whole situation.'

'Yeah, I had the same friggin' dreams,'

'You disguised your sleepless night very well.'

'They were deep dreams,' He grinned and kicked his way out of his sleeping bag.

'Get ready,' she said and headed for the already crowded washroom.

'Yeah, yeah,' he stretched and cut through other pilgrim's headlamps, swiping the dawn like swords of Jedi knights. He looked at Karl's bunk. His eyes were open. 'Awake, Karl?'

'Ya yaaa,' He rolled and showed his back.

'Sleep ok?'

Ya yaaa,' his voice was deep within the sleeping bag.

'Comin' to breakfast?'

'Ya yaaa.'

'Karl, have you ever thought of walkin' for a bit the Camino?'

'Ach nein! Why? When I have four healthy tyres under my ass.'

***

'Sugar! You're early. Is it light outside?' Is anything wrong?'

'It's light. It's six o clock. I couldn't sleep.'

'Mommy?'

'Yes, ma Sugar.'

'I want to stop.'

Both remained silent. The sheets rustled. She pulled the sheet away. He gasped. The taut, acid scarred mask still shocked him. He looked at the floor.

'Stop?'

Yes, Mommeee! I want to stay here. With you!'

A long silence hung between them. Seconds ticked by. He waited. The silence got even louder with every second, and other sounds, normally suppressed became audible, her breathing with a slight rasp, a gurgle in the water pipes, a moan of a jet twenty thousand feet above their heads, a radio three rooms down, all became thunderous screams in the growing silence, making him fidget.

'Alright, Sugar,' her voice broke the terrible disorientating silence 'Get the woman with Brady. She's the mistress of Satan. You must rid the earth of her no matter what! Get her and you can come here, Sugar. Do it for Mommy, Sugar!'

'I'll do it.'

'The sooner you get that last Succubus, then the sooner you can come here,' she paused. 'Here to me, Sugar.'

'Here. For my remaining time, Mommy? Can I?'

'Get that whore, an' you can come here till it is

time.'

Thankful sobbing filled the bare room.

'Ah, I will, Mommy. I don't care what it takes. No more in the dark. I'll get them. No matter where they are! Day or night. I'll get them, Mommy.'

'If you don't Sugar, you might fail and end up in hell yourself.'

Sugar's sobs seemed to have no effect on Mommy. Her disfigured face was again hidden under the sheet. 'I spent years teaching you obediance to the Lord. Don't let me and the Lord down, Sugar.'

He fled the room, leaving another small box on the bed next to her hand.

* * *

Jane clasped her stomach as if she had won a gluttony contest. She sat at an outside table of the albergue where she had gobbled down two breakfasts. She wriggled a bit from damp panties that hadn't dried after washing them the previous evening. The sun bathed the church belfry that supported a big bundle of sticks that were a storks nest. It's inhabitant glided, wings curved like landing flaps, and made three landing attempts before wheeling away and soaring out of sight. She went inside the restaurant. Most pilgrims had departed on the chilly heels of dawn. Jane and her band were the last people left. Angie dozed. Karl checked his phone messages while Dan stared at his laptop screen. Jane poured a cup of hot water and dipped a fennel teabag into it.

'Have you got enough for your magazine?' Karl asked.

'I've heard so many stories, but I need to edit them. And I dunno if my editor will like any of it. About two hundred thousand people walk the Way of Saint James each year with two hundred thousand reasons. I tried to outline some of them,' he closed his laptop and looked into the distance.

'I talked to a man riding the Camino on horseback,' Angelique smiled. 'That's cool!' she giggled.

'So did I. And I met a woman who had her dead teenage daughter's age on the clam shell hanging from her backpack, Jane added.

'Ach ya! I talked to a German priest who is trying to regain his lost faith,' Karl rubbed his tattoo. 'At the same table there was a man from Switzerland who was bullied at work. He is going back home to quit his job while a Danish woman said she left her husband for her lover and then she left her lover for a woman.'

'I met some nuns who were frigg... er, human,' Dan smiled.

'Many reasons, as Dan says,' Jane's eyes went from one to the other. 'When I was at dinner in an albergue, a Russian and an American both cried with joy in each other's arms before strangers at the table.' They all chuckled.

'I talked to an American army soldier who is marching day and night, stopping only to nap at the edge of the trail,' Angie said.

'That's friggin' fantastic!'

'Of course *he* was!'

'Typical Angie!' Jane squeezed her arm.

'Why not!' she chuckled and threw Dan a look to make a good catholic priest break his vows. Dan laughed out loud. Jane kicked his foot.

'Did Jane, kick you Dan?' Angie grinned. 'She always does that under tables.'

'Well, some of my interviews were pretty good. I met a Jewish woman with her deceased mother's name round the heel of her right boot, and a group of Irish lads raising money for a friend with cancer. One told me a nice story about a pilgrim in a wheelchair. Other pilgrims passed him along the way. Then he came to a point where the ground was steep and rocky. He was stunned to find a group of pilgrims, who were all strangers to each other, had spontaneously waited for him. Then they carried him in his wheelchair to the top,' Dan sniffed and paused. He swallowed. 'That is the sort of story that moves a fella!'

'I would shake them all by the hand,' Karl nodded. 'That is true soul.'

'Do programmers have souls?' Dan grinned.

'Puh!' Angie slapped Dan across the back of his head.

Dan grinned. 'And I met Jane, seeking Debbie's soul. But I think I found my own.'

'Allez, that is better than pissing in a violin, wasting your time.'

They fell into silence. A man cleared his throat. A white beard stooped at the end of the table. 'Hi!' he smiled showing gaps in his teeth in a face lined like a road map. 'I couldn't help but hear what you guys were saying.' His accent was somewhere north of New York. 'Those stories of other pilgrims are great.' Everybody nodded. He took a slow deep breath. 'The factor in all those stories is time.'

'Ya, time,' Karl nodded. 'That is logical.'

'Sure!' a gnarled finger stabbed in Karl's direction. 'Time! You need it, and you sure can't find it lying around on the ground.' His one good eye followed their faces. 'You can lose it, but never find it.' His gaze roved over them. 'You gotta make it! Make it!' He placed a hand on the back of a chair to steady himself. His toothy gap flashed again. 'Listen!' he snapped like a commander, forty years younger. 'I'm very old. I'd thought about the Camino,' he nodded and stared Angie out. 'You're a pretty girl, if I may say, young lady. Both of you ladies,' his gap flashed again. 'But time is loaded like a dice against beauty. Like everything.' He seemed to nod off, then raised his head. 'Well, I always put it off till later. Always another time, later. Years flooded by in a torrent. Then I realised, one comes here *now*. Now or never!' He raised a preaching finger. 'Now or never,' he nodded. 'Like that Italian love song,' Recollections of the past drew a tired smile. 'But,' he returned to the present. 'I'm here. I came *now*. God said to me, if I don't grab my *now* with both hands, it's gonna become a never. I decided not to waste life grumbling about the past nor worrying for the future. If I have a future!' the gaps flashed again. 'I'm living my *now*, right *now*! The Camino *is* now. All those pilgrims have that in common. They are all doin' it *now* before they miss it and regret it till they die.' He stared. Everyone stared back in silence, like a contest. His gap reappeared. 'Well, that's all I got to say, I guess. That's the end of my preaching for today. God bless you and the things you dare to do.' He turned away. They erupted into spontaneous applause.

Angie and Jane dabbed their eyes. They all smiled

as if all their troubles were over but faded as Alonso appeared with a tense face.

Jane looked at him and said, 'Hi Lonsey. What happened to your dicky bow?'

'Oh!' he furrowed his brow as if trying to remember. 'Too much of a hurry, I think.' His forced smile wasn't convincing. 'I've come to warn you Dan.'

'Warn me about what?'

'Ramos is on the warpath.' Jane noticed that Alonso hadn't shaved. 'He found about the shooting incident in Afghanistan.' He looked at Dan. 'His brother was shot and killed by a British soldier. He thinks it was you, Dan.' They all looked at Dan in silence.

'I didn't shoot him! My mate shot him. I was hit by a Spanish soldier who was drunk. My mate shot him before the bastard shot me again! Self defence.'

'Ramos decided that you are to blame. He's looking for you!'

'He's fuckin' crazy!'

'And crazy enough to kill you. There is no logic in the thinking of a mad man.'

'What do you expect me to friggin' do?'

'Dan, now the suspected killer is in a cell, Jane can continue and you can lie low. In fact, I would say you have to, Dan. For Jane's sake.'

'You mean I should hide?' Dan's lip curled.

'Dan!' Jane bundled her fists. 'Don't be a hero!'

'Yes, Dan, you've done more than enough,' Angie's dark eyes were pleading.

'And, what's more,' Karl fingered his tattoo. 'It would mean violence. That will not solve anything! You will be hurt or worse.'

Alonso rested his arm on Dan's. 'Listen to them, Dan! They're right. Step back and let Jane get on with her mission. She's safe now without you worrying.'

'Dan. Think of your *kids*.' Jane's voice was a command. 'Go! You've been doing a balancing act trying to decide to go or stay. Now you have a good reason. So, go. Please, Dan. You've done enough for me. Go to your job and kids.'

'But..!'

'Please, go.'

'But, Jane..'

'Go!'

'After Rabanal.'

'Very well, but then you go.'

'Or maybe I...'

'Go!'

EL GANSO

The shadows stayed ahead of them. Jane, Angie and Dan followed the pilgrim's morning ritual of chasing their shadows across almost flat terrain of lush grasses and dark green bushes at the foot of the León Mountains. A few horses grazed in a nearby field. It was easy walking. Today's real climb had yet to begin and Karl was already heading to El Rabanal.

Jane's heart leaped. A tall wooden cross stood as if it had grown in tall grass ahead to her left. The thoughts of the murder victims left at other way crosses flooded back. *Could there be anyone under that cross?* She looked at Dan to see if he reacted at seeing another cross. He didn't. *He looks sad,* she told herself. *He feels he's giving up. He's not the type that gives up easily.*

They walked in silence and within an hour they passed the El Baracco Cowboy Bar in El Ganso. A stork flapped leisurely westward to the Cruz de Ferro that lay hours ahead of them.

They had read so much about El Baracco and the great evening parties, but this morning they wouldn't see much. The gates were barricaded and streets deserted. They came to a STOP sign at a street junction. Somebody had scrawled Don't above the STOP and Walking, below.

'Don't stop walking,' Jane said. 'That's good.'

'When are you leaving us, Dan?' Angie asked.

'As soon as I see a good café to have a second breakfast. That's the sole reason I have for walking with you lot.'

Jane saw through his bravado. *If only there weren't so many different issues! The killer and I, Debbie and I, my father and me. Then there's Mendoza and Dan, that horrible Ramos and Dan, his editor and a judge, all against Dan! Oh, God help him, please!*

'El Ganso means The Goose,' Angelique suddenly said.

'Named after the women who live here,' Dan grinned.

'Macho idiot!'

'I resemble that remark!' he chuckled.

Jane laughed and stared at him. 'Dan. You're impossible.'

'I know. My ex...!'

'... wife told you ten times a day, I know,' Jane finished for him. They filled their water bottles at a running tap protruding from the corner buttress of El Ganso church, it's bell tower flanked by two twiggy stark nests, one occupied by a grubby looking stork. It loudly clappered its beak and looked down with distain.

'God be with you,' said a priest next to the tap. The baggy knees of his trousers showed years of praying. 'The bible tells us to love.' The priest smiled.

'The Kamasutra tells us *how*.'

'You're back on form, Angie old girl,' Jane squeezed her arm. Angie's lips pressed together.

They passed a mix of abandoned houses and bombed looking cottages, on the verge of collapse, the signs of the exodus of youth fleeing the land and farming. At the last house the overhead cables ended, and the Camino dirt trail began, sounding like breaking toast beneath their boots.

'Hi Jane,' a high soft voice greeted behind. Jane swirled around. 'Li Li! How are you?'

'I'm good. Can I join you?' The Chinese woman fell into step.

'What will you do after the Camino?' Jane watched her from the side.

'Go home to my parents in China. I have been away six years in the USA. It is time to return and help them. We don't leave our old people alone.'

Jane nodded and thought of her father alone after her mother's sudden death. *I don't know if I want to go home again,* she told herself. *I don't even know if he wants me around after Debbie, his favourite, and my mother are gone. I wonder if Debbie would have taken care of him if she were still around. Debbie was a taker not a giver.*

She marched in silence, envying the solidarity that the Chinese woman described. *Another world, another culture. Why had dad preferred Debbie?*

'I wonder if we have lost something in our scattered-families-society.' Jane thought aloud.

'Your spirits and energy are not much connected,' Li Li said.

'My family is completely disconnected,' Jane said.

They followed their shadows west in silence under a blue sky, mottled with puffs of cumulus sailing above the steep mountains ahead.

The buzz of Dan's phone distracted her. She listened to Dan's voice.

'Hi Mr Prosser-Jones.' He listened. Jane saw his face fall.

'But, Mr Prosser-Jones, the deadline is still two weeks away!' He clicked on hands free and Prosser-Jones' whining voice filled the air.

'Sorry, Daniel, but the printers are calling a strike. I have to bring the deadline forward.'

'How much forward?'

'To now.'

'Now! Mr Prosser-Jones, I planned to edit the stuff here in case I need to redo any interviews.'

'Work around it, Daniel. Otherwise mother will cancel the project.'

'This is damned short notice!' Sweat beaded Dan's brow.

'The strike will ruin us. Be here, Daniel.

'The strike's not my friggin' fault!'

'I thought you wanted to keep your special projects job with us, Daniel.'

'Of course I do!'

'Good. Be here in two days.'

He stared at his phone. 'Fuck!' Dan was talking to himself. Worry and anger collided across his face. The three women watched his face and worried with him.

'He sounds rather cold hearted,' Jane said.

'A heart like his makes a four star freezer feel like a friggin' n oven.'

'That means you have to go,' Angie said.

'Yeah, and better yesterday than today!'

RABANAL

'Fried eggs!' Dan tried to sound cheerful as they reached the first house at the edge of El Rabanal de Camino; a village clinging to a steep hill like a limpet. The beginning of serious uphill walking to the Cruz de Ferro. A black metal wrought pub sign hung up high on the wall of the stone building. It boasted that it was the "Posada El Tesin."

'I can have another breakfast and record a few last-minute interviews,' Dan blinked into the sun strobing though the waving leaves opposite.

'Are you ok with your decision to leave, Dan?' Jane watched his face for signs of regret.

'I thought it over for the last kilometres. Now I have no choice. At least I know you are all right with Karl and Angie keeping your company. Plus Alonso.

The killer's in the slammer. I'm not needed,' he shrugged. 'My plan B wasn't needed. I'll do a few interviews here then order a taxi and make my editor happy. That'll go down well with the judge.'

'Then will you get your visiting rights back?'

Dan's eyes shone. His face squashed into a broad smile. 'Yep. I'll get to see Lisbeth and Antony,' his face split into a huge smile with a sparkle in his eyes that she had never seen before.

'I'm happy for you, Dan,' Angie hugged him, almost knocking him off balance. 'Keep in touch.'

'I will, t'be sure.'

'We'll buy some food to take with us and push on,' Jane said and went inside the bar where Johnny Cash was telling everyone He'd walk the line. Minutes later she returned with food in her mouth and in both hands. She shoved two fat bocadillos into Angie's side pockets. 'These are to eat at the very top of the Camino.' She stood before Dan. Her breath came in short gasps. She looked into his eyes. 'Thanks Dan. I don't think I'd have made it without you.' She hugged him and kissed both cheeks. 'We'll stay in touch. I have your phone number.' She punched his arm.

'Get up that mountain, girl and do your thing,' he winked.

She walked a few paces and turned. 'See you in England sometime,' she called back.

'I hope I don't have to go to England to see you,' Angie kissed and squeezed Dan tight. 'Visit, ok?' she pulled free. Her eyelid flickered.

'See you somewhere in France, I guess.'

'Don't wait too long!' She blew a kiss and turned to follow Jane. Dan watched them go. He sighed. He was used to moving on, dammit. That what life was about. Moving on. He sat, stretched his legs into his boots and relaxed. He watched Jane and Angie begin their steady climb with short, slow, measured steps, their boots tilted upward on the steep street. This was where the climb really started to reach the highest point of the Camino in the mountains of León. His eyes followed them till they disappeared behind the houses.

Karl watched in silence.

Dan felt a little lighter. He went inside and ordered and came back and stretched with the sun on his face, enjoying American country music that goes so well with bacon and eggs under a big blue sky. 'This is the life!' He stretched his arms and smiled into the sky until his breakfast plate slid onto the small table, joined by a giant, lighthouse-like bottle of ketchup.

'I read that an army marches on its stomach. You are the living proof,' Karl smiled.

'Sure. I joined the friggin' army just for the free meals,'

'Dan.' Karl rubbed his tattoo. 'Do you regret the past. Joining the army, getting shot. Would you change the past if you could go back in time?'

Dan thought, chewing on his food. 'Jane asked me that. She said she'll like to go back in time and stop her sister Debbie comin' here.'

'I wonder if that would be good.' Karl said.

'Well, I told her no. Somethin' else would have gone wrong. It's Sod's law. Life is like a train ride, Karl. Friends get on. Some get off. One day parents get off, new people get on, and all bring their new experiences, sorrows, joys on your journey of life.

One day you'll get off, and other friends will continue the journey without you. With luck, the good times outweigh the bad. No matter what, you should never go back and change the points on the line. The points move very little, but they can send you down a new track a thousand kilometres from where you are. You'll lose all the good times along with the bad. You will lose all the people you know, an' like, and maybe even love,' He stared Karl in the eye. 'That my friend is too high a price to pay. That tiny change back in time could destroy what you have today.'

'Mathematically, that's a hell of a ratio,' Karl screwed up his face.

'Ride your train and make the friggin' best of it,' Dan looked stern and had stopped eating.

'You know, for once I think you are right, Dan.'

They sat in silence watching pilgrims pass by.

'Can I ask you something, Karl?'

'Why do you ask? You will anyway,' he smiled.

'Jane and I were havin' a conversation about Debbie.'

Karl looked at the table and touched his tattoo. 'What about her?' His eyes showed he knew more that he wanted to say.

'What was she like?'

Karl toyed with the sugar shaker. A few grains spilled across the table. 'Not much to say. A girl,' he pursed his lips. 'Why?'

'Jane's remark friggin' shocked me.' Karl's eyes flickered across Dan's features. Johnny Cash was walking the line again. A man laughed. Two women sat at the next table and rested their feet on their back packs. One drank water like a camel tanking to cross the Sahara. The other filed her nails with a beauty salon expression. A man lay on the grass snoring lightly into his backpack.

'She said Debbie was a bitch.'

Karl stared at Dan. Eyes searching. 'That could be true.'

'Then I really wonder why she is doin' this pilgrim thing.'

'Angie told me that Jane feels guilty. I saw Debbie only once. When visited Jane at London university.' He rubbed his tattoo again. 'She was, what you say in English, a man eater?'

'Were you in love with her?'

'Gott no! She was very flighty. Jane warned me not to get involved.'

'Did you?'

'Jane's warning made me curious. I went out with her. Once was enough. I think she was a veteran of countless mattresses. She knew what the world costs, but not the value.'

'A cynic?'

'I'd rather not talk about her, Dan.' He stood and lay some money on the table. 'Breakfast is on me. I'll get the car and try to get back on my train of life,' he grinned. 'I'll leave you to your mega breakfast while I drive up to the Cruz de Ferro.'

'Why don't you let Angie drive that old wreck so you could walk a bit of the Camino?'

Karl shook his head. 'I cannot walk long distances on rough ground. Flat feet,' he rubbed his tattoo and patted Dan's shoulder. 'Take care, Dan! And good luck with your boss!'

Dan nodded and watched Karl walk with his slight limp back down the road to the car under a grove of fat trees. Blue smoke belched from the exhaust as it backfired. Dan smiled as it roared away like an unresolved Rubric Cube. A shadow fell across the table.

'May we join you?' A stocky man watched Dan from above.

'Be my guests,' Dan smiled.

'Does that mean you're buying?' the man smiled.

'Hm, not that much of a guest. Ireland isn't it?'

'Cork in county Cork,' he smiled. He's from France,' he indicated his companion.

'Paris in Paris,' the man joked in an accent to make a girl weak at the knees.

Dan wiped his mouth. 'What brings you to the Camino?'

The French looked at the other man and shrugged. 'I had Leukaemia. Many long months of treatment. I swore that if I was cured, I would walk the Camino.'

'You're here, so you're tellin' me good news,' Dan watched the man's sparkling eyes.

He nodded. 'A German organisation DKMS found a match for my blood group. They had a donor and his stem cells were used to replace mine and reproduce till I was healthy again.

'Have you met the donor?'

'Two years have to pass before donor and recipient can write to each other. If both parties agree.' He looked at the sky and swallowed. 'I'm looking forward to meeting the person who helped save my life. But this is only half the story. When I was completely down, a friend gave me a book by a guy called Joe Dispenza. He recovered from a severe bicycle accident when he was a young guy. Then spent years investigating why some people have spontaneous recovery from terminal illnesses. This book made me understand that nobody could cure me from outside unless something *inside* also was able to heal. I realised thoughts and feelings had a lot to do with my getting ill! I realised that holding grudges against things in the past would stop my healing progress,' he stopped and stared into this distance.

'What did you do about it?' Dan asked.

He smiled. 'I began meditating. Every day.'

'Does that work?' asked the man from Cork.

'I continued every day and felt a love for life. A hard thing when you lay in a hospital bed and fears are chasing around your mind like an express train. But within weeks I noticed I felt better! Then this love for life felt very real, more real than my diagnosis. From that point on I knew I would be fine and it took only two weeks more and I could be released from hospital. Cured. And now I am walking the Camino. In a way, the illness and what I learned out of it is the best thing that happened in my life.' They fell into silence, broken by the waiter placing plates on their table.

'Good morning,' a man with a guitar joined them.

'Are ye goin' to give us a song?' the Irish man from Cork in Cork pulled back a chair for him to sit.

'I'm a bit tired for that,' the man yawned like the Channel tunnel, his tonsils waved at Dan. 'I've been walkin' through the night. The albergues were all full. I'm playin' for food along the Camino.'

'Why do you have that bell round your neck?' The Frenchman asked reaching over and tapping a bell the size of an apple.

'In case I get lost,' he grinned a little embarrassed.

'They can alert wildlife so you don't surprise them. It's not every day you see a man with a bell around his neck,' Mr Cork from Cork chuckled and covered his mouth to hide bad teeth.

'There are lots of strange things along the Camino,' Mr guitar man said. 'I met a young Belgian woman wearing homemade clothes!'

'Belgium is not exactly the fashion centre of Europe,' Mr French accent purred.

'She wore a long, felt cloak and homemade shoes in bright colours. She was carrying a violin.'

'They be sendin' friggin' marchin' bands next.'

'Yes, well, I'll give you a tune if you buy me breakfast.'

'Ok, Dan said. 'I'm in!' Cork from Cork and Mr French accent nodded.

The man ate a big breakfast. The Frenchman ordered more food each time the guitar man finished a plate. In the end the guitar player leaned back. 'I'm full!' he gasped, then reached for his guitar and started to sing "Country Roads". After several songs they fell into silence for a few moments, baking in the sun. Dan let his eyelids droop. He was satisfied he could add more funny side stories to his article.

'Is this seat free?' A woman's voice opened Dan's eyes. 'Help yourself,' he smiled.

'Thank you.' She smiled back. 'Oh, may I see your guitar?'

'Sure, it's nothing special,' the guitar man grinned and handed it to her. 'You sound Irish.'

'You, too,' she chuckled. 'Haven't picked up one of these for ages,' she twisted the tuning keys and started to hum. Dan thought she was beginning a lullaby, but then she started to sing Hallelujah. He was mesmerised by her soft, angel like voice. People around put down their cups as her voice got stronger and resonated in a pure tone. People from the other tables joined in. Passing pilgrims stopped to listen. Some cuffed their eyes and smiled. Her song came to an end and for a few moments, a magical silence hung over the trail, broken by a cheering applause. She reddened and handed the guitar back. 'Haven't played in a while,' she said and pulled her backpack from the ground. 'Well, I'll leave you in peace,' she wrinkled her nose in an impish grin.

'Where are you from in Ireland?' the guitar man said.

'County Down. I've taken a sabbatical from my convent to experience the Way of Saint James.'

'You're a nun!' Dan's face hung in blank surprise. She nodded. 'You're in civilian clothes?'

'It's not the clothes it's the mind that makes us what we are,' she smiled and nodded at the silver Mercury pin on his rucksack. 'You're a soldier. Royal Signals isn't it?' Dan nodded, dumbstruck. 'My father was in the Royal Signals. I recognise the pin. But *you're* not in uniform either.'

'Got the push,' Dan looked at the ground. 'Wounded.'

'It meant a lot to you,' she placed her hand on his shoulder. Dan didn't draw away from the nun, as he did in the past. 'A new life awaits you. Just go for it.'

'Will God help?' a bit of cynicism tinged his voice.

'Maybe. But that's not important. You were born with free will. You can do it. I see that.' Her hand squeezed his arm and fell away.

'Thanks, er, sister.' Dan flushed. She smiled. The

guitar man winked.

'May God be with you,' She smiled, slung her backpack over her shoulder and blended with other pilgrims walking past.

'I'll be getting along, too,' guitar man took his leave. Dan nodded. He had lost his voice. The others got up to go. They patted Dan's shoulder and transferred a sort of magic. Dan watched the merry group of new found friends tramping the trail to the Cruz de Ferro. Two of them had quick dry Micro-Fibre towels swinging from their backpacks like skirts, drying in the rising sun.

He finished his breakfast and leaned back. A trail of ants scurried alongside his chair across the paving, each with a mini shadow running alongside them, giving the illusion they were running in pairs, shoulder to shoulder.

He became absorbed until a larger shadow swamped them. Dan looked up.

A piranha smile bent the long scar, making it uglier below the large sunglasses.

* * *

'Are you here to chill with me? Or start an old comrades reunion club?'

Ramos' hand moved to his open jacket.

'My brother is past meeting an old comrades association.'

'Too bad. Drinkin' was somethin' he was good at.' Dan shook his head in wonderment while watching Ramos with careful eyes. 'Listen, Ramos. What happened was years ago and it was his own fault.'

'I'll finish what my brother failed to do in Afghanistan.'

'He was drunk, Ramos. Drunk. He was pig wild! Shootin' at people and anythin' he saw. He hit me!'

'You shot him like a dog!'

'He was worse than a dog!' Dan sprang from his chair, finger pointed in Ramos' face. 'He was a fuckin' stupid dog!'

'He was my brother!'

'And you were the lousy drive-by shooter outside the Elvis bar,' Dan sneered in a show of bravado he did not feel.

Ramos' scare deepened with his snarl. 'The next shot won't miss, bastardo!'

'My death won't bring your brother back. Everyone nearby will hear it. You prick! You won't get far.'

'I will not desecrate the Camino with the blood of a bastardo! Your blood. I take you with me.'

People round them stirred. Ramos grinned and put a hand inside his flashy leather jacket. His hand stayed put. His eyes bulged, his face almost purple.

Two arms had locked around him.

'Don't try, lad, that's a good boy.' The Yorkshire accent sounded most reasonable and calm.

'Puta Madre!' Ramos cursed, tried to kick back and struggled.

Pilgrims at the next table went inside.

A sun burnt face looked over Ramos' shoulder. Mr Tennis shoes winked at Dan. 'All right, lad?'

'I'll say!' Dan skipped towards them.

'Puta Madre! You'll pay for this! 'Ramos tried to sound convincing while the air was pressed out of his lungs.

'Now, now, don't be a naughty boy.' He squeezed and Ramos' eyes almost popped out of his head. 'Jus' thought you might want a little assistance.'

Ramos gasped, winded. His leather jacket lining ripped as Dan's hand reappeared. The snout of a grey automatic protruded from his hand. Dan stepped back. Fear filled Ramos' eyes.

'A suppressor.' Dan unscrewed it and cast it into the grass. 'Never very effective. Everyone would still hear it.' Rapid click clacks followed. Eight gleaming bullets sprang from the breach and were swallowed by grass.

'His van's down there.' Tennis shoes nodded over his shoulder. 'I'd take it if I were you. There are trains leaving from Astorga to Madrid. Be on one.'

'Who the friggin' hell are you?'

'Not here, lad. Not in front of this bugger! Be off with yer! I can't hold him here forever.' He tightened his grip. Pain drained colour from Ramos' face.

Dan grabbed his rucksack and sprinted towards the van. He held the pistol like a trophy. The van was unlocked. Keys sticking. Tyres spat dust. Dan didn't need a map, just a heavy foot on the accelerator.

CRUZ DE FERRO

Jane learned a headful of new French swear words from Angie during the climb. The tiring way up the mountain to the Cruz de Ferro through white, purple and yellow mottled lavender was rewarded by a panoramic blanket of hills and forests stretching to the mountains. Their feet rhythmically beat the trodden path as they followed the periodic clam shell symbol on short jutting posts or yellow arrows splashed on rock pile walls or trees.

The Way climbed steadily. Pain sneaked back into Jane's calf and thigh muscles, her lungs laboured. Neither Jane nor Angie spoke, each alone in their own spiritual thoughts, but still listening, and watching.

'Your cuckoo's calling you,' Angie broke the

silence. They stopped and listened.

'My mascot,' Jane nodded and then continued.

'I read that there's gold in these hills,' Angie waved an arm direction south of their path.

'I've found only blisters so far,' Jane smiled grimly as they reached a flat shelf of grassland. The thin earth path cut through a green landscape dotted with white blossom bushes and isolated young trees, part of a national planting programme.

'Hola!' a German man and girl greeted them. They were sprawled on the grass near a pale grey donkey chomping plants hanging from its mouth. Everyone who walked by paused and patted or photographed the donkey, which stared blankly into the distance.

'We stop when the donkey stops. Then we rest while he eats,' the man said. 'We've been walking with him for more than three months.'

'Donkeys kill more people annually than plane crashes,' a man nearby said. Everybody stopped smiling and stared at the donkey, expecting it to explode or morph into a monster. Jane tried to read the man's expression to tell whether he was joking or not. The couple's heads turned towards the donkey and watched it intently as if it were a ticking bomb. A group of pilgrims stopped and took the opportunity to drink, looking like a bugle band with bottle bottoms pointed skyward like a medieval group of heralds.

Jane and Angie trudged onward.

'Is it always this tiring?' Angie gasped.

'Not always, but almost,' Jane smiled, inwardly proud at how much she had walked till now.

'I don't know how you do it. My energy is drained and this little backpack is biting my shoulders harder than by boyfriend does!' she panted.

'Don't worry. That's Foncebadón ahead. We can rest there.'

'Where? All I see is ruins!'

'It's abandoned.'

'This is desolate!' Angie stopped and gasped and surveyed stone piles jutting out of the ground like decayed teeth.

'It is, in fact, the most ruined village of the Camino,' Jane nodded as they stopped at another wooden way cross, like the one before El Ganso. A notice said, "Place no stones". There were none.

'It looks as if it was bombed!' Angie surveyed the fields. Jagged ruins crowned the bleak peak.

'It was destroyed in the Napoleonic wars, rebuilt, but still died out when young people left for the cities. It was originally a Roman outpost, and they built roads for traders. There is an albergue and a café though.'

'Thank, God for that! I'm completely out of water.'

'You'll need it, there's more climbing ahead.'

'I was mad to do this! Can't we stay the night here?'

'No.'

'Merde.'

'We'll make it.'

'I hope so!' She watched a bus parked across the road from the café. 'Look at all those cyclists!' Angie pointed at a mass of riders in tight cycling clothes unloading bikes from the hold of the bus. 'They have no luggage! Just bikes!' They watched the cyclists mount their bikes, tighten chinstraps and start freewheeling back down the slope. The bus growled, exhaust belched smoke round nearby pilgrims' ankles. The brakes groaned as the last cyclist passed with a wave to the driver and followed the group picking up speed.

* * *

Half an hour later they had clambered higher with full water bottles.

'Do we need this extra weight?' Angie panted.

'There's no more water available until we have left the Cruz de Ferro and get down to the next village,' Jane said and stowed her bottle and followed Angie along a very narrow dirt path winding through head high bushes. A million small white flowers closed in so close around her that they brushed her face and shoulders. They climbed all the way, rested and drank more water, and massaged their calves. Eventually, they crossed a road to a steep stony path that suddenly flattened out in a gentler gradient.

They had reached the plateau between dense forests and bushes bursting with white, yellow and lilac blossoms and all shades of green flanking the earth path.

'There it is,' Jane pointed with her chin at the tall solitary post on the skyline between the gaps of the forest. Angie gasped for breath. 'How could anyone do this for fun?'

'Many reasons, Angie. As Dan said, more than two hundred thousand people come here every year for two hundred thousand reasons.'

'Wow!' Angie cut her off and stopped. 'Wow! Look at that, Jane! The place I have read so much about and seen in so many pictures!' They both stood on the path and looked at the mast ahead pressed against the sky. 'Quite a walk, but worth it,' Angie laughed. 'Sorry I complained back there.'

'Be warned, it's really rugged going down the other side. You might want to drive down with Karl.

'No way! After all we've gone through, and now we're safe with that maniac locked up! No way!'

'Just wanted to mention it,' Jane said, pulled out her small camera and clicked a dozen times at the distant mast. Gradually the forest opened out showing the Cruz de Ferro atop a giant wooden post rooted firmly in a hill of stones, which had been brought by millions of pilgrims from all over the world over time.

'So this is the highest point of the Camino,' Angelique looked back the way they had come from Santa Catalina far below. 'Quite a climb.' Her mood had changed to joy.

Jane sighed with satisfaction. *This was certainly a highlight for Debbie.*

'It's all downhill from here.' Jane said as she perched on her backpack before the stone mound. 'I'm glad that most of our luggage is with Karl in the car.'

'Me too!' Angelique scanned the dark impenetrable pine forest around them.

'Tour groups,' she said and looked down on the huge earth parking area across the nearby road. A day tour bus pulled up and spewed gaudy tourists. Small groups and individual pilgrims trudged past and gathered around the mound and touched the grey weather-beaten mast, smiling at the small cross at the top of it. Cameras and cell phones clicked nonstop. Many tugged open their backpacks, rummaged around inside and pulled out a small stone to place on the stone hill at the base of the cross.

Jane saw one or two pilgrims discreetly pluck a stone from the ground and carry it to the mount.

Tears streaked the cheeks of a man praying loudly in French. His wife found her cell phone far more interesting. A group of Spaniards all knelt with their backs to the sun and prayed in silence with pious, mournful faces.

'Some of them have expressions as if they're on the gallows.'

'Makes them feel good,' Jane said. 'But not everyone's here for religious reasons.'

'Neither are you if it comes to that.'

The increase in volume from the Frenchman turned their

heads. His wife finally acknowledged his existence by stopping her cell phone gossip to snap close-ups of his face.

'They'll love the tonsil shots back home,' Angie giggled and watched a group of Americans pouring from a coach, without backpacks, waving their tablets about as if taking part in a mass ping pong game as they shot selfies.

'Can't find my stone!' An Englishman next to Jane rummaged through his backpack.

'You're not having mine,' a woman with him said. 'I brought it all the way from Scunthorpe. She opened a buttoned-down pocket and held a stone up to the light. 'There,' she lay it down to accompany the others at the base of the cross.'

'That's not a stone! That's cement!'

'It's the bottom lip of Clarence.'

'The garden dwarf?'

'Yes.' She patted the piece of red cement lovingly.

'The one with Tom Berenger lips?' I though you put him in the dustbin after he fell down the steps and broke to pieces.'

'I did, but I kept the lips. I love those lips of his.'

'Of a dwarf?!'

'No! Tom Berenger.'

'Of a Portland cement lip?! You're as daft as y'mother.'

'Get your camera out to take a photo of you and me.' He rolled his eyes and plucked a camera from his backpack and waved it in the faces of various pilgrims who started to give him a wide berth. 'Do you speak English?' they all shook their heads – including pilgrims with USA flags on their backpacks - and moved away warily. A Spanish guy muttered the word 'Loco,' while nodding in Mr Scunthorpe direction.

'I'll do it,' Angelique offered.

'Oh! Thanks love,' he grinned. 'D'you know how to work one of these...?'

'Make sure you get my stone in,' his wife commanded.

'It's cement!' he rolled his eyes.
'Say cheese,' Angelique called.
The middle-aged couple clenched their teeth at the camera. 'Ceeement,' the man said hardly moving his lips.

* * *

A school party swarmed the sidewalk in Astorga. Teachers flapped their arms with less success than penguins trying to fly. Dan swerved round the kids outside the noble ochre villa that houses the Museo del Chocolate, showing Astorga as the first place where chocolate was produced in Europe.

'Shit! Dan stamped the brakes. Tyres shrieked with the kids. Something slid to the front of the van. A kid scurried back on the sidewalk. Teachers glared. And yelled. 'Out the way!' he shouted and continued along the Avenida la Estación looking in the rear-view mirror in case he was followed.

Dan parked the van badly in front of the ochre station building and hoped it would be noticed quickly by a traffic warden looking for promotion. He was sure Ramos had a tracer bug hidden in his own van. It was the nature of the man as well as his job. He would soon roll up with his thugs but Dan didn't plan to be around to meet them.

He shouldered a modern door in an old wall. The light gleamed on the stone floor of the station foyer. It was brighter than a highly bulled barracks. A bald pilgrim sagged over his backpack on a bench. His light snores were almost musical. Dan ignored the ticket machines. He wanted to be remembered. His knuckles on the ticket window attracted the ticket clerk hanging over a newspaper. He placed a piece of Astorga chocolate next to a steaming coffee.

'Hola,' the clerk screwed up his face at the disturbance and eyeballed the ticket machine in case it was missing.

'A ticket to Madrid, please.'

The clerk pushed his glasses above his forehead and looked cool. 'Madrid? Sí, Señor.' His fingers boogied on the keyboard and kick started a printer. It whined and spat a white slip of paper. The clerk pushed it through the slot.

Dan looked at the ticker price and peeled off a fifty Pound note.

'No. Euro! Euro!' the man in the ticket office said. His fingers pulled back the ticket.

'Cards?'

'Sí, card.'

'What cards?' Dan grinned. 'Poker? You want to play poker?'

'Poker! No! MasterCard?' The ticket clerk pushed the English pounds back through the window, spilling some coffee on the counter. The man grimaced.

'Card! Maestro?' Dan shook his head. 'Visa?' He slid it toward the man who shoved the card into a cash machine. The machine whined and gave birth to a curled piece of paper.

'Which platform? Que plataforma?'

'The one next to the line,' the clerk said. Dan thanked the man profusely hoping he would remember him. The employee ignored Dan while he dried the counter shaking his head.

On the platform Dan relaxed. Beside the station building stood a ghost locomotive dripping rust on short rails going to nowhere. A tinny speaker squawked and the Madrid train purred alongside the platform. Its wheel brakes squealed. The carriage doors sighed and opened. A mother with a squealing child, a priest with a fixed smile and a few pilgrims with packs alighted. Dan's phone buzzed.

Moments later the almost silent train glided out of

Chocolate town.

* * *

The mound shifted and clinked under Jane's feet as she and Angie reached the top.

'Hallehello!' Karl's voice called. He slowly climbed the mound.

Jane waved briefly and then held the mast in both hands, feeling the rough grey weatherbeaten wood. She squinted up along the length of the post and prayed silently. She stepped back as a pilgrim knelt and pressed his forehead against the mast.

Angie touched a small nylon Canadian flag hanging from the many cords and ribbons tied round it. She smiled and poked a tiny grey teddy bear, next to a new looking wrist watch flanked by pictures of Jesus and saints. Notes fluttered in the breeze. A ribbon above them held a blue cap. Another held a white straw sun hat amid clam shells. Tiny bunches of lilac blossoms plucked from the bushes around them lay lovingly at the stones.

'We could start a boutique with these,' Angie grinned. She poked at the debris with her toe and read aloud messages on smooth stones. 'Norma, Sue, & Loopy' she squinted at another in Italian. 'Hey!' she picked up a larger flat grey stone. 'First Battalion Scots Guards twenty-one May. Yesterday!' She saucer eyed Jane. 'A whole battalion of men!'

'Missed your chance by one day,' Jane chuckled as Angelique elbowed her.

'It reminds me of a sailing ship's mast,' Karl leaned back to take in the famous icon against the blue sky atop the parched wood. 'Fifteen hundred metres above sea level,' Karl took a deep, satisfied breath as if he had scaled Everest single handed. He poked a toe between an empty wine bottle, coloured hair bands, stones with messages and an abandoned pilgrim pass. 'Look! These are house bricks. Builders' rubble.'

'Don't spoil it, Karl!' Angie punched his arm. His phone rang. He grunted and walked favouring his leg on the way down the mount with his phone on his ear.

'I'm starving!' Angie said. 'Come on! It's bocadillo time!'

'I'll catch you up,' Jane opened her backpack took the suede leather bag and extracted a small empty jar. The spoon scooped gravelly dust and let it run into the tiny jar.

'You and your rituals,' Angie shook her head.

'I have to,' Jane twisted the cap closed and wrote CdF on the top with her marker. 'I promised.'

* * *

Jane picked up their paper wrappings as well as a few other people's trash. 'I'm off to the little girls. Back in a minute,' she dumped the collected trash in a bin and headed for the Chapel of Saint James in the middle of the huge clearing. As she turned the corner her face squashed in disapproval. Steam rose before the toes of a row of guys facing the back wall. One turned and raised his hand. Lars the Dane.

'Delightful,' Jane's mouth turned down. She hastened into the new forest of young trees, planted in multiple curving rows. She walked further through the rocky gorse until enough trees hid her from the open space round the chapel. Jane shied back. A startled bird shot out from the long grass. Her view was channelled along the rows of trees. *Privacy and comfort*, she thought and trudged between the trees looking for a spot without long grass to avoid insects. A stony patch of earth without grass looked good. Flies buzzed. It stank. She saw the reason and wrinkled her nose at the tissues rotting round lumps of fly infested excrement.

'Damn!' *Why can't people bury it?* She screwed up her face and pressed her lips tight together and batted flies away. She walked deeper into the cultivated forest. She double checked the next clearing, sniffing and searching the ground before deciding. She let her backpack slide to the ground and fumbled with her pants. Birds called, and the sun speckled through the trees around her. It was peaceful, she thought.

A cracking sound startled her. She tried to look around, but squatting made it difficult. A dry twig popped.

Jane cocked her head. Another crack broke the silence. She tensed. Looked around. She wanted privacy but now she felt isolated. *Relax and go with the flow*, she told herself. *It's normal that you're over sensitive after all that has happened to you.* She swallowed, eyes darting everywhere. The trees reduced line of sight to less than ten feet. Another loud crack made her leap. Jane rubbernecked, eyes wide open.

'Anyone there?' She dragged up her pants. A blurred form crashed through the branches behind her. She screamed and without any other thought started to run. A figure crashed against her. They tumbled. Breathe shot from her as they thudded to the ground. Hot air rasped in her ear.

'Help!' she cried.

Knees pinned her arms into the gorse. The shadowy silhouette, black against the dappling rays, raised an arm. Jane tried to move. Knees crushed her biceps and made her scream in agony. A smothering hand stifled her scream against glove.

The figure released her. Jane's lungs wheezed in air.

'Jane!' Angie hollered as she climbed to her feet.

An arm shot out. Angie screamed. Clapped her hands to her eyes. The attacker plunged through trees. Gone.

Jane grabbed Angie who was crying in pain. Her hands covered her eyes. 'Can't see! Can't see!' She gasped and retched.

Jane knelt by her. 'Angie!' she yelled.

'Can't see!'

'CS spray!' she heard Karl panting behind her. 'Don't rub your eyes! Don't touch your face!'

'I'll call an ambulance?' Jane panted. Water splashed over Angie's eyes from Karl's water bottle. 'Give me your water,' he limped over and grabbed Jane's bottle from her backpack without waiting for her reply. 'Call an ambulance! Call Dan!' He tipped the bottle splashing over Angie's' eyes.

'It's alright,' Angie gasped. 'It's all right. Thanks, Karl,' she shook her head and sat on the grass. She pulled her own bottle and rinsed her face and blinked rapidly. 'It's alright, Karl...' She looked up with her red rimmed eyes and took long deep gulps of air.

'Ach, Jane! Why did you go in the woods alone?'

'Allez! She wanted to pee *alone*!' Angie wiped her eyes.

'You should have *told us* first,' Karl said and walked a few yards with his hands outstretched in wonder.

'I thought there was a loo behind the chapel!' Jane shouted and wiped her eyes. 'One would think there would be a loo here,' she stared unfocused at the ground.

'You're right, Jane. Then this would never have happened!'

'It can't be the killer!' Karl grunted. 'Alonso told us he has been arrested!'

'Then who was that?' Her pointed finger quivered at the woods.

'He must have escaped arrest!' Jane's eyes were wide in alarm.

'No.' Karl rubbed his tattoo. 'Alonso would have warned us. And, if he escaped, how would he know we'd be here at this exact place at this exact time? No, not logical.' he shook his head. 'Whoever it was knew we would be here now. Only with that knowledge would he have been in a position to attack.'

'I'd say, call Dan!'

'Ach, why? He's gone!'

'Call Dan!' Jane shouted.

'Do you think I am not good enough to protect you?' he rubbed his tattoo, his brow knitted above a black scowl. 'I also have things to do, you know? I cannot stay here forever! I have a business to run! But I am still here, but you think I am useless compared to Dan!'

'No, Karl. You protect us with the information you get.'

'And you've got my car,' Angie slapped the back of his head.

'Ach, don't do that!' he barked at Angie. 'Just because I can't walk so good!'

'Sorreeee!' she held her hands up in surrender.

'Call, Dan. Please. I want him here.'

'Ok, ok. First we get out of this forest and back to the car.'

* * *

The crunch of tyres on gravel as the car braked next to them in the parking area got their whole attention.

'Hola! What's going on?' Alonso slammed the door behind him.

Jane looked up. Her eyes widened. 'You look as if you've been partying none stop!'

'I *never* party, Jane.' His smile was tired.

'Then where's your bow tie and jacket?' I don't like scruffy men,' Angie winked. He blushed.

'Actually, you look like an unshaven pilgrim.'

'There's nothing wrong with that. I've been a pilgrim many times. With my parents. It's *our*

Camino, you know?'

'It's just that you don't look well,' Angie's voice was concerned.

'I'm all right,' Alonso sounded irritated. His eyes darted between them all. 'I was up all night on duty.' He ran his hands through his dishevelled hair and focused on Angie. 'What I want to know is how you are, Angie?'

'I'm ok now thanks,' Angie smiled. The sun glinted on the little arrow piercing in her ear.

'You were lucky it was only CS gas,' Alonso smiled at her.

'Is it? It didn't feel lucky no matter what gas it was!'

'You got here very fast,' Karl said looking Alonso up and down. 'I only called ten minutes ago.'

'I was nearby following up on a few things when you called,' he rubbed his stubble chin. 'Did you get a look at your assailant?'

'It happened so quickly.' Jane folded her arms round herself. 'I thought you had the man in custody!'

'We do,' Alonso assured her. 'And you, Angie?'

'I saw a figure over Jane. I ran and jumped on him.'

'Did you see his face?'

'How could I? The pig blinded me with gas.'

'If he's in custody, why is he free?' Karl folded his arms and stared at Alonso.

'It was someone else,' Alonso said emphatically. 'Definitely a different person. It has to be.'

'Are the police coming, Lonsey?' Angie's eyes roamed over his clothes.

'Did you call them?' Alonso sat and closed his eyes

for a second.

'We called you.'

'We thought you *are* the police.'

'Of course I am the police. I am off the murder case as you know, but, I am still here to help you. And here I am,' Alonso said and tapped his chest.

'If the killer is still in your custody, who was it?' Karl rubbed his tattoo and looked thoughtful.

'I would say it looks like Ramos,' Alonso said.

'Ramos!' Jane and Angie furrowed their brows.

'Why him?' Karl eyeballed Alonso. Jane noticed that Karl looked sceptical.

Alonso mopped his brow. 'Mendoza got rid of him after complaints by the public. He feels he lost his job because of Dan. Then this thing with his brother. He has many reasons. He obviously came looking for Dan, and attacked you in frustration,' Alonso looked from one to the other and saw confusion in their faces. 'He probably thought if Dan was nearby he would try and intervene.'

'Ach, that would be too risky!'

'Ramos is not normal. Remember,' Alonso raised a finger. 'He was discharged as psychologically unfit. He is unpredictable and could do anything!' He spread his hands to show helplessness. 'He is carrying a gun as well.'

'Merde! This is getting like the Wild West!'

'Well, we have our man so Ramos is the only one I can think of,' Alonso said. 'What is your plan now? Will you carry on by car?'

'If the killer really is in gaol,' Jane looked thoughtful, 'I'd prefer to walk.'

'Ach! That is stupid and illogical!'

'Jane! It is too dangerous!'

'If Dan were with us...'

'Dan! Dan! All I hear is Dan. Always Dan!' He rubbed his tattoo. 'Look!' He levelled a finger at Jane. 'Dan the action man is gone!' he spluttered. 'He has enough problems of his own! If he were here and Ramos found him he would shoot him! Bang bang bang! if you are near him, you'll get shot, too!'

'I have an idea,' Alonso said. 'I'll walk with Jane and she'll have my protection.' He smiled and clapped Karl on the shoulder. 'You see, Karl? Nothing to worry about. You don't need Dan around all the time.'

'Ach, he also tends towards violence. Violence against violence! Is that what you want to be part of? Violence?'

'Karl, let's not be too dramatic. I agree, it's good of Alonso to escort me.'

'Us,' Angie cut in. 'Us. I'm coming with you, remember?'

'And I?' Karl challenged. 'Aren't I part of the team?'

'You've got the car,' Angie said, and went to slap his head, but hesitated and lowered her hand. 'Or shall I drive and let you walk.'

'My leg is not good.' Karl reddened. Alonso smiled. Jane rolled her eyes. Angie folded her arms like a matron. 'You know I can't walk big distances over rough ground.' He turned away.

'Well, it looks like I am your best bet for now,' Alonso raised an eyebrow at Jane.

'That sounds good,' Jane looked at Angie. 'Are you in for it?'

'If he's being grumpy,' she nodded at Karl, 'then I'd prefer to walk with you.'

Karl stomped three rapid paces and turned full circle. 'I am not a grumpy!' he shouted. 'He looks grumpy!' He pointed to Alonso.

'Me? Grumpy?' Alonso forced a grin.

'Well you don't seem to be yourself, Lonsey! You don't seem to be logical! You are looking very messy. So I am asking myself what is wrong.' He took three strides and turned a circle and stared at them all.

'I think you are mistaken.' Alonso measured his words. 'I admit I'm not feeling so good, and I have had a late duty that kept me up all night, but I *am* all right. And,' he grinned. 'I am not grumpy.'

'Neither am I!' Karl bellowed and stomped away.

'Karl!' Angie sprang after him.

'Angie! Let him go.'

'Merde! I don't like to see him upset because of something stupid.'

The engine revved, full of aggression. Gravel stung a group of Tourgrims as Karl's driving raised a dust plume. A door flew open and flapped like a broken wing. They watched the colourful car howl along the road west and out of sight round a sinking curve; its exploding exhaust still audible long after it disappeared. They listened in silence as it faded away.

'Well, ladies,' Alonso broke the silence and smiled. 'Shall we begin our walk?'

THE FALL

'Not so fast, Jane!' Angelique's voice broke into her thoughts. Her voice sounded irritable and strained. Jane stopped in a curve in the trail to look back. Angie was breathing as if in labour.

'Come on, Angie, old girl!' Jane smiled and waited for her.

'Must you keep using that expression?' she scowled. 'Old girl, old this, old that!' She mimicked and stomped by, her stick clicking hard against the rocks.

'Sorry, Angie,' Jane looked back. She felt uneasy about Alonso. In the brightness of the open sky, Alonso's face had lost its natural tan. Dark rings emphasised his hollow eyes. 'Are you all right, Lonsey?' The worry in her voice was unmistakable.

His eyes focused on her without expression as if looking into her brain. He nodded and caught her up. 'You look as if you haven't slept for a week.'

'Summer flu. It's going around.' He followed Angie descending the earth trail edged by heather and gorse. He stopped and turned to Jane. His chest was heaving and his breath rasping. In that moment, Jane saw that Alonso was not just out of condition but ill. More ill than he confessed.

'You shouldn't be doing this, Lonsey. I know you mean well, but, you don't look good at all.'

Alonso looked at the ground, panting. He coughed. 'I too have a mission, Jane.' He turned and continued walking with heavy steps. Jane followed in silence. He disappeared around a curve in the rocky trail. Jane pulled her water bottle and sucked long and deep to relieve her tongue sticking thirst. Water ran down her gullet, almost in time to sweat coursing down between her shoulder blades. It was sticky, itchy, and horrible. She felt like dropping everything and ripping off her soaked top. Now the trail down was no longer a trail. It was a series of treacherous foot trapping, V clefts in rock slabs, between claustrophobic tunnels of bushes pressing in on her. Each turn exposed more craggy gashes. She stepped with extreme care. Jagged hungry teeth of granite threatened to twist her ankles in a complicated fracture at every step. There was no time to notice the beautiful wild flowers fighting for space either side of the torturous way. *This is not a trail! It's like a tight rope with knots and curves!*

'Can't stop. Can't go back,' Jane muttered through clenched teeth. She dreamed of their next stop and the end of this part of the trail. The part with the worst reputation for accidents. Bushes grabbed at her, whipped her face, plucked at her clothes. Visibility was short and each hairpin bend invisible till almost too late. An infamous path of twisted fractures. *Slip here and your walk is over!* The warning voice in her head said. *This is far worse than the descent from the heights of Alto Perdón.* She reached yet another steep cleft without any sure footholds. She glimpsed Angie and Alonso disappearing behind a monster rock. *How is he managing this?* She wondered. *He looks terrible!* She recalled his saying he'd grown up here. *He knows the Camino like the back of his hand. It was his own back yard.*

Jane stopped with a foot pressed against each side of a split rock gully. She considered calling them back. They could make their way back to the road. It would be longer but safer. She opened her mouth. It was parched. No sound came. *Angie won't go back*, Jane thought. *When she starts anything she always goes bull headed for it until the end. But Alonso. He shouldn't be here! He should be in bed and getting a long rest. Too late now. They're here because of me.* She shuffled centimetre per centimetre along the granite fissure. A second's inattention could snap and spread an ankle. No way for an ambulance to reach any of them. Sweat poured down her brow into her eyes. It stung. She halted, pulled off her scarf and dabbed them dry. Her hat felt hot. Her shirt sucked sweat and clung like a wet-suit. Air burned inside her nostrils. Hot knives pierced her calves. Tumbling stones rattled both the silence and her nerves, bouncing like hail below her. Jane was exhausted.

She tried to catch up with the others at the hollow ruins of Manjarín. Another dead village. A few volunteers in charge of a solitary albergue were the sole inhabitants. A limp and tattered Templar flag looked like the colours of the loser's side of a battle.

A group of pilgrims stood around looking helpless. Two lay on the ground. Faces masks of pain. A boot lay among a spaghetti of laces. Others bandaged their ankles with grim expressions. One victim grimaced and pulled his sneakers off with a curse.

'Can I help?' Jane didn't want to stop but felt she should. It was part of the pilgrim spirit and also in her nature.

'Thanks a lot, but we'll manage.'

'Wrong footwear,' another said in a Told-you-so tone of voice.

A man sitting with a roll of bandages in his hand glowered daggers. Others grinned or shrugged. Two lay down in the shade and smoked.

Jane was relieved she was not needed. Normally she would have done everything possible as she had learned from her Girl Guide days as a thirteen-year-old.

Where the devil are Angie and Alonso? She wondered, feeling isolated and alone. It never failed to surprise her that when walking with a companion, leaving the trail for a minute, on returning, your companion is a mile away.

Alonso, despite his poor condition had also vanished. She halted. Pebbles rattled and hissed to a stop. She listened. 'Aaangiee,' she called. Cocked her head like a budgie. Her labouring breath and heartbeat were her sole company. Not even an echo answered. She balanced her way along the edge of a ridge path flanked by immense boulders. Gorse flowed above and below. Her steps had her full attention. Her whole world shrank to the size of her footprints. *You're going to have to speed it up a bit to catch the other two. Move it!* she ordered. Perspiration trickled into her eyes. Her pack pressed her wet shirt cold against her back. A toe felt cramped. Flies buzzed her face. The wheezing of her lungs filled her ears. Eyes locked on the stony thread of the way. Walking the plank. She sensed rather than felt the sudden pressure against her backpack.

Don't lean over! A voice in her head warned. *I didn't!* She mentally snapped back.

The pressure was back. Stronger. Firm. She tried to turn. The path tilted. Breath burst from her lungs on impact. Her nose smelt earth. She saw the path an inch away. She was hanging from a ledge. Facing the drop.

They're my fingers! She thought, watching her hand grasping the edge of the ridge in slow motion. Fingers closed on rough grass. Its roots tore free.

'Help!' She heard her own voice far away. 'Help!' *That can't be me!* 'Help!' It *was* her! She panicked. The grass sounded like tearing paper. That's loud! The roots appeared spraying dirt on her face in slow motion. *That will dirty my clothes!* The world spun around her. She tumbled into darkness.

* * *

Grass prickled her nostrils. She sneezed.

'She's comin' round.' A voice she recognised spoke. Jane sneezed again and rubbed her nose.

'Jane?' Angie's voice penetrated her mind.

'No broken bones, as far as I can tell,' Alonso's voice said.

Dear Alonso. Always so concerned, she thought.

'She's very lucky she didn't land a yard to the right, she'd be down there.'

Jane tried to imagine where "Down there" was.

'This ledge stopped her,' Alonso's voice said.

'Jane? Can you talk?' This was Angie.

What a silly question! Jane thought and made herself speak. 'Angie?' Jane opened her eyes. 'Hello, Angie. Ouch!' Pain seized her body.

'Keep still, Alonso's silhouette stood over her like a giant against the sky. 'Can you move your fingers? Jane did. 'Your toes?' Jane did and nodded. Your legs? Jane did. Alonso watched her open and clench her fists and start to rub her arms. Her legs drew up and straightened.

'Everything feels alright.' She slowly sat up. 'Oh, my God!' She looked at the edge of the ledge where she had landed. The jagged rocks below made her feel dizzy. 'Gosh! I'm glad I didn't end up down there!'

'You were more than lucky, Jane.' Angie stroked her back.

'You must have fallen,' Alonso told her.

'Fell? When?' she rubbed her temples searching her memory. She was confused. She remembered nothing. Just voices waking her up.

'I don't know when. I reached Angie and she asked where you were.' Alonso explained.

'We back tracked and found you,' Angie said. 'I almost died when I saw you down on this ledge!' She wiped tears from her eyes. 'Oh, merde! Jane, I can't forgive myself for not waiting for you.'

Jane reached out and touched Angie's cheek. 'Don't blame yourself, Angie. It was my fault for not taking more care.'

'I thought you had been attacked.' Angie's voice was worried.

'Who says this was an attack?' Alonso was peevish. 'She must have fallen. An accident.'

'I'm trying to reach Karl. We need the car. I'll tell him to come to Majarín. Will you manage the way back?' Angie looked at her with a serious expression. Jane nodded. Angie scrambled up the slope and at the top pulled her phone.

'How do you feel?' Alonso watched her roll onto her hands and knees.

'Better,' she groaned as she got back on her feet.

'We'll drive to Ponferrada when Karl gets here with the car.'

'But my walk! Debbie...!'

'Debbie isn't the issue now. *You* are,' Alonso took her arm and helped her up the slope. At the top they looked down at the ledge where Jane had landed.

'I cannot remember too well, but,' she looked up at them. 'Someone pushed me.'

'If that's the case,' Alonso said with a serious expression. 'I will get back to my office from Ponferrada and make an official report about this. Then you don't have to worry about it.'

PONFERRADA

'This is an albergue without Wi-Fi,' said a big round albergue warden who looked as if he had been expelled in disgrace from weight watchers. He stared at them with a totem pole expression as if he had been switched off.

'Ach!' Karl rolled his eyes.

'We are both traditional and religious.' The phase came out pat, as if he said it a hundred times a day and was also bored with hearing it.

Karl stared with his mouth open. 'Both are boring.'

'There's Wi-Fi at the bar across the square.' The hosteller's tone was disapproving, as if they had requested the albergue's fornication statistics. Wi-Fi seemed to be something sinful. He pointed across a grassy expanse to shops that seemed to be near

France.

'Ach, Gott! That's a kilometre away!'

'Yes, it is,' the hosteller looked pleased.

'Ach, Scheisse!' Karl rolled his eyes.

'Do you offer a pilgrim menu?' Angie asked.

'Kitchens are available if you bring your own food,' the man said.

'Where's the nearest place to eat?' Jane felt she knew the answer. The hosteller's eyeballs swivelled across the grassy no man's land, as if it were the red-light district of Ponferrada.

'Allez! Let me guess! Across the plaza. Right?'

'Right in one,' the man beamed and turned away to dole out more unhelpful answers to other pilgrims.

'I'm going to have a very long shower to ease my aching body and change my plasters,' Jane picked up her backpack and limped down the gardens to the shower building.

'I'll join you,' Angie hobbled after her.

' And then we can eat,' Karl called after her. 'I'll be at the bar. See you there.'

'If my feet will carry me to wherever that might be,' Jane called back.

A bunch of pilgrims sitting on their shadows on the grass with heads full of beer started bawling 'I did it. Myyyyy waaaaay.'

* * *

The guillotine blade was poised to drop. Dan imagined Mendoza pulling the release lever with the blade over his neck. He ran a fingertip along the edge like a connoisseur. A mass of grinning skulls along the wall looked like a football crowd whose team was winning. He glanced at comic skeletons in red silk lined coffins against the walls and said, 'Quite the place to give a guy an appetite. And you should see the toilets, black and white tiles smeared with blood.' He beamed as if he had come to the Camino only for this experience. 'Did you tell them that I'm back?' He asked Karl with his back glued to the bar.

'No. I thought it would be a surprise.' Karl grinned mischievously.

'What sort of place is this?'

'It's called the Morticia. A well known club here in Ponferrada,' Karl rubbed his tattoo and started to thaw out. 'Morbid but dark. A good place to meet and not be seen.'

'Nor friggin' heard,' Dan glanced at the DJ dancing with himself.

'It is discrete,' Karl grinned.

'Ok as long as you don't ask me to put my neck on that thing,' Dan looked at the blade decorated with blood stains. 'Where did you find this place?'

'Internet. I told the girls where to meet us.'

'Let's stay here at the bar till they arrive.' He perched on a stool ordered so they could practice their drinking.

'Hey, Dan!' Angie's voice filled the club, turning heads along the bar. Dan's head turned with foam on his lip. Angie's bosom collided pleasantly against his chest and her arms grabbed like tentacles. 'Where did you come from! I thought you were on the way back to the country that stole the Channel Islands from us!' She twisted. 'Hey, Jane! Look who's here!'

Jane pushed her way between the tables looking in disgust at the decorations around her. It was a quiet night in the club, so everyone turned to look at the impromptu reunion as an alternative to the missing floor show. 'Factually, Dan, I'm glad to see you. But what about your job?' She squeezed his shoulder.

'I had a run in with friggin' Ramos. He was as crazy as a loon and tried to pull a gun.'

'Oh my God!' Angie and Jane chorused. Karl listened in silence.

'That guy in bright red tennis shoes saved me. I stole Ramos' van and dumped it outside Astorga station, bought a train ticket for Madrid at the ticket counter and another one to Barcelona at the ticket machine. When I got Karl's call, I let the trains go without me, phoned my editor and sent the data from an Internet café in Astorga with high speed connection. He confirmed reception, so everything is fine for the moment.

'Puh, but Ramos won't give up. Be careful, Dan,' her finger touched his chest.

A waitress with a wide mouth redder than the blood smears round the club, hovered nearby as if she was about to wet herself. Angie and Jane looked at the ghoulish decorations and pictures of horror people and lost their appetite. Dan told them about his pantomime at the ticket office to mislead Ramos.

Jane watched Karl frowning with a puzzled gaze and fingering his tattoo. She knew something was disturbing his logical mind. But what?

'I have something to say,' Jane announced as they took seats at a circular table and ordered drinks. Her eyes saddened. 'Debbie didn't reach here.'

'How do you know?' Dan said.

'I simply have the feeling, and no more of her postcards.'

'Are you sure, Jane?' Angie took her hand.

Jane nodded. 'I've always felt her presence along Saint James' Way, from the very beginning up to El Acebo. But not here in Ponferrada.'

'Did you feel it everywhere else?' Dan looked at her.

'Almost the whole time,' her chin sank, and she stared at the table. Small marks formed from tears dropping from Jane's cheeks. They all reached out to her and rubbed her hands and arms. Angie hugged her.

'What do you want to tell us?' Karl's eye flickered over her face.

All eyes remained on Jane as she covered her face with her hands. Nobody spoke. The smell of cigarettes and loud music in the background distracted them.

Jane took a tissue from Angie, blew her nose and took a long deep breath and nodded. 'I'm all right now. Thanks. What I want to say is we ought to get moving to Santiago. Here in Ponferrada could have been the last place she reached. If she reached it.' She dabbed her eyes again and balled the tissue in her fist.

They sat in silence until the waiter came and occupied their thoughts. Jane looked at the mummy standing against the far wall. A few people started dancing. Obviously pilgrims and obviously tired.

'So it looks like our friggin' footie days are over.'

Jane nodded. 'Factually, it was the end of the line for her. I'm sure.'

They sipped their drinks and after another silence, Dan rested his hand on Jane's arm. 'What's the plan now, Jane?'

Jane looked at each one in turn, as if weighing up whether to tell them or not. They watched her intently. As if on cue, the music stopped. It was suddenly so quiet one could hear shadows moving. 'My final mission is to make a public announcement in Santiago Cathedral.'

'Ach Gott! Will they allow it?'

'Yes. I've already contacted them. I'll publicise the scandal of women disappearing along the Camino and that the authorities have been suppressing it. I arranged with the cathedral for a video crew to be there.'

'Wow! How? When?' Karl stared at her.

'I have my contacts,' Jane smiled. 'The camera crew is available at short notice. The church back home helped me set it up, and the bishop here approved it. They are also angry that young women have disappeared, and that news was distorted to make them look like accidents, or even completely covered up. They have got a private Spanish TV company who wants to expose the negligence of the authorities. It should go out as a special documentary within a week. This is the only way this can be exposed. The Cathedral administration will provide a place for me with a microphone. They just need one day's notice.'

Jane looked at all eyes round the table. 'We drive to Santiago de Compostela tomorrow.'

Karl raised a warning finger. 'Let's hope that Ramos does not hear about it. He would be sure to turn up, and that would be very bad for Dan,' his eyes searched their faces.

'Either way, I could use another friggin' drink!'

'Factually, alcohol doesn't solve problems, Dan,' Jane said primly.

'Neither does café con fuckin' leche.'

* * *

'Sugar?'

The figure stood in silence.

'Is that you, Sugar? Talk to Mommy, Sugar. What time is it? It must be late.'

'The Succubus has a plan, Mommy. I cannot save her the way I saved the other Evas.'

'Why? What's so different?' The sheet before the form's mouth dampened from her breath and fluttered like wings of a butterfly.

'Usually, I find a red head, follow them a few days, get into conversation, get to know them, get their trust.'

'Yes, Sugar, I know. People always trust a monk. Especially along our Camino.'

'When I know where they are staying I turn up,'

'By coincidence,' she chuckled. 'And *what* a coincidence!' her chuckle rattled in her throat.

'Sometimes I reserve a place to sleep ahead, and offer it to them. That always makes them happy.'

'And you know exactly where they are. That's good, Sugar. Very clever.'

'Then I play up my football injury.'

'That makes 'em helpful,' her chuckled rattled again.

'I always have a package of bibles that I drop.'

'Oh praise the Lord! I bet they always fall for that one.'

'I ask them to help loading the bibles in the car.'

'Then your chloroform cocktail,' the sheet jerked as her chuckles gurgled deep and louder.

'Hah ha!' he chuckled with Mommy. 'I call it Chlor de Camino!' he guffawed.

'Aha, ha, ha! I like that, Sugar,' she laughed unable to stop. 'I love it, I love it, I love it, my Sugar!'

'Then we go for a lil' ol' drive,' he snorted, 'with their noses full o' Chlor de Camino!'

'Haaaaah! That's good!' the sheets convulsed with her laughter. Her feet kicked free. Sugar noticed her incredibly long toe nails curving like talons.

'Then I save them for the Lord.' Mommy's! Save them for the Lord! Her blind eyes could not see the fanatical gleam in his eyes. Her laughter subsided into gasps for air, sounding like a steam train pulling a hundred wagons.

'But, but Mommy, there's no time for that with the Succubus! No time!'

'Save her, Sugar! Or you'll be damned from your place by the Lord.'

'I could shoot them both dead.'

'Nooo!' she shouted. 'You goin' mad, Sugar?' The sheet pulsed. 'Only with the cross I gave you. The pointed cross from the wood of the cross on which Jesus himself was crucified. Nothing else, Sugar! Nothin'!'"

'But Mommy...'

'No! Pierce them with the cross of holy wood! Even if you sacrifice yourself!'

'But...'

'Do it! Do it! Do it! Do it! Do it!' she screamed. He

fled her room. 'Do it! Do it! Do it!' Her voice chased him as he ran out of the building. It echoed in his ears. 'Do it! Do it! Do it! Do it! Do it!'

* * *

Jane climbed down the metal ladder for the third time that night. She crept along the corridor like a cat in a dogs' kennels to the albergue kitchen in stocking feet. She made coffee three times. It got cold three times. She splashed it away three times. A squadron of flies cruised the food wreckage abandoned by pilgrims, tight on budget but wasteful in cooking. The flies woken by Jane's presence were the only sound except for a couple of distant snore heads. Before she went back to her bunk the first early risers entered the kitchen.

'Morning,' they greeted, grabbed coffee pots and ransacked the fridge faster than the Huns in ancient Rome.

You won't get back to sleep now, Jane returned to the dormitory and packed her backpack as quietly as she could under the beam of her Petzl headlamp and left the room. She sat down on the grass in the long garden outside and watched the sun peeking over the edge of the earth sending daylight swarming over the town.

'Morning, Jane!' Dan appeared, cheerful and as fresh as a daisy, which pissed her off after her bad night.

She wanted to say, "Is it?" or "What's good about it?" but she limited herself to a nod and let the sun flow over her face.

'Sleep well?'
'Factually, no.'
'I slept very well.'
'You snored.'
'Did I?' he frowned. 'I never heard a thing! Had breakfast yet? I could eat a friggin' horse. You coming?'
'There is no breakfast. It's self-catering.'
'Are you sure?'
'Ask the flies.'
'I'll take a look,' he wandered off to the kitchen.
'Good luck.' Jane murmured, lay back on the grass and closed her eyes to wait until Karl came with the car. She was pleased that Angie had insisted on bringing her old rattle trap to the Camino, although she had not expected Karl to do all the driving. He should have brought his own shiny luxury chariot with hand controls. She smiled. He probably didn't want it to get dirty.

* * *

Bruce Dickinson, singer and pilot of Iron Maiden, sounded as if he had a front seat in the car. Heavy Metal hammered with stunning loudness out of the radio. But Karl was driving. Karl was in charge of the car. Captain of the ship. So Karl chose the music. Dan photographed the stream of swaying backpacks of pilgrims skirting the soaring ramparts of the castle of Ponferrada. Angie reduced the volume yet again. Jane hung on to the door with its broken handle to stop it flying open.
'I wonder why they say the Templar knights built

it?' Dan mumbled from the back seat. 'None of those guys had a brick in their hands in their whole lives.' He squinted up at the soaring castellations. He felt a slight pang as pilgrims headed down a side road to the trail.

Angie followed his gaze. 'Don't tell me you're missing it, Danny boy?'

Dan shrugged. 'It's grown on me in a way. I feel I'm cheatin' a bit and should be there with them. I get a slight feelin' of desertin' the colours.'

'Typical army man! What did the colours ever do for you?'

'Gave me a home. A job. A life. A meanin'. A family. Belongin',' he paused. 'Should I go on?'

Angie switched to her classical music. 'Then they kicked you out on your proud English arse. Some family! Real family doesn't do that, Dan, Mr soldier man.'

'What a fuckin' cheek! How dare you! You've no fuckin' idea how things work!'

'Dan!' Jane shouted. 'Stop this!'

'She fuckin' started it!' His finger quivered at Angie.

'Merde!'

'You, too, Angie.'

'Let's be peaceful...'

'Oh. Fuck off, Karl! You and your fuckin' peaceful sh...'

'Dan!' Jane screamed and jolted everyone into silence.

The sound of the loud exhaust filled the car. Karl changed down a gear to make it louder and took corners a bit too fast.

'Karl! Slow down!' Jane shouted like a captain in a

hurricane.

'Another dent won't hurt,' he said. 'If you all talk reasonable, I will drive reasonable.'

'Angie, I apologise. It's just a sore friggin' point.'

'Sorry, Dan,' Angie searched to connect with Dan's eyes in the mirror.

'Lots of pilgrims use some transport,' Karl slowed down. 'Taxi, bus, even the train, or use an auto like us. Sometimes they are exhausted or frightened they won't get a bed before dark. Many reasons. All are OK.' He punched the Metal station and raised the sound.

'Listen! If you want to walk you can. I'm not stopping you!'

'No, no, Jane!' Dan smiled lamely. 'My feet want to be with you.'

They left the town behind. Karl never removed his hand from the gear stick and stirred the gears like a one-handed drum solo as they swayed along the winding road heading west.

Dan felt his eyelids drooping and nodded off against Jane's shoulder. She didn't move and watched the countryside whirl by. It reminded her of the waltzers at the fair as a child with Debbie and her dad. Debbie always wanted to go on the waltzers again and again and dad always obliged. *What Debbie wants Debbie gets,* Jane remembered saying out loud at Chester fun fair. *Dad didn't speak to me for the rest of the day. And now I'm still doing things for Debbie and it's almost cost me my life. First in the albergue and at Cruz de Ferro,'* Jane thought. *Then the fall from the precipice. Fall or pushed? Was I really pushed? Or did I slip? If I was pushed, then by whom?* She tried to recall the moments before. *I was walking behind Angie and*

Alonso. I lost sight of them. The way was steep, difficult, rocky, narrow. But factually I was very careful. So why should I fall? She sighed, unable to find an answer. *He might try again. Was it Ramos?* She wondered. She frowned. *Dan told me he took Ramos' van and left him stranded back in Rabanal. So how could he get up to the Cruz de Ferro before us? And he couldn't sneak past us down the narrow hairpin trail where I fell or was pushed. What's more, Dan told me that Mr Tennis shoes actually saved him! God I'm confused!*

'Galicia!' Angie interrupted Jane's thoughts. She caught a glimpse of a sign announcing the province. 'The land of a thousand rivers!' She prodded the classic station button.

Angie's announcement pulled Jane's mind back to the present. Her library memory reminded her that the lush green countryside of hills, mountains and valleys was a region that neither the invading Romans nor the Moors were able to subdue. The proud Celtic tribes in mountain strongholds ensured the survival of their traditions, evident to this day.

The car lurched and stopped. A small herd of white and black mottled milk cows stood shoulder to shoulder between hedges. They collectively stared Karl out. He did a Moses by sounding the horn and the herd parted like the red sea.

'Who lives in those tiny houses? Midgets?' Dan had woken up and indicated at another long, narrow tiled roof stone building on stilts between sprawling eucalyptus groves. Patches of lilac foxgloves nodded in the breeze. He snapped a grey, moss covered wagon wheel rotting against the fence. Its steel hoop a rusty halo.

'Nobody lives there, Dan. They're called hórreos.

They are the unofficial symbol of Galicia. They were grain stores. Rodent proof because of their long legs.' Dan's camera swallowed scene after scene.

'Ach, It's so green here. Reminds me of Germany.'

'Yeah, completely different from the Meseta.' Dan's camera buzzed non stop.

'These eucalyptus forests were planted for wood production. They deprived other plants of water. The government levies high fines and forces owners to remove them now,' said Angie.

'Factually, the Galician culture is very different from the rest of the provinces along the Camino.' Jane's teacher tone was back. 'Don't expect flamenco or sombrero hats here. Bagpipes are the traditional instrument in Galicia. Their music and clothing are similar to the Scots and Irish.'

'Yeah? Then they're the people for me,' Dan lounged in the rear seat inspecting pictures in his camera screen.

'I dislike bagpipes,' Karl switched to Metal and used up the gears while the others acted like tourists. They entered a small town and Karl drove aimlessly around the streets full of people.

'Where are we? Jane asked.

'Sarria!' Karl said. 'Most pilgrims start here. To get a Camino certificate, a pilgrim has to walk at least 100 kilometres. Tour groups start here and busses carry their backpacks.'

'Camino Lite,' Dan sneered.

'Puh! Why not? That sounds like my kind of pilgrimage,'

Jane watched a crowd of pilgrims standing outside cafés, chatting, staring at maps and watching their luggage being loaded into mini busses before they' started on their hike. 'The largest number of pilgrims start their Camino here. It is just over a hundred Ks to Santiago from here.'

'I'll find a place to park,' Karl said. 'Does Alonso know we are here?'

'I text him,' Jane replied. 'He'll meet us in Santiago. He said to phone when we arrive.'

'I'm hungry,' Karl swerved and jolted to a stop in a parking spot. Angie leaned between the seats to the radio, switched back to classic and grinned at Dan. They got out with more arm stretching and knee bending than a football team. Jane looked around with the feeling they could have been followed.

'Here,' Karl announced and they walked into a bar with a blue metal sign outside displaying a Camino shell above Km111.

'Good name,' Dan said.'

'Factually, it's exactly the remaining distance to Santiago,'

They had a coffee inside at a table with four different styles of chairs.

'It's sure friggin' crowded in this town,' Dan watched people walking by. 'What bullshit is that to start the Camino here?' Dan scoffed. 'Why don't they walk the whole way?'

'Factually, many have short vacations'

'Take a look at this!' Angie chuckled at the sight of a lady dressed to kill walking into the bar.

'I say!' she called imperiously. She had high heels and even higher voice. A red patent leather handbag swung from her arm. 'Where can I get a pilgrim stamp?' She held out her pilgrim pass as if expecting caviar to be spread. Everyone ignored her. 'A stamp thing for my pass?' she demanded from the bar keeper. He smiled and took her pass and stamped it and handed it back.

'Obliged, I'm sure.' Without looking, she placed it in her handbag and snapped it closed with a distinct click. 'Gosh! This makes me feel like a real pilgrim!' she squealed and strutted out to a chauffeur driven Bentley with its engine idling at the curb.

People shook their heads in wonder.

Karl rubbed his tattoo. 'The Camino will get quite full from here on.'

'Can we stop in Portomarín? Angie asked. 'I'd like to see that.'

'The original town is submerged by a reservoir but you can still see it during the summer month when you look down from the bridge,' Karl explained. 'I read you can hear the old church bell ringing when the water is rough.'

'What's up, Dan?' Jane's eyes were anxious. She followed his gaze to a van with darkened windows across the road.

'Don't turn round. It looks like one of Ramos' friggin' scouts.'

'Where?' She looked. 'It could be anyone.'

'Why wait to find out?' said Angie.

'Let's get back to the car,' Karl said.

'It's me they want. You three get y'selves to Shitty-shitty-clang-clang and be ready to clear off. I'll wait here to see what happens.' Dan sat slowly on a bench outside.

'Merde!' Angie planted hands on hips. 'Don't be crazy! Come with us!'

'They won't do anythin' here on the friggin' street. I don't want them to try anythin' with you lot. Go!' he waved them away. 'I'll catch you up.'

'Don't do anything silly, Dan,' Jane said.
'Clear off, f'fuck's sake!' His face flamed.
'But...'
'Park at the train station. I'll get there after I've shaken them off.'
'How will you find us,' Jane frowned?
'Start the engine and I'll hear the friggin' exhaust a mile away,' He took the menu, pretending to read while looking over the top at the van.

The van engine revved, swerved in a tyre squealing U turn and stopped outside the café like a getaway car.

Dan watched.

The door opened.

A man built like a bunker got out. Rubbernecked the street and headed for Dan.

Dan pushed his hand inside his deep thigh pocket. His fingers clasped round the knife. The man strode towards his table. Adrenalin flooded Dan's veins. He tensed. A coiled spring. Every muscle rock hard.

The man stopped. Grabbed a menu from the next table, looked at it, turned and called, 'Sí! Está bien!' The van side door slid back with a clunk. Six chattering family members squeezed out, and seated themselves at the tables near Dan. The powerful man ruffled a bright eyed little girl's hair. She beamed at Dan showing two missing front teeth and said, 'Hola!'

SANTIAGO DE COMPOSTELA

'Jesus was kidnapped here.'
  'Another friggin' joke?'
  'I hope not,' Jane nudged Angie who rolled her eyes.

Dan and Karl were on wobbly legs after their visit to a Santiago bar the night before. The bartender had served everyone, including himself, with each round.

They now waited at the bottom of the steps up to the Pórtico da Gloria, the main entrance to the gigantic, Romanesque cathedral. Its towers soared over the city of Santiago de Compostela where the late morning sun pasted short stubby shadows to their feet. Jane and Angie examined Jane's notes.

'No joke!' Karl continued. 'The Baby Jesus was kidnapped from his crib. Here in the Plaza do Obradoiro. Activists wanted to make the public aware of the plight of people who had been evicted. You should write that in your magazine, Dan. Jesus later was discovered next to a teller machine in a bank.'

'Good. Gives it a money angle. Adds to the drama,' Dan's gaze roamed the square.

'It's a happy end.'

'Anymore stories like that?'

'Yes!' Jane broke in. 'A few years ago, the Codex Calixtinus was stolen.'

'Sounds like a Latin secret service thing,' Dan smirked.

'Factually, I wouldn't expect you to know what it is,' Jane said in her teacher tone.

Dan smiled. 'An' I bet you're going to tell me.'

'A medieval illuminated book. You could say it's the first Camino guide about the travels of Saint James.'

'Don't tell me everyone should read it.'

'One doesn't read it. It was chanted aloud. It contains musical pieces. Most interesting,' Jane pressed her lips in a tight line and nodded.

'Worth a friggin' fortune, I bet. Did they get it back?'

'Police found it in a garage with two million euros in cash.'

Dan's eyebrows and jaw jerked in opposite directions. 'Where did it come from? The Jesus bank?'

'The cathedral electrician systematically milked the collection boxes. The dean of the cathedral had to resign.'

'So he should.'

'In fact, in the same year, the mayor was accused of tax fraud.'

'Don't ruin my new vision of the Camino,' Dan said.

Jane adjusted her pony tail and watched pilgrims arriving alone and in ad hoc groups. She saw them smiling, laughing, and some dabbing moist eyes in a euphoria of accomplishment. They had made it. Cameras and phones held the moment, in a continuous barrage of selfies or groupies. A huge sense of happiness buzzed through the plaza. Nearby a pilgrim stood apart, in silence, hands in pockets and lost deep in thoughts. A company of cyclists in yellow cycle gear piled their bikes high in a mound of interlocked steel. Nearby, five women lay like starfish in a row on the warm, crazy paving. The air was filled with happiness and goodwill.

Jane felt like joining them.

No time, she prodded herself. *I've a mission to accomplish*.

A crowd of Japanese in identical white bill caps and nylon wind jackets seemed oblivious to the joy around them. Their tour guide barked instructions.

'He reminds me of my old sergeant major at boot camp,' Dan said.

'Look at her!' Karl pointed. A girl's face was pure rapture as she juggled a set of clubs before the cathedral steps. Dan nudged Karl, who smiled at her. She caught his eye and smiled back.

Dan turned full circle and took in the whole square. 'Despite the bad things we've experienced, the Camino has shown me a lot about my own life. That is a special magic.'

'You believe in magic, Dan?' Angie pursed her lips.

'I don't know. But this is magic!' Dan looked across the square. 'You start as a walker and finish as a pilgrim.'

'And the total rest of your life?' Karl frowned. 'Will that be magic?'

Dan shrugged. 'Depends on the magic.'

'I don't believe in magic. Life is a total programme. You have to make it right.'

'I thought the past was my programme. I used experience from the past as my gospel, and judged people by events from the past. There's something I've learned from Angie. Let go of the past. Look forward. The future starts now. Live your future now, and that's how it will be. You're too serious, Karl. I believe in happenstance. It's amplified by your actions. We all have multiple destinies that activate according to our actions. The more you try to do, the more things happen. Happenstance.'

'Serendipity,' Karl grinned and touched his tattoo.

'If you're friggin' lucky.'

'I still think you have to programme your life right.'

'If it is how you want your future to be, then, ok. I respect what you say, and I think we should do it our own way. The important thing is to make a positive decision and then do it and live it. Then there's a big chance it will happen.'

'Dan.' Karl's tone raised Dan's eyebrow. Karl

rubbed his tattoo as if it itched. 'Dan.' His tone was wary. 'I didn't like you when we first met.'

'That's ok, Karl.' Dan playfully punched his shoulder. 'The feeling was two hundred percent mutual, so we've got that in common,' his face split in a big grin.

'But I have learned to respect you,' Karl added.

'That's friggin' mutual, too, Karl.' They stared in silence at the cathedral, lost in their thoughts.

'Hi dreamer,' Angie's voice pulled them back to reality. 'Midday pilgrim mass is about to start. Jane's already up there.' Dan looked up the steps. A camera crew and Jane waved down at them.

He waved back and spotted the teacher he had interviewed after Puente la Reina. It seemed ages ago. 'We'll follow,' Dan said.

'Hello. Dan, isn't it?' she said. 'How are you today?'

'I, er,' Dan was tongue tied. His gaze frozen.

'I'm going in for the service.' The woman in front of him made a little skip.

Dan stared at her garb. 'But, you're dressed!'

She looked down at her robes. 'I hope so!' her light chuckle giggle tinkled like a bell.

'Like a nun!'

'That's most observant,' her laugh tinkled again. 'I'm in a teaching order.'

'You seemed so nice!' Dan reddened. 'Sorry, I mean...'

'It's alright. Some people think we're stern old virgins,' she chuckled. 'Well? Are you coming?'

'I'm waiting for someone.' Dan's face was a ripe tomato. 'I'll follow...!'

'Very well,' her eyes sparkled. 'Good luck with

your article, by the way.'

Dan watched her go. 'A frig..., a nun!' He shook his head in disbelieve. 'They ruined my childhood.'

'You have carried your problems too long, Dan,' Karl rubbed his tattoo. 'Like you said, the past was your bible. Close the bible, Dan.' They watched the nun merge into the throng of pilgrims streaming up the steps into the cathedral.

'Hola!' Alonso was suddenly at Dan's side.

Dan was shocked. 'Jesus! You look really friggin' fucked, Lonsey.' Dan focused on Alonso's hollow eyes. He coughed and tugged a rag of a hankie from his pocket.

'Lot of late night duty,' he said. 'Where is Jane?'

'Inside the cathedral.'

'Good,' he coughed. 'I shall escort her myself so nothing goes wrong.'

'Are you going on vacation?' Karl nodded at a big leather bag in Alonso's hand.

He nodded. 'Personal odds and ends, before I take a trip.'

'We will come with you.' Karl said

'No. Stay here until I check if Ramos is there. I'll come out and wave if the coast is clear. If I see Ramos, I won't wave and you stay away till Jane has finished.'

'I don't like that, Lonsey.'

'There's totally no choice, Dan,' Karl said.

* * *

The massive stone walls kept the inside of the cathedral cool. Cool enough to chill Jane into a sudden shiver. She turned her back on the shadowy, gloomy central nave filling up with pilgrims. She followed Alonso up three steps onto a carpet covered low platform before the altar. Her eyes took in the dazzling Baroque surroundings designed to awe. Above it a canopy covered in gold leaf where she picked out the three statues of St. James; the Moor-Slayer, James the pilgrim, and the Apostle James. All this was flanked by golden twisted pillars and a bewildering assemblage of figures. *It looks as if they hose piped it with molten gold.*

'Sit here,' Alonso took her elbow indicating two chairs behind a wooden lectern to their left.

Jane turned and sat down. The shining Botafumeiro, one of the largest censers in the world, hung from a thick white rope holding it twenty feet in the air before the altar to her left. She was now facing the central congregation where arriving pilgrims took their seats. The murmured words of the people became louder. Their voices hung in the air, blending to become a growing hum that echoed from the high barrel vaulted ceiling. Pilgrims in the long pews pushed tighter together, shoulders pressing against shoulders, sharing obliging smiles.

Jane's lips parted as her jaw sagged taking a long look at Alonso. He placed the big leather bag at his feet. 'I wanted to brief you;' he whispered. 'Stay here. Don't move until I come for you.'

Jane nodded. She tried to estimate how many days of beard he had. *Two? Three?*

'Stay behind the lectern. It has a microphone, see?' he pointed to the mic on a thin flexi stem. 'Everything is arranged and approved. You'll be facing the main congregation and the people on the left and right wings can also see you.'

'Great.' She grasped his arm and saw dark eyes regarding her. 'Thanks for everything, Lonsey. We couldn't have got this far to do this without you.'

He nodded, looking away across the arriving crowd in front of them. 'Just don't step in front of the lectern while the Botafumeiro is swinging,' he pointed at the fat bellied vessel above them. 'It's sixty kilos and swings at eighty kilometres an hour!'

She nodded again. 'Where will you be?'

'I have a few things to discuss about the arrangements. I'll come after the mass has started.' He smiled and walked away along the aisle of the transept.

Jane looked down at her speech in her hand. *My shoes are dusty.* She shook her head and looked around. *What would Debbie have made of this? She liked the good things for herself but was quick to cry decadence when others showed wealth. She would have found this vulgar*, Jane decided.

A tall nun with a man's face appeared in front of her. She smiled and turned to the lectern. The speakers thudded as the nun tapped the microphone with her finger tip. She began to rehearse the chorus with the congregation. They obediently chanted the words after her, line by line. Photo flashes speckled the cathedral and bounced off the stone walls like summer lightning. The cameramen checked their equipment on the nearby aisle to her right. One of them looked at Jane. His thumb popped up. Jane took a deep breath and smiled. Her forehead was damp. Things ran around inside her gut.

Angie came through the open gate in the metal balustrade and slid onto the seat next to Jane.

'Everything okay?' She squeezed Jane's arm, her lips spread in a wide smile. Jane nodded and read her text again, lips moving slightly. The organ boomed long and deep. The congregation fell silent, necks craning for a view of the altar. The pilgrim mass began.

* * *

The Japanese group in the plaza scattered before a cream sight-seeing road train with kitsch gold trim. Its bell filled the air like a fire engine and bored relentlessly past the cathedral steps. A few shot karate chop looks at the driver.

'There's the train to Disney Land,' Karl smiled and turned and limped towards the cathedral. Dan's laugh was cut off by hard metal ramming his spine. His face paled.

'This has a suppressor,' Ramos' garlic breath hissed over Dan's shoulder. 'You thought you fooled us with the train trick, amigo.'

'D'you expect to get away with this?'

'Shut up! Get into the van over there!' Ramos nodded toward the front of the Parador hotel. A van stood at a down sloping ramp and punched the air with heavy beat music.

'Move!'

'If I don't?'

'I'll shoot. The music will help this suppressor.' His breath made Dan gag. 'People will think you had a heart attack and I'll be gone. Your girlfriend will get the same, amigo. Walk, Mr corporal Brady! Walk!'

Karl looked back. 'Hey, Dan! What's up?'

'There's a fuckin' pistol in my back.'

'He's coming with us, amigo! Stay back!' Ramos called over Dan's shoulder.' Dan saw Karl's eyes widen. 'Karl! See that Jane makes her speech!'

'Shut up, you bastard!' Ramos' free hand pulled nylon straps from his pocket and pushed Dan. His face slammed the van. A double click-clack told Dan a live round was in the gun breech. Dan gagged from Ramos' breath. A crony turned up the van radio to disco levels. People around were too intent on reaching the cathedral to care. Dan's back prickled with sweat. The pistol muzzle was steel hard and ice cold.

CATHEDRAL

'Ramos!' a loud hoarse voice roared.

Dan saw Mendoza, flanked by several blue uniforms, striding towards them. 'Ramos! You are under arrest!' Mendoza stopped. Eyes cold. No sign of panic or alarm. 'Watch out! He called over his shoulder and rapidly spread his arms twice. The uniforms fanned out in a horseshoe and pulling guns and crouching.

Ramos sprang away from Dan and raised the pistol. Dan heard nothing. His ears were numb and then ringing. He was deaf. Cordite filled his nostrils. A blow on his foot made him look down. The pistol lay between his feet, with Ramos sprawled on the ground. Karl bent over him, rubbing his knuckles. He smiled at Dan and shrugged apologetically. Police officers swarmed over Ramos and his cronies like a tsunami. Dan picked up the grey pistol. 'Made in Switzerland,' he looked at Ramos. 'You'd better stick to buying only their watches in future,' he grinned at the livid scar face as police officers hustled Ramos away. Dan sensed he had an enemy for life, and might, one day, have to watch his own back.

'Are you in order, Dan?' Karl rubbed his tattoo.

'Wow! Karl! I thought you were a fuckin' pacifist!'

'Sometimes a man must jump over his own shadow.' Karl grinned.

'Jasus!' Dan started toward him. 'You've been hit!' Dan knelt to examine a hole below the knee on Karl's jeans.

'Didn't feel a thing,' Karl's face was serious. He bent to roll up his trouser leg. The sun reflected from a silver tube ending in his boot. 'Motorbike accident. I was twenty.' He saw Dan's expression, laughed and tapped the prosthesis with his knuckle. 'Good German engineering,' he winked.

'So that's why you never walked the Camino with us.'

'I could have, but all day long walking could be a bit much. So, I did the driving.'

'Wherever you are there is chaos, Mr Brady,' Mendoza's voice interrupted. He smiled and regarded Dan for a few seconds. 'Ever since I found out about that man's past I have been wanting to remove him and get him committed.' He held his hand out to Dan. 'Mr Brady, I apologise about things that happened in the Camino and the complications for you because of this Ramos man,' he wrinkled his nose. 'This is not what law enforcement is about.'

'Then why have you been chasin' me?'

'Me?' Mendoza's eyebrows arched. 'Why should I

chase you, Mr Brady? I always knew where you were,' he smiled and smoothed his moustache. 'I knew you were innocent after we found the first skeleton. The forensic team proved it was buried long before you arrived.'

'Skeleton? First skeleton?' Dan face was pure puzzlement.

'All I heard was that the killer had been arrested.'

Mendoza's mouth and eyes were round like a fish out of water 'Who told you that?'

* * *

'So that's the famous Botafumeiro,' Angle's mouth hung open slightly as she admired the dazzling giant incense burner above. 'It looks like an elaborate giant salt cellar!'

'Tut!' Jane dug her elbow at Angie. 'That you, the sister of a priest could show such disrespect.' They chuckled lightly. 'Factually, the smoke comes out of the slanted slots around the upper half.'

'Puh! I guessed that, teacher Jane.'

'It is the one of the largest in the world. In fact, it means smoke expeller and the smoke was thought to prevent the spread of disease from the unwashed pilgrims.' They stared at the gleaming Botafumeiro with its intricate design. It hovered before the altar, possessing a latent undefinable silent power.

'Puh. That must have been the first preventative medicine,' Angie whispered. 'Is it gold? It looks worth a million dollars!'

'Silver,' Jane whispered. 'Look. There are the eight Tiraboleiros,' she nodded at a group of scarlet robed men at on side of the transept.

Lips apart, their expectant gazes followed the men. Each man grasped a separate tail spliced into the thick main rope and carefully paid out the cord.

'Looks heavy,' Angie whispered.

'Eighty kilos.'

Angie looked at Jane. An amused smile flickered. 'Ms facts,'

'Of course. It's my job,' Jane grinned smacking Angie's leg.

The Botafumeiro sank to waist height of three priests and two scarlet robed men who encircled it. A flame leaped. White smoke erupted. Organ music burst through the cavernous building. The smoke thickened rapidly, expanding with the organ's volume.

'Puh!' she wrinkled her nose. 'It makes more smoke than a bushfire!'

A priest blessed the Botafumeiro and stepped back. The faces of the Tiraboleiros grimaced as they heaved, bowing in a circle towards the rope. The Botafumeiro soared upwards like a rocket on a tail of grey smoke. The choir joined the bellowing Mascioni organ. The congregation rippled following the swinging gold comet. Faster. Higher. Camera flashes dotted the congregation. Jane's head swung side to side as if at a tennis match. The dense trail of smoke shrouded the altar area in a thick fog as the gleaming meteoroid swept by. Jane sucked in her breath, thinking the censor would crash against the barrel vaulted roof. It returned in its down flight. Heads of people in its path ducked between shoulders.

Jane breathed in the scent. She felt a squeeze on

her arm. Angie gave a thumbs-up. 'This is your moment, Jane.'

Her eyes met Angie's. 'For Debbie,' she whispered, her fingers grasped the suede sack of little Wilkins marmalade bottles holding the different soils of the Camino trail. The sack had become quite heavy since she started. She rose and took three short nervous steps to the lectern holding the thick heavy open bible. The Botafumeiro passed her from left to right; four seconds later it tore passed in the opposite direction. The smoke prompted a short cough. Her fingers felt clumsy fumbling with her sheet of paper and the now weighty, suede sack. She looked at thousands of faces pointed upwards at the Botafumeiro streaking over their heads. Her chest rose as she took an extra deep breath and stood. Her nervousness subsided. Suddenly she felt secure in the thick protective walls of the cathedral among the pilgrim congregation. She thought of Lonsey watching over her somewhere nearby. She took a step. Pride rose in her chest. 'Made it!' she clenched her fist. 'Made it! Made it! Made it!' She resisted throwing an air punch. She felt the cold dull metal of the microphone. It looked unfamiliar. *How far away should I stand? Stage fright? Not now I hope. Just speak as loud as you can, the way you did on graduation day,* she ordered. That day opened before her eyes like a photo slide. She saw herself on the stage. The day she publicly told the dean what she thought of him and his way of giving female students better grades. She smiled at the memory of the applause from students and staff. She bent towards the microphone. The Botafumeiro flashed past engulfing her in scented fog.

'Not yet Jane!' Angie hissed in a stage whisper. 'Ten more swings!'

Jane grasped the paper, brought from England. She could deliver it by heart, but she kept the paper with her. Security, in case a word played truant. She lay it on the open bible and smoothed it flat; her eyes found the cameraman just outside the balustrade. He swayed from the short jerking tugs as his assistant tightened the Steadicam harness. He aimed the camera at Jane. He looked up, smiled, gave a nod. Action! *He's filming! Oh my God! He's actually filming!'* Her mouth was tinder dry. Her heart ratcheted up a gear. *Should I have used a little more make up? Too late*. The camera was rolling.

A voice turned her head. She hesitated. Looked about her.

'*No!*' a child's high pitched voice echoed.

Heads turned. A red robed figure dashed through the balustrade gate past the Tiraboleiros occupied in their task. Jane froze, mouth agape.

'Whore!' The child's voice screamed. Hate filled eyes blazed above a bandanna in the deep red hood. 'Devil's whore!' The child's voiced morphed into a male bellowing voice. He bounded up the three steps to the altar toward her, narrowly missing the Botafumeiro. Smoke thickened and covered the altar, engulfing . the whole transept in a dense fog of incense. The red monk pulled Jane hard from behind the lectern toward the altar. The Botafumeiro slipstream ruffled her hair. Jane's spine slammed against the cold marble of the holy table. She tried to cry out but fingers crushed her throat cartilage to splitting point. Her eyes fixed on a sharpened wood crucifix held up by the monk and poised to stab. The suede sack hit her feet. Her heart skipped a beat, stuck in her throat choking her. 'He's killing me!' she gurgled.

Angie's wild face pressed over the monk's shoulder. Her teeth sank into his hand. The monk roared and slashed. Angie's face contorted in a silent cry. Jane kicked with all her force. The monk staggered. A nearby priest rushed towards them. The cross plunged. The priest fell back. Blood bloomed on his vestments. The monk swung back, raised the cross and grabbed Jane's throat. She choked. The point quivered. A figure thudded against the monk. Both men hit the floor. Jane tried to move, her legs failed. Dan rolled aside, knocking the lectern flying, his shoulder bleeding. The monk sprang to his feet and raised the wooden dagger.

'Look out!' Jane shrieked. The Botafumeiro tore by.

'She has to die!' the monk's voice bellowed through the smoke. The Botafumeiro blew passed leaving more smoke. The red figure swivelled back to Jane. He stumbled. Dan lay, arms clamped the monk's feet. Jane's foot felt the brown sack. She bent, scooped and swung with desperate might. The sack cracked on the red hood. The monk staggered back. A sickening thud. Jane saw Dan with shoes in his hands and the buckled Botafumeiro, haemorrhaging a spiralling pillar of white smoke. It twisted slowly above the broken form of the monk contorted against the balustrade.

Dan clambered to his feet. 'Y'finally found somethin' useful to do with all that friggin' soil.'

'Dan!' Angie leant against the altar holding her shoulder. She was pale but smiling weakly. 'Where the fuck's Lonsey? He promised to keep an eye on you.' Dan's lips clamped tight in anger and helped Angie to her feet.

Jane shook her head gagging at the stench of scorched skin and cloth. The habit smouldered from pieces of glowing incense. A Tiraboleiro looked inside the monk's hood and threw up. Security men yelled into mobiles and pushed people back. Pouring smoke created a dense fog, hiding much of the scene from the congregation. Some collapsed in each other's arms or stared blankly. Others contributed to a barrage of photo flashes. First aid men ripped open their bags and knelt over the priest and helped Angie. The organ strangled mid note and the Tiraboleiros heaved on their ropes and pulled the wrecked Botafumeiro to a safe height. An unnatural hush hung over the congregation.

Security men surrounded them. A first aid man who pushed the hood back. His hand peeled back the blood sodden bandanna. He shook his head. The bloodied features were unrecognisable. The unseeing eyes of the killer moved slightly. A red bubble grew from his lips. His unfocused eyes searched. 'Mommy... I'm com...' More blood bubbled from the corner of his mouth. The eyes fixed on the ruptured Botafumeiro and froze. A Tiraboleiro lay his red robe over the body, its bones and organs shattered by well over a ton force of moving kinetic energy.

Karl lay an arm across Jane's shoulders and led her away. Angie approached Jane, supported by Dan's arm and hugged Jane as if she never wanted to release her.

Police quickly moved in and began to politely direct people to the doors. 'An accident! An accident!' a police offer repeated to the exiting pilgrims. 'PLease leave the cathedral. A sad accident.'

A photographer and detectives arrived and rapidly photographed the scene. Dan stared at grey socks protruding from under the cloak. A pool of blood seeped onto the floor.

'You were all very lucky, Mr Brady,' Mendoza's gravelly voice brought Dan back to the present. The Comisario stood next to Dan. 'He would have killed you and Ms Downer.' Mendoza nodded at the body.

Dan picked up the wooden cross between his thumb and fore finger. 'He executed his victims with this. Do you know who he is?'

'Yes, Mr Brady. A man we have been watching...,'

'Comisario!' a uniform interrupted. They talked in Spanish with the speed of a machine gun. Mendoza launched into a barrage of orders, then turned back to Dan. 'We raided a farm house last night. We found the backpacks of his victims with details of each owner.'

'Jasus! A real monster.'

'That's not all. We found three most detailed dairies in the farm. Each was written by a clearly different personality. He recorded the names of every single victim and where he buried them.'

'Do you mean my...?'

'Yes, Ms Downer,' Mendoza nodded. 'We now know where your sister is buried. We'll take you there as soon as possible.'

'Oh, God!' Jane swayed unable to hold back her tears. Karl steadied her.

'It was clearly the act of an ill mind. His mission was to rid the Camino of red headed women who he believed were Satan's helpers and reincarnations of a prostitute called Eva. She and her pimp murdered his father. You were very lucky to remain alive under this circumstances Ms Downer.'

'Comisario?' another police officer interrupted.

Mendoza turned back and took Jane's hand. 'Ms Downer, you can be assured that you shall get all the help you need to repatriate your sister's remains.'

'Thank God,' she whispered.

'What will happen now?' Dan watched three men zipping up a green plastic body bag.

'We can finally close this sad chapter of the Camino.' He tugged his moustache.

'But who is the man?' Dan frowned. Mendoza's phone rang. He pulled it from his pocket, stared at the back, twisted it to see the display and sighed. 'Excuse me,' he said to Dan. 'Sí, Señor Presidente!' He listened and walked away a few paces.

'Now I can finally close this horrible chapter in my life,' said Jane, covering her eyes to banish everything she had seen.

'We all can. It's been so horrible.'

'I am glad we stuck together and saw it solved;' Karl rubbed his tattoo.

Mendoza was back. 'I have to go. There's a lot to be taken care of,' he thrust his hand out. 'Goodbye Ms Downer, Mr Brady. I'll be in contact with all the details and help you need. Maybe one day you will all return to the Camino under better circumstances.' They watched him walk down the centre aisle behind the stretcher carrying the body-bag.

* * *

'Ms Downer.'

Jane turned to the voice. Mr Tennis shoes pulled a card from his wallet. 'Rolls Investigation Service, at your service. Beam's the name, as in sunbeam.'

'Have you been following me?' Jane's brows were a straight line across her forehead.

'Guilty as charged. May I call you Jane?'

'Factually I don't know yet.'

'I wondered who you friggin' were. But thanks for savin' me back in Rabanal.' Dan said.

'You're welcome, lad,' Mr Beam winked then turned back to Jane. 'Ms Downer, your dad's used our services for years.' Everyone stared at him like a zombies' meeting. 'An unusual assignment for me, I can tell you.' He held Jane's gaze. 'Your father wanted you to be safe. He employed our agency to keep an eye on you.'

'Were you always behind me? Following?'

'Since you checked in at Stansted.' His smile was shy. 'Your dad wants to tell you that he's sorry for what happened in the past.'

'There's a lot of that,' she stiffened. 'A lot.'

'He says he should have been fairer to you.'

Jane's eyes welled. 'He said that?' She wiped them. 'Why couldn't he tell me himself?'

'He's frightened you might not hear him out.' He smiled as the stress in her features fell away like a veil.

'Is that true?' A gradual smile began at the corners of her mouth and spread slowly with a slight uncertainty. Her heart started to beat faster. She thought of Debbie, who had it all, but lost; mum whose eyes never lost their sadness again; dad's emotions shutting down and his silence. An awful deafening silence that had isolated her, left her hurt and lonely; and no longer at home in her parents' house.

'Jane,' Mr Beam said, encouraged by her smile. 'Your dad said to tell you, he loves you, and to come home.' Everyone had gathered round Jane. They were all here because of her. Their silence magnified their respect.

'Jane?' Angie nudged her. Karl rubbed his tattoo. Dan sighed. 'It's your friggin' call, Jane.'

Goose bumps crept over her skin. She studied the stone floor. She thought of dusty boots, the trail, pilgrims she met, laughs, fears, hopes, blisters, pain and tears. Especially tears. Tears that returned to her eyes now. She cried unashamedly. Those around her touched her shaking shoulders. Angie clung to her and bawled her eyes out with her. Karl lay his arm around the them both. Jane took a body shuddering breath, removed her hands from her face. Someone gave her a cloth. She wiped her eyes and stared at the floor and thought of Debbie, the sister she had once loved, the sister she had hated, the sister she'd let down but, maybe, repaid.

'Jane?' Angie prompted. 'Everything will be good. Believe me.'

'Do it, Jane. Friggin' do it,'

Jane's chest filled out, her smile grew, her eyes sparkled. She looked at Mr Beam through wet eyes. 'Yes. I shall come home, Mr Beam. In fact, I'll come home with my sister, Debbie.'

'Then call him, lass, go on,' Beam winked.

She pulled out her cell and pressed a button. The ringing at the other end squeezed out of the phone. It stopped. A voice buzzed faintly.

'Hello? Dad? It's me! Jane!' Her face lit up in a

dazzling smile, and all the strain and stress dropped from her shoulders like a discarded cloak. She babbled a thousand words in a non-stop barrage, tears rolled and her smile was the biggest Dan had ever seen. She cut off the phone. 'I'm going home,' she whispered.

Dan smiled and stepped forward and gave each of them a silent hug. 'Y'know what? I still have my friggin' ticket to Majorca and my kids are still there,' his smiled slashed his face and his eyes sparkled with a new open energy. 'Listen, Jane. I'm not one for long goodbyes. You've got my number. Ok?'

'So have I!' Angie's lashes fanned her cheeks.

'Good. See you use it,' he grinned. 'I'll be on my way.'

'Must you?' Jane looked at him sadly.

'You've got enough to do now, and I can't help there, so I'll be saying; adios amigos.' He raised his hand in a mock salute.

Jane nodded and flung her arms around him and squeezed. 'Adiós, Dan. Keep in touch.' She kissed his cheek.

'Sure, I will. We went through too much to simply forget each other,' he pulled back and squeezed her shoulders. 'Live a good life, Jane.'

'You, too. And, mind your manners,' she laughed through her tears.

'What manners?' he winked. 'Y'know, Jane. I came to the Camino and thought I knew everything. Through you I learned that I knew very little about people, but I also learned that I can still learn. I realise that we are all responsible for our own luck, and not to go blaming others for everything that goes wrong. Thanks for that, Jane. I owe you,' he smiled and pointed his finger like a gun.

'What about your job?' Karl scratched his tattoo.

'I'll get something better. After the Camino, and getting to know you guys and many other good people, I finally know who I am. And, I know I'm worth more than I ever believed.'

'Factually, you are even better than you know.'

'You have my address in France, Mr Irishman,' Angie squeezed him tightly for a long minute, kissed both checks and stroked his lips with hers like a butterfly. Dan stepped back with flushed cheeks.

'If I remember it, I'll certainly visit,' he winked.

'Puh! Don't you *dare* forget it!' She dabbed her eyes and turned away.

'Ach, I can drive you to the airport.'

'Er, no thanks, Karl. Too dangerous,' Dan gave a cocky mock salute and disappeared into the crowd.

Angie blew her nose loudly. Jane's eyes followed Dan till he disappeared.

* * *

Dan exited the cathedral and walked down the steps toward a gleaming, yellow ambulance with a blue stripe below the windows. He stopped next to Mendoza. A cigarette jutted from under his moustache. They silently watched four men slide the green body bag into the back of the ambulance. A few passers by stopped or hesitated with craning necks, but two police officers politely moved them on.

'Comisario, have you seen Detective Amador? I'm leavin' an' I wanted to say goodbye. Although he did promise to stay near Ms Downer!'

Mendoza's eyes studied Dan's face. 'He did, Mr Brady. He did stay near her.' Mendoza bent his head back and blew a stream of blue smoke into the air.

'Hah! Like hell he did!' Dan stopped. Mendoza's eyes were hard to read. Dan followed his gaze to the ambulance.

'*That* is Detective Amador, Mr Brady.' Mendoza nodded towards the body bag inside the ambulance.

'Lonsey?' Dan's voice was hoarse. 'That's Lons...?'

'Amador,' Mendoza nodded with wet eyes.

'Jasus effin' Christ! *That's* how he covered his tracks, and always knew where we were! He knew everything! Our itinerary, overnight stops! Everythin'! Jasus effin'....!'

Mendoza touched his moustache, 'I'm sorry to say that we were all completely misled. He suffered not from two, but multiple personalities.' He sucked urgently at his cigarette as if it were oxygen.

'You mean split?'

'More than that. Multiple. He was a brilliant police officer; a little obedient boy dominated by his mother; a ritual killer on a mission; a musician; an artist. Each of those three personalities kept separate dairies in his home. Three!' Mendoza stared at Dan and held up three fingers to make his point. 'He smuggled sedatives into the clinic where his mother committed suicide last night. His mother was probably the real guilty person.' The slam of doors turned Dan's head. The rear ambulance doors cut off the sight of the body bag.

'He was near Ms Downer all the time,' he said and trod his cigarette into the stones.

'This will look friggin' bad in the news.'

'What news, Mr Brady? The only news I know is

that detective Amador died bravely fighting lung cancer. He'll have a funeral with honours. That will be the official announcement.'

'Fuckin' honours!' Dan's eyeballs bulged. 'What about today? His attempt to kill...!'

'Mr Brady,' Mendoza spoke quietly. 'In that ambulance lies the body of an anonymous drunk who had an unfortunate accident trying to make a name for himself,' Mendoza pursed his lips. 'It happens from time to time, you know? Look at the running of the bulls in Pamplona for example,' he stroked his moustache as his eyes danced across Dan's angry features. 'Misadventure, as you so quaintly call it in English.' He patted Dan on the shoulder. 'Misadventure, Mr Brady. Nothing more, nothing less.'

'I cannot friggin' believe..!'

'Call it the shadow side of life, Mr Brady. The Camino also has its share of shadows.' He thrust his hand out. Dan didn't take it. 'Then, good luck, Mr Brady,' he said as he pulled his buzzing phone. 'Aah! Señor Presidente!' he twisted away. 'Sí, sí, sí,' he opened the rear door of a blue and white police car and slumped into the rear seat. The slam of the door cut off his voice.

'Too friggin' near,' Dan muttered. 'Too near for any of us to see him.' He thrust his shaking hands deep in his pockets to try and steady them. His eyes, deep blue in anger stared at the ambulance. This was a secret he should keep to himself. For him and him alone.'

* * *

Jane came out of the church alone and stood at the top of the steps with a commanding view of the Plaza do Obradoiro below. She needed a break from everyone inside. She needed some moments alone. Everything that happened had been so much horror, but in another way, some joys. She felt vindicated in her mission that had helped resolve a terrible secret.

The movement of the ambulance below attracted her attention as it pulled away, followed by a little police convoy leaving a solitary man standing.

'Dan!' she recognised him, hands deep in his pockets. She instinctively raised her hand to wave. It froze as she realised he hadn't seen or heard her. She watched him turn and walk slowly across the plaza towards a taxi and a new future. A passing nun tapped him on the shoulder. He stopped. Turned. Jane watched them talking. Dan gesticulated like a windmill in a storm. He threw back his head and laughed. Suddenly Dan hugged the woman.

'Another life changed for the better,' Jane whispered. The bells of the Cathedral de Santiago de Compostela boomed across the cobalt May sky. Jane's smile was the broadest she had enjoyed in a long, long time.

AUTHOR'S NOTES

I wrote Fatal Camino in a hurry when I considered walking The Camino in September 2014. I walked my Camino in May 2015 and visited the locations in the story. It was an exceptionally dry and hot May, which is reflected in this story. Despite the theme of this story, my experiences convince me that The Way is one of the safest places I know. I had the good fortune to talk to various women of different nationalities who were walking alone. They showed no sign of fear, especially after their initial week, and, despite the universal reaction of friends back home - 'You? A woman alone!' - they confirmed that they were treated with the greatest respect and consideration. This is remarkable when one considers that almost a quarter of a million people a year walk The Way: I cannot imagine another place with a population of quarter of a million that is as safe.

Murder is a gruesome business, and more horrible if committed along such a setting. Naturally, it was this contrast that intrigued me when I had one of my "What if" thoughts. Nevertheless, The Way is engraved on my heart as one of the most positive experiences of my life. If I see pictures, it brings back memories of the faces of wonderful people I was privileged to meet. I still tell endless tales to anyone who will listen. I will always say – "Don't dream it! Do it".

All the locations truly exist - I was there - but three have been slightly modified, a couple moved, and the clinic invented, the rest is an entirely fictional story. Enjoy. Walk The Way and change your life, if you haven't done so already. Maybe we'll meet along the Way. Don't worry, I'll leave the chloroform at home.

Most of all I dedicate this books to the thousands of pilgrims who make the existence of The Way, the Camino, possible. Good ordinary people displaying extraordinary strength and discipline during this extraordinary walk. It is these people that convince me that many humans are better than our reputation.

John Douglas Fisher
August 2015

John Douglas Fisher